TIGRIS

EUPHRATES

THE · HANGING · GARDENS
OF · BABYLON

CRUSALEM

PERSIAN · GULF

D0434850

MILES

0   100   200   300   400   500

THE CURSE OF THE KING

The Tides Turn

THE
CURSE
OF THE
KING

PETER LERANGIS

HARPER
An Imprint of HarperCollinsPublishers

Seven Wonders Book 4: The Curse of the King
Text by Peter Lerangis, copyright © 2014 by HarperCollins Publishers
Illustrations copyright © 2014 by Torstein Norstrand
Map art by Mike Reagan, copyright © 2014 by HarperCollins Publishers
All rights reserved. Printed in the United States of America.
www.harpercollinschildrens.com

ISBN 978-0-06-207049-4 (trade bdg.)
ISBN 978-0-06-237819-4 (int'l ed.)

Design by Joe Merkel
15 16 17 18 19   CG/RRDH   10 9 8 7 6 5 4 3 2
❖
First Edition

FOR MOM AND DAD,
WHO HAVE READ EVERYTHING
SINCE THE VERY FIRST SENTENCE

CHAPTER ONE

THE WRATH OF YAPPY

HAVING LESS THAN a year to live doesn't feel great, but it's worse when you're in a cop car that smells of armpits, cigarettes, and dog poop. "Don't New York City cops ever clean their cars?" Cass Williams mumbled.

I turned my nose to the half-open window. Aly Black was at the other end of the backseat, but Cass was stuck in the middle. Outside, music blared from a nearby apartment window. An old woman walking a Chihuahua eyed us and began yelling something I couldn't quite make out.

"Okay, what do we do now, Destroyer?" Cass asked.

"'Jack' is still my name," I said.

"'The Destroyer Shall Rule,' that was the prophecy," Aly replied. "And your mom pointed at you."

1

"We were invisible! She could have been pointing at . . ." My voice trailed off. It was after midnight, but the way they were both glaring at me, I felt like I needed sunglasses. I was beginning to think throwing that last Loculus under a train might not have been a great idea. "Look, I'm sorry. I really am. But I had to do it, or everyone would have died. You would have done the same thing!"

Aly sighed. "Yeah, you're right. It's just . . . an adjustment, that's all. I mean, we had a chance. And now . . ."

She gave me a sad shrug. *We're dead*, is what she didn't say. A genetic mutation was on target to kill us before the age of fourteen. And I had sabotaged our chance to be cured. Seven Loculi was what we needed. Now one of them was in pieces under a train.

I sank back into the smelly seat. As the car slowed to a stop in front of a squat brick police station, our driver called out, "Home sweet home!"

She was a tall, long-faced woman named Officer Wendel. Her partner, Officer Gomez, quickly hauled himself out from the passenger side. He was barely taller than me but twice my width. The car rose an inch or so when he exited. "Your papa's inside, dude," he said. "Make nice with him and make sure we don't see you again."

"You won't," Aly replied.

"*Wait!*" cried the old woman with the Chihuahua. "*Those are devil children!*"

2

Officer Gomez paused, but another cop waved him in. "You go ahead," he said wearily. "We'll take care of Mrs. Pimm."

"I recognize her," Aly whispered. "She's the person who shows up in movie credits as Crazy New York City Neighbor."

As Officer Gomez rushed us inside and down a short, grimy hallway, I eyed my backpack, which was slung over his shoulder. The Loculus of Flight and the Loculus of Invisibility formed two big, round bulges.

He had peeked inside but not too carefully. Which was lucky for us.

Officer Wendel walked ahead and pushed open the door to a waiting room. Dad was sitting on a plastic chair, and he stood slowly. His face was drawn and pale.

"Officers Gomez and Wendel, Washington Heights Precinct," Gomez said. "We responded to the missing-persons alert. Found them while investigating a commotion up by Grant's Tomb."

"Thank you, officers," Dad said. "What kind of commotion? Are they in trouble?"

"Healthy and unharmed." Gomez unhooked the pack and set it on a table. "We had reports of noises, people in costume—gone by the time we got there."

Officer Wendel chuckled. "Well, a few weirdoes in robes near the train tracks, picking up garbage. Guess the party was over. Welcome to New York!"

3

Dad nodded. "That's a relief. I—I'll take them home now."

He reached for the backpack, but Officer Wendel was already unzipping it and looking inside. "Just a quick examination," she said with an apologetic look. "Routine."

"Officer Gomez did it already!" I pointed out.

Before Gomez could respond, a sharp barking noise came from the hallway. The old lady was inside, with her dog. Officer Wendel looked toward the noise.

I reached for the pack, but Wendel pulled it away. She opened my canvas sack and removed the basketball-sized Loculus of Flight. "Nice . . ." she said.

"A world globe," I blurted. "We have to . . . paint the countries onto—"

"What the . . . ?" Officer Wendel's hand had hit the invisible second Loculus.

"It's nothing!" Cass blurted out.

"Literally," Aly added.

Wendel tried to wriggle the Loculus out. "Is this glass?"

"A special kind of glass," Dad said. "So clear I'll bet you can't see it!"

"Wow . . ." Wendel said. She lifted her hands high, holding up . . . absolutely nothing. Nothing that the human eye could see, that is. "I can feel it, but I can't—"

"I am not crazy stop treating me like I'm crazy, I saw them, I tell you—they were floating like birds!" Mrs. Pimm's voice was rising to a shriek—and I remembered where I'd heard

4

her voice and seen her face.

An open window, a dim light. She had been staring at us as the Shadows from the Mausoleum at Halicarnassus lifted us through the streets. She'd been one of the only people who'd noticed the flurries of darkness, the fact that we were being borne down the street in the invisible arms of Artemisia's minions.

I darted toward the door and looked out.

Yiiiii! The Chihuahua saw me first. He wriggled out of her arms and skittered down the hallway toward me, baring his teeth.

"There—those are the wicked children!" Now Mrs. Pimm was heading our way, followed by two burly cops. "They were floating above the ground . . . talking to spirits! *Come back here, Yappy!*"

I sprang back into the room as Yappy clattered inside, yapping away.

Officer Wendel let go of the backpack. She and Gomez surrounded Yappy, reaching for his collar. Mrs. Pimm began lashing at them with her cane. Two other cops grabbed at her shoulders.

"Where's the Loculus?" Aly whispered.

There.

I couldn't see it, but I saw a perfectly rounded indentation in the sack on the table—a logical place where an invisible sphere might be resting. Shoving my hand toward the air above it, I felt a cool, round surface.

Now I could see the Loculus. Which meant I was invisible. "Got it!"

Aly sidled close to me. I reached out and grabbed her hand. Just before she disappeared, Cass reached for her, too.

Dad stood there against the wall, looking confused. Now Cass and Aly both had hands on the Loculus, so I let go of Aly and reached toward Dad with my free hand. "If you touch us," I said softly, "the power transfers."

He flinched when I took his arm. But it was nothing like the looks on the faces of Mrs. Pimm and the group of police officers. Their jaws were nearly scraping the floor. A cup of coffee lay in a puddle below them.

I could hear Yappy heading for the entrance as fast as his little legs could carry him.

We followed after him, but we didn't rush.

Even the NYPD can't stop something they can't see.

CHAPTER TWO

TWERP PERPS, SNALP, AND THE FAT LADY

DAD'S DISGUISE WAS a porkpie hat and a fake, glued-on mustache that made him sneeze. Aly's hair, colored blond with cheap spray-on hair color bought at Penn Station, was bunched into a baseball cap. Cass wore a hoodie and a fake scar on his cheek, and I opted for thick sunglasses, which were now hurting my nose.

Dad and Aly sat on one side of a narrow table, Cass and I on the other. We were the only ones in our little train compartment, which made our disguises kind of ridiculous. At least I thought so.

None of us had been able to sleep. Now the countryside was aglow with the first hints of the morning sun. "We are two hundred forty-nine miles into Pennsylvania, fifty-four point three miles from the Ohio border," Cass announced.

"Thank you, Mr. GPS," Aly said.

"Seriously, how can you do that?" I asked. "The angle of the sun?"

"No," Cass replied, gesturing out the window toward a narrow post that zoomed by. "The mile markers."

Dad covered his mouth. *"Ahh-haaaa-choo!"*

"Guys, maybe we can take off the disguises?" Aly said. "I've been checking news sites, feeds, social media, and there's nothing about us."

"What if we're America's Most Wanted?" Cass asked. "What if our pictures are in every post office from here to Paducah?"

Wincing, Dad pulled off his mustache. "Cass, let's examine that word—*wanted*. The best way to predict how people will act is knowing what they *want*. One thing the New York police don't want is the press to know that four people vanished from under their noses."

"'Tonight's headline: Twerp perps pop from cops! Details at eleven!'" Cass said.

Aly pulled back her newly blond hair into a scrunchie. "When we get to Chicago, I'm washing out this disgusting color."

"Your hair was *blue* before this," Cass remarked.

Aly stuck out her tongue.

"I think it looks nice," I said, quickly adding, "not that

blue wasn't nice. It was. So was the orange."

Aly just stared at me bewildered, like I'd just said something in Sanskrit. I turned away. Sometimes I should just keep my mouth shut.

Cass cracked up. "Maybe she can borrow the red coloring from your skin."

"Once we're in Chicago, Aly, you're getting on a plane to Los Angeles," Dad said. "To see your mom."

"What am I going to tell her?" Aly asked.

"The truth," Dad replied. "She has to know everything. And she has to keep what happened to you a secret—"

"She won't do that!" Aly said. "I mean—I vanished for weeks. She's going to open a federal investigation!"

Dad shook his head. "Not when she realizes what's at stake. That there's still a hope of curing you kids. Our job now is to create an airtight alibi, which we all will use. It has to explain why three kids disappeared and then slipped back weeks later, all at the same time. We have to somehow contain this. People in our hometown are going to ask questions. Yours, too, Aly."

"So . . . um . . ." Cass said uneasily. "How do I figure into these snalp?"

"Snalp?" Dad said.

"*Plans*," I translated. "It's Backwardish. Remember? He uses it when he's feeling silly. Or nervous."

"Or deracs," Cass added.

9

Dad looked him straight in the eyes. He knew about Cass's background. Honestly, I couldn't imagine what Cass was thinking. Mainly because I don't know what's it's like to have two parents in jail on a robbery conviction. What I did know was that he'd be sent back to child services until he was eighteen. Which meant, under our circumstances, forever.

"Of course I have plans," Dad said. "Don't you y-worr . . . wy-orr . . ."

"Yrrow?" Cass said. "As in, *worry?*"

Dad was already scribbling on a sheet of legal paper. "Exactly," he said.

"Okay then, I won't," Cass said, looking very, very worried.

* * *

"Next station stop, Chicago, Illinois!"

As the conductor's voice echoed in the train car, the sun burned through the window. Aly and Cass had fallen asleep, and I was almost there, too.

Dad's eyes were bloodshot as he put the final touches on the list we'd been working on for hours. I read it for about the hundredth time.

"Um," I said.

Aly sighed. "Complicated."

"Out of our minds," Cass added.

"I think we can make it work," Dad said with a deep breath.

10

1. Jack loses memory in B.ville hospital. Wanders off in middle of night.

   Get corrob. From Dr. Flood. All true.

   Rick S. will vouch. Lives in H'ville, works for med supplier to MGL, never met J.

2. J. ends up in woods in Hopperville, falls asleep. Found by anonymous homeless guy.

   Email Walsh. He owes favor or 2.

   Get applic. papers ASAP. ← − − −

3. Homeless guy contacts Rick S*, who can't ID Jack but recognizes he needs sophisticated treatment. Sends J. to Stanford, CA.

4. In Stanford, Dr. Walsh* brings back J.'s memory.

5. Walsh contacts Dad, who flies out to get J.

6. While in hospital, J. rooms with accident victim who is a hardened street tough but nice guy (Cass). They bond.

7. Upon meeting Cass, Dad decides to begin legal adoption.

NOTE: call Aly's mom, work out alibi for her.
* college friends of Dad. Will work with us.

"I like the 'hardened street tough' part," Cass said.

"Now for your story, Aly," Dad went on. "We need something your mom can jump on board with."

"Mom and I are no strangers to alibis," Aly said. "I've been working with covert government groups for a long time. We can say I was on a CIA project. Much less complicated than your epic lie."

Dad removed his porkpie hat and ran his fingers through his steadily graying hair. "One thing you need to know, guys. Your disappearances have been in the news. Luckily for us, the reports have stayed local. Three separate communities, three separate disappearances, three different times. Well, four, including Marco. Now three of you are showing up at once. Up to now, no one has connected the disappearances. That's our task—containing the stories. Keeping them strictly local news."

"No publicity," Aly agreed, "no photos on the web, play it down on social media."

Dad nodded. "Ask—insist—that your friends not blab about it. For privacy's sake."

"I will keep the news away from hardened-street-tough circles," Cass said.

"Contain, concentrate, commit—that's the only way we are going to solve this genetic problem," Dad said.

No one said a word. We were all trying our hardest to avoid the great big fat imaginary elephant in the room—and on its side was an imaginary sign that said HAPPY FOURTEENTH BIRTHDAY crossed out in black with a skull underneath.

"This may be the last time we see each other," Aly said in a tiny, weak, unAlylike voice.

"I will die before I let that happen to any of you," Dad replied. His face was grim, his eyes steady and fierce. "And I won't rest until my company finds a cure."

"What if they don't?" I asked.

Dad gave me a steady *have-I-ever-let-you-down?* look. "You know the McKinley family motto. It ain't over . . ."

"Until the fat lady sings." I couldn't help smiling. There were about a dozen McKinley family mottoes, and this was one of Dad's favorites.

"La-la-la," Aly sang, smiling.

Dad laughed. "Sorry, Aly, you don't fit the bill."

Cass, who hadn't spoken in a long time, finally piped up softly. "Mr. McKinley?" he said. "About number seven on your list . . . ?"

Dad smiled warmly. "That's the only one we don't have to worry about. Because it's the only item that's one hundred percent true."

CHAPTER THREE

THE ENEMY OF INTERESTING

"IT MEANS A soprano," I said, scrolling through a Wikipedia page on my trusty desktop. We'd been home for ten busy days, buying a bunk bed and a desk and a bike and clothes for Cass, catching up with teachers and friends, telling the alibi over and over a thousand times, buying hair dye to cover up the white lambda shape on the backs of our heads, blah-blah-blah. Today was going to be our first full day in school, and I was nervous. So of course it was a perfect time to procrastinate—like looking up Dad's odd saying about the singing fat lady.

"I hated that show," Cass called out from the top bunk.

"What show?" I asked.

"*The Sopranos,*" Cass said. "My last foster family

binge-watched all seventeen years of it. Well, it *felt* like seventeen."

"No, I'm talking about 'the fat lady,' " I said. "It means a soprano—like, an opera singer. It's a way of saying the opera's not over until the soprano sings her big showstopping tune."

"Oh," Cass said. "What if she's not fat? The show keeps going?"

"It's a stereotype!" I said.

Cass grunted and sat up, dangling his legs over the side of the bed. "I hate stereotypes, too."

Since returning, Cass had been a thirteen-year-old curly-haired version of Dr. Jekyll and Mr. Hyde. Half the time he was his bouncy self, thanking Dad a zillion times for agreeing to adopt him. The other half he was fixated on our . . . timetable. Our predicament. Dilemma.

The fact that we were going to die.

There. I said it.

I'll admit, I hated actually putting that idea into words. I tried not to think of it as a fact. Or even think of it at all. Hey, the fat lady hadn't sung, right? Dad was trying to keep the show going.

I had to stay positive for Cass and me.

"It's weird," Cass murmured.

"What's weird?" I said.

"G7W," Cass replied.

"Of course it's weird," I said. "It sits in DNA for generations and then, *bam*—it shows up in people like you and me."

"No, I mean it forces us all into stereotypes," Cass said. "That always bothered me. You know, like when P. Beg called us Soldier, Sailor, Tinker, Tailor. It's like another way of saying Jock, GPS-Guy, Geek, and . . . whatever Tailor is supposed to be."

"The one who puts it all together," I said. "That's what Bhegad said."

"He slices . . . he dices . . . he figures out ways to find Loculi in ancient settings! But wait, there's more! Now the new improved Jack is also the Destroyer!" Cass let out a weary laugh. "How does that make any sense? It doesn't. At first this whole thing seemed so cool—we were going to be superhumans, woo-hoo! But the last few weeks have been like this bad dream. Don't you wish we could be normal— just kids like everybody else?"

"Cheer up, Cass," I said, scooping stuff up from my desk. "Normal is the enemy of interesting."

I dumped my pen, phone, change, and gum into my pockets. The last thing I picked up was the Loculus shard.

It was my good luck charm, I guess. For ten days I'd been carrying it with me all the time. Maybe because it reminded me of my mom. I really did believe that she had dropped it at my feet on purpose, no matter what Cass or Aly thought.

Besides, it really was awesome to look at. It felt smooth

16

and cool to the touch—not like metal exactly, or plastic, but dense and supertough. I held it up to the sun for a quick glance:

"You've been wearing that thing out," Cass said. "It looks like it shrunk."

"*Shrank*," I corrected him.

"Thunk you." Cass hopped down from the bunk. "Anyway, you're much more Tailor than Destroyer. That description fits Marco."

"Now who's stereotyping?" I said.

Cass giggled. "Somewhere in this world, the Massa are training Marco Ramsay to be the new king of Atlantis, while you, me, and Aly are going off to seventh grade. I think we get the better deal."

As he disappeared down the hall and into the bathroom, I heard the front doorbell ring—which seemed kind of weird for 6:39 A.M. Dropping the shard into my pocket, I glanced out the window. I saw a white minivan parked at the curb. The van's sides were emblazoned with the call letters of a local TV station WREE-TV.

Uh-oh. So much for keeping things under the radar.

"Sorry, no interviews." Dad's muffled voice echoed upward.

"We think the nation will want to hear this brave story," a woman's voice piped up. "It's got heart, grit, pathos—"

"I appreciate that," Dad said firmly. "Look, I know your station owner, Morty Reese. He'll understand as a father, we'd like our privacy."

The woman's voice got softer. "If it's compensation you're concerned about, we are prepared—"

"Compensation?" Dad shot back with a disbelieving laugh. "Wait. Morty asked you to bribe me?"

"Mr. Reese has your best interests at heart," the woman said. "This story could lead to awareness of traumatic brain injury. Hospitals will realize they need to increase security—"

18

"I'm sure Mr. Reese can donate directly to the hospitals if he's so concerned," Dad replied. "My private life is not for sale, sorry. Between you and me, he should learn how legitimate news organizations operate."

"Mr. Reese is an excellent newsman—" the woman protested.

"And I'm an excellent trapeze artist," Dad shot back. "Thanks but no thanks."

I heard the door shut firmly.

CHAPTER FOUR

THE BARRY

"SO, DID HE work there before or after you were born?" Cass said as we walked up the street toward school.

"Did who work where?" I asked.

"Your dad, in the circus," Cass said. "Did you get to see him?"

Trapeze. It took me a moment. "Dad was being sarcastic," I explained. "He doesn't like Mr. Reese."

"Your dad has a weird sense of humor," Cass said.

"Reese is like the Donald Trump of Belleville," I said. "Except with normal hair. Dad says he owns half the town, but still Mr. Reese wants to be a media mogul. He's the head of Reese Industries, the Bathroom Solutions People."

"Whoa. As in 'Reese: The Wings Beneath Your Wind'?" Cass asked.

"Yup," I replied. "Those little plastic toilet thingies that attach the seat to the bowl. Everyone has them. That's billions in profit. And billions in profit buys local TV stations. Anyway, the most important thing is that Dad's trying to protect us. To keep our faces out of the news so he can work on saving our lives."

"Hope springs eternal," Cass said, kicking a stone up the sidewalk.

I smiled. That was the first positive thing Cass had said all day. "You know, that's one of my dad's favorite sayings."

"That's a sign!" Cass said with a grin. "I *do* belong in your family!"

I put my arm around his shoulder, and we walked quietly along a wooded area.

When Cass spoke again, his voice was soft and unsteady. "It's so hard to stay optimistic. How do you do it?"

"I try to list all the good things," I said. "Like number one, I have a new brother."

"Is there a number two?" Cass asked.

"We both feel healthy," I suggested. "We haven't needed treatments yet. Your turn."

"Um . . ." Cass replied. "Number three, it could be that this whole thing will blow over? I mean, it's possible the

Karai Institute was lying to us—you know, about needing those Sesulucol?"

"Ilucol," I corrected him.

Cass laughed. "Number four, you are getting really good at Backwardish!"

I veered off the sidewalk onto a dirt path that led into a tangle of trees that sloped downward to a creek. "Come on, this is a tuctrosh . . . tushcort . . . *shortcut.*"

"Wait—what? There's a stream down there!" Cass protested. As he walked, his foot kicked aside a busted-up baseball glove, festooned with a banana peel. "This is disgusting. Can't we take Smith Street to Whaley and then the jagged left-right on Roosevelt? Or bypass Roosevelt via the dog run?"

"Even *I* don't even know my neighborhood that well!" I said over my shoulder.

"Wait till I learn to ride a bike," Cass grumbled. "Then we'll have great options. And I won't seem like such a doofus."

"You're not a doofus," I said.

"I am the only kid in the country who can't ride a bike!" Cass replied.

"Yeah, well . . ." I said. "You had a different kind of childhood."

"As in *none,*" Cass said. "You try growing up with criminal parents."

WHOOOOO . . . WHOOOO! An eerie call made me stop in my tracks.

"Cool," Cass said, bumping into me from behind. "An owl?"

Slowly a plaid shirt appeared among the rustling leaves—and then the moonlike, grinning face of Barry Reese. *"Whooooo do we have heeeere?"*

He jumped in front of us—well, if you consider slowly moving nearly two hundred pounds of well-fed and expensively dressed flesh into a narrow dirt path *jumping.*

"Not owl," I said. "Foul. Cass, meet Barry Reese."

"Son of Donald Trump?" Cass said.

Barry ignored the comment, or maybe he was too busy thinking up his next move. Barry had a hard time doing two things at once. He held up three pudgy fingers to my face, then five, then one. "How many fingers? I heard you had some mental problems, like losing your memory. Just want to test to see if you're okay, Amnesia Boy."

There were approximately three hundred middle-school kids in Belleville who would be quaking in their boots at this kind of bullying. But after facing up to killer zombies, sharp-taloned griffins, and acid-spitting vizzeet, I wasn't bothered by Barry Reese. "Stick two of them into your eyes and I'll count slowly," I said.

He shoved both of us backward. His face was covered with a sheen of sweat as he grinned sadistically at Cass.

"Look! It's Cash! The hardened LA stweet tough who still wides a twicycle!"

"Wait, how did you know that?" Cass said.

"Um, maybe because you just announced it to the world?" Barry replied. "Can I have your autograph? It's okay if you want to use cwayons."

I lunged forward and gave Barry a shove. "It's *Cass*. And he only gives autographs to people who know how to read."

Unfortunately pushing a guy of Barry's bulk was like trying to move a boulder. He bumped me hard with his belly and grabbed my backpack straps. "That was disrespectful, McKinley. The Barry sent you to the hospital once and he can do it again. Now give me your phone."

"My *phone?*" I said. "Doesn't the Barry have a phone?"

His beefy fingers were already in my jeans pocket. As I wriggled to get away, the pocket popped inside out along with Barry's hand. All my stuff spilled out onto the ground, including the Loculus shard.

Cass and I scrambled to grab it, but Barry was shockingly fast when he was excited. "What's this?" he asked, scrunching up his face at the shard.

"Nothing!" I blurted.

"Then why did you both grab for it first?" As he lifted it upward, the shard glinted in the sunlight. "What's that weird star shape on it? A symbol from a secret nerd society?"

"Mathletes!" Cass said. "It's . . . a club. Of math people. We talk about . . . pi. And stuff like that."

"I like pies, too . . . but I don't like *lies!*" Barry snickered at his own idiotic joke. "Especially lies about anti-American world-domination cults that kidnap kids for weeks at a time!"

Cass was shaking now. "Jack, is he going loony tunes on us? Should we be calling nine-one-one?"

Barry stepped closer, his beady eyes shifting from me to Cass. "You're not a street tough, Casper, are you? And, Jack, you didn't lose your memory and travel across the country. Your little story? It's full of holes. My dad thinks your dad has connections with terrorists. Where does he fly all the time? What's with all the long trips to Magnolia?"

"Mongolia," Cass corrected him.

"Wait—*terrorists?*" I said. "There are no terrorists in Mongolia!"

"Ha—so you *were* there!" Barry said.

"My dad runs a genetics lab there," I replied. Barry's face went blank, so I added, "That's the study of genes, and not the kind you wear."

Barry grabbed my shoulder and turned me around. He cradled the back of my head in his right hand. "Where's the white hair, Jack?"

"*What?*" I squeaked.

He let go of my head and spun me back around. "That

day you fell into the street—I saw this, like, upside-down V shape on the back of your head. Now it's gone. It means something, doesn't it? A secret symbol from some hidden organization?"

Cass's eyes were huge. Leave it to Barry, the dumbest person I knew, to come the closest to the truth.

"Uh . . ." Cass said.

"I'm right, huh?" Barry barked. "Go ahead, tell the Barry he's right!"

Let your enemy give you the lead.

Dad had recited that one to me at least a thousand times. And now, in this moment, I finally understood it.

I stepped right up to Barry and refused to blink. Then I took a deep breath and spoke fast. "You want the truth? Okay. My hair and Cass's? Yup, it did go white in the back, in the shape of a Greek lambda, which is their letter *L*. Now our hair is dyed. The lambda means we inherited a gene from a prince who escaped the sinking of Atlantis. See, the gene unlocks part of our DNA that turns our best ability into a superpower. But it also overwhelms the body, and no one who's ever had it has lived past the age of fourteen. In the last year of life, the body begins to break down. You get sick every few weeks. You can stay alive for a while if you get certain treatments, but eventually you die. We learned this from a group called the Karai Institute on this island that can't be detected. They told us we can

26

be cured if we find seven magical Loculi that contain the power of Atlantis, which were hidden centuries ago in the Seven Wonders of the Ancient World. As you know—well, maybe you don't—six of the Wonders don't exist anymore. The thing in your hand is a piece of a destroyed Loculus."

"Jack?" Cass mouthed, as if I'd just lost my mind.

Barry's mouth was sagging. His eyes narrowed, as if he were still stuck on the second sentence. Which he probably was.

Would he try to repeat his own mangled version of what I'd just said to his dad? I hoped so, because any sane human being would send him straight to a psychologist. And he knew it.

"Well, that's everything," I said, reaching to grab the Loculus from Barry's hand.

He pulled it back.

"Okay, so if you're supposed to get sick every few weeks . . ." he said quietly, "how come you're not sick?"

"The fresh, rejuvenating Belleville air?" Cass said.

Barry's face curled. "You guys are playing me. That was the obvious-est lie! I'm going to get to the bottom of this. You watch, I'll find out the truth."

"Great," I said. "Meanwhile, will you give me that back?"

"Why should I give you a piece of a destroyed Oculus?" Barry asked. "It might be worth something."

"Loculus," Cass said. "With an *L*."

27

"Trust me," I said, "it's worth absolutely nothing to you."

"Awwww, really?" Barry said. "Nothing?"

With an exasperated sigh, Barry held out the shard to Cass. Both of us reached for it at the same time.

Before our fingers could touch it, Barry spun away. With a grunt, he tossed it far into the scrubby, trash-strewn woods.

"Fetch," he said. "With an *F*."

CHAPTER FIVE

SHARD LUCK

"WHAT HAPPENED TO your face?" Dad stared at me oddly, standing in the front door.

I peeked past him to the sofa, where a strange man dressed in black was rising to his feet. "Thorns," I said, touching my cheek, where the edges of thin gash peeked out from behind a Band-Aid. "We lost something in the woods."

I didn't want to mention the shard in front of a stranger. It had taken us about a half hour on our hands and knees in the woods to find it. Which made us very late for school. The cool thing was, no one seemed to care. Cass and I were like returning war heroes. Everyone was nice to us. The nurse cleaned us up and gave me a whole box of Band-Aids.

The principal herself, Mrs. Sauer (pronounced *Sour*), brought a Welcome Back cake into homeroom. Barry ate most of it, but it was still nice. I even had a session with the school psychologist, who said she was screening me for PTSD. At first I thought that was some kind of a sandwich, like pastrami, turkey, salami, and dark bread, but it means post–traumatic stress disorder. The only stress I felt was from thinking about the great sandwich I wasn't going to eat.

"Jack . . . Cass," Dad said, "this is Mr. Anthony from Lock-Tite Security. After that strange little visit from the TV station this morning, I figure we'd better make ourselves safe from intrusions, wiretaps, recording devices. Somebody in this town—who shall remain nameless—thinks he's going to win an Emmy Award for investigative journalism."

Cass nodded. "I understand, Mr. McKinley. I met his son. I don't blame you."

"We'll go upstairs," I said.

We raced each other through the living room and up the back stairs. Cass reached the second-floor landing first. He quickly tossed off his shoes and socks before walking on the Oriental rug that lined the long hallway. "I love the way this feels. This house is so cool."

"You could have a whole room of your own, you know," I said. "We have a lot of them. There's more on third floor, too."

"We already decided we were going to share," Cass said. "Are you changing your mind?"

"No!" I said. "I just thought . . . if you ever felt like you needed space. It's a big house and all."

Cass shook his head, his face darkening. "Besides we have to be prepared. We can't be separated if it happens . . ."

"*It?*" I said.

"You know . . . *it*," Cass repeated. "Dying."

I leaned over, softly banging my head on the wood railing that looked out onto the first floor vestibule. "I thought we talked about this. We're going to stay positive, remember? We're feeling good so far, Dad is on the case—"

"Right," Cass said. "But doesn't that first part seem scary to you? About us feeling good?"

"*Dying* is scary, Cass!" I said. "Feeling good is not scary!"

"But we shouldn't be feeling good!" Cass replied. "By now, both of us—or at least you—should have had an episode. Which would mean we'd need a treatment. No one knows how to give us one!"

"Dad is working on it," I said.

"He has no contact with anyone in the KI, so how can he figure it out?" Cass said. "I've been thinking all day about what Barry Reese said. Why are we still healthy, Jack? We shouldn't be!"

"Uh, guys?" Dad's face appeared directly below me. He was scowling. "Can you please take it inside?"

31

Cass and I ran into our room and shut the door tight. I emptied my pockets onto the desk, yanked off my ripped pants, and quickly pulled on a pair of sweats I'd left on the floor. That was another agreement Cass and I had made. I could keep my side of the room as messy as I wanted.

Feeling more comfortable, I began pacing. "Okay, let's think about this. The intervals are irregular. Always have been. We know that."

"Yeah, but the older we get, the *closer* they should be," Cass said.

I couldn't argue that. Professor Bhegad had warned us exactly that would happen as we neared the Day of Doom.

Closer. Not farther away.

"I think it's the shards," Cass said. "Remember, it was the Loculus of *Healing*. It was supposed to restore life to the dead."

"You mean *shard*," I said.

"Shards." Cass shrugged. "I took one, too."

I looked at him. "You did? Why didn't you tell me?"

"I didn't think it was important," Cass replied. "I just took it as a souvenir. It's not as nice as yours. No designs or anything. I thought it was just a busted, useless piece of junk. But now . . ."

He went to his desk and pulled open a drawer. From the bottom he took out a hunk of material maybe three inches long, wrapped in tissue. "It's kind of ugly."

32

I heard a rustling noise from my pile of junk on my desk and jumped away.

Cass dropped the shard. "Whoa. Did you bring in a *mouse?*"

The rustling stopped. I darted my hand out and pushed aside some candy wrappers. No critters there.

Just my shard.

"Pick it up, Cass," I said softly. "Your shard."

Cass swallowed. He lifted the little disklike thing from the floor. On the desk, my shard began to twitch like a jumping bean. "Whoa . . ." Cass said.

I leaned over, peering closely at my shard, then Cass's. "They're not two random pieces," I said. "It looks like they may have broken apart from each other."

"It feels warm," Cass said.

"Hold the long side toward me," I said.

As Cass angled his arm, I reached out to my shard and turned it so its longest side faced Cass's.

"Ow—it's like a hundred degrees!" Cass said.

"Hold tight!" I said.

I felt a jolt like an electric current. As I pulled my fingers away from the shard, it shot across the room toward Cass.

With a scream, he dropped his relic and jumped away.

Bluish-white light flashed across our room. As Cass fell back on the lower bed with a shriek, the two shards collided in midair with a loud *DZZZZZT* and a blast that smelled like rotten eggs.

Flames shot up from the carpet as the pieces landed. I raced to the bathroom for a glass of water and doused the small fire quickly. I could hear Dad yelling at us from downstairs.

But neither Cass nor I answered him. We were too busy staring at what remained in the singed, smoking patch of carpet.

Not two shards, but one.

They had joined together, without a seam.

CHAPTER SIX

ALY-BYE

"WAIT, THEY JUST flew together and joined in midair," Aly said, "like snowflakes?"

Her hair was purple now, her face pale on my laptop screen. Belleville, Indiana, may have been overcast, but the Los Angeles sunshine was pouring through Aly's bedroom window.

"It was more like massive colliding spacecraft," Cass said. "Only . . . tiny. And not in outer space."

I held up the joined sections. Together they formed one larger shard. "You can't even tell where they were separated."

"That's awesome," Aly replied, as her face loomed closer to the screen. "Absomazingly ree-donculous. It means that—" Aly turned away from the screen and let out a loud sneeze.

And then another.

Cass's eyes widened. "Are you okay?"

"A cold," Aly said.

"Because Jack and I were wondering, you know, about the treatments," Cass went on. "It's been a while since your last episode . . ."

"It's *a cold*, that's all," Aly said, clacking away at her laptop. "Let's get down to business. I've been doing research. Tons. About the Seven Wonders. About Atlantis."

"Why?" Cass asked.

"Because what else am I going to do?" Aly said. "I know you're feeling bad, Cass. But I refuse to give up. We start by trying to get back in touch with the KI. They're lying low, but I'm betting they'll want to be in contact with us. Which means we need to protect our alibi. So I pretended to be, like, an evil spy searching for clues to break our story. All kinds of things didn't add up. That doctor friend of your dad's? His employee records showed he was in Mexico the day he supposedly treated Cass. And the convenience store where Marco was last seen? Its video feed showed a seven-foot-tall, red-bearded barefoot guy who bought three peanut butter sandwiches and a dozen doughnuts. The owner was suspicious, so he sent the feed to the local cops, who ran a primitive facial ID scan. They came up with three hundred and seven possible suspects. Including one Victor Rafael Quiñones."

"Who's that?" Cass asked.

"*Tor* from Victor, *quin* from Quiñones," Aly said. "I'm figuring Torquin is a nickname."

"Wait. His name is *Victor?*" Cass said.

"So of course I deleted the footage of Torquin from the FTP servers," Aly said. "Even the backups. And I altered the doctor's hospital records, too. I even hacked into his Facebook account and deleted the pictures of Mexico. I am covering our tracks so the alibi is clean. But the point is, I can't do everything. Things can go wrong. What if there are off-line copies of the originals? *Arrrrrghh!*" Aly shook her fists in frustration. "Okay. Okay, Black, stay calm and hack. I will try to locate Torquin or anyone who seems connected to the KI."

"Is that possible?" Cass asked.

Aly shrugged. "Anything's—" She broke off in a fit of coughing, swinging away from the screen. All we saw now was her bookcase.

"Aly?" Cass said.

Something thumped. I heard a choking noise. A pounding on the floor. *"Mo-o-om!"* came Aly's voice.

A blur passed across the screen—a woman with salt-and-pepper hair, wearing a T-shirt and jeans. She passed from top to bottom, falling to her knees and out of the screen. "Aly? *Aly, wake up!*"

I was on my feet now. *"ALY!"*

The image on the screen juddered. And then all went black.

CHAPTER SEVEN

DOWN AND OUT IN LA

"GALLUP, MCKINLEY!" CASS said, staring out the window of the jet.

"I'm not piloting this plane, Captain Nied is," Dad replied. "And he's going as fast as he can."

"That's not what I meant." Cass gestured to the distant ground below, which was clearly visible even in the dimming sunlight. "That little town near the river? It's called Gallup, New Mexico. Right near the Arizona border. It also happens to be in McKinley County. So it's Gallup, McKinley."

I took a deep breath. I could barely focus on what Cass what saying. Except for the "Gallup" part. Because my heart was galloping.

"I think it's named for US president William McKinley," Cass said. "He was shot. But he didn't die right away. He died because no one got to him in time."

"That's cheerful," Captain Nied said.

"Cass," Dad said softly, "we're doing the best we can. We'll get to Aly. She's with the best doctors in Southern California. Dr. Karl has promised me she'll see to her personally."

Dr. Karl was another college friend of Dad's. She was the head of emergency medicine at St. Dunstan Hospital, where Aly had been taken. I was becoming convinced Dad knew at least half the doctors in the United States. In my left hand I clutched my phone. Before leaving, I'd sent Aly three unanswered texts. There was no cell reception up here, but that didn't stop me from looking at the screen for about the thousandth time.

In my right hand I turned the shard around and around as if it were a magic charm. As if I could somehow massage it to full size. "I wish we were taking her a whole Loculus of Healing."

"That wouldn't cure her," Cass said. "Or us. It takes seven of these things to do that."

"Yeah, but it would buy some time," I said.

"You and I are feeling fine without a Loculus of Healing," Cass remarked with a deep sigh. "Why us and not her? Why does she get the bad luck?"

I stopped turning the shard. My hands felt warm. My first thought was body heat.

My second thought was, *Are you* crazy?

Spoons and forks didn't heat up in your hands when you fiddled with them. Neither did joysticks, worry beads, action figures, whatever.

I handed it to Cass. "Notice anything?"

"Whoa," Cass said. "Do you have a fever or something?"

"It's warm, right?" I said. "Like, unnaturally warm?"

Cass turned it around curiously. "It looks smaller to me."

"Cass, what if that heat isn't just heat?" I said. "What if it means something—like, it's active in some way?"

"Like, alive?" Cass said.

"No!" I said. "It's the shell of a Loculus that's existed for thousands of years, right? What if it absorbed some of that healing power? Maybe that's what's keeping you and me from having episodes."

Cass's eyes were as wide as baseballs. Dad was staring at the shard, too, from the copilot's seat. Together we looked at Captain Nied.

He yanked back the throttle, and the jet began to dive. "Fasten your seat belts, gents. And welcome to LA."

* * *

It is amazing what $200 will do to a Los Angeles cab-driver.

As we twisted and turned through the city streets, palm

40

trees and white stucco houses zoomed by in a blur. We could see the freeway in the distance, the cars at a total standstill. "Freeway is not free!" the cabdriver said in an accent I couldn't quite figure out. "Is prison for cars!"

No one laughed. We were too busy keeping our stomachs from jumping through our mouths. Dad was on his cell phone with the hospital the whole way.

According to Dr. Karl, Aly was alive, but it wasn't looking good.

As the taxi screeched to a stop in the hospital parking lot, we pushed our way out. I hooked my backpack around my shoulders and sprinted after Dad. He flashed his ID left and right, fast-talking his way past guards. In a moment we were on the fifth floor, barging into the intensive care unit. It was a massive room, echoing with beeps and shouts and lined with curtained-off areas.

A dark-haired woman with huge eyes peered out from behind one of the curtains. "How is she, Cindy?" Dad asked, marching across the room as if he were a regular.

"Breathing," Dr. Karl said, "but unresponsive. Her fever is spiking around a hundred four."

I pulled the shard out of my pocket and held tight. I almost didn't recognize Aly. Her skin was ashen, her eyes were only half-open, and her hair was pulled back into a green hospital cap. A breathing tube snaked from her mouth to a machine against the wall, and a tangle of tubes connected her arm to an IV stand with three different fluids.

Over her head was a screen that showed her heartbeat on a graph.

Aly's mom was holding her daughter's hand. Her face was streaked with tears, and her narrow glasses had slipped down her nose. She looked startled to see us. "Doctor . . . ?"

"Sorry," Dr. Karl said, "I'm going to have to ask the kids to stay in the waiting room. Standard procedure for intensive care."

"I have to speak to her," I insisted.

"She won't hear you," Aly's mom said. "She's completely unresponsive."

"Can I just touch her?" I said.

"*Touch* her?" Mrs. Black looked at me as if I were crazy.

"This is way beyond ICU protocol," Dr. Karl said. "If you don't leave now, I will have to call security—"

BEEP! BEEP! BEEP!

Cass and I jumped back. "Are they coming to get us?" Cass asked.

"It's not a security alarm. It's something to do with Aly!" I said. Aly's monitors were flashing red. Her eyes sprang open and then rolled upward into her head. She let out a choking sound, and her body began to twitch. As three nurses came running from the center of the room, Dr. Karl strapped Aly's arms down.

"What's happening?" I demanded.

"Febrile seizure!" Dr. Karl said. *"Clear the area!"*

"But—" I said.

A nurse with a barrel chest and a trim beard pulled me back, and I nearly collided with Cass. As the hospital staff closed in around Aly's bed, we both stumbled back toward the entrance.

"They're killing her, Jack!" Cass said. "Do something!"

I dropped my pack. "I'm going invisible. It's the only way I can get to her."

"There's no room for you," Cass said. "If you barge in, they will feel you, Jack. It'll freak everybody out. Total chaos, and it won't be good for her."

"Any other ideas?" I said.

Cass nodded. "Yeah. I'll distract them. Give me three seconds."

"What?"

But Cass was already running away, heading toward the table that contained the medical equipment and monitors.

One . . .

I reached into the pack and lifted out the Loculus of Invisibility.

Two . . .

As I stepped forward, the loud beeps stopped. I looked toward the monitors. They were dark. Aly's equipment had shut down completely. Cass was scampering away from the wall socket, where he had pulled out the plugs.

43

Three!

I heard a shout. Two nurses broke away from Aly, scrambling toward the equipment, leaving her right side wide open. I raced toward her, clutching the Loculus of Invisibility with one hand and the shard with the other. Dr. Karl was injecting something into her left arm, concentrating hard.

Aly's chest was still. She wasn't breathing. I placed the shard on her stomach, just below her ribs.

"The pads—now!" Dr. Karl shouted. "We're losing her!"

"Come on . . ." I said under my breath. "Come on, Aly. You have to live." Aly's eyes stared upward, green and bright, dancing in the light even in her unconsciousness. I felt like I could talk to her, like she'd answer me back with some kind of geeky joke. I wanted to see her smile.

But there was no reaction. Not a fraction of an inch of movement.

A doctor was racing toward Aly with two pads strapped to his hands. They were going to try to shock her alive. I pressed the shard harder into her abdomen. I guess I was crying, because tears were falling onto her face.

Aly's mom bumped into me and screamed. It wouldn't be much longer before my invisible presence was going to be a big deal.

"We have power!" a voice barked. With a soft whoosh, the monitors fired up and the lights blinked on. The heartbeat graph showed a long, horizontal, flat line.

Dead. A flat line meant dead.

The doctor placed the pads on either side of Aly's chest but I did not take my hand away—not even when they shot electricity through her, and her body flopped like a rag doll.

It wasn't working.

Aly was ghost white and still. Her chest wasn't moving. As Dr. Karl finally called off the electric shocks, I pressed harder than ever, leaning toward her face.

"I'm . . . I'm so, so sorry," Dr. Karl said to Aly's mom.

I had failed.

She was the first to die. One of us would be next, then the other. And then there would be none.

I brushed my lips against her cool forehead. "Good-bye, Aly," I whispered. "I—" The words clogged up in my brain, and I had to force them out. "I love you, dude. Yeah. Just saying."

I let go of her and walked away toward the center of the room. I felt numb. My eyes focused on nothing.

"Jack?" Cass whispered, wandering toward me, looking all teary and confused. "Where are you?"

I picked up the backpack and slipped the Loculus of Invisibility back inside. As I became visible, I noticed I was next to two doctors who must have seen me materialize out of thin air.

But they hadn't seemed to notice. They were both

staring over my head toward Aly. Gaping.

Cass turned. His jaw dropped. "What the—?"

As I wiped away tears, the first thing I noticed was Aly's mom. She was on the floor, fainted away.

The second thing I noticed was Aly sitting up, staring straight at me.

"You *love* me?" she said.

CHAPTER EIGHT

THE HUMPTY DUMPTY PROJECT

SHE WAS ALIVE.

Half of me wanted to jump with joy. The other half wanted to sink down and melt into the linoleum. Dad and Dr. Karl stood by the bed, gaping as if their mouths had been propped open by invisible pencils.

"I heard you say it, Jack McKinley!" Aly laughed as if nothing bad had happened. "You said, 'I love you'! I heard it!"

My mouth flapped open and shut a couple of times. "The shard . . ." I finally squeaked. "It worked."

Aly's smile abruptly vanished. She looked around the ICU. "Wait. *Jack? Cass?* What are you doing here? Why am I in a hospital? Why is Mom on the floor?"

I rushed over. Dad and I both lifted Mrs. Black to

her feet. Her eyes puddled with tears. As she hugged her daughter, the place was going nuts. Cass was screaming, pumping his fists. The hospital staff high-fived each other like middle school kids. Dr. Karl looked bewildered. I thought I could see some tears on her cheeks as Aly's mom hugged her, too.

"You are a miracle worker, doctor," Mrs. Black said. "Thank you."

"I—I'm not sure what did it," Dr. Karl said. "I guess . . . the pads?"

Aly pulled me closer. "What happened?" she whispered. "I had an episode, right? And you guys flew out to see me."

"Um, yeah," I whispered back.

"So how did the doctor figure out—?" she asked.

"She didn't," I replied.

"Wait—so *you* did it?" she said. "You saved my life?"

"It's a long story," I said.

Aly smiled. Her eyes moistened. "Backsies."

"What?"

"About what you said," she said, "into my ear . . ."

I felt my face heating up. "That's because I thought you were dead!"

Doofus. Idiot.

She was looking at me like I'd just slapped her. But before either of us could say anything, the crowd of medical people began elbowing me away. Dr. Karl was shouting orders. All kinds of tubes were being hooked up to Aly's arms.

I backed away, standing with Cass. "Boj emosewa," he said.

"Thanks," I said.

I took a deep breath. I felt a million things. Happiness. Relief. Embarrassment. Pride. I could finally feel my body relaxing. That was when I opened my clenched palm and looked at the shard.

It was the size of a quarter.

And the only thing I felt was scared.

* * *

"What if it just . . . vanishes?" Cass paced back and forth in our hotel room. Behind him was a huge picture window. The sunset looked like an egg yolk spreading on the Pacific Ocean. "We use up its power, it gets smaller and smaller, and then, poof, it's gone?"

"I wasn't expecting it to shrink like that," I said.

"Jack, it's been getting smaller all along," Cass said. "I tried to tell you that back home. It must be like a battery. You and I used up some of its power. Aly used up a lot more."

"We have to preserve it somehow," I said. "But we can't exactly hide it away. It's buying us time."

"I wish we could contact the KI," Cass said with a sigh. "I wish we hadn't been cut off like that. Don't you think that's weird—they take Torquin away and then . . . radio silence?"

"Maybe they've given up on us," I said.

Cass flopped on one of the double beds and stared out the window. "Now you sound like me."

I could feel my phone vibrating in my pocket. Aly was calling. "Hello?" I said.

"I'm bored," Aly's voice piped up.

I put her on speaker. "Hi, Bored. I'm Jack. Cass is here, too. How are you feeling?"

"Good," she replied. "Too good to be sitting here in the dark in a hospital room. The doctors have finally stopped coming in and gawking. They're talking about releasing me tomorrow. I'm like the Miracle Girl. I feel like an exhibit at the Museum of Natural Hysteria, and I'm tired of talking. So it's your turn, Jack. *You* know what happened to me, and I want you to tell me now."

I explained it all—the shards, the shrinkage, the healing power, the trip to LA, and my stunt with the Loculus of Invisibility.

When I was done, the phone fell quiet for a long moment. "Um, are you still awake?" I finally said.

"That silence," she said, "is the sound of my mind being blown. Do you realize what this means? If your two shards fused like that, we may be able to put the whole thing together again."

"Like Humpty Dumpty!" Cass added.

"Which means we have to get to the other pieces," Aly went on.

50

Cass hopped off the bed. *"Yes!"*

"Whoa, hold on—the Massa took the other pieces," I said. "They're probably back on the island right now, trying to fit them together."

"Exactly," Aly said. "So there are two possibilities. They manage to do it, and they realize there's a piece missing. In which case they will be coming after us."

"Or?" I said.

"Or they won't be able to do anything with those shards at all," she said, "because you guys are G7W and they're not. Don't forget, the Loculi get their power from us. Without us, there's a good chance those shards will just be shards."

"You are a genius," Cass said.

"How do we get to the island?" I said. "My dad can get us anywhere from Chicago to Kathmandu in a private plane. But even he can't get to an island shielded from detection. Torquin's the only person who can get us there, and he's gone."

"It's findable by the KI, and by the Massa," Aly said. "If they can do it, so can we."

"How?" Cass asked.

"I'm thinking," Aly said.

I was thinking, too. I was thinking about Brother Dimitrios and my mom, heading across the ocean. Dimitrios was probably happy to have the Loculus pieces. Maybe the Massa couldn't fuse the shards, but they could try to fit

51

them together like puzzle pieces. Would Dimitrios find out that Mom had dropped one? What would happen to her if he did?

I began to sweat. Even now, I wasn't sure which side Mom was on. She seemed to want to help us. Which would make her a mole inside the Massa organization. But she had left Dad and me to join them—faked her own death and kept it secret all these years. How could I trust her? *How could I not trust my own mom?*

My mind was firing in all directions. I pictured Mom on a plane with the Massa, staring out the window, scared.

"The Massa," I said. "Somehow we have to get the Massa to take us there."

"Are you crazy?" Cass said. "We just risked our lives escaping them!"

"Jack, we don't know where they are," Aly said.

Something Dad had said on the train was still echoing in my head. *The best way to predict how people will act is knowing what they want.*

"Maybe not," I said. "But we know what they want. And it's the same thing the KI wants."

"World domination?" Cass asked.

"Loculi," I replied. "And we still have two of them. At some point—probably after the heat is off us—they will come after us."

"We don't have time to wait," Aly said. "It may take

them weeks, or months. That shard is going to shrink to nothing."

"Exactly," I said. "We have to make that happen ourselves. We have to make them find us. There are four likely places they are monitoring right now—four places that have the unfound Loculi."

"The four remaining Wonders of the World!" Aly blurted out.

"I'll work on my dad," I said. "You work on your mom, Aly. Explain that it's a matter of life or death. We get ourselves back to the island and find Fiddle. He's hidden away with some KI operatives. They've got to be planning something. They'll help us. The moment you get out of the hospital—"

"Wait," Cass said. "We're supposed to sneak away, travel to one of the sites, and look for the Massa?"

"No." I shook my head. "All we need to do is go there. And let them come to us."

CHAPTER NINE

MAUSOLEUM DREAM

I LOOK OVER my shoulder. He is not here yet. But he will be.

WHO?

All I know, all I recognize, is that I am back in Bodrum. The last place in the world I want to be. The place where we failed to find the Loculus. Our last stop before NYC, where all our hope was lost—

The others—Dad, Cass, Aly, Torquin, and Canavar—are nowhere. The hotels and houses are gone, too. I'm wearing sandals and a robe. My mind goes from confusion to panic. Before me is an expanse of blackness, the contours of surrounding hills lit only by moonlight.

Bodrum is Halicarnassus. I am in another time. And my Jack thoughts are being crowded out of my head.

In rushes a flood of other, more distant memories. Of beauty and pain. Of deep-green forests and smooth blue lakes, happy laughing families, scholars teaching children, athletes wrestling deadly piglike vromaskis, sharp-clawed red griffins swooping overhead.

Of smoldering clouds and raging fires, blackened corpses and shrieking beasts.

Over my shoulder is a leather sack. Inside is a sphere. It looks like the Loculus of Healing, but I know it's not. It is fake. I planned it this way. I am also heading in the wrong direction—away from the distant silhouette of the great half-finished structure in the distance. The Mausoleum.

I planned that part, too.

I hurry onward quickly, keeping the sea to my left.

I know now. I am Massarym. And I have a plan.

Not far ahead, maybe a half mile, is a hill. Trees and thick bushes. A team of mercenaries awaits there. They will take me to safety. After my plan is fulfilled.

I want to be found before I reach them. I must be found. The plan depends on this. My mind conjures up an image: the real Loculus, I see, is safe underground. Or so I hope.

I am scared. But I slow my steps, deepen my breaths.

When the explosion happens, I am barely prepared for the blast of light, the cloud of dirt like a giant fist. I stagger back. I fall to my knees.

Then the cloud begins to lift, and a tall, bearded man emerges. He wears a white, gilt-edged robe. Although his hair is gray, he stands straight, like a warrior, his shoulders thickly muscled. His body radiates power, but his face, which is familiar to me, is etched in sadness.

Part of me wants to run to him, to hug him. But those days are over. The lines have been drawn. He is my enemy now, because he is an enemy of the world.

"I am hoping you have come to your senses," he says deeply, forcefully.

I am both comforted and repulsed by the sound of my father's voice.

As the old man comes nearer, his robe snaps in the sea-thick wind. I see the hilt of his sword, his prized possession, jutting from its scabbard. But the scabbard's leather is frayed and ragged looking. I know Father must not be happy about this indignity. Slowly I sidestep closer to the edge of the cliff. Below us, the waves crash against the shore.

"My senses," I say in a voice with false confidence, a voice that isn't my own, "have never been lost, Uhla'ar."

The old man's face softens slightly into a rueful smile. He holds out a powerful arm, his palm extended.

I step closer and then turn. With a swift, sure thrust, I toss the Loculus into the sea.

I watch the sphere turning and growing smaller in the dull light of the moon. My father's eyes bulge. His mouth becomes a black hole.

As he dives into the raging churn below, his scream slices me like a dagger.

CHAPTER TEN

IF IT LOOKS LIKE A HOAX...?

TWO DAYS.

That was how long it took the doctors to release Aly. I thought about the dream a lot during that time. But neither Cass nor I could figure out what it meant.

The more important thing was convincing Dad about our plan. He tried hard to act like we were happy beach-going tourists in la-la land, but we pounded him with logic and pleading, to no avail. I'm surprised he didn't drop us both into the La Brea Tar Pits.

When Aly was released, we had a great reunion, on two levels. On the top floor of her house, Aly, Cass, and I pored over her research materials, trying to figure out where to get ourselves captured.

On the first floor, her mom and my dad were having lunch. And arguing. Well, okay, *discussing.*

"My dad doesn't love the idea," I said.

"He's gone from 'Are you out of your minds?' to 'Can we change the subject?'" Cass said.

"I think Mom is willing," Aly said. "I told her this was the only way to keep me alive. She said she'd already seen me die and didn't want it to happen again. Give her a chance. She can be very persuasive." Her fingers clicked over the keyboard. "Okay, take a look at this."

www.magicalRouthouni.gr

EXPERIENSE THE
MAGICK OF ANCIENT
ROUTHOUNI

• With it's healing waters and cultures of great marvell, that makes Routhouni famous!!!

• Dine in style with so many of our delictious caffés by the water side!!!!!

• While the ancient Wonder Of The World, "KING ZEUS" who every one talks of throgh all histories, waethes over YOU!!!!

"Looks like Torquin on a bad hair day," Cass said.

"Is this a joke?" I asked.

"Stay with me," Aly said. "I thought this was cheesy, too, but there was something about it. So I did a little digging around. And I found this."

Now she was clicking away to another page:

MYTHDEBUNKERS.org
Exposing hoaxes since 1998

Statue in Routhouni Square, Greece,
Is the Statue of Zeus at Olympia

FALSE.
An email message has been circulating since 2001, citing an archaeological claim that a statue in a small Peloponnesian town is actually one of the Seven Wonders of the Ancient World: the Statue of Zeus at Olympia.

THE LEGEND: The statue appeared in an olive grove near Routhouni in AD 425, around the time of the demise of the statue of Zeus. At the statue's feet was the dead body of a young man, impaled by Zeus's staff. Amazed locals brought the statue into town, convinced it was a manifestation of Zeus himself. With proper honor and worship, they thought, Zeus would remain a silent and benevolent protector.

THE FACTS: the statue in Routhouni Square looks nothing like the statue of Zeus, which was seated. Its obvious crudeness strikes many as laughable. Some nineteenth-century scholars claimed it was a study for the Zeus statue, or perhaps the statue's "first draft." But in the face of no evidence, modern scholars conclude that this is old-fashioned Victorian thinking at its most fanciful.

I took a deep breath. "If it looks like a hoax and the experts say it's a hoax . . ."

Aly clicked the back button and returned to the Routhouni website. "Take a look at the thing in the statue's hand."

She zoomed in to the image:

"A bowling ball?" Cass said.

Aly smacked him. "What if it's a *Loculus*? Think about it. The Seven Wonders were built to protect the Loculi. When we found the Colossus, he tried to kill us. What if the statue of Zeus came to life, too?"

"So it went after somebody who tried to take its Loculus, stabbed him, then went back to being a statue?" Cass asked. "Who would try to take a Loculus? Who would even know what it was?"

THE CURSE OF THE KING

"Another Select, I guess," I said with a shrug.

"So Zeus the statue came to life and went after the thief," Aly said. "He actually transformed into Zeus the god. And he chased the thief until he caught up to him. After killing the thief, Zeus turned back into a statue."

Cass gave her a dubious smile. "Okay, that's one possibility. What about the other Wonders?"

"Well, there's the Lighthouse at Pharos," she said, "but that's in Alexandria, which is a big bustling city—too exposed. The Temple of Artemis is in a big tourist area—Ephesus, Turkey. We've been to the Pyramids, and we know the Massa cleared out of there. I think Zeus is our best shot. Look, the question is not *Is this convincing?* The question is *Would the Massa think this is convincing?* I'm betting yes. I'm betting they have this thing staked out."

Before she finished the sentence, I could hear footsteps on the stairs.

We froze. Dad and Mrs. Black appeared in the doorway. Their faces were grim and drawn. Dad had his phone in his hand. I could practically read the *no* in their eyes.

I decided to talk first.

"January, August, April, July," I said. "Those are the months Aly, Marco, Cass, and I turn fourteen. I know what you're going to say, Dad. MGL is hard at work on a cure. But—"

"We had a setback at McKinley Genetics Lab," Dad

61

said. "Our team was developing a shutoff mechanism. But it doesn't work. The gene mutates, Jack. When you attach anything to its receptors, they change shape. It's like a beast that grows a new heart after you kill it."

"That so totally sucks," Cass said.

"What does it mean?" I asked.

Dad sighed. "It means we'll need six months of new research, maybe a year . . ."

I felt the blood drain from my face. "We don't have that time."

Aly's mom ran her fingers through her daughter's hair. "No, you don't."

Dad nodded. "We're going back to the hotel. How long will it take you to be ready, Aly?"

"Five minutes!" Aly shot back. "Maybe four."

Dad turned toward the door and said the words I hadn't expected to hear. "Wheels up in one hour. Wherever you guys want to go."

CHAPTER ELEVEN

GOD OF COUCH POTATOES

LEAVING THE LOCULI at home was out of the question. Dad and I were both paranoid the Massa—or some snoop hired by Morty Reese—would break in and steal them. So we took them with us on Dad's jet. For protection. We also packed flashlights and supplies in our packs and made sure our phones were charged.

The ride was bumpy. We argued for six hours about how to proceed. Aly was still thin and quiet from being sick. But by the time we reached the Kalamata International Airport, we had a plan. Cass, Aly, and I would grab a taxi. Alone. Bringing Dad with us, we decided, would make the Massa suspicious. Plus, it would do us no good if he wound up captured along with us.

So Dad and the Loculi stayed behind with the plane.

I was a nervous wreck. The taxi had no air-conditioning and there was a hole in the front passenger floor. Rocks spat up into the car from the road as we sped noisily across Greece. Soon the mountains of the Peloponnese rose up in the distance to our right, and Cass had a revelation. "Whoa," he cried out, looking up from his phone. "The meaning of *Routhouni* is 'nostril'!"

"Is geography!" our driver said. (Everything he said seemed to come with an exclamation point.) "Just north of Routhouni is long mountain with—how do you say? Ridge! To Ancient Greeks, this looks like straight nose! Greek nose! Strong! At bottom is two valleys—round valleys! Is like, you know . . . *thio Routhounia* . . . two nostrils!"

"And thus," Cass announced, "Routhouni *picked* its name."

"Cass, please . . ." Aly said.

Cass began narrating like a TV host. "Our car develops a moist coating as it enters the rim of the *Routhouni*. It is said that the people here are a bit snotty, tough around the edges but soft at the core."

"Ha! Is funny boy!" the driver exclaimed.

Cass gestured grandly out the window. "Exotic giant black hairs, waving upward from the ground and dotted with festive greenish globs, greet visiting tourists as they plunge upward into the—"

"Ew, Cass—just *ew!*" Aly said. "Can we leave him by the side of the road?"

On the outskirts of town, goats roamed in vast, sparse fields. Old men in ragged coats stared at us, their backs bent and their hands clinging to gnarled wooden canes. Black-clad old ladies sat knitting in front of rickety shacks, and a donkey ignored our driver's horn, just staring at us in the middle of the street. I felt strangely paranoid. I clutched the backpack tightly.

As we drove slowly through a flock of squawking chickens, I read the English section of a big, multilingual road sign:

You are aproching Routhouni the Prid of the Peloponnese!!!

"Prid?" Cass said.

"I think they mean 'pride,'" Aly answered.

Where on earth *were* we?

"Maybe we should have brought Dad along," I said. "This is pretty remote."

"We want the Massa to think we're alone," Aly said. "That was the plan. If we need to, we can call him."

I nodded. Dad had promised to hire a chopper if necessary, if anything were to go wrong. Which seemed weird, considering that "going right" meant being captured.

I tried to imagine Brother Dimitrios and his gang actually traveling to this place. I couldn't imagine *anyone* in his right mind traveling here.

We rounded a bend, following a narrow alley lined with whitewashed buildings. The car began swerving around potholes, bouncing like crazy. "Who paved this road," Aly grumbled, "Plato?"

"Is funny girl!" the driver barked.

He slowed to ten kilometers an hour as we crept toward the town center. I knew we were getting close by the sound of Greek music and the smell of fried food. Soon the dark, tiny street opened up into a big cobblestoned circular plaza surrounded by storefronts. We paid the driver and got out. I don't know what they were cooking, but I had to swallow back a mouthful of drool.

Did I say I was starving?

I was starving. I hadn't eaten in five hours.

Most of the shops were shuttering for the evening, but the cafés and restaurants were jumping. People strolled across the plaza, slowly and aimlessly, arm in arm. Kids chased each other and played catch. In the restaurants, stray cats wove around people's legs, looking for scraps, while entertainers in flowing costumes sang and played tambourines, guitars, and strange instruments that sounded like oboes. Old men sat silently outside the cafés at backgammon tables, sipping coffee and amber-colored drinks. An outdoor bar called America!! had two huge flat-screen TVs, one blaring a soccer game in Greek and the other an old rerun of *Everybody Loves Raymond* in English.

In the center was Zeus.

Or something Zeus-ish.

The statue glowered over the surroundings like a creepy, unwanted party guest. No one seemed to be paying it much notice. Its face and shoulders were peeling and pockmarked, like it had a skin disease. Its eyes were pointed in the direction of a flat-screen TV. Over time the eyeballs had eroded, so it looked like a grown-up Child of the Corn. In its raised hand was a big soccer ball–like thing, but I could barely see it under a dense crowd of birds.

"Behold, the Loculus of Pigeon Droppings," Cass mumbled, as we slowly walked around the plaza. "Held aloft by Zeus, God of Couch Potatoes, now approaching his record two millionth consecutive hour of TV viewing."

"Can't you be serious for once?" Aly hissed.

I could feel the curious eyes of the café-dwelling old men. One of the musicians moved toward us through the crowd—a girl about our age, maybe a little older. The hem of her skirt was raggedy, but the fabric was a rich patchwork of reds, purples, and blues, spangled with bright baubles. Her ankles and wrists jangled with bracelets. As she caught my eye, she smiled and then said, *"Deutsch? Svenska? Eenglees?"*

67

"Uh, English," I said. "American. No money. Sorry."

One of the café waiters came running toward us, shouting at the beggar girl to chase her away. As she ran off, he gestured toward the café. "Come! Eat! Fish! Music! I give you good price!"

Now customers and coffee sippers were staring at the commotion. "This is bad," I whispered. "We don't want to attract public attention. This is not how you stage an abduction. Kidnappers need quiet."

"Don't look now," Cass said, "but they're here. Other side of the plaza. We're six o'clock, they're twelve. Just to the left of the big TV!"

The TV was no longer playing *Everybody Loves Raymond* but an old black-and-white episode of *I Love Lucy*. Sitting at a small round table were four men in brown monk robes.

The Massarene.

I couldn't tell if they were the exact same goons who'd tried to kill us in Rhodes. We were too far away. Those pious robes hid a gang of thugs who would shoot at thirteen-year-old kids from helicopters.

"What do we do?" Aly asked.

"They tried to murder us once already!" Cass said.

"That was before the Massa knew who we were," I said. "Remember, they need us."

"So we just walk up to their tables?" Cass asked. "Like,

'*Yia sou,* dudes! Can we offer you some baklava for dessert, or maybe a kidnapping?'"

"Just let them see us," I said. "Come on, follow me."

The shortest route was directly across the plaza. People crisscrossed back and forth in front of us, as the sitcom's laugh track washed over the town square. The monks were eating and talking quietly, ignoring the TV. As we passed the statue, one of them looked up toward us. He had a thick brown unibrow and an intense, angry stare.

Aly tugged at my arm. "Where's Cass?"

I whirled around. I could see Cass a few feet behind us, at the base of the statue. He was helping up a crying little boy who had fallen on the cobblestones. The kid's parents smiled and thanked him, jabbering away in Greek. Cass backed away and tripped over a stone, too, landing against the statue. It looked like he was doing it on purpose, to cheer up the little boy and make him laugh. "I'll get him," I said.

But as I stepped toward Cass, I heard an odd cracking noise, like the turning of an ancient mill wheel.

The little boy shrieked, jumping into his father's arms. I could hear chairs scraping behind us, people screaming.

Pop! A jagged projectile of broken stone flew toward me and I ducked.

Pop! Pop! Pop! They were flying all around now.

I scrambled backward toward the café. The monks had

69

left their seats and were backing away. Desserts and dinners lay abandoned on tables, dropped to the ground.

"Jack!" Cass screamed.

High above him, the statue of Zeus turned, shedding more marble pieces. And it reared back with its staff, pointing it toward Cass.

CHAPTER TWELVE

BIIIIG TROUBLE

"CASS, GET AWAY from it—it thinks you're trying to steal the Loculus!" Aly screamed.

She dived toward Cass, pulling him away from the statue.

Zeus was moving by centimeters. Each jerk of his arm cracked the marble that encased him. "Lll . . . oc . . . ul . . . ssss . . ."

The word was just barely recognizable. Each syllable was accompanied by a sickening creak.

"Um . . . um . . ." I crawled backward. My tongue felt like a strip of Velcro.

I heard a chaos of noise behind us. Screams. Chairs clattering to the pavement. Children crying. The square was

71

clearing out. Aly clutched my left arm, Cass my right.

Within minutes, the square had completely emptied. No more old men. No bumbling waiters. No begging gypsies or bouzouki-playing musicians. Just us, the sound of the TVs, and the deep groans of the marble cracking.

A mist swirled up from the ground now in tendrils of green, yellow, and blue. It gathered around the statue, whistling and screaming.

The statue's expression was rock stiff, but its eyes seemed to brighten and flare. With a pop of breaking stone, its mouth shot open, and it roared with a sound that seemed part voice, part earthquake. The swirls sped and thickened, and in moments Zeus was juddering as if he had been electrocuted by one of his own thunderbolts.

In that moment we could have run.

But we stayed there, bolted to the spot by shock, as a bright golden-white globe landed on the stones with barely a sound and rolled toward a café. Its surface glowed with an energy that seemed to have dissolved the centuries of grit and bird droppings. I felt my body thrumming deeply, as if each artery and vein had been plucked like a cello.

"The Song of the Heptakiklos . . ." I said.

"So it *is* a Loculus!" Aly said.

I couldn't take my eyes from the orb. I staggered toward it, my head throbbing. All thoughts were gone except one: *If we could take this and then rescue the Loculus of Health, we would have four.*

"Jack, what are you doing?" Cass screamed.

I felt Aly grabbing me by the arm, pulling me away. We rammed into Cass, who was frozen in place, staring at the statue. We all looked up. Before our eyes, the statue's veins of marble turned blue and red, slowly assuming the warm, fluid texture of human skin.

Zeus was shrinking. The massive statue was becoming a man.

Or maybe a god.

As the mist receded, Zeus lowered his head. His eyes were a deep brown now, his face dark, and his hair iron gray. The muscles in his arms rippled as he stepped toward us, lifting the staff high above his head. *"Loculussss . . ."* he murmured.

"Give it to him!" Cass screamed. "He doesn't see it! He thinks you stole it! *Yo! Zeus! Your godliness! O Zeus! Look— it's on the ground!"*

"He doesn't understand English!" Aly said.

"IIII'LL GUB YOUUUU, MY PITY!" the statue bellowed.

"That sounds like English!" Cass said. "What's he saying?"

"Wait. 'I'll get you, my pretty'?" Aly said. "From *The Wizard of Oz*?"

The statue was moving slowly, creakily. It clearly hadn't

moved in a long time and its eyesight wasn't good. I had no intention of backing away. I wanted that Loculus. "Guys, I'm going after it. Back me up. Distract Zeus."

"Are you out of your mind?" Cass screamed. "We came here to be kidnapped!"

"We came here to win back our lives," I said. "Who knows if we'll ever have this chance again? *Back me up!*"

"B-but—" Cass stammered.

Aly placed a hand on his shoulder. Stepping between Cass and the statue, she straightened herself to full height. "Yo! Lightning Boy!"

The statue turned to face her.

And I moved slowly, step by step backward, through the shadows, toward the Loculus. The statue's eyes didn't waver from Aly. He was speaking a string of words in a strange language. It sounded vaguely Greek, of which I understand exactly zero, but the rhythms of it seemed weirdly familiar. Like I could hear the music but couldn't identify the instruments.

Go, McKinley. Now.

I turned. The pale moonlight picked up the contour of the fallen orb in the shadow of a café. As I crept closer, my head was jammed up with the Song of the Heptakiklos now. Gone was the noise from the TVs, from Aly's conversation. The Loculus was calling to me as if it were alive. As I reached for it, I heard something behind me, in a deep, growly rasp.

"OHHHH, LUUUUCY, YOU ARE IN BIIIIG TROU-BLE NOW."

I turned. Aly and Cass were both gawking at the statue. "Could you repeat that?" Aly said.

The statue lifted one leg and hauled it forward. It thumped to the ground. *"TO THE MOOOON, ALIIICE!"*

"What's he saying?" Cass asked.

"I Love Lucy," Aly said. *"The Honeymooners.* Those—those are lines from old sitcoms."

From behind me came the sound of a laugh track. "That TV . . ." I said. "Zeus has been watching it for years. Decades. It's the only English he knows. The sitcoms and the ads."

The former statue was staring at me now. Its pupils were dark black pools. The muscles in its face seemed to be tightening, its mouth drawing back. As I grabbed the Loculus, I felt a jolt up my arm, as if I'd stuck my finger in an electric socket. I tried to hold back a scream, gritting my teeth as hard as I could.

"Jack!" Aly screamed.

I turned just in time to feel a whoosh against my cheek. Zeus's staff flew past me, embedding itself in the ground.

Holding tight to the Loculus, I ran for the edge of the town square. In a moment Aly and Cass were by my side. "Follow me!" Cass shouted, leading us down an unlit alleyway.

75

As we raced out of town, I could see pairs of eyes staring at us out of darkened windows. Mothers and fathers. Children.

A voice behind us thundered loudly, echoing against the stucco walls. *"LOOOOCUULUUUUS!"*

CHAPTER THIRTEEN

THE FOURTH LOCULUS

IF I THOUGHT Zeus was a creaky old has-been, I was dead wrong.

We were running so fast I could barely feel my feet touch the cobblestones. But I could hear the steady thump of leather sandals behind us. The street was ridiculously narrow. We were running single file, with me at the rear, Aly in the middle and looking over her shoulders, and Cass in front.

"COWABUNGAAAA!" the statue shouted.

Aly's eyes widened. *"Duck!"* she cried.

I hit the ground. And Zeus's staff hurtled past us overhead like a javelin, impaling itself in the grate of a steel sewer basin with a metallic clunk.

I leaped to my feet, holding the Loculus under my arm like a football. Zeus wasn't more than twenty yards away now. I was going to be shish kebab unless I got the staff before Zeus did.

I scrambled and slid to a stop at the staff. Zeus roared when he saw what I was trying to do. The weapon was pretty well jammed into the grating, but on the third tug, I managed to pry it loose—along with the sewer grating, which went flying across the sidewalk.

"GGEEEEAAAAAGGHHH!" I didn't recognize the sound of my own voice. I lifted my arm and felt the weight of the staff. The thing must have been nearly as heavy as I was, but it felt impossibly light in my hands.

Zeus leaped toward me, arms outstretched. My body moved into action. I spun to the left. My arm swung the staff, connecting with the statue's legs in midair. He flipped forward, his face smacking hard onto the street. Without missing a beat, I raised the staff high and stood over him.

He rolled over and scrambled away on his back, a look of terror spreading across his face.

I could see Cass and Aly now, looking at me from behind the building in astonishment.

I was pretty scared, too. What had I just done?

"I WOULD HAVE GOTTEN AWAY WITH IT, TOO . . ." the statue said, *". . . IF IT WEREN'T FOR YOU MEDDLING KIDS . . . !"*

78

"What?" I replied.

*"I THINK THIS IS THE BEGINNING OF A BEAU-
TIFUL FRIENDSHIP."*

"Scooby-Doo!" Aly shouted. *"Casablanca!"*

"Is that his only English?" I said. "Aly, you're an old
movie geek. Can you give him an answer he'll understand?"

"Um . . . 'Surrender, Dorothy'?" she said.

But Zeus wasn't listening. Cocking his head, he stepped
forward, staring at me. I raised the staff, and he stopped.

"Masssarrrymmm?"

His voice was softer now. It was a question. A real question. And in a flash I was beginning to understand this
thing. "Wow . . ." I said. "He thinks I'm Massarym. He
thinks I'm the one who gave him the Loculus."

"M-m-must be a family resemblance," Cass said.

I stepped forward. "Jack," I said, pointing to myself. "I
am Jack."

"Dzack," the statue said, pointing to me.

"Right—Jack, not Massarym," I said. "So. Can't you
leave us alone? *Go back!* You don't need this Loculus. What
are you going to do with it? You're *Zeus!* You can throw
thunderbolts and stuff. Do you understand? *Go back!"*

Zeus shook his head. His cheeks seemed to sag.
"GO . . . ?"

"Home!" I said.

"PHONE HOME . . . ?" Zeus growled.

Oh, great. *E.T.* He was stomping closer to me now. That was the only way to describe it. His legs were muscular but still a little stiff. I could see now that his eyes were not a solid color but a roiling mass of shapes and colors, all tumbling around like a miniature storm. I backed off, keeping Cass and Aly behind me. With one hand I held tight to the Loculus, with the other I kept the staff firmly pointed.

"Just give it to him or he'll kill us!" Cass said, grabbing the Loculus out of my hands.

He caught me by surprise. As the Loculus came free, the staff fell from my grip. It was too heavy for me to hold. With a crack, it broke into three pieces against the cobblestones.

And in that moment, I knew exactly what kind of Loculus we had. Lifting that staff, leaping like a ninja—it wasn't adrenaline that let me do those things.

"Cass, that's a Loculus of Strength!" I cried out. *"Give it back to me!"*

Zeus and I moved toward him at the same time. With a scream, Cass jumped back and dropped the Loculus like it was hot. It rolled away down the street and I dived after it, landing with a thud on the sidewalk. As I hit the side of a building, I saw the Loculus resting against the bottom of a rain gutter opening a few feet away.

As I closed both hands around it tightly, I turned.

Zeus was coming at me now. In his hand was a dagger.

80

Its hilt was huge, its blade jagged like the edge of a broken glass bottle.

I heard Aly and Cass screaming. But I had the Loculus, and it gave me a power I never thought possible. I felt my free arm swinging downward, picking up a broken section of Zeus's staff.

I whirled, swinging the shaft like a bat. It connected with Zeus's torso and sent him flying across the narrow alley. As he hit the wall and sank down, I grabbed him by the collar and lifted him above my head.

I, Jack McKinley, had Zeus in the palms of my hands!

A thick, rusty nail jutted from the outer wall of a stucco building. I thrust Zeus against it, taking care that the nail ripped only through his thick tunic, not him. Because that's the kind of guy I am. At least when I have a Loculus of Strength.

Zeus roared, flailing wildly as he dangled from the wall. I knew he wouldn't stay up there long.

At the end of the alley were a couple of abandoned pushcarts. One of them was full of leather goods—satchels, sandals, sacks, clothing.

I ran over and grabbed an extra-large vest. Tucking the Loculus under my arm, I ripped a long shred of leather as if it were paper. "Stay calm," I said, approaching Zeus with caution. "This isn't going to hurt."

I grabbed his arms. I couldn't believe I was actually

wrestling them into position. As I tied them together tightly, Zeus cried out, *"I'LL GET YOU, YOU SKWEWY WABBIT!"*

As I backed away, Aly was laughing.

"What's so funny?" Cass said. "Did you see what Jack just did?"

"Sorry . . . sorry," Aly said. "It's just . . . Elmer Fudd?"

"Yeah, well, he doesn't look so godlike," I said, "but he'll break loose. Trust me, he's not going to stop until he gets his Loculus back. And I don't want us to be near him when that happens." I glanced over my shoulder. In the moonlight, the steep foothills of the Peloponnesian mountains looked to be about a mile or so away. They were dotted with trees and small black holes.

Caves.

"Let's book," I said.

We ran up the alley and wound through the streets away from the center of town, leaving Zeus's anguished cries behind.

Just behind a shack at the edge of town, I stopped. "Wait a second."

"Jack, we have to keep moving," Cass said. "We can't stay here. That thing is going to get loose and kill us."

"He turned into Zeus because we got close to him— we activated him," I said. "The same way that the other Select did, centuries ago. I'm hoping he goes back to being a statue once we're far enough away."

"Yeah, but he *killed* that guy, like, centuries ago," Cass said. "What if he doesn't turn back into a statue until he gets the Loculus back—and *then* kills us?"

"I say we call your dad," Aly suggested. "He can get us out of here. This was a bad choice. We need to put an ocean between us and him."

I thought a moment. Leaving Routhouni now, when I knew the Massa had spotted us, didn't seem like the best idea. We didn't have time before one of us had another episode and we used up the last of the shard. "We'll hide for a while up in the mountains," I said. "That way, if Zeus escapes, we'll see him coming. There's a chance the Massa will come after us there; you know they're going to want to get this Loculus. But at least we'll be safe. For a little while."

"If Zeus comes after us, we're going to need more than the Loculus of Strength," Cass said.

"I'll text Dad on the way," I said. "Maybe he'll have some ideas."

We turned and ran, leaving Zeus hanging.

CHAPTER FOURTEEN

Escape from the Nostril

I MANAGED TO strap my flashlight to my head by making a kind of cap with leather strips. Holding the Loculus in one hand, I used the other hand to scrabble up the side of a rocky cliff. The Loculus was making this as easy as walking.

By the time I reached the first broad ledge, Cass and Aly were way behind me. "Show-off," Cass called up. His flashlight beam surfed up and down the scrubby mountainside.

"Take your time, mortals," I said.

I sat, unhooked my pack, and took a look at the text Dad sent me as we were leaving Routhouni. Just as I figured, he did have some ideas about what we should do:

84

> Not keen on your plan. Am airlifting a package to you by chopper. Hoping you will regain your senses and return to the airport, fast and unseen. If not, what's in the bag should give you a fighting chance. Keep your GPS on. Never thought I'd say this, but hope the Massa find you soon.

I didn't know what was in the package. I hadn't had time to ask. But already I heard an engine roar overhead.

From the direction of the airport came a helicopter. I stood, waving. As it hovered overhead, a bay opened in its keel. A sack, tied to the end of a sturdy rope, lowered toward me.

He was sending us the Loculi!

"Honey, we're home," Aly announced, her arm appearing over the rim of the ledge.

I reached down and hauled her into the air and onto the ledge with one hand—as if I were lifting a rag doll. She sprawled in the dust.

"Curb your enthusiasm, Superboy," she said.

"Sorry, I'll try a different method." I sat on the ledge, dangling my legs just over Cass's head. "Grab on!"

"What?" Cass said.

"My ankle," I said. "Go ahead."

When I felt his hand clutching my ankle, I rolled onto my back. Curling my legs upward, I lifted Cass high. With a scream, he sailed clear over my head and came down onto the ledge near Aly. "Welcome," I said. "You're just in time for Santa."

Cass dusted himself off and looked upward. "What the—? Why is your dad giving us those?"

The sack was just over our heads now. I reached up and untied it. "He thinks that we're going to change our minds. Like, we'll take one look at the Loculi and say, 'Hey, let's go invisible and fly back to the airport!'"

"Actually, not a bad idea," Cass said.

"We're going to stay put and wait," I said.

We untied the rope and then I gave it a sharp tug, to indicate we were done. The rope rose back up into the bay. In moments, the helicopter was disappearing into the night, toward Kalamata.

Dad had attached a handwritten note to the sack: *Good luck and hurry back!*

I quickly stuffed the note into my pocket and shone the flashlight around the ledge. Behind me, in the mountain face, was a cave about four feet high. It was empty, its rear wall maybe twenty feet deep and covered with Greek graffiti. "If we need to, we can hide the Loculi in here," I said. "I'll try to text Dad to pick them up, after the Massa find

86

us. I wish he hadn't sent those things to us."

Aly was scanning the countryside. Routhouni was a distant cluster of dim lights in the darkness. The only other building between here and there was a tiny white house with a cross on its roof, in a field farther down the base of the mountains. "I don't see any headlights yet," I said.

"Do monks drive?" Cass asked.

"Of course they drive!" Aly said. "How else would they travel?"

"Sandals?" Cass said. "Camels? I don't know. We're just sitting ducks here."

I wanted to face the Massa. I wanted that badly. I don't know if it was the Loculus of Strength, or just the incredible rush of feeling that the hunt for the Seven Loculi was still alive. "We can't count on the Massa following us," I said. "Let's wait out the night here. If nothing happens, then we can get back to Routhouni in the daylight."

Cass was pacing now, squinting into the distance. "What about the lightning?" he said.

"What lightning? It's a clear night," Aly pointed out.

"He's *Zeus*, right?" Cass said. "What if he throws lightning bolts at us?"

"Zeus is mythological," I said.

"Oh, *that's* a relief!" Cass shot back. "I mean, whew, myths aren't real. That's as ridiculous as, like, I don't know . . . statues coming to life!"

"Easy, Cass," I said.

"He has a point," Aly piped up. "We're in the middle of nowhere. We saw a bunch of monks and we're assuming they're the Massa. Maybe the real Massa know enough not to be anywhere near this place."

Cass threw up his hands. "Yeah, well, maybe this whole thing was just a dumb idea."

"Whoa, what happened to our team?" I said. "We came up with this idea together. We can't just give it up. Not only that, we found another Loculus—so the way I see it, we're one step ahead. Plus, I just saved our lives and hung Zeus on a nail, and no one even said thanks. You guys want to call my dad and be picked up? Fine. But I'm going to finish this quest or die trying. I'll do what we're supposed to do, by myself."

I walked to the far end of the ledge and leaned against the rock face. I could hear Aly and Cass mumbling to each other. As far as I was concerned, I'd go back to the island alone. I had nothing to lose.

After a quiet moment I felt a hand on my shoulder. "Hey," Aly said.

"I don't know what's bothering you, Aly," I said. "You and Cass."

She was silent for a long moment. "When I came so close to death, Jack, it changed me. I'm not as afraid of it anymore, I guess. Part of me just wants to go home and be with Mom and my friends."

"I don't want you to die," I said. "Or Cass. Or me. Fourteen is too early."

Aly nodded. "Yeah. I think you're right. Thank you for nailing Zeus, Jack. You came through for us. I guess what I'm trying to say is, we are in this together. To the end."

"Bad choice of words," I said.

Aly laughed. "Sorry."

We sat, dangling our legs over the cliff. Cass joined us, leaning his head against Aly's shoulder. "I'm tired. And don't say, 'Hi, Tired. I'm Jack.'"

"I'm tired, too," Aly said. "We're twins."

"You guys get some sleep," I said. "I'll keep a lookout."

"How do we know you won't sleep, too?" Aly asked.

I grabbed the Loculus. "Popeye had spinach. Superman had the power of Krypton. I, Jack, have the Loculus of Strength."

Cass's eyes fluttered shut. A few seconds later, Aly's did, too. I was worried about both of them. I wasn't Popeye and I wasn't Superman. I needed them both, and I could feel them pulling away.

Overhead another military plane zoomed by, but neither of them stirred. I held tight to the Loculus and cast a wide glance over the barren countryside from left to right and back again.

And again.

By the fourth time, my eyes were heavy, too. There would be no fifth time until daybreak.

The "Strength" in the Loculus of Strength did not include staying awake.

CHAPTER FIFTEEN

THE DREAM CONTINUED

HE HAS FOUND me.

Again.

I thought I'd lost him in Halicarnassus. But here he is in Olympia, standing before me in the shop. Standing before a great, massive lump of marble that has traveled here by the work of twenty slaves over three months.

He has that look in his eyes. The Betrayed Commander. The look that caused troops to quake in their sandals. The look that made me cry when I was a coddled little princeling. But now, after all I've been through—after all my land has been through—he annoys me.

"You would do this to your own flesh and blood, Massarym?" are his first words. "This trickery? This disloyalty?"

I look deeply into his gray, stern eyes, trying to find the man I once adored and respected. "I would ask the same of you," I say. "As the king, your people are as your own flesh and blood. And you have allowed them to die. The ultimate disloyalty."

"The queen is at fault," he shouts, "and you, ungrateful wretch—"

"You cast a blind eye to Mother's actions then—but now you protest," I say. "You did not protest while she disturbed the balance of Atlantean energy. While she dissected and analyzed the power like some curious experiment. When she trapped it away from the earth itself into seven spheres—"

"Stealing those spheres is what caused the destruction!" he bellows. "Playing with them! Showing off!"

I am tired of this argument. I have work to do.

"Of that last part I am indeed guilty," I say. "But I realized early on that I was wrong. I returned them. If you are correct, everything should have been perfect again. Was it?"

The king is silent.

"Why the earthquakes, my king?" I say. "Why the monsters?"

He turns away.

"Mother's actions—not mine—depleted the energy," I say. "She doomed Atlantis. Had we left the Loculi in place, they would have sunk away with the rest of the continent. Only by taking them and making them safe—stealing, as you say—could we have any hope for rebuilding. Minds of the future, minds greater than ours, will figure out what to do. I am not seeking

*glory; I am not foolish. I want to house the Loculi for future gen-
erations, in the most magnificent forms imaginable." I gesture
toward the block of marble. "Behold Zeus, Father! Does he not
look like a living man?"*

*It looks nothing like a man. One can discern only the back of
a giant throne—and the outline of what will one day become,
according to plan, a likeness of the mighty god. The architects
would have liked Zeus to be standing tall, but no temple could
have been built high enough to do justice to this vision. So he will
sit on a regal throne, his feet planted firmly. His staff has been
separately sculpted, and it leans against the marble block. By its
side is the Loculus of Strength.*

It is this I want my father to see.

*The lines of his face deepen, his eyes hollow. I have been
waiting for this moment. In my time since leaving Atlantis, I
have marshaled my own powers.*

IMMOBILITUS.

*My father is rooted to the spot. He tries to move toward the
Loculus but cannot. "I will not allow this," he bellows. "I command you to return that to me!"*

"I am not your soldier," I say.

"You are my son!" he replies.

*I must fight a desperate pang of guilt. Shall I show mercy?
His words tug at my heart.*

But the deaths of thousands of Atlanteans tug harder.

I have much work to do. Structures to build. And I will not be stopped. Not by any army. Not by Uhla'ar.

"You wish for your hands to be around that Loculus, rather than Zeus's?"

"Immediately!" he thunders.

"Then your wish, my father, shall be granted," I say. "Now and forever."

I feel the power welling up from my toes, spreading through my body like an intruder. It hurts. It blinds. I raise my hand toward my father, and I feel a jolt as if a hundred knives course through my veins.

Father's mouth drops open. His feet leave the ground, and he floats.

He is in midair now, screaming. I have never heard the king scream before. I know it is the last time I will ever see him.

But I turn away. I have already mourned the loss of my father. The loss of my people. My family now is the future. The people of the world yet unborn.

I walk away, forcing my ears to hear nothing.

CHAPTER SIXTEEN

A GOAT MOMENT

MY EYES FLICKERED open. I tried to hold on to the dream, but it was fading. I wanted to remember the details, to trap them in my brain, because they always seemed to mean *something*.

Already, in early versions of the dream, I'd seen Atlantis destroyed and the Loculi stolen away. Back then, it was as if I'd been trapped in the body of Prince Karai. But in these latest dreams, I'd been Massarym.

Somehow, being Massarym felt a whole lot worse.

"Hey," Aly said softly. "Are you okay?"

I sat up. The images were drifting away like smoke. I was on the ledge outside Routhouni. It was still dark. Middle of the night. Aly lay next to me on the ground, and

Cass was curled up into a fetal position behind us. I blinked myself deeper into reality.

"I wanted to kill him . . ." I mumbled. "Not me. Massarym."

"You wanted to kill Massarym?" Aly asked.

"No! *I* was Massarym," I said. "In my dream. I wanted to kill my father. The king of Atlantis, Uhla'ar. It was the second time I dreamed about him. The first was back when you were getting sick. I was Massarym then, too. Back then, the king was mad at me for stealing the Loculi. I threw a fake Loculus over the cliff in Halicarnassus. To fool him. This time we were near the Statue of Zeus. But it wasn't a statue yet."

The details were growing faint. Aly put an arm around my shoulder. "I have nightmares, too, but they're not like *that*. Shhh, it's okay."

"Yeah. Just a dream." Her arm felt warm, and I let my head touch her shoulder. In the distance, the lights of Routhouni flickered faintly. "Is it almost morning? We're going to have to make our move."

I heard a dull thump from above us.

Cass's eyes flew open. He spun around, looking up the hillside. "Did you hear that?"

Aly and I stood. "What kind of animals live on Greek mountains?" Aly asked.

"Goats?" I said.

My flashlight was still strapped to my head. I shone it

upward just in time to see something small and sharp hurtling downward.

Cass fell back, almost to the ledge. *"OWW!* The goats are throwing rocks!"

Another rock flew downward. And another. "I don't think those are goats."

"Let's get in the cave," Cass said.

As Aly and Cass headed for the opening, I grabbed my backpack and the Loculus of Strength. I meant to follow them, but something happened when I tucked that thing under my arm.

I didn't want to hide. I was angry. Someone was trying to scare us. What if this was a trap, bandits trying to force us into a cave, a place we couldn't escape? After all we'd been through, no way was I going to let this happen. I held tight to the Loculus and dug my foot into the mountain wall.

"Jack?" called Aly from inside the cave. "Jack, what are you doing?"

My fingers dug into the dirt wall like hooks. They were both yelling at me from the cave opening, but I blocked it out. My muscles felt like steel coils as I climbed the cliffside.

"Woo-HOO!" I couldn't help shouting. I mean, come on. Jack McKinley, the last guy picked for any sports team. The boy who collapsed after one push-up. The winner of

the Most Times Shoved to the Ground by Barry Reese
Award five years running. Now my friends were in danger
and I could do something about it. I was climbing with the
ease of . . . a goat!

This felt awesome.

Concentrate.

I hauled myself upward, maybe fifty feet, and reached
my fingers over the rim of the next ledge. Then I hoisted
myself straight upward and managed a three-sixty somer-
sault in midair. Well, maybe three-forty, because I landed
on my back. It wasn't the Loculus of Perfect Coordination,
I guess.

Still, it didn't hurt at all, and I sprang to my feet. I
turned my head, training the flashlight beam right and left.
This ledge was narrower but longer from side to side.

There.

Above me. A tiny movement. Black against the blackness.

"Hello?"

As I looked up the hill, an outstretched body leaped at
me. It knocked me off-balance, spinning me around. I fell
to the ground, dropping the Loculus.

As I rolled away, my flashlight slid off my head. I
grabbed it, the leather strips dangling. "Who's there?" I
shouted, shining the light into the blackness.

"Jack? Are you okay?" Aly yelled from below.

I felt a hand land heavily on my shoulder. Leaping away, I spun to face my attacker.

Two eyes glared at me as if they contained light sources of their own. They were silvery white and definitely not human. "What do you want?" I said.

"*WHAT DO YOU GO-O-O-OT?*" came the reply, as the massive figure of Zeus hurdled toward me.

CHAPTER SEVENTEEN

BATTLE ON THE MOUNT

IT FELT LIKE a cow had dropped out of the sky and landed on my chest. I couldn't breathe under the weight. Zeus's mouth was inches from my face, but I felt no warmth and smelled no breath. He had one hand on the Loculus and it took all my effort to keep hold of it myself.

As long as I had contact, I could match his strength. I twisted my body hard. I kicked. Finally I just reared back my head and butted him on the forehead.

It hurt like crazy. But I guess it didn't feel too great for him either. He roared with surprise. And I took that moment to curl my legs upward, between his body and mine, and push hard. He fell away.

Unfortunately, the Loculus fell the other way. I

scrambled to my knees, swinging the flashlight.

The god-statue stood before me, legs planted wide, the broken section of his staff in his right hand.

"We're coming!" came Aly's voice from below.

I swung the beam around, looking for the Loculus. Zeus saw it first. He dived like a shortstop, reaching with his arms. I threw myself into his path.

Big mistake. Without the Loculus, my body took the hit hard. I bounced away, but I'd managed to knock him slightly off-balance, too, and we both tumbled to the rim of the ledge.

The Loculus rolled out of reach. Zeus and I lunged toward it at the same time. I was closer and my finger grazed the surface. But all I did was knock it over the ledge.

As it disappeared, I cried out, "Catch!"

Zeus roared and came for me, his fingers reaching for my neck. I could see the tempest in his eyes. So I did the only thing I could.

I bit him on the shoulder.

His eyes bulged. His arm froze. I jumped to the rim and flung myself over, praying I wouldn't overshoot the lower ledge.

"Jack!"

Aly was climbing up from below, her body pressed against the mountainside. She had caught the orb and was clutching it to her. I tried to jump clear of her, but my foot clipped the Loculus, dislodging it from her grip. Cass, who was below her, jumped back down to the ledge to get out of my way.

I landed beside Cass. Aly landed on top of me. It hurt but we were basically unharmed.

"Where's the Loculus of Strength?" I said, leaping to my feet.

"At the bottom," Cass cried. "I saw it falling."

I glanced upward. Zeus was at the edge, scanning the area. I would need to get down there, fast. I unhooked my backpack and took out the sack with the two Loculi. "I'll fly down there," I said, carefully removing the Loculus of Flight. "You and Aly take the—"

"GERONIMO!"

Zeus had jumped off the top ledge and was diving straight for me like I was a pool on a hot summer day.

I left the ground. Zeus landed at the spot where I'd been. He reached toward me, swinging with the broken staff. I heard it crack against my ankle, and I winced. But I was aloft, hanging tight to the Loculus of Flight.

I fought back the pain. The Loculus dipped and rose crazily. I felt like a disoriented bat.

Don't let it throw you off. Control. Think.

As I took a deep breath, the Loculus leveled out. The sun must have just risen above horizon, because I could see the outline of Zeus now. He was on our ledge, staring at me open-mouthed with astonishment. Cass was nowhere to be seen, but Aly was lowering herself downward from the ledge.

Of course. She had to let go of the Loculus of Invisibility. She needed two hands. *"Jack! Cass fell!"* she called out.

I looked down quickly, but the base of the cliff was a black pit, angled away from the moonlight.

"Cass!" I called out. *"Caaasssss!"*

I swung around and flew straight downward, landing on the ground harder than I meant to. My ankle throbbed so bad I expected it to fall off. I pulled out my flashlight and shone it around. The bushes and trees were a scraggly, dusty green, like fake props in a movie.

It took me three sweeps of the light beam before I saw a wink of solid-colored fabric from beyond the thick copse at the base of the cliff. I kept the light trained on it as I limped through brambles, somehow managing to step into every small animal hole along the way.

Cass's body was twisted so that he was facing up, while his torso was nearly turned to the ground. I knelt by him, cupping my hand around his head. The backpack, with a telltale round bulge, was on the ground next to him. He hadn't even gotten the Loculus out. "Cass," I said. "Are you all right?"

His eyes blinked. He seemed to have trouble focusing on me. "Aside from the pine needles in my butt," he said, "I'm pretty comfy. Owwwwww . . ." Grimacing, he rolled into a fetal position—just as Aly let out a scream from above.

I felt my blood run cold.

"Grab . . . the Loculus . . . of Strength . . ." Cass said.

I followed his glance with my flashlight until I saw the Loculus of Strength resting about ten feet away on a small, flat bush. I ran to it, flicked off the light, and dumped it back into my pack. "Thanks, Cass."

Holding one Loculus under each arm—Strength and Flight—I shot upward. The statue was scrabbling down the mountainside, inches from Aly. "Hey, Zeus!" I called out.

He turned to face me, his gnarled fingers digging into the dirt.

I circled above him. His teeth shone in the moonlight, gritted with anger. With my hands full of Loculi, I would have to use my legs. "You'll get a kick out of this," I said.

Swooping down, I smashed my foot into his jaw. His grip slipped. As he tumbled down the mountainside, head over heels, pain shot up my leg and my vision went totally white.

"Jack!" Aly cried out.

I steadied myself and flew up toward her. She reached out, grabbing my arm. "Are you okay?" she said.

"I'm glad I have Strength," I replied, sailing down toward Cass. "But at the moment, I kind of wish I had Healing."

I dropped to the ground, taking care to land on my good leg. "Can you . . . move, Cass?" I asked, grimacing at the pain.

"Break dancing, no," Cass replied. "Running from a deranged killer god, yes. What about you? You don't look so good."

I sat next to him, my eyes scanning the horizon. "Where is he—Zeus?"

"It was a pretty bad fall," Cass said. "If he wasn't dead, he might be now."

"He's a god," Aly replied. "How can he be dead?"

"We have to book before he sees us." I glanced around and noticed the small white shack in the distance. There was a cross on the roof. A church. "There."

"Wait. I thought we were going to go back to where the monks are," Aly said.

"I thought the statue would turn back to stone," I said. "He hasn't. He's going to come after us. Those innocent kids and families and old people in Routhouni—you think none of them will be hurt?"

"But—" Aly said.

"We have three Loculi, Aly," I said. "The Massa will know this. Wherever we go now, they will follow. We can't put all those people at risk. So let's move on!"

I put the Loculi down, reached for my phone, and sent Dad a text:

in trouble! come now.

white church agnst mtns outside
Routhouni.

"Vamanos," I said, standing up.

On the other side of the bush, a great black shadow rose like a wave from the sea. *"WHO YOU GONNA CALL?"*

A fist slammed against my chest and I fell backward.

Zeus crashed through the bush. I tried to stand but my ankle collapsed, shooting pain up the side of my body.

Through slitted eyes, I watched the god-statue sprint back toward town, the Loculus of Strength tucked under his arm, as another jet passed overhead.

CHAPTER EIGHTEEN

LOSER, LOSER, LOSER

on my way. u ok? what happened?

LIMPING TOWARD THE white church, I stared at the message from Dad.

My ankle felt like it had been twisted off and shoved back on again. Cass's shirt was in tatters, his face scarred by branches. Aly looked like an extra from *The Walking Dead*. Now that the sun was peeking up, I could see every painful detail of my friends' injuries.

Zeus was long gone. By now he'd probably turned back into a statue again. Maybe back in Routhouni, maybe on the way.

I didn't want to find out. There'd be time to battle him again later. "How do I begin to answer this message?" I muttered.

"How about: "Sup, Pop?' " Cass said. "'We tried to steal a Loculus from a god who learned English by watching TV sitcoms. Jack pinned him to a wall, but he came back and nearly killed us. How was your sleep?'"

"It's not only sitcoms," Aly said. "Movies, too. When Jack asked him what he wanted, he answered, 'What do you got?' That's a line from *The Wild One*. Marlon Brando, 1953."

Cass nodded. "For you, that counts as a new release."

I blocked them out and began typing out a message to Dad:

> long story. c u at white church.

Shoving the phone into my pocket, I continued the trudge across the rocky terrain. No one said much. I tried to look on the positive side. We were alive. We had located a Loculus.

That was about it for the positive side.

Destroyed Loculus of Healing? Check.

Lost Loculus of Strength? Check.

Brought maniac god to life and possibly set him loose on innocent Greek townspeople? Check.

Didn't even come close to attracting Massa, which was the whole reason we got into this mess in the first place? Check.

We were a team of losers, alone in the dark in the middle of nowhere, without a clue.

Loser, loser, loser.

I took a deep breath. Professor Bhegad had had names for the four of us. *Soldier, Sailor, Tinker, Tailor.* Cass was the Sailor who always knew how to navigate. Aly was our geeky Tinker of all things electronic. We'd lost our Soldier, Marco the Great and Powerful, to the Massa.

As the Tailor, I was . . . well, nothing, really. *The one who puts it all together,* according to Bhegad. As far as I was concerned, that was his lame way of saying *none of the above.*

There was nothing inside me for the G7W gene to make awesome.

Looking at my bedraggled friends, I figured the least I could do was put on a good face. "Hey, cheer up," I said. "It ain't over till the fat lady sings."

"Loo-loo-loo-LOOOOO!" Cass crowed like a demented soprano.

I had to laugh. But my ankle buckled again and I stopped.

Aly knelt by my side, touching my leg gently. "Is it broken? Zeus hit you pretty hard."

"No, I don't think it's broken," I replied. Her touch did nothing for the pain, but I liked the way it felt. "He did hit it hard, though. If my leg were a baseball, it would have been over the center field wall."

"Let's rest," she said gently. "Oh. And, by the way—thanks, Jack."

"For what?" I said.

"For your bravery," she replied. "You really took one for the team."

My temperature shot up about ten degrees.

"Um, I don't want to spoil your magic moment, but we have to move." Cass fumbled around in his pocket and pulled out the shard of the Loculus of Healing. Squatting next to Aly, he wrapped his hand around my ankle, pressing the shard into my skin.

"No! Cass!" I cried, pulling my leg away. "Save it. Look, we've missed our chance with the Massa and we don't know when we'll see them again. Let's save the shard."

I stood and balanced my weight from leg to leg. It hurt, but I knew I could make it.

"You sure?" Aly said, and I nodded.

We began trudging to the church again. My ankle throbbed, but the pain seemed to get better the more I walked. "One thing—let's all promise to stay healthy from now on," I said. "So we don't use that thing up any faster than we have to."

Aly and Cass both grunted in agreement.

For all the good it will do us, I did not say.

* * *

Sleeping isn't easy when the saints are staring at you.

The little church had white stucco walls. In it were a few rows of pews, a small altar made of polished wood, and a hard marble floor.

Plus gigantic paintings in brilliant reds and golds that were so realistic it felt like you were being judged from all directions.

Somehow Cass and Aly had nodded off, but I was wired.

I looked at my watch. It had been nearly an hour since I'd texted Dad. Where was he?

Outside the sun had risen. The air was cool and crisp. I scanned the horizon but it was completely still.

Taking out my phone, I tapped out a quick message:

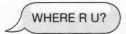

It didn't take long for the reply:

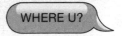

Oh, great. For all I knew there were tons of these little churches and he was completely confused.

R U LOST?

YES. LOCATION? TELL.

R U on the rd out of nostril?

??

ROUTHOUNI = NOSTRIL, REMEMBER? go toward mts. we r in white church rt by the bottom of the mt. like i said.

OK. STAY.

I figured Dad was either panicked or driving. Or both. Those short texts were not his usual old-school style, with complete sentences. "Later, guys," I said to the saints as I headed outside to wait.

The moment I stepped out the door, I spotted a movement on the horizon. My pulse quickened. *"Here! Over here!"* I shouted.

Cass stumbled outside, yawning, his hair all bunched on one side. "I hope he's bringing breakfast."

Aly emerged behind him. Her purple hair hung at her shoulders, and her face seemed softer somehow. I smiled. "Good morning."

"What are you staring at?" she asked.

"Nothing." I turned away, gesturing out toward the horizon. "Dad's coming!"

Cass squinted into the distance, shielding his eyes against the sun. "Uh . . . did he grow a huge black beard since yesterday?"

I could see the shape of the car now. Dad had rented a Mercedes coupe at the airport, but this was a minivan jammed with people. The driver's window was down, and as the van got closer, I could make out a guy with gray hair, glasses, and a ZZ Top beard. He called out something in Greek, waving his arm.

"A priest," Aly said. "Oh, great, we're trespassers in a house of worship."

I didn't like the looks of these guys. But then again, I wasn't used to seeing Greek priests. *"Hello!"* I called back.

"No speaky Greeky!" Cass chimed in.

As the car pulled up to the church, the man smiled. I could see now that he was wearing a dark robe. "Americans?" he asked. "Early for the service?"

"Right!" Cass squeaked.

Now the back doors were opening. Two other men, all in long robes, climbed out of the minivan. It seemed like a lot of priests for such a little church.

And priests did not usually carry firearms.

"Jack . . ." Aly said, taking my arm.

My eye was on the person now emerging from the

passenger door. As he stood and walked toward us around the minivan, he smiled and held out his arms.

Cass and Aly stiffened.

"Good morning," said Brother Dimitrios. "I always had faith I would see you again."

CHAPTER NINETEEN

DEIFIRTEP

THE BACKPACK.

I still had it. We hadn't hidden it away.

Great. The plan was to be captured by the Massa, but not to give them the whole store!

Cass and Aly were both staring at the pack. It was too late to do anything about it now. "What did you do to my father?" I asked. "How did you get his cell phone?"

"Jack, whatever are you talking about?" Dimitrios said, laughing. "Your father is still with his plane. We don't need to steal a cell phone to find you."

He stepped forward, open arms, as if he wanted to give me a hug hello. But I knew enough about Dimitrios's friendliness. It was as fake as a plastic jack-o'-lantern.

I shrank away, out of his grip. "Come now, no need to be afraid. You should be delighted."

One of Dimitrios's goons was opening the back door of the minivan.

"So . . . we're supposed to go with you?" Cass squeaked.

"It's not uncomfortable," Dimitrios said. "We will drive smoothly."

"So, um, what are you going to do to us?" Cass blurted out.

Dimitrios chuckled. "Celebrate, of course. Over the triumphant news—that there is new hope for your lives!"

Cass and Aly eyed me warily. Neither of them moved.

"Children, let's be open," Dimitrios said. "The Massa, as you know, are all about openness. You are carrying two Loculi. And, if I'm correct, you also have the remaining pieces of the Loculus of Healing."

I gasped. *"How did you know?"*

"Because, dear boy, we could not find them in New York," Dimitrios said. "And we recovered everything. Think about it—with your pieces and ours, we may be able to resume the search for Loculi! We will have three! Look around. Do you see the Karai Institute coming after you to save your lives? No! But, voilà—here we are!"

"Who loves ya, babe?" grunted Dimitrios's helper, gesturing toward the back of the van.

Three. He hadn't said a thing about Zeus's Loculus.

"So . . . how did you know we were here?"

"We have spent years recruiting agents," Dimitrios replied. "Our man in this area drives a taxi. He found you very amusing."

"The taxi driver?" Cass said. "He was too nice to be a Massa."

Brother Dimitrios's smile faded. But all I could think about were the monks. They weren't Massarene after all. They were actual monks.

Which meant Dimitrios didn't know about Zeus or the fourth Loculus.

I took a deep breath and headed into the back of the minivan. Aly and Cass climbed in beside me, and the door shut with a loud thump. With a *shussssh* of tires in the dirt, the van turned and began heading back across the stubbly plain. *"Remind me why we're doing this,"* Cass hissed.

"To get to the island," I whispered back. "To reconstruct the Loculus of Healing. Remember? Our plan?"

"Were we out of our minds?" Cass said. "Did you see these guys? What if they kill us?"

"What are you going to do to us, Brother D?" Aly demanded.

"Are you afraid?" Dimitrios asked, turning to face us.

"Deifirtep," Cass said.

Dimitrios looked at him blankly for a moment, then burst into laughter. *"Petrified!* Oh, yes, I got that. What fun

117

we'll have with your witty little habits! Well, you needn't be scared. You'll see. Now. I have a question for you. I confess your visit defies a certain logic. Do you fail to grasp the significance of what you did in New York City? Destroying the Loculus meant destroying yourselves."

"Yeah, we grasp it," Aly said. "Do you grasp that we saved your life? You'd be a zombie by now, wandering around in Bo'gloo, if we hadn't jumped in."

"Drooling," Cass added. "Really bad skin. No blood. You'd hate it."

Dimitrios blanched. "You are so right—how rude of me not to thank you. I was headed for the underworld. As was Sister Nancy. You acted bravely by destroying that Loculus and thus closing the gates."

Sister Nancy. As in Nancy Emelink. An anagram of Anne McKinley, aka my mom. How long would she be able to use that name? I worried about her. All those years we thought she was dead, she'd risen incognito to the top of the Massa—but now she seemed to want to help me. And I wanted to protect her secret. What would they do to her if they found out?

"You're welcome," I said. "And we do know we're as good as dead, if that's what you're asking."

"Not anymore," Brother Dimitrios said with a smile. "You will be happy that we are well along the way to assembling the pieces of the Mausoleum Loculus. Piece by piece.

Except for the sections you have. Which you will hand over now."

Dimitrios held out his palm toward me. I could feel Cass and Aly stiffen.

"No!" I blurted.

"No?" Dimitrios said. "That disappoints me. I would hate for someone to have to search you. We were just getting to be friends."

I quickly took out the shard and showed it to him.

"Jack!" Aly cried out.

"You're welcome to take this," I said, "but you don't want to."

I explained that the shard was keeping us alive. That if he took it away, one or all of us would go into a coma. "Of course, maybe that's what you want," I said. "For us all to die right here in your van. But it would be a shame to lose the only people who can find the other Loculi . . ."

Brother Dimitrios's fingers were millimeters from the shard. He raised an eyebrow high and sighed. "All right," he said. "But don't try anything rash. Like trying to escape. We need you and care about your lives dearly."

"Sir!" a voice called from the front of the van.

Dimitrios spun around. We were heading east, the sun rising in front of us, huge and swollen like an angry furnace. Where it met the pavement, a black dot shimmered as it slowly drew closer.

Dad.

I shoved the shard into my pocket, sneaked out my phone, and quickly typed out a text:

> PLAN WORKING! IN BLK MINIVAN W BROTHER D. GO AWAY. PLS DO NOT MEET US!!!!

Brother Dimitrios leaned forward. The dot on the horizon was growing larger by the second. It was a dark car, sending up clouds of dust behind it, traveling ridiculously fast. As the Massa driver veered to the left to avoid its path, the car veered with it.

I squinted against the glare of the sun as the car headed toward us.

A Mercedes coupe.

"No, no, no, no," I murmured. "Not now . . ."

Aly gripped my arm.

"What is that idiot doing?" Brother Dimitrios shouted, his eyes focused on the road ahead. "Shake him, Mustafa!"

"He's crazy!" the driver shouted back.

We lurched back and forth violently as Mustafa tried to avoid collision, but the Mercedes was bearing down on us. I had never seen Dad drive like this.

I felt myself falling to the floor in a tangle of limbs with Aly and Cass. Grabbing the back of the seat, I hoisted myself up enough to see a brief flash of blue metal through the windshield.

The sound of the collision exploded in my ears. I somersaulted forward, jamming against the minivan's backseat. The minivan spun twice, then came to a stop. As Brother Dimitrios pushed me away, I caught a glimpse through a side window.

Dad's car was upside down, its roof crushed in.

"Dad!" The scream ripped upward from my toes. I pushed open the rear door of the minivan and jumped out.

Outside, I could see one of the Massa slumped in the passenger seat of the minivan, groaning, clutching his bloody forehead. I limped past him toward Dad's car. It was about ten feet away. A plume of black smoke belched out from the hood, and the whole thing looked like it was about to blow, but I didn't care. I knelt by the passenger window, hoping to see him. *"Dad! Are you okay? Say something!"*

I was answered by a loud metallic *grrrrrrock!* from the other side of the car, accompanied by the tinkle of broken glass.

The driver's door.

I leaped to my feet in time to see a thatch of coppery red rising over the car's upended chassis.

"Something," said Torquin.

121

CHAPTER TWENTY

IN THE MATTER OF VICTOR RAFAEL QUIÑONES

I HAD NEVER been so unhappy to see the belching, bearded, barefoot giant in my life.

"What did you do to my father?" I screamed. "How did you get his car?"

"Stole car," he said, shrugging as he waddled past me, a black leather bag in one hand and a metal crowbar dangling from the other. "At airport. He was there. I was there. I needed car. He didn't." His small green eyes stared out from under the shelf of his blood-soaked forehead, intent on Brother Dimitrios.

"Ah, my good man . . ." Brother Dimitrios approached Torquin with a wary hand outstretched. "Surely we can discuss this like two civilized—*augh!*"

122

Torquin took his hand, lifted Dimitrios over his head, and tossed him to the ground like a sack of potatoes.

Two of the other priests were racing away, kicking up dust across the field, their sandals flying off in midair. "Come back!" Torquin bellowed after them, rearing back with the crowbar. "No fun!"

Torquin dropped the leather bag. With a couple of strangely delicate steps, he heaved the crowbar like a javelin. But my eyes were distracted by a glint of metal from the minivan. I heard a soft click.

Mustafa was leaning out the driver's window, taking aim at Torquin with a rifle.

I ran toward the shooter, screaming at the top of my lungs. Cass was way ahead of me. Directly in the gun's line of sight.

Brother Dimitrios sat up, his face taut with urgency. *"Don't hurt the boy!"* he shouted.

A *craaack* split the morning air. A puff of smoke.

Cass and Torquin dropped to the dirt. Aly was shrieking, taking off after them in a sprint.

I grabbed the passenger door handle and yanked it open. The driver swung his head to look at me, his eyes wide with shock. Before he could bring his arms back through his window, I rammed him with my head. Then I reached for the window button and squeezed as firmly as I could.

The window slowly rose, trapping the driver's arms. His

curses turned to screams as I switched off the ignition key, trapping the window in position. "Get the rifle!" I yelled.

Aly was already running toward Mustafa. She grabbed the rifle and yanked downward. With a cry of pain, Mustafa let go. The rifle went clattering to the dirt.

"Cass!" I shouted. "Torquin!"

My feet barely touched the ground as I ran toward the two bodies. Cass was struggling to sit up. "I'm okay," he said. "Torquin jumped into the path of the bullet. He fell against me."

We hunched over Red Beard. His face was covered in dirt and his eyes rolled upward. A trickle of blood ran from his mouth down the side of his cheek. Aly slapped his cheeks, screaming his name. *"Don't die! Torquin, you are not allowed to die!"*

"Arrrgh, why did he do this?" Cass said.

I reached into my pocket for the shard. It was so small. If we used it again, we risked losing it.

"Do it, Jack," Aly said.

I nodded. Torquin's bratwurst-sized fingers were twitching. I knelt next to him. I felt the shard growing warm in my palm.

I brought the shard carefully toward Torquin's chest. Cass leaned over the big man and said, "Hang in there, dude."

Before the shard made contact, Torquin shuddered and sat bolt upright. "Arrrmmgh . . ." he grunted.

Cass lurched away from him. "Auuu, Torquin, what did you eat for lunch? Dog food?"

What was left of the shard slipped from my palm, fell against Torquin's leg, and disappeared in the grass.

* * *

The Massa priest with the bloody forehead had made a run for it. Torquin was thirty yards away, dragging the other priest toward us by his clerical collar.

But my attention was focused on a patch of pebbles and scraggly grass. "Found it!" I cried out, closing my fingers around the shard.

It was the size of a pebble and nearly weightless. I could barely feel it in my hand. "What if we lose this?" Cass asked.

"We can't afford to," Aly said. "Put it in a supersafe place. Like, surgically, under your skin."

I did the next best thing. I tucked it into my wallet. It wouldn't get lost there.

"Alive," Torquin's voice rasped. He flopped the unconscious priest down in the dirt beside us. A welt the size of a small boulder was growing from the top of his head.

Proudly, Torquin held up the crowbar. "Set high school record for javelin."

"You threw that and actually hit him?" I asked.

"You went to high school?" Cass asked.

I looked around. The van driver and Brother Dimitrios were both as unconscious as the crowbar victim. "Okay,

125

time out," I said. "This is all wrong. *So* wrong. But before we start yelling at you, Torquin, tell me what exactly happened with you and my dad."

"Said hello," Torquin said. "Asked if he wanted to come. He said no. Frustrating. Torquin asked to borrow phone when he went to bathroom. Took phone. And took car."

I took it with two fingers. "So those texts from Dad . . . were from you?"

Torquin nodded.

I lowered my voice. "Didn't he tell you—we're trying to be captured."

"Um . . ." Torquin said.

"Where have you been, Torquin?" Aly said. "You just disappeared on us in New York!"

"And is your name really Victor Rafael Quiñones?" Cass said.

Torquin took a deep breath. Then he belched.

"That is so gross," Aly said.

"Happens when Torquin is excited," Torquin said. "Hate the name Victor."

Cass laughed. "I hate my real name, too—Cassius!"

"Shakespeare," Torquin said. "From *Julius Caesar*. The 'lean and hungry look.'"

"I can't believe you know that," Cass said.

"Torquin with Omphalos now, head of Karai," Torquin barreled on. "Omphalos gave jet to Torquin. Slippy—nice jet." He pointed to the leather bag he'd dropped on the ground. "In case meet Massa, supposed to use meds . . . injections. Pah! Crowbar easier."

"So wait, you were here to get Brother Dimitrios?" Aly asked.

"No!" Torquin replied. "Orders to get you back. Meds just in case."

"Back to where?" Cass asked. "Where is the KI now?"

"Can't tell," Torquin replied.

"Who is the Omphalos?"

"Don't know," Torquin said.

I took Torquin aside, far from any potentially listening Massa ears, and explained our whole story—Aly's healing, the fused shard, the plan to let the Massa kidnap us. He listened carefully, grunting and frowning as if this were a crash course in advanced calculus.

As he looked over the unconscious Massa, his eyes welled up. "So Torquin made big mistake . . ."

"They'll wake up," Aly said. "We can salvage the plan."

"Professor Bhegad would be mad at Torquin!" The big man pounded his fist into his palm. "Missing Professor Bhegad. Very very m-m-much . . ."

Cass looked aghast. "You're not going to cry, are you? Maybe you've been reading too much Shakespeare?"

"We all miss him, Torquin," Aly said. "But before you get too upset, let's figure a way out of this."

"Come with us," Cass said.

"He just drove Dimitrios into the dust," Aly said.

Cass shrugged. "Maybe he can stow away? Or follow us with Slippy?"

"We can't let our plan fall apart," I said.

"No. Your lives most important." Torquin scrunched up his brow, looking at the unconscious Massa. He took a couple of locomotive breaths, like a bull. Closing his eyes, he held the crowbar high over his head. "Do it."

We looked at each other, baffled. "Uh, do what?" I said.

Beads of sweat had formed at the edges of Torquin's forestlike beard. "Before Massa wake up," he said, "you knock out Torquin."

CHAPTER TWENTY-ONE

SLIPPING AWAY

I **WASN'T EXACTLY** expecting Brother Dimitrios to break out into a Greek dance, but I thought he'd be happy to see Torquin flat out on the ground.

Instead he wiped his forehead with a handkerchief, shaking his head in disbelief. "I thought we'd already taken care of that ape."

If only he'd known how hard it had been to knock out Torquin. The guy's head was as hard as granite. So I, Jack McKinley, swung the crowbar like a cleanup hitter. With a loud *craaack*, I whupped him so hard upside the head that he flew through the air like a rag doll. My brave action caused Aly to swoon. She declared at the top of her lungs that Marco was a distant memory. Because of my own awesomeness.

I hope you don't believe that.

Truth was, I couldn't possibly hit Torquin. None of us had the stomach to do the dirty deed. He may have been crude and weird, but he'd been our friend and protector. Sort of. So we finally convinced him to use the meds in his black bag. One of them was a tranquilizer that got the job done in a few seconds. And out he went.

Dimitrios reached inside the minivan. "I suppose I should take care of him permanently," he grumbled.

"*No!*" we all shouted at the same time.

"Please," Aly said, "leave him alone and we promise we won't resist going with you."

"Torquin is harmless," I quickly added. "Now that the Karai Institute has been destroyed, he's just . . . deluded. Really. He's harmless."

Brother Dimitrios stood over the unconscious priest. "Doesn't look so harmless to me."

With a loud *whoosh*, flames began shooting up from the crashed rental car. It was maybe fifteen feet away from Torquin.

"I'd better not regret being merciful." Scowling, Brother Dimitrios grabbed the knocked-out priest and dragged him toward the minivan. "Let's get out of here, now," he called out.

"Wait, what about Torquin?" Aly asked.

But Dimitrios was already starting the engine and extracting Mustafa from the window. As he shoved Mustafa to the passenger side, he grabbed the rifle. *"Get in! Now!"*

Cass eyed Torquin. "He'll be okay, Jack. He can find his way back after he comes to. Come on, let's go."

We climbed into the minivan. With a screech of tires, the van swerved around Dad's rental car and peeled down the highway. I stared at Torquin's inert body, a receding black lump near the smoking car.

A moment later a deep boom shook the road, and the minivan's rear wheels rose off the ground. As we thumped down, Cass, Aly, and I pressed our faces against the van's rear window. My throat closed up.

Torquin's body was nowhere to be seen. A thick, fiery black cloud billowed from where he'd been lying.

* * *

Losing Torquin was like a knife to the gut.

"I can't believe this . . ." Aly murmured.

"I don't," Cass said, his face ashen. "I don't. He's alive. He escaped. He . . ."

Cass's voice trailed off. As the black cloud billowed, the acrid smoke reached us clear across the deserted plain. We must have been two miles away. Even the wildest wishful thinking wasn't going to bring him back.

"He saved our lives so many times . . ." Aly murmured.

In Egypt after an explosion, on the island during the Massa attack—time and time again he'd been there for us. I thought about the first time I'd met him. He'd caught me

trying to escape the island and forced me back to Bhegad—
even that may have saved my life.

We all owed him, big-time.

And we'd never be able to repay.

I fought back tears. Aly and Cass were slumped against
one side of the van, holding hands tightly. "He didn't
deserve that . . ." Cass said softly.

"I guess he's with P. Beg now," Aly replied, forcing a
wan smile.

I nodded. "Bhegad's probably happy. He's got someone
to scold."

Cass looked as if he'd aged three years. "It's my fault. I
said he'd be all right. I said we should leave him there . . ."

"Cass, don't even think that," Aly said. She put an arm
around him, but he was stiff as a plank.

"It's all our fault, Cass," I said. "We knocked him out."

"He *asked* us to," Cass said. "We never should have said
yes. It was the dumbest thing we ever did."

The trip was slow, the Kalamata streets jammed with traf-
fic. It was just after noon by the time the minivan pulled up to
the private-terminal gate of the airport. I felt numb. My brain
kept asking if there was something I could have done.

By now Mustafa was awake and groggy. A guard
checked Dimitrios's papers but he seemed distracted by
messages coming in through his headset. "Better hurry, sir,"
the guard said. "There's been some trouble at the military

base and flights are limited."

We sped across the tarmac, past about a half dozen private aircraft. "Look," Aly whispered, pointing to a sleek jet that was being hosed down by a chain-link fence.

Slippy.

There was no mistaking the Karai stealth jet we'd flown in so many times. I wondered how long it would take the Omphalos—whoever that was—to realize the jet wasn't coming back.

I looked around for Dad. I had no idea where he was right now, but I half expected him to come running out.

Wherever you are, I thought, *don't worry. We'll be back.* Maybe if I repeated that enough times, I'd believe it myself.

The van came to an abrupt stop. "Move!" Brother Dimitrios shouted.

We emerged from the minivan and ran up a set of metal steps to a small black eight-seater jet. Dimitrios pushed me into a thick, comfortable seat by the window.

I watched Slippy shrink to the size of a toy as we headed out over the Mediterranean.

CHAPTER TWENTY-TWO
MASSA ISLAND

I DRIFTED IN and out of sleep. Dimitrios offered us lunch, but even though I hadn't eaten in a gajillion hours, I wasn't hungry. In my waking state, I couldn't shake the image of Torquin on the ground.

For about the hundredth time, I absentmindedly touched my pocket to make sure the small shard was still there. We couldn't lose that.

A flurry of Greek words filtered back to us from the front of the aircraft. Mustafa happened to be the pilot, and after what I'd done to him in the minivan, he was not a happy camper. If Dimitrios hadn't been there, I think he would have pounded me into hamburger by now.

"Seat belts!" Mustafa snapped.

We buckled ourselves in. The sky became thick with clouds, and sharp strips of lightning crackled all around us. The plane bucked and rolled. My shoulder slammed into the airplane wall. I heard a metallic *grrrrockkk* from the underside of the plane.

I vowed to stay calm. We'd been through this before. Strange weather always surrounded the island. These were signs the plane was getting close. "Did you ever think . . ." Aly said, bouncing left and right, "that the island has a mind of its own . . . and it doesn't like the Massa?"

"Maybe if you show your smiling face out the window, it'll know friends are arriving," I said.

Aly gripped my hand tightly. My stomach was fluttering. I should have hated the idea of returning to this sweltering, half-destroyed home of deadly creatures and horrible memories. But I was more excited than scared. "Can I confess something to you?" I said. "I hate this place but I feel a little . . . excited. Like, happy to be back. Tell me I'm not crazy."

"You're not crazy," she replied. "I feel it, too."

I braced myself, expecting her to talk about seeing Marco again. But she quickly added, "We actually have a chance to live now."

"True," I said.

"You know what else?" Aly added. "I sense Torquin is at our backs, cheering us on."

We looked at Cass, who hadn't said a word the whole flight. He was staring out the window as if tracking the flight of a ghost. Aly leaned forward and put a gentle hand on his shoulder. "Still thinking about the big guy, huh?"

Cass shifted away from her and exhaled without answering.

In truth, I wasn't thinking about our plan, or about Torquin. As Aly settled back, I said, "I'm nervous about seeing my mom again, Aly. I don't know how to feel about her."

"She slipped you that shard, Jack," Aly said. "She must be on our side."

I shook my head. "It doesn't add up. I mean, *no contact* for seven years? And then, boom, she shows up at Massa headquarters in Egypt—and she's like one of the heads of the whole organization?"

"Jack, she was the one who made it possible for you to escape that headquarters—with the Loculi!" Aly said.

"And look where we are now," I said. "Aly, what if she's fooling us—making us *think* she's a spy? This may all be a trick to get us over to the Dark Side." I took a deep breath and watched as the clouds began to clear and the plane to steady. "I don't trust my own mom. But I really, really want to see her again."

The island became a kidney-shaped green dot in the midst of a bright turquoise sea. Most of it was carpeted with a jungle of dense green, broken only by the solid black peak of Mount Onyx. Bright yellow beaches ringed the northern coast. Soon I could make out the orderly geometry of the Karai Institute campus—red-brick buildings surrounding a quadrangle crisscrossed with brick paths.

From a distance it looked as though the Massa attack had never occurred—the soldiers hunting us down, the fires and the bombings, the chases through the trees. But as we flew closer to the campus I saw uncut grass and weed-choked paths, blackened sections of buildings that had been bombed or torched. People in ragged white uniforms were dragging equipment into the buildings, guarded by others in black suits with rifles strapped across the backs. "Those must be KI prisoners," Cass muttered.

I looked over toward the jungle. With Torquin's help, a band of Karai had escaped there with our friend Fiddle. But my eyes fixed on three plumes of black smoke deep in the jungle. "I hope the rebels aren't in that . . ." I said.

"Or Marco . . ." Aly added.

Marco. There it was. I could see her eyes lighting up.

"Marco's one of the Massa," I reminded her. "Probably safe and well fed and shooting three-pointers from the top of Mount Onyx."

"That would be, like, three-thousand-pointers," Aly said.

The plane dipped its wings. Way down below, I could see black-suited guards waving at us. We dropped fast and touched down smoothly at the airport. This was where Fiddle would always greet us, his geeky ponytail swishing left and right as he eyeballed the jet for damage.

As the pilot pushed open the door, a severe-looking woman with the trace of a mustache stood at attention. "At your service, Brother Dimitrios!" she barked. "Welcome back to Massa Island! I have prepared a report when you are ready."

"'Massa Island'?" Aly grumbled, unstrapping her seat belt. "Guess they've made themselves comfy."

With a smile, Brother Dimitrios gestured for us to exit. As Aly stepped toward the door, Mustafa stood from his pilot seat, turning toward me. His eyes radiated pure hate. At first I thought his arms were covered with tattoos, but I realized they were bruises from the window I'd shut on him. "This will not be comfy for you," he said in a thick Greek accent.

Brother Dimitrios exhaled. "*Vre*, Brother Mustafa," he said with weary amusement. "Cannot we let bygones be bygones? Serves you right for being trigger-happy."

I felt Mustafa's eyes like lasers burning into my head. As I stepped into the hatch, he shot his arm out and ripped my backpack off my shoulders. "Hey!" I shouted.

Dimitrios clucked wearily. "I will speak to Mustafa about his roughness, Jack. But of course we must have the Loculi. As a precaution, that's all. We will take extraordinary care of them."

As I stepped out onto the tarmac, I felt my heart sinking.

Shake it off, a voice scolded in my brain. *What were you expecting? They'd let you keep them?*

"Jack . . ." Aly said, tugging on my shirt sleeve.

She and Cass were staring at a commotion at the edge of the tarmac, where a line of ragged people in filthy white uniforms was being led out of the jungle. They were heading to one of the supply buildings, whose front door was guarded by two sentries.

"Ah yes, I imagine you know some of these people," Brother Dimitrios said.

I nodded, examining the grim, familiar faces. "Cobb—she worked in the kitchen. Made the salads. The tall guy, Stretch, could repair anything mechanical. Yeah, I know them."

"Good," Dimitrios said. "They will be happy to see you. They are going through the welcoming process."

"In chains?" Aly said.

"Well, they were hostile when we found them," Dimitrios said. "They were among a much larger band of escapees near Mount Onyx."

"What happened to the others?" I asked.

His smile sent a shot of ice up my spine. "Let's just say these are the lucky ones."

CHAPTER TWENTY-THREE

GOOD ENOUGH FOR THE COCKROACHES

I WATCHED THE prisoners being led into the distant building, keeping an eye out for Fiddle's ponytail. I didn't see it. They all looked like their hair had been cut by a lawn mower. I didn't see anyone who resembled him or Nirvana at all.

I was afraid to ask Brother Dimitrios if those two were among the "others."

At the moment, I couldn't ask Dimitrios anything anyway. He was in deep conversation with the woman who'd met him outside the door. She towered over him, looking down a long, bumpy nose, and as she spoke, her silver-black ponytail seemed to wag excitedly. She was yapping away in clipped Greek sentences and gesturing toward us with a bony, olive-green finger.

"Margaret Hamilton," Aly said.

"You know her name?" I said.

"That's the name of the actress who played the Wicked Witch of the West in the *Wizard of Oz* movie," Aly said. "She looks just like her."

The woman looked at us and flashed a snaggletoothed grin. "Cue the flying monkeys," I murmured.

"Jack, this is Almira Gulch," Dimitrios said. "She will be turning you into a newt and eating you for lunch."

No, he didn't actually say that. What he actually said was, "Children, this is Mrs. Petaloude. She is in charge of recruit training. We have a bit of an emergency, alas, so I will be turning you over to one of my associates. Just stay here for a few moments, will you?"

"Wait, *training*?" I said. "Training for what?"

But they were already walking toward a Jeep, with Mrs. Petaloude bending his ear about something.

"Jack, who has the Loculi?" Aly whispered.

"Mustafa," I said.

"One more thing to worry about. I wish your dad hadn't sent them to us." Aly groaned, shaking her head. "I'm thinking about that shard, too. We should rotate it, each of us taking it for a while. To keep ourselves healthy. I'm good for now, and you've been holding it all along. Let's give it to Cass."

Cass turned toward her blankly, as if he hadn't understood

a word. I was worried about him. Since Torquin's death, he had completely checked out.

I pulled the tiny shard from my wallet and slipped it to him. "Can you keep this safe?"

Cass nodded, slipping the shard into his own wallet. I heard the voice of Brother Yiorgos calling us from the edge of the tarmac. He did not look happy, to say the least. His scowl had deepened and his skin had been darkened by the sun. In the deep crags on his face, you could imagine families of mosquitoes frolicking happily. We hadn't exactly left him on good terms. Somewhere in the jungle near Mount Onyx was a tree tattooed with the back of his head, courtesy of Torquin.

"Follow me," he called out. "Now."

"Nice to see you, too," Aly grumbled.

We walked behind him as he tromped down the thick jungle path. He was wearing a bag slung around his shoulder that slapped against his sides as he walked. I swatted away bugs by the dozen. "At least they could give us repellent," I grumbled.

"Brother Yiorgos is repellent," Aly said.

Yiorgos spun around. "I would save up that sense of humor if I were you," he said. "You will need it."

As we moved out of the jungle and into the campus clearing, I could see what Brother Yiorgos meant. Nothing was funny about what the Massa had done here. We'd

142

seen hints of the transformation from the air, but I wasn't prepared for this.

The Karai had fashioned their institute to look like a college—all red-brick buildings with stone steps, connected by grassy lawns and brick pathways. Now the brick paths were being replaced with cement, and the grass patches were being filled with gravel. The Massa attack had totaled a couple of the buildings, and in their place new structures were rising—drab concrete slabs with tiny windows. I was relieved to see that the magnificent, museumlike House of Wenders still stood across the quadrangle. But its sides had been damaged by bombs, and now the bricks were being removed for a makeover. The seven columns still stood at the top of the stairs, but the word *Wenders* had been chiseled from the marble pediment. On the ground, ready to be hoisted into place, was a cement block carved deeply with another word:

"Soon, this will all be perfect," Brother Yiorgos said in his thick Greek accent. "Massa strong. No more like Karai. No more froufrou Harvard-bricky college-la-la-la heads in clouds."

Aly scratched her head. "Could you repeat that?"

Brother Yiorgos grunted, pushing us into a bunkerlike building next to the House of Wenders.

I was sort of hoping we'd go back to our old dorm, which was now surrounded by scaffolding and teeming with Massa workers. Not that the dorm was a cozy place to begin with. But it looked like a palace next to the long metal-sided box they were taking us to now.

The doorknobs contained massive locks and the windows were barred. Inside, the place had the welcoming smell of wet cement and freshly cut tin. Our footsteps clonked on a metal floor as we passed tiny, unfurnished rooms. We had to duck through an open metal doorframe as Yiorgos led us into a large boxy space with a square hole for a window. "Living room," he said.

"Sofas and flat-screen TV arriving tomorrow?" Aly asked.

Yiorgos's eyes blazed. "You are here to work." He zipped open his shoulder bag and threw a pile of clothes onto a metal work table. On top, a white polo shirt unfolded. It had an *M* insignia on the left breast pocket. "Wait for Brother Dimitrios. Wear these. You smell bad."

"Where are we supposed to sit?" Aly asked.

"On the floor," Yiorgos said with a sneer. "If it's good

enough for the cockroaches, it's good enough for you."

As he stomped away, Cass turned to the window and stared silently. Around us, the jungle was growing dark. It was hard to believe a whole day had gone by since we'd awakened in Greece.

Aly slumped against the wall. "Okay, Tailor, sew us up something quick. Because I don't like this at all. I have a feeling we out-stupided ourselves by coming here."

"Stay focused," I said resolutely. "The key is finding Fiddle and the rebels. They're still out there. They've got to be."

"You saw those prisoners, Jack," Aly said. "And those are the ones the Massa spared!"

"That's what Brother Dimitrios told us," I said. "And Brother Dimitrios lies. Fiddle rescued a lot of people. Once we find them, we have a team. Experts. Fighters. We take the island back, reconstruct the Loculus of Healing, find the backpack, and book it."

"Five," Aly said, holding up her hand.

As I slapped it, Cass spun around. His face was bright red.

"Are you two serious?" he said, his voice a garbled rasp. "What planet are you on? Do you think we're really going to survive this? *Do you think we deserve to?*"

"Cass . . . ?" Aly said cautiously. She and I exchanged a look. It was the first thing Cass had said since we left Greece.

145

"They're dead, Jack," Cass said. "They're all dead, like Torquin. Did you see the fires in the jungle? The Massa smoked them out."

"It's just smoke, Cass," Aly said. "It's not proof of anything."

"Think about it, Jack—they escaped with *nothing*, no weapons, no communication, no food!" Cass was practically yelling now. "If the smoke didn't get them, starvation did. Don't you guys see? We're dead people, all of us! This was a terrible plan. They're going to separate us, take what they need from us, and then kill us! They're evil. *Bhegad is dead and Torquin is dead and Fiddle is dead and we're dead!*"

His voice echoed sharply against the metal walls. I felt paralyzed. Tongue-tied. "You—you didn't kill Torquin, Cass," I said lamely. "It wasn't your—"

"If you say that to me one more time, I'll kill you, too!" Cass blurted.

Tears had formed at the corners of his eyes, and he turned back to the window. Aly walked toward him and stood inches away—not touching him, just standing. She took a deep breath. "Hey, you want to know something I never told you?"

"No," Cass said.

"This will sound dumb," she went on, "but my mom was really impressed with you. She's a psychologist, and she really knows how to read people. She said you had an

146

incredibly strong emotional core."

Cass snorted. "You're right. It does sound dumb."

"You know what else she always says?" Aly went on. "Lack of sleep is the number-one thing that can mess up a person's brain. At least fifty percent of all psychological pain can be eased by regular sleep."

Cass turned away.

"We've been up more than twenty-four hours, Cass," Aly said gently.

"I—" Cass's voice broke. "Aly, I can never forgive myself . . ."

"For Torquin. I know. But you can't stay awake the rest of your life because of what happened. Torquin would want you to continue, Cass. He would want you to live. And you need sleep. We all do." Aly knelt on all fours, sweeping aside scraps of metal and bunching up a thick blue plastic sheet. "Come on. We'll catch a nap right here. The Massa Hilton."

I saw a trace of a smile cross Cass's face. He sank to one knee as if gravity had reached up an invisible hand and yanked him down. As I watched him and Aly settle into the makeshift resting spot, my own head began to feel heavy. I slid down against the wall, yawning. "Good night, guys."

"'Night, Jack . . . Aly," Cass squeaked. And then he added, "And I didn't mean what I said, about wanting to kill you."

Aly smiled. "We didn't think so."

* * *

The tap on my shoulder came about ten hours later by the clock, but it felt as if I'd been asleep for fifteen minutes.

As I blinked my eyes open, Brother Dimitrios stared down at me. He looked haggard and tired himself. "So sorry for the interruption . . ."

I yawned. My body was aching. We were all wearing our clean Massa clothing, and the room smelled of laundry detergent and sawdust. "Can we do this later?" I said. "I'm getting used to my new dorm."

With a weary smile, Dimitrios held out his hand. "Oh dear, did Yiorgos tell you this was your dorm? That scalawag. We wouldn't house you in a place like this—it's a temporary way station while your rooms are being prepared. Anyway, I'm afraid that there are some things that you must take care of, Jack."

"Now?" I said. "It's the middle of the night."

Cass was stirring now, and Aly bolted to her feet. "What's going on?" she demanded.

"Go back to sleep," Brother Dimitrios said. "Someone will come soon to take you to your quarters."

"But you just said we had to leave—" Aly began.

"I *said*," Brother Dimitrios snapped, "just Jack."

Aly raced to the doorway and stood there, arms folded. "Sorry, but no."

"Excuse me?" Brother Dimitrios said with a curious smile.

"We go together," Aly replied. "You've already brainwashed Marco, and you can't have Jack. So, no."

Cass looked at her in amazement. "You go, girl."

"I assure you, dear Aly, brainwashing is the furthest thing from my mind," Brother Dimitrios said. "You three are very different people with different talents. We must interview each of you, to develop individual plans. Surely you can't expect to stand over each other's shoulders forever."

"You need us, Dimitrios," Aly said. "So here are our terms. Jack stays. You bring Marco to us, show us he's still alive. We talk to Marco for an hour. Privately. *Then* we negotiate."

Brother Dimitrios looked confused. "Yes, we do need you. But I daresay you need us more. And for us to help you—to preserve your lives, my dear—we must follow our orders or *we* suffer consequences—"

"What consequences?" Aly demanded. "And who gives them?"

"So if you'll pardon my rudeness, here are *my* terms," Dimitrios barreled on. "If Jack expects to see you—and his father—again, he will do as I say and come with me. Alone."

CHAPTER TWENTY-FOUR

THE ILLUSION OF CONTROL

AS WE PASSED the place of eating we used to call the Comestibule, two horrifying things happened:

One, the sun peeked over the horizon. Which meant we were officially going to begin a full day of misery in Massaville.

Two, the smell of coffee and fried eggs from inside the building actually made me drool. As in, a string of liquid escaped my mouth and made a straight line down to my shoes. "You are ailing?" Brother Dimitrios said.

"I am hungry," I replied, wiping my mouth.

"The cafeteria is not yet open," he said, "but I have some pull here. You will need nourishment for what we have planned."

"Okay, enough mystery," I said. "What's the plan?"

But Brother Dimitrios was already heading into the building.

Seeing the interior was a shock. The place looked totally different. The paintings and the huge antler chandelier were gone, and all the wood paneling had been painted white. Brother Mustafa the pilot was swigging down some coffee, but he left the moment we arrived. Dimitrios snapped his fingers and immediately a sleepy-looking goon with a runny nose padded into the room, setting a plate of food in front of me.

I stared down at a yellow lump oozing about a pound of smelly white cheese.

"Chef's specialty, feta omelet," Brother Dimitrios explained.

"I think I just lost my appetite," I said. "Do you have any cereal?"

Brother Dimitrios leaped up from his seat, running into the kitchen to demand another meal. As I pushed the plate aside, I looked around the room.

Memories flooded in. I pictured the great banner that had once been strung across this hall: WELCOME TO YOUR KARAI INSTITUTE HOME, JACK. Back then I'd been too scared and creeped out to appreciate the welcome. Or the food.

Dimitrios reappeared with a bowl of soggy granola and

some weird-tasting milk. I bolted them down. I was still chewing as we walked out the back door. We hadn't gone ten feet before I saw something that made me nearly spit out the remains of my breakfast.

The KI game building, where we used to have unlimited entertainment possibilities, had been gutted. Now it was being merged with the enormous hangar building next to it—the place where all the KI repairs used to take place. It was where I had nearly been hit on the head by Fritz the mechanic because of my own clumsiness.

Its roof had been raised even higher. It was a fretwork of curved, thick wooden beams, and I could see that the building's final shape would be like a gigantic egg. All around the building, massive cranes made of lashed-together tree trunks groaned loudly, hoisting beams on steel winches.

"Behold the future Tharrodrome," Brother Dimitrios said. "From the word *tharros*, which means 'courage.' Perhaps you will remember our task chamber in the compound in Egypt, where your remarkable friend Marco performed some extraordinary feats of strength."

I did remember the chamber. And I remembered what the Massa had unleashed on Marco. A mutant beast. A warrior swordsman. "Is that what you're building here? A place where you torture kids and put their lives at risk?"

"A place where we test our Select and grow them to their

full potential," Brother Dimitrios said. "Which the KI, in their foolishness, never thought to do."

"Why did you bring me here alone?" I asked.

Brother Dimitrios opened a wood-frame, windowless door. "For your test, of course."

I stepped inside. The room had a coffee machine, a sink, a door, two office chairs, a wall clock, and a desk. I figured the door led to a toilet. A string of curly fluorescent lights hung from the unfinished ceiling. On the desk was a tablet with a keyboard. A slideshow flashed on the screen—photo after photo of Massa goons tearing down the Karai Institute. "So this is it?" I said. "I have to watch the construction of Six Flags Over Horrorland?"

"Sit, please." Brother Dimitrios rolled back the office chair. As I sat, he opened a desk drawer and pulled out a set of earplugs connected to a small tablet. "During your task, you will wear these, with the tablet hooked onto your belt. This way you can communicate with me if you need to."

"Wait. Where will you be?" I asked.

"This does not matter," Dimitrios said. "Let us begin."

He touched the screen. The slideshow disappeared to reveal a screen full of strange-looking apps with Greek labels. "Do I get a lifeline?" I asked. "If it involves any tech, I'll need Aly."

"You, Jack, will be *their* lifeline." Dimitrios leaned over and tapped an app that resembled a camera. Instantly the

153

screen showed Aly and Cass in a dorm room, much nicer than the one we'd just been inside. Cass was holding a phone and Aly was touching her fingers to the wall.

"Aly appears to be placing a wad of chewing gum over a spy lens," Brother Dimitrios said. "We placed three of those lenses in the room—small, dark globes about a quarter inch in diameter. Just large enough for a bright young person to spot. You see, she believes she is blocking us from seeing into the room."

"Because the lenses are fake," I said.

"Very good, Jack," Dimitrios said. "This is our way of giving her the illusion of control."

"If the lenses don't work, how come we see Cass and Aly?" I asked.

"We are actually watching through another lens, the size of a pinhead," Dimitrios replied. "It blends in with the grains of cement on the ceiling. I would like you to keep an eye on your friends. If they try anything funny, they will ruin your test. And there will be consequences. Oh, yes, just in case . . ."

He tapped another app and a kidney-shaped map appeared on the screen. In the northern section, two dots glowed. "This, of course, is the island, and the dots are Cass and Aly. Should they move outside the cabin, you will be able to track their movements."

"That's my trial—to spy on my own friends?" I asked.

Brother Dimitrios shook his head. "Your trial is to decode this."

Another app, this one revealing an image of an old document.

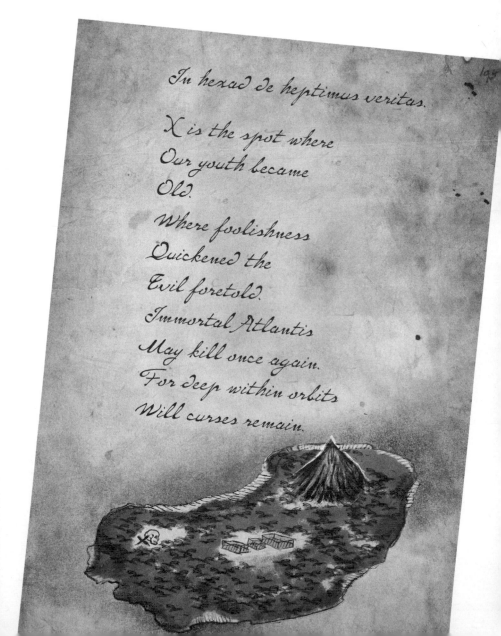

In hexad de heptimus veritas.

X is the spot where
Our youth became
Old.
Where foolishness
Quickened the
Evil foretold.
Immortal Atlantis
May kill once again.
For deep within orbits
Will curses remain.

"What the heck does that mean?" I asked.

"You tell me," Brother Dimitrios said.

"Wait," I said. "I have to do *your* work? You guys couldn't figure this out?"

"Who says we haven't?" Brother Dimitrios shot back.

"Any hints?" I said.

"The answer to this is the name of a great danger that exists on this island." Dimitrios held a remote to the wall clock. It instantly became a timer, which read 20:00:00.

"You have twenty minutes," he said. "If you fail, one of your friends dies."

"Wait, you're joking, right?" I said. "You wouldn't do that. You said you needed us!"

"Unfortunately, Jack, I am not the one who sets the rules," Dimitrios said.

"Then who is it?" I demanded. *"Let me talk to him now!"*

Dimitrios backed out of the room shaking his head. "I am sorry, dear boy. But twenty-three seconds have gone by."

The door clicked shut as he disappeared.

CHAPTER TWENTY-FIVE

IN HEXAD DE HEPTIMUS VERITAS

17:58:13.

This was insane.

Impossible.

I couldn't concentrate. My eyebrows were raining sweat. Nearly two whole minutes had gone by and I hadn't done a thing except stare at the dumb poem. I couldn't make any sense of it.

Curses? Deep within orbits?

Youth became old?

The words swirled in my head until they had no meaning at all. Like I was looking at a foreign language.

Do something. Print it out. Take notes. First things that come to mind.

157

That was what my creative writing teacher, Mr. Linker, always told us. *Sometimes it looks different when it's on paper.* So I went to work.

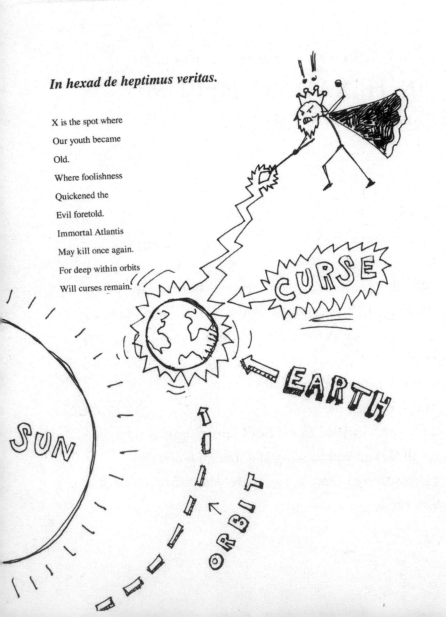

In hexad de heptimus veritas.

X is the spot where
Our youth became
Old.
Where foolishness
Quickened the
Evil foretold.
Immortal Atlantis
May kill once again.
For deep within orbits
Will curses remain.

CURSE

EARTH

SUN

ORBIT

I felt like an utter idiot.

This was a waste of time.

15:56:48.

"Code . . . it's a code, it must be a code . . ." Now I was talking to myself.

I thought about the codes we'd seen.

The rock at the top of Mount Onyx.

No. Not like this at all.

The door to the Hanging Gardens of Babylon.

Nope.

The letter from Charles Newton we'd found at the Mausoleum at Halicarnassus.

Uh-uh.

Wait.

I stared at the heading, which was in bigger type than the rest of it. *In hexad de heptimus veritas.*

The Charles Newton letter had a heading, too. It was the key to understanding the rest of the letter. Where the date was supposed to be, there was a message: *The 7th, to the end.* That meant we had to count every seventh letter.

My eyes fixed on the word *Heptimus.* It was like Heptakiklos.

Hepta was seven; *kiklos* was circle.

I wiped the sweat from my brow. *Duh.* So much of this quest was about the number seven. Everything always came back to sevens.

159

Carefully I wrote down every seventh letter of the poem.

Looked like a word scramble. Great. Cass was good at those. Probably Aly, too. For all I knew, Marco ate them for lunch. Me? It's about the same level as my gift for ballet dancing. Zero out of ten in the Jack McKinley Scale of Loserdom.

But Brother Dimitrios's words clattered around in my brain: *If you fail, one of your friends dies.*

The threat of murder has a way of bringing out the best in a person.

Okay, the *Q* had to go with a *U*. In the letters I saw a *query* . . . also a *require* . . . and an *I am* . . . I began scribbling as fast as I could:

WARM SQUIRRELS, ICY FOE

MY CALF WORRIES SQUIRE

FORMERLY ICIER SQUAWS

i SCARE SQUIRMY FLOWER

SORCERER QUALIFY SWIM

ACQUIRE LESS FROM WIRY

MR. WOLF is QUEASY CRIER

"Arrrghhh!" I cried out.

Useless. I slammed down my pen.

7:58:34.

Eight whole minutes, down the toilet!

Okay. Calm down.

I needed to go further. Figure out the other parts of that heading. *In hexad de heptimus veritas.* My fingers shook as I opened the tablet's browser. I typed "in hexad de heptimus veritas" into a search engine page but got nothing. So I entered the words one by one.

Definition: hexad. A group of six.

Definition: heptimus. Sevenths.

Definition: veritas. Truth.

This was weird. The first two words were from the Greek, the last was from Latin. It was a mishmash. This wasn't Atlantean. Or even ancient. Brother Dimitrios and his pals must have made it up.

"Just go with it, Jack," I muttered to myself. "Okay . . . in a group of six of sevenths truth . . ."

7:14:32 . . .

I glanced away from the clock and then back again.

7:14:29 . . .

7:14:28 . . .

Seven-one-four-two-eight.

For that one second, the clock showed a number that meant something to me—the magic sequence of sevenths, 714285!

I hated fraction conversions. But I knew this one cold.

Divide seven into any single digit. You get the same

digits in the same sequence. Well, they may start in a different place, but it's all the same.

Like .142857. Which is one seventh.

Or .285714, two sevenths.

Or .428571, three sevenths.

Or .714285—five sevenths, same as on the clock.

The same six digits over and over again, starting in different places.

That would be a group of six.

A hexad!

We were getting somewhere. Maybe.

In hexad de heptimus veritas.

Okay.

That would mean . . . *Truth in the hexad of the sevenths.*

But which hexad?

I figured, start with one seventh: .142857. Maybe if I pulled out the right letters, it would spell something. So the first letter, the fourth, the second, the eighth, and so on from each line. . . .

Impossible. One of the lines only had three letters.

Wait. Wait.

There was another possibility.

Down the side of the printout, I wrote out the magic sequence, one digit for each line of text. Then I circled the corresponding letter—for number 1, the first letter, for number 4, the fourth . . .

In hexad de heptimus veritas.

1   Ⓧis the spot where

4   Our yⓄuth became

2   Olⓓ.

8   Where foⓞlishness

5   Quicⓚened the

7   Evil foⓡetold.

1   Ⓘmmortal Atlantis

4   May ⓀIll once again.

2   Fⓞr deep within orbits

8   Will curⓢes remain.

Underneath I wrote out the letters:

XYLOKRIKOS

"What the heck?" I quickly typed the word into the search engine. The first hit made me gasp:

164

Der Xylokrikos

Xylokrikos—jungle creature—Journals, Herman Wenders
Von "Xylos" (Holz) und "Krikos" (Kreis), ein sagenhaftes Geschöpf
der Mythologie selten angeführt. Entstehen der Kreise von Jahr

I clicked on it and looked at the page:

DER XYLOKRIKOS

Von "Xylos" (Holz) und "Krikos" (Kreis), ein sagenhaftes Geschöpf, in Erzählungen der Mythologie selten angeführt. Entstehen der Kreise von Jahresringen im Baumstumpf.

Finally I clicked on the translation button and read what it meant:

THE XYLOKRIKOS
From xylos (wood) and krikos (ring), a mythological figure rarely sighted by sources. Arises from the rings of a tree stump.

I leaped up from my seat, pumping my fist in the air. *"Woo-hoo! I got it! Brother Dimitrios, I know you must be watching this! The answer is Xylokrikos!"*

Dimitrios's face appeared on the tablet screen. I jumped. I didn't realize he was controlling the screen like that. "Ah, bravo, Jack," he said.

"Thanks," I said quickly. "So you'll let them alone, right? Cass and Aly—they're going to be okay?"

"For now," Dimitrios said. "Your friends will indeed be pleased that you passed part one. Let's tell them."

The image dissolved. Now I was looking into Cass and Aly's room.

It was empty.

"Well, will you look at that . . . tsk-tsk-tsk," came Dimitrios's voice.

"Where did they go?" I demanded. *"If you hurt them . . ."*

"They are fine. I am a man of my word," Dimitrios said. "Ten minutes ago they received a handwritten message from a fellow named Fiddle."

I froze up but said nothing.

"It seems this musically named fellow directed them toward somewhere on the island," Dimitrios continued.

The screen's image dissolved to reveal a patch of jungle. "You have hidden cameras?"

"All throughout the island, of course," Dimitrios said.

In the midst of the patch was a dull glow. As the camera zoomed in, the glow became a hatch, half-hidden by vines. On it was a carved Λ.

"Don't get too excited," Dimitrios said. "If they reach this hatch, there is a . . . surprise waiting for them."

"What *kind* of surprise?" I demanded.

"You will be given sufficient information to figure that out."

"Just tell me if they're in danger!" I said.

"I would recommend that you make haste, Jack," Dimitrios replied.

The image vanished. In place of Brother Dimitrios's face was a map of the island, marked like a radar screen. I could see two blue dots moving from one of the compound buildings into the jungle, toward a big *X*.

Farther south in the compound was a third blue dot. As I walked the tablet to the door, the dot jiggled slightly.

It was me.

"You will be allowed one lifeline," Brother Dimitrios's voice said. "And that will be me. You may ask one question after you begin."

"What am I supposed to do?" I shouted into the tablet. *"And that doesn't count as my lifeline question!"*

Dimitrios's answer was one word:

"Hurry."

CHAPTER TWENTY-SIX

LIFELINE

"UCCCHH." I STOOPED down and plucked the tablet out
of the jungle grass.

I was running too fast, being too hasty. The jungle
humidity drenched me. My hands were slippery. I needed
the tablet to check my bearings, my blue dots, but I kept
dropping it.

Where were they?

There.

Their two dots were looping around from the north.
They'd had a big head start, and they were way closer to
the hatch than I was. My dot was at the extreme western
part of the screen. I'd never catch up to them. I'd have to go
straight to the hatch.

Clutching tight to the tablet, I ran. I lifted my feet as high as they could go. Overhead, birds and monkeys screeched as if they were watching a soccer match. As I got closer I shouted, *"Aly! Cass!"*

My answer was a chorus of hoots, caws, and shrieks. My friends were never going to hear me.

My blue dot moved toward the goal faster than Aly's and Cass's did from the north. When I was on top of the big *X*, I stopped.

I looked around for a hatch, but all I saw was the same old jungle mess. I leaned over, clearing away brush with my arms. A snake hissed, slithering away. A huge lizard eyed me from beneath a nearby bush.

"Where is it?" I cried out in frustration.

EEEEEE! came the shriek of a monkey. Torquin had understood those cries. He'd made friends with some of these creatures. What were they telling me?

My eyes were watery and stinging. I didn't know if it was sweat or tears. I caught sight of the corner of a high tree stump and leaned on it, rubbing away the moisture with my free hand.

EEEE-EEE-EEEEEE!

EEEEEEE!

I had to jump back. Monkeys were dropping out of the trees like parachute jumpers. They landed just beyond the stump in two lines.

I narrowed my eyes. "What do you guys want?"

EEEE-EEE-EEEEEE! One of the chimps pointed to the stump, slapping his head.

"It's a stump! What's wrong with . . . ?" *The research.* I realized Brother Dimitrios had given me a big fat clue. "Okay . . . the xylokrikos . . . is that what you're warning me about? This thing is really a monster?"

I stared at the remnant of the old tree. Was this where Brother Dimitrios was leading us all—some kind of portal, where the monster would morph out of the wood to attack us?

I backed away. But then, out of nowhere, a rock went flying past my ear. The monkeys were trying to get my attention. They were divided down the middle into two groups, each screaming and gesturing toward the other.

"What?" I said. "Come on. This is a magical island. Be magical. *Talk to me!*"

They were pointing to something between them. I stepped closer until I could see a silvery filament like a taut spiderweb, a line so thin that it was barely a shimmer. It emerged from the jungle behind them and seemed to be connected somewhere near me, like some weird zip line for insects. Squinting against the sunlight that flashed through the trees, I followed the line to its source.

It ended at the stump.

From their reactions, I thought the monkeys were going

to have a heart attack. At the place where the filament attached to the trunk's bark was a set of metal electrodes.

An electric fence. That's what it had to be. Back when we were first on the island, Aly had discovered a network of these, placed by the KI around the campus.

How extensive was this fence? How far away were Cass and Aly? I checked my tablet, lining up my location with theirs.

I was at the bottom right of the *X*. Aly and Cass were coming closer to the top left. They would be crossing the *X* soon. But the monkeys were all here, all warning *me*.

"Lifeline!" I screamed into the tablet. "What is this—this *wire*, Dimitrios? Where does it go, and what does it do?"

Dimitrios's face did not appear. Instead, I saw footage of Aly and Cass tromping through the woods. This was his answer: a video feed from some hidden security camera in a tree. They were headed for a broken-down cottage in the distance. Around the cottage was a perfectly round wooden fence.

You will be given sufficient information to figure that out.

That's what Dimitrios had promised me. But this information was wack. How was any of this meaningful? Screaming monkeys, electric filaments, hatches that didn't exist, tree-stump monsters . . .

The xylokrikos.

From xylos *("wood") and* krikos *("ring")* . . .

No. It wasn't about the stump monster. Not really. It was about its name—wood plus ring. A ring of wood!

The fence.

That was what the poem's code meant.

"It's not about a monster, is it, Dimitrios?" I shouted. "The puzzle—xylokrikos was the answer. But it's about that wooden fence. The wire is attached—and if they cross it they'll be electrocuted! *How do I turn it off? Lifeline! Lifeline! How do I turn it off!*"

A soft chuckle arose from my tablet. "I said one question, and you just asked three. Well, I have a heart and I shall address the last one. The only way to de-electrify that filament is to break the circuit. It is constructed of carbene, an extremely thin, extremely strong material developed by our scientists. So you will not be able to break it with, say, a stick. I suppose the only way to disable it would be contact with a grounded water-containing carbon unit that will conduct the electricity."

"Meaning what?" I demanded.

"A living being, Jack," Dimitrios replied. "There are candidates in your vicinity, I'd say."

The monkeys were backing away, hopping and gesticulating, slapping themselves obliviously. If I could trap one of them . . .

No. They seemed to sense what I was thinking and were

already in retreat. I'd never be able to do it in time.

But letting Cass or Aly touch that fence was worse.

Unless I did it first.

I closed my eyes. This was the right thing to do. I was the Tailor, who figured things out. I was the Destroyer. In this one act, I would be both.

People say your life flashes before your eyes just before you die. Not me. All I could see was the photo on my old hand mirror—Dad, Mom, and me as a toddler in the snow, playing Boom to Daddy. The photo I'd been looking at every day of my life since Mom disappeared. It calmed me down. Made me realize I'd once had some happiness in my life.

I would be dead in a few seconds. But at least I was smiling.

Stretching out my arms, I dropped the tablet.

And I dived into the filament, chest first.

CHAPTER TWENTY-SEVEN

THE SEVENTH CODEX

MY FIRST TASTE of death was a mouthful of wet leaves.

I sprang up. My feet were still on the jungle ground. The monkeys were still chattering. My eyes darted toward the tree stump. I saw the black electrodes where the filament had been attached.

Just the electrodes. Nothing else. The unbreakable carbene filament was . . . *broken?* "No . . ." I murmured.

They'd touched it first. They'd gotten to it before I had. I'd been too slow to save my friends' lives.

"Aly! Cass!" I screamed.

The monkeys screeched back at me. But they were hiding now, no longer helping me. Without seeing them, I didn't know where the filament had been. I had no idea

175

where to go. Everything in the jungle looked the same.

I scrambled for the tablet, scooping it off the ground. The screen was cracked, and pressing the power button did absolutely nothing. Tossing it into the jungle, I reared back my head and shouted Brother Dimitrios's name.

Among the cacophony of monkeys and birds, I heard a woman's voice directly behind me. "Remarkable. I would not have predicted it would have been this one."

I spun around but all I could see was a suffocating scrim of dense greenery all around. *"Who are you?"* I shouted. *"Where are Aly and Cass?"*

"Remarkable indeed. He is still concerned about them. Bravo." Dimitrios emerged, with an enormous smile. Next to him was a woman in commando gear. From the weathered wrinkles on her face, I could tell she was much older than Mom. But her carriage was straight and upright like a soldier's, her eyes sharp and smart. Despite her advanced years she looked as if she could handle herself against anyone.

"First," the lady said, "be assured that your friends are safe."

"Wh-what?" I stammered. "If they . . . then I should be . . ."

"The filament held no electrical charge," Brother Dimitrios said.

I wasn't sure I heard that right. "Wait. It was a fake? *You made me think I was going to die?"*

"It seems inscrutable, I know," the woman replied, "but it was necessary."

"And who are *you?*" I demanded.

Dimitrios stepped forward. "Jack, my boy, I know this is upsetting but manners are always important when among your elders. Before you is—"

The woman held up her hand to quiet Dimitrios. "You may call me Number One," she said.

"Wait . . . Number One?" I said. Okay, maybe it was just the shock of being alive. Or the distant ridiculous jabbering of monkeys. Or the solemn way she called herself a potty name. But I started laughing like a five-year-old. "That's your name—Number One? I mean, really, *Number One?"*

"It's more of a rank, I suppose," she said with a bemused smile.

"I guess it could be worse—*you could be called Number Two!"* I was howling now. "That would really be rank!"

"Jack, stop that now!" Dimitrios said. "Apologize!"

"Sorry . . . sorry," I replied, taking deep breaths.

I expected Number One to be as stuffy and upset as Dimitrios. But she was smiling curiously at me. "I had a brother once," she said. "You remind me of him."

"So. Number One," I said. "Nice to meet you. How come I haven't ever seen you before?"

"I haven't needed to be seen until now." She nodded

177

toward Dimitrios, then turned back toward the campus. "We have much to talk about. Follow me, please."

I stood my ground, looking at the back of her head in disbelief. My giddy mood was curdling fast. Into rage. "Okay. Just a second. You nearly scared me to death. You owe me an explanation. I want to see my friends. I want to talk now."

I heard a rustling in the bushes behind me. Brother Yiorgos emerged, blocking my path, along with another goon who wore an eyepatch. Neither was smiling.

"You know Yiorgos, of course," Brother Dimitrios said. "And this is Brother Plutarchos—er, Cyclops, for short."

"Enough. Your friends are fine. Come. I am not fond of mosquitoes, Jack." The woman turned to go, calling over her shoulder, "And you, I suspect, are not fond of being carried."

* * *

I had a bad case of WWF, Walking While Furious. I could barely see straight. My heart was like a jackhammer.

I wanted to find Cass and Aly, tell them the story, and begin an assault on the Massa—*somehow*. But whenever I slowed down, Yiorgos began breathing down my neck. Which, trust me, is enough to keep anyone moving.

The woman led us through the jungle, into the campus, and up the stairs of the building formerly known as the House of Wenders. I barely recognized the lobby. During the KI days, it had been a soaring, dark-wood-paneled atrium with a towering dinosaur skeleton. Now it was a construction site. The skeleton had been removed, and the grand mahogany balcony was shattered and patched up with crudely cut wooden planks.

"We sustained quite a bit of damage," she said.

"In the attack *you* caused," I reminded her.

She smiled. "Ah well, the old fortress needed some sprucing up anyway."

As I followed her to the second floor, I felt a tug in my chest. She'd taken over Professor Bhegad's office, complete with his rickety old leather chair and wooden desk. His mess was gone—no more piles of papers and bursting file cabinets. No more creaky, dust-encrusted metal fan and grimy windows. But the old Oriental rug remained, and I could see a straight path worn by Bhegad's footsteps, leading from desk to door.

Somehow the sight of that path brought him back in my mind. I could see his heavy footfalls and stooped gait, the way he pushed his glasses up his bulbous nose, his stiff and formal language. Here in this office, on the day Marco had fallen into the volcano to save our lives, the professor had actually cried. For us.

For the first time, I realized how much I missed the old guy.

"Sit," the woman said, gesturing toward an empty chair.

Looking straight at this gray-eyed Massa leader, I wondered if she could cry. I wondered if she had emotions about anything.

Just over her shoulder were two framed black-and-white photos. One, of a dark-eyed boy, looked like a faded school picture. The other was a dark-curly-haired man with watery eyes and a huge, ridiculous-looking smile.

"Family resemblance, no?" the woman said. "Both my father and my brother are long gone."

"Did you play chicken with their lives, too?" I muttered.

The woman raised an eyebrow. "Excuse me?"

I didn't care if she was an adult, or if that ridiculous name "Number One" meant she was the head of the Massa or Queen of the Universe. For all I knew, those family photos were just more lies. *I thought I was going to die!* I rose to my feet and gripped the edge of her desk. "The poem was a lie. The code was a lie. The xylokrikos meant nothing, and you made up that stuff about the unbreakable wire. Was that your idea of a joke?"

Brother Yiorgos grabbed me and held my arms behind my back. The lady known as Number One stood up sharply. "Release him. He's more angry than dangerous."

With a grunt, the monk pushed me down into a chair. Number One came around her desk, sat on the edge, and leaned toward me. When she spoke, her voice was soft and sad. "Until you have experienced the death of your own blood before your eyes, you will not appreciate what it means to love and lose someone."

"What makes you think I don't know that?" I snapped.

I looked away so I wouldn't be tempted to blurt out any truths about my mother.

"If you do know, then we may begin to understand each other." The woman stood, looking at the two pictures on the wall. "My brother's name was Osman. He and you were very much alike. He was a Select, you know. There is not a day that I don't think of him."

"Your brother was a Select?" I said. "So you knew about all of this back then?"

"I did," Number One said. "In fact, I lost both Osman and Father to Artemisia, just as you lost Radamanthus Bhegad."

I thought of Bhegad's soul being ripped from his body. I thought of the last time I'd seen him, hanging from my ankle as I flew on a griffin. I began to shake. In my mind's eye he was falling to the earth below, falling fast, without a scream . . .

"We have the resources to prevent further deaths, Jack," the woman said, her voice softening. "To restore the world to its glorious destiny that ended at the fall of Atlantis— reason and equality, health and progress, cooperation. Since the fall, the world has become a battleground among barbarians, all of them blind to the coming destruction. You

181

are our hope, Jack. Show him, Dimitrios."

Brother Dimitrios spun a tablet toward me.

"Does this look familiar?" the woman asked.

"Yes," I said. "There were a bunch of these paintings at Brother Dimitrios's monastery in Rhodes—all about the life of Massarym."

"Now look at this," Number One added, swiping the screen with a bony finger and revealing another image:

"The two images are the same painting," Dimitrios explained. "In this image, I used infrared imaging to reveal the pentimento."

"Penti-*who?*" I said.

"When words are written onto a canvas, and then artists paint over these words to hide them," Brother Dimitrios said. "That is *pentimento*. The history of Atlantis was written in six books, or codices. Massarym, fearing these books would be destroyed, wrote his own history. We call it the Seventh Codex. And it is hidden in these paintings."

"The Seventh Codex," Number One went on, "told of two curses. When Massarym stole and hid the Loculi for their safekeeping, Uhla'ar blamed his son for the kingdom's destruction. He suspected Massarym wanted to rebuild a new Atlantis with himself as king. Massarym tried to explain the truth: that the queen's tampering had upset the balance of Atlantean power—that he, Massarym, merely wanted to preserve the Loculi. But Uhla'ar would not hear of it. He placed a curse on his own son, that Massarym would never live to see the Loculi retrieved."

"Well, that sure happened," I said.

"Ah, but Massarym, in turn, placed a curse on his father," Number One said. "Uhla'ar would not die, but would be condemned to remain on earth, neither dead nor alive."

"He turned Uhla'ar into a ghost?" I asked.

Brother Dimitrios chanted as if reciting by memory. "'The Curse of Uhla'ar shall not be lifted until the seven Loculi are placed within the Heptakiklos by the actions of the Rightful Ruler. Only then shall the Curse be lifted and the continent raised once again.'"

"Wait—*raised*?" I said. "Like, this whole island? Right here?"

Number One was beaming. "Kind of quickens the heart, doesn't it?"

"Okay . . . okay . . ." I said, trying to make sense of what she'd just said. "Uhla'ar chased Massarym—right, I know that because I have these weird dreams about the past. But about the Loculi. I thought we just had to bring them back and put them in the Heptakiklos. Bam, done and done. No one told us about any Rightful Ruler."

"Dimitrios, continue," Number One commanded.

"'By two indicators shall the Ruler's identity be revealed,'" Brother Dimitrios recited. "'The first shall be an act of Locular destruction. The second, an act of self-sacrifice.'"

I flopped back into my chair. "Oh, great—he's the only one who can activate the Loculi. But he has to destroy one, and then kill himself. Sure. I think I know where you're going with this."

"It is a paradox," Brother Dimitrios said.

"Massarym was all about mysteries," Number One said. "One must read the prophecy carefully, in the original language. *Destruction* sounds so final in English. But broken things can be fixed, no? And what if the act of self-sacrifice is just that—an *act*? An *attempt*."

185

I closed my eyes and took a deep breath, trying to piece this craziness together. "So you saw me throw the Loculus under the train. Boom, Locular destruction. And just now, you faked me out to see if *I* would *attempt* to sacrifice myself."

They both nodded.

"Didn't you try this with Marco already?" I snapped. "Back in Babylon, he told us *he* was going to be king. Is this your trick—you tell him, then me, then Cass, then Aly . . . ?"

Brother Dimitrios sighed. "You will forgive us for being impulsive about Marco. We had heard how jumped into a volcano for his friends. In our judgment, he had fulfilled the second part of the prophecy—"

"He didn't jump," I said. "He was fighting a vromaski, and they both fell off the edge."

"So we learned," Brother Dimitrios said. "But alas, only later on. So when in Ancient Babylon, he *destroyed a Loculus*, well, that was the first part of the prophecy! But there, too, we were wrong. He merely destroyed the replacement, your so-called Shelley."

"He never destroyed a Loculus," Number One said. "You did, Jack."

I thought about what happened when I was standing by the tracks in New York City, invisible—when Mom was looking straight at me, somehow knowing I was there.

186

The first to leave the scene had been Dimitrios, muttering something under his breath. We all heard what he'd said—Cass, Aly, and me. Mom had waited till he was gone—and then she'd pointed at me.

I recited those words under my breath. "The Destroyer . . ." I said, repeating Brother Dimitrios's words, "shall rule."

"You have fulfilled both requirements, Jack the Destroyer," the woman said. "Marco has indeed an extraordinary destiny based on his gifts, and Aly and Cass on theirs. But yours is the most important gift of all."

Brother Dimitrios's eyes were intense. "We must keep this a secret until the training is complete."

"And then the real work can begin"—Number One's mouth curved upward into a smile that was half ironic, half admiring—"my liege."

CHAPTER TWENTY-EIGHT

HIS JACKNESS

THERE'S A FINE line between destiny and doofusness, and I was walking it.

All the way back to the dorm, I felt like two people. One of them was trembling with excitement and the other was cackling out loud.

My liege.

Was that supposed to be a joke? Was she flattering me? What did her little smile mean?

And really, what did that painting say? For all I knew, the words in that painting could have been anything—a diary, an Atlantean laundry list, whatever. Did it make any sense that out of the zillion people born in the world since the sinking of Atlantis, I, Jack McKinley the Painfully

Average, would be the future king?

No, it didn't make sense. But neither did magic beach balls, or invisibility, or living statues, or time rifts, or zombies, or acid-spitting creatures.

My worn-out sandal clipped a vine, and I nearly fell over. Massa construction workers looked up and stared at me weirdly. Did they know? Maybe the good news had been sent out to them over some kind of Massaweb. What were they thinking?

All hail, King Jack!

His Royal Highness, Jack the First of Belleville!

A good day to His Jackness, Master of the Kingdom of Atlantis and Ruler of the World!

Sooner or later everyone was going to have to adjust to King Jack. Including me.

I stood up, drew myself up to full height, and gave them a kingly wave with a cupped palm. "Carry on!"

And then one of my new subjects spoke:

"Uh, kid, you just stepped in monkey turds."

* * *

Cass was the first to run toward me from the dorm. "Did they suck out your brains and replace them with Jell-O?"

"Did you see Marco?" Aly asked, her face full of excitement and hope.

"No and no," I said.

189

Cass crinkled up his face. "What stinks?"

The last hint of kingliness flew out of my head. I wiped my sandals in a wet, grassy spot. "Sorry, I thought I got it all off."

"We need to talk, now," Aly said. "And here, where no one will hear us."

"And fast, because we're starving and the cafeteria's open," Cass said.

"I guess you're feeling better," I said.

Cass nodded. "Oh. That. Yeah, well, sorry about yesterday. Aly and I have been talking. She was right. I'm not going to blame myself, and I'll promise to be more like Torquin. The bravery part, not the grunting and bad driving."

Aly looked like she would explode from excitement. "Jack, we want to hear about your meeting with Brother Creepo. But we have to tell you what happened to us. We got this note from—"

"Not here." I looked around, thinking about the secret cameras the Massa had planted in the jungle. "There are bugs."

"In the trees?" Cass asked.

"My room is safe," Aly said, turning to go back into the dorm. "Leave the sandals and follow me. I destroyed the surveillance cameras."

"Not all of them," I said. "There's one the size of a

pinhead, probably up where the wall meets the ceiling, directly above your desk."

Aly turned back. "Excuse me? How do you—?"

"I'll help you disable it," I said. "Show me the way."

I kicked off my stinky sandals and followed Cass and Aly into the new dorm. It was about twice the size of the old building. Instead of being greeted in a cramped hallway by our old Karai guard, Conan the Armed and Sleepy, there was a big empty entryway two floors high. A hallway led to the right, and I found a door marked with my name. I ducked inside to look. It was a big corner room with screened windows, tons of sunlight, and a shelf with a few used books and an iPod dock. I think the dresser had been Marco's in the old dorm, because one of the drawers had been kicked in and repaired with glue.

I could hear Cass and Aly clomping into the room next to me. I washed my feet, then put on a new pair of sandals I found in the closet and sprinted to meet them. Aly was standing on her desk, staring at me as I entered. In her hand was a piece of twisted metal. Just above her, wires jutted from a spot near the roof. "How did you know, Jack? About this camera?"

"Dimitrios showed me," I said. "The other lenses that you covered with gum? Those were fakes. I was tracking you. They made me think you were in danger."

"Jack, you're scaring me," Cass said.

191

Aly stepped down, eyeing me warily. "So, that note from Fiddle—?"

"A fake, too," I said. "The Massa led you to that hatch. They made me watch. They told me you were going to be killed. But they were lying. They were testing me. To see if I would sacrifice myself to save your lives."

They both stared at me silently.

"Well . . . ?" Cass asked softly. "Did you?"

I nodded.

"So . . . they're brainwashing you," Aly said.

Cass shrugged. "Sounds like bravery to me."

"It's called behavior modification," Aly barreled on. "You see it in a million movies. They make you feel like you're going to die. Or that someone you love is going to die. They start breaking down your free will. After a while you don't know what's real or fake. Then they can worm their way into your brain and make you believe anything. Like the *Manchurian Candidate*."

"The *who*?" I said.

Aly rolled her eyes. "Classic movie. Don't you have any culture?"

"Don't you ever watch any *new* movies?" Cass replied.

"The point is, the Massa are sneaky and weird." Aly went on. "They deluded Marco into thinking he's going to be the next king. Watch it, Jack. They're probably working on you, too. I think they're trying to separate us—divide and conquer."

"What exactly did they say to you?" Cass asked.

Number One's words burned in my brain: *We must keep this a secret until the training is complete.*

No way. I needed to tell Cass and Aly the truth. Once you start lying to your best friends, it's hard to go back. But right this moment, I didn't know what was true and what wasn't. What if I really did tell them that Number One anointed me future king? They'd say I was a sucker and a traitor, like Marco.

And I wasn't.

I had to think this through myself. Calmly. Without being influenced.

If what Number One told me was a lie, then nothing changed. But if it was true, I had to do it right. I needed to be very, very cautious.

"Well," I said, "it turns out that the head of the Massa is this woman called Number One. She's, like, my grandmother's age—"

"Wait," Aly said. "You met the *head* of the Massa? Just you? Why?"

"I'm special, I guess." I wanted that to sound like a joke, but I'm not sure it worked. "I think she wants to raise the continent of Atlantis."

"Like, from under the ocean?" Cass said. "The whole island?"

"It's a Massa thing," I replied. "When Massarym stole the Loculi, raising the continent was part of his long-term plan. He wanted to bring back the glory that was Atlantis, blah-blah-blah."

Cass punched a fist in the air. "That is so emosewa!"

"Are you serious?" Aly leaned closer, all red in the face. "Um, tell me neither of you knuckleheads know what a disaster this would be."

"Right, tons of vromaskis and griffins and stuff," Cass said. "That would suck."

"No, that's not the point!" Aly said. "Millions of years ago, the entire middle of the United States was a sea. New York City had a mountain range like the Rockies. But the continents drifted. *Slowly.* Meteors collided, sea levels shifted, earth moved, air quality changed, continents sank, species died. *Incredibly slowly.* Raising an entire continent—*voom*, just like that? We're talking massive disaster. Tidal waves and earthquakes, to start. Changing wind and water currents, rising seas, coastal floods, shifting tectonic plates. New York City, Boston, Los Angeles, Seattle, Chicago, New Orleans, Athens, Capetown— gone. Don't even think about the Netherlands. Dormant fault lines burst open coast to coast, followed by fires. Dirt and dust clouds will block the sun, just like the time of the dinosaurs. And you know what happened to them. We'd be lucky if anyone survived!"

"Chicago's not coastal," Cass said.

"You get the idea!" Aly stared at me, her face a mixture

of fear and disbelief. "Do they really believe they can make the continent rise?"

"Maybe you're overreacting," I said. "How do you know it will be so bad? Maybe Atlantis isn't big enough to cause all that."

"It doesn't have to be that big to do a lot of damage, Jack!" Aly said.

"Well, people have been predicting ecological disasters and stuff anyway," I said. "At least this way, Atlantis would appear, with all its energy restored. And if the world had, like, good leaders, they could help."

Aly looked at me in disbelief. "How? Stop the floods with a proclamation?"

"They could think ahead," I said. "You know, evacuate people from the coasts. Look, we're already changing the climate by burning fossil fuels, right? And people are bombing and killing each other. There's genocide everywhere. It's not like the world is on a path to such a great future. Don't you think we *need* Atlantis?"

"I don't believe I'm hearing this," Aly said. "From Marco, yes. *He* thinks he's going to be king. But not from a reasonable, intelligent person like you. I say we kill this ridiculous discussion and stick to our plan. We contact the rebels, find out where the shards are hidden, get the other Loculi back, and kick some butt and figure out how to get off the island. That's going to be hard enough. Now, let's go to eat in the cafeteria, which probably *will* be bugged. Cass, if they drag you and me away to meet with Number One, we have to stay strong."

Cass giggled. *"Number One?* That's seriously her name?"

As she and Cass marched out the door, my head felt like it was whirling off my neck.

CHAPTER TWENTY-NINE

WHAT'S A FEW MILLION LIVES...?

I WAS GOING crazy.

I couldn't concentrate.

I thought about Aly's lecture on the great value of sleep. As she and Cass went off to the Comestibule—sorry, cafeteria—I tried to doze off. It didn't work. Being alone scared me.

So I got out of bed and trudged down to the cafeteria myself.

I found Cass downing powdered scrambled eggs as if they were about to go extinct. Old Mustafa the pilot was sitting at a table full of men, all laughing at some joke. Mrs. Petaloude sat a table all by herself with a plate full of bugs. Well, at least that was what it looked like. Aly was chatting up this skinny old scarecrow of a guy with a stiff gray beard that looked like it could scour pots.

"Jack!" she called out, waving me over. "Meet Professor Grolsch, the Most Interesting Man on the Island. He has like thirteen PhDs—"

"Phineas Grolsch," the old guy said, extending a bony hand, "and only two PhDs, plus an MA, MD, LLD, and MBA—Oxford, Cambridge, Yale."

"Um, Jack McKinley, Mortimer P. Reese Middle School," I squeaked.

"Cass Williams, starving," Cass said, bolting up from the table. "I'm getting seconds."

"We were discussing meteorological hypotheticals," Professor Grolsch said.

"Who?" I said.

Aly gave me a meaningful look. "You know, what would happen to the world if, say, I don't know, a *whole continent* was raised from the deep—"

"*Gro-o-olsch!*" Brother Dimitrios's voice snapped.

I spun around. Against the wall, at a long table, sat Dimitrios, Yiorgos, and the guy they called Cyclops, along with a bunch of sour-faced people in black robes. If eyes could kill, Professor Grolsch would be in the ground.

Grolsch's pale skin turned ashen. "Lovely to meet you," he said quickly and scooted back to his seat. "My oatmeal is getting cold."

Aly leaned close to me. "You see their reaction? They could tell what we were talking about. Grolsch was stalling. They *know*. About the destruction they're going to cause. But they don't care. What's a few million lives if they can rule the world?"

Out of the corner of my eye, I saw Brother Cyclops lumbering toward us. He nearly collided with Cass, who was carrying a plate of muffins, bacon, and doughnuts. "Sorry, you can't have any," Cass said, placing his tray at our table.

"Neither can you," Brother Cyclops said. "You have to meet someone."

"Wait—I—hey—!" Cass yelled as Cyclops pulled him toward the entrance.

Aly and I followed. At the front door, about ten Massa were gathered, busily chattering with someone in their midst. "Clear, please," Cyclops growled.

The crowd stepped aside, and Number One stepped through. She was dressed in layers of gossamer blue fabric embroidered with gold. As she lifted her hand, tiny jewels caught the morning sunlight. Neither Aly nor Cass shook the outstretched hand, so I did. "Guys, this is Number One."

Aly stared her square in the eye. "Do you have a real name?"

Number One threw back her head with a laugh. "I am so glad you asked. Yes, dear girl, my given name is Aliyah.

Come. We have much to talk about."

As the Massa turned back into the cafeteria, Number One turned the other way.

"*Number One* to you," Cyclops grumbled.

"And to you, too," Cass said.

Number One led us across the campus. Left and right, people stared in awe. I had the feeling she didn't appear in public very much. As she pointed out this and that new construction project, her voice was clipped and hurried. "As opposed to the Colonial-era foolishness of the Karai, we will have a facility light-years ahead of the technological curve," she said. "As Jack has seen, our security is quite comprehensive—and, trust me, he has not yet seen everything."

She gave me a sharp look and suddenly I was worried about our conversation outside the dorm. Had she heard us?

Easy. She's trying to rattle you.

We were headed toward the long brick building that was once the Karai Command Center. From behind it, I could see a cloud of dust. High-pitched voices rang out, yelling and laughing. But not Massa goon voices.

They were little-kid voices.

"What the—?" Aly said. "Your people bring their *kids* here?"

"Oh, great," Cass whispered, "we're going to be the Babysitters Club for the Massa nursery."

As Number One reached the back wall of the building, she turned. "I thought you'd like to see how we are preparing for a glorious future."

Behind the building, completely hidden from the campus, was a field of sparse grass that stretched at least fifty yards to an old barn. Fifteen or so kids were playing on it, arranged into groups with color-coded shirts. The oldest were about ten years old, the youngest around seven. Some were practicing jumps and headstands. A fire-hydrant-sized girl sprang past us doing backflips. Another girl was commanding a robot made from a dead stuffed monkey, making it walk in circles. Two others were racing up a huge tree, scaling it at impossible speed with only their hands.

"These aren't kids, they're freaks," Aly muttered under her breath.

Number One's eyes scanned the field. "Their teacher is supposed to be with them. . . ."

But I was looking toward a sudden commotion at the side of the field. There, three kids were reaching through a hole in a six-foot-high chain-link fence, taunting a pig using sticks and a cape, like matadors.

I stepped closer, and I realized it wasn't a pig.

"Is that . . . a *vromaski*?" I asked.

Number One's face stiffened. "They disabled the electrical protection. Children . . . children! *Where is your trainer?*"

She and I ran toward them, but the kids ignored her. As

201

one of them poked the vromaski, the bristles along its back stood on end. It swung around fiercely, spraying drool, its rubbery nose slapping against its own cheek. It eyed the attacker, a girl with dark skin and wild curly hair. She stuck out her tongue and did a mocking little dance. "Heeeere, piggy, piggy, piggy!" she called out.

"That kid is crazy," Cass said. "She's going to be killed!"

The vromaski coiled its hind legs and leaped up on to the side of the fence, grappling up the chain links with all four legs. It hauled its thick body upward before perching at the top, eyeing the dancing little girl. Its jaw dropped open, revealing a row of knife-sharp teeth.

Licking its lips, the vromaski leaped at its prey.

"Watch out!" I sprinted toward the girl, knocking her out of the beast's path.

Above me I heard a noise like a lion's roar crossed with a broken vacuum cleaner as the beast landed behind us. I scrambled to my feet. The vromaski turned and leaped again, its hairy ears swept back, a spray of drool flying from both sides of its mouth.

"No-o-o-o—"

Before I could move, its belly connected with my face.

CHAPTER THIRTY

ESIOLE

I FELL TO the ground. I struggled to keep my nostrils open, but the stench of the beast closed them back up again.

Pushing against the mud-encrusted belly of the beast was like trying to lift a subway car. It planted its clawed feet on the ground to either side of me, roaring, as it raised one tightly sinewed leg like a hawk after its prey.

Jamming my knees into the beast's underside, I rolled to the right and dug my teeth into the vromaski's other leg. It jerked away, its claws ripping a small hank of hair from my head.

I tasted blood. My mouth was on fire. I thought my tongue would shrivel up in my mouth. The spot where my hair had been ripped out felt as if someone had sliced it with a knife. The vromaski was jumping around now, letting out a sound between a squeal and a roar, pawing the ground wildly.

I sprang away from the slavering creature. It was surrounded now—kids with sharp sticks poking its sides, the curly-haired girl yanking on its neck with a lasso. Cass, Aly, and Number One ran over, grabbing the beast's collar, pulling it toward the pen.

"Trainer!" Number One cried out angrily.

Out of the corner of my eye, I spotted a pair of thick-muscled legs heading from the direction of the barn. A body hurtled toward the vromaski, colliding against its flank. The beast fell over, flailing its legs.

"Vromaski-tipping, my favorite pastime," a familiar voice said. "Wait till he farts. That's really fun."

I scrambled to my feet and caught a glimpse of my rescuer. The mop of shoulder-length hair was unmistakable. Not to mention shoulders as thick as a side of beef. His skin was tanned and his hair looked a shade lighter than I remembered, almost blond. His T-shirt and shorts were emblazoned with the Massa insignia, and an arsenal of weapons and instruments hung from his black leather belt.

He looked amazingly powerful, but you would expect that of a Select whose main talent was sports.

Aly's jaw was shaking as if the muscles were loose.

"Mar-*co*! Mar-*co*! Mar-*co*! Mar-*co*!!" the kids screamed.

204

The little girl, with a few quick motions, hog-tied the beast's feet together. "Ta-da!" she cried out.

Marco turned. "Good work," he said. "Okay, time to go home, Porky."

Grabbing the rope, he threw the squealing beast back into the pen.

"I did not just see that," Cass said.

Marco bounded toward us, a big smile on his face. "Heyyy, it's a Select reunion!"

I had never been so happy to see a traitor I hated so much. But what could I say to him? *Good to see you?* That wasn't true. So I settled for "Thanks, Marco."

"You know how much I hate vromaskis, Brother Jack." Marco held his arms wide. I think he expected us to rush toward him, but we didn't. Not even Aly.

Standing there a moment, he cast a nervous glance toward Number One. "So, you left your charges alone," she said.

"Yo, sorry, Numero Uno," he said. "I was teaching Gilbert to tie his shoes . . ."

"Ah, very important task indeed," Number One said dryly, "but important enough to put the rest of the trainees' lives at risk?"

"*I* lassoed it!" the curly-haired girl cried out. "It was *me*! Marco came out afterward!"

A group of boys giggled and began chanting, "Eloise,

205

smelloise, brain is made from Jelloise."

"*I'll lasso you, too!*" Eloise screamed, stepping toward the boys, who ran off giggling.

"Yo, little sister, *ssshhh*, put a lid on it," Marco said.

Eloise scowled at Marco. "Put a lid on your ugly face, Dumb Butt."

"My butt," Marco replied, "is actually pretty intelligent."

Number One glowered at him. "Then it compares favorably with your brain. Now go untie that beast, and *safely*. We need it for agility sessions."

Marco's cocky grin vanished. "Yes, ma'am."

As he turned and jogged back toward the pen, Eloise stomped away, back toward the big house.

"Just a moment, young lady," Number One said, following her.

Cass watched them go, shaking his head in awe. "She insulted him like that and all Marco could say was 'Yes, ma'am'?"

"He respects her," I said.

"He's afraid of her," Aly said. "Marco Ramsay is actually afraid of something."

Now Number One was returning with Eloise, whose arms were folded defiantly at her chest. "Eloise, dear, these are the other three of the Karai Select."

"So?" Eloise said.

"Well, you know how good Marco is at sports—Aly is

that good with computers," Number One replied.

Eloise put her hands on her hips. "Can you build one using strands of DNA to transmit data?"

"No one can do *that*!" Aly said with a laugh.

"Pffff," Eloise replied with an unimpressed shrug.

"And Cass is like a human gyroscope," Number One said. "Plus he can speak whole sentences backward."

"Iksamorv taht dekcor yllatot uoy, yeh!" Cass said.

Eloise rolled her eyes. "Gnirob yllatot."

Cass's eyes popped wide. "Cool, Esiole! You speak Backwardish?"

"Who can't?" Eloise retorted. "I stopped when I was seven. It's such a loser thing to do." She spun toward Number One. "Can I go now?"

With an exasperated sigh, Number One nodded. As Eloise went skipping away, Cass scowled. "Requesting permission to spank that little brat Eloise with a wooden elddap."

What was going on here? Who *was* this girl? Who were all of these freakish children?

In the vromaski pen, Marco and the other kids were hauling the beast through a gate. Outside the pen, other kids popped triple and quadruple midair spins.

"These are not normal kids," I said.

Number One managed a faint smile. "Unlike the Karai, we selected these children for G7W when they were very, very young. We thought with proper advance training, their bodies

SEVEN WONDERS

would become stronger, resistant to the gene's deadly effects."

I squinted my eyes, trying to make out the white lambda shape on the backs of their heads. "But they're too young to be Selects. None of them has the mark yet. How can you be sure?"

"A while back a brilliant geneticist joined our team," Number One said, "defecting from the Karai, by the way. Her technique revolutionized the diagnosis of G7W. With her genetic mapping analysis, we are now able to recognize the gene at birth. We no longer need to see the lambda."

I felt Aly's and Cass's eyes on me. We all knew a former Karai geneticist. I had spent my first seven years with her. "A while?" I said, trying to sound all la-di-da. "What's her name?"

"I believe you've met her," Number One said. "Sister Nancy."

I swallowed hard. How was this possible? My own mom, grooming Massa recruits? How could she do this?

Don't. Let. It. Show.

"Um, yeah, right, we did meet her, I think," I said. "But if she's from the Karai, how are you so sure you can trust her?"

"She came to us in a state of panic," Number One replied. "The Karai had placed a kill order on her. Because of a disagreement with your beloved Professor Bhegad."

"P. Beg?" Cass said. "He was disagreeable, but he wasn't a killer."

208

"Ah, but Professor Bhegad did not call the shots," Number One replied. "He followed whatever the Omphalos decreed. And when anyone crosses the Omphalos, they . . . disappear and never resurface. I would keep this in mind if you still harbor any crazy notions."

My head was about to explode. Seven lost years of my life finally made some horrible sense. Mom had disappeared because she had been afraid. Because her life had been on the line. "And . . . these kids," I said. "What will happen to them, now that we're here?"

"I suppose they will be our B team," Number One replied. "We don't have years to train them anymore. Your actions at the Heptakiklos changed everything, Jack. Our seismologists tell me the rip in the caldera of Mount Onyx is growing. If it bursts before the Loculi are returned, Atlantis will be lost forever."

"And if we return them," Aly said, "we raise an entire continent and destroy the world as we know it?"

"Evacuating coastal cities is difficult but possible," Number One said. "Losing Atlantis is a crime against humanity. But of course you wouldn't be here to see it, because if you don't return the Loculi, your time will have run out. Not to be cruel, but you'll be dead. So, children, it seems you have no choice but to join us. Can I count on you?"

Aly and Cass were staring at me. As if I were the only one who could sort this out. I averted my eyes, looking out across the vast field. Marco was nowhere to be seen.

Jack, you are the one who puts it all together. Professor Bhegad's words echoed loud in my brain.

We were losing sight of the plan. The plan was everything.

"Okay," I said. "We're with you."

"Jack!" Aly cried out.

"Under one condition," I added. "If you return the two Loculi to us, we will agree to reconstruct the third one."

Number One smiled patiently. "No conditions. We will construct it ourselves."

"You're not Select," I replied. "You can't."

"Let me ask you something, then, Jack," said Number One, stepping closer to me. "Haven't I been straightforward and honest with you?"

"I—I think so," I said.

"And you understand your own destiny on this island, don't you, Jack?" she asked.

Cass and Aly looked at me curiously. "Um, yeah . . ." I said.

"Then why on earth would you lie to my face right now?" she said.

My legs locked. *Lie?* Did she know about the plan? Or about Mom's identity?

"Wh-what do you mean?" I said.

"Earlier this morning, our Loculus shards went missing from their hiding place," Number One replied.

210

"Missing?" Cass squealed. "Who—?"

"Perhaps you can tell me," Number One said.

"Wait," Aly said. "You think *we* did that?"

"My dear, there are no other people on this island with any motivation." Number One held up her hand as if to stop us from protesting. "You're children. You do foolish things. I understand that. I will go away and let you return them, no questions asked. You have until nightfall."

"Or else what?" Cass said.

Number One turned to go. "There will be no 'or else.'"

CHAPTER THIRTY-ONE

THE KING OF TOAST

"YOUR OWN DESTINY on this island?" Aly was doing a great imitation of Number One's strange, faint accent. As she paced my dorm room, she ripped apart long strands of beef jerky, shoving the pieces into her mouth. "Don't tell me they're feeding you the same line they fed Marco."

My eyes strafed the room. Aly had disabled the spy cam, but I didn't trust the Massa. They might have had another one embedded in a cobweb or a speck of cockroach poop. I tried to catch her eye, to get her to be quiet, but Aly was on a roll.

"You're not answering me," she barged on. "Did they tell you you'd be king? Because you are King of Toast, Jack, unless you have some brilliant idea. Marco's turned into a camp counselor, your mom is a Massa recruiter, we're sup-posed to create global catastrophe—and just to make things more interesting, we were just accused of stealing the *only things that can save our lives.*"

"Who could have stolen the shards?" Cass asked. "No one has any motivation!"

I eyed the iPod in a dock on my shelf. It was grubby and well used, probably stolen from a Karai worker, I figured. Quickly I flipped through the songs, mostly old pop tunes I would never listen to. Cranking it up, I hit shuffle and let her rip.

As the room echoed with sound, Aly covered her ears. *"Justin Bieber?"*

I walked right up next to her ear. "This place may be bugged," I said.

"But I—" she protested.

"They're smarter than you think," I said. "If we speak softer than the music, they won't hear us."

They both sidled closer.

"I think it's Fiddle," I whispered. "By taking the shards, the rebels may be sending us a signal. They know we're here and they want us to find them."

"Then why didn't they come for us directly?" Cass asked.

"We have been under constant surveillance," I said. "Finding the shards would be easier than reaching us."

"How do you figure that?" Aly asked.

"The rebels know this island," I said. "There must be at least one Karai security expert among them who can help them get past the Massa defenses and figure out where the likely hiding places are. So it's up to us to find the rebels."

"The last time we were here, when Fiddle liberated those Karai prisoners, he mentioned where he'd be taking them," Cass said. "He gave the location a name . . ."

"'*MO twenty-one—near Mount Onyx.*' That's what he said," Aly piped up.

A giant green bird flew past our window, disappearing into a tree bordering the jungle. Despite the brilliant tropical sunshine, the area beneath the tree canopies looked almost pitch-black. "We need to be careful, though. There are cameras in the jungle," I continued. "I don't know how many. We'll have to disable them."

"I can cross the signals," Aly said. "So one camera's feed will actually be another's. That way we'll pass by unnoticed."

"What if they track us?" Cass asked.

"I disabled our KI trackers," Aly reminded him.

"But they had some kind of tracking mechanism on us when I had to find you in the woods," I said.

Aly turned her shirt sleeve inside out and gave it a sharp tug. It ripped open, revealing a tiny, super-thin, wafer-like plastic chip. "That's why they made us wear these shirts," she said.

Cass and I quickly ripped out our chips and threw them

on the floor. I ran to the window and flung it open. It was a short drop to the ground and maybe a ten-yard run into the jungle. "Number One told us we had until darkness, 'no questions asked.' My feeling is they'll leave us alone. They'll see we ripped out the trackers but they'll think we're trying to cover up our hiding place. And they won't care where we hid the shards, so long as we bring them all back."

"What if we can't find the rebels by darkness?" Cass asked.

"The Massa need us," Aly said. "What could they possibly do?"

"They have a whole other team of Selects now," I reminded her. "I wouldn't count on kindness anymore."

I jumped out the window first. Together we raced into the jungle, leaving Justin Bieber far behind.

* * *

Within minutes, my shirt was sweat drenched.

We ran until we had to catch our breaths. I looked at my watch, and then upward into the deep green sameness. I could see the distant black peak of Mount Onyx above the tree line. "It's two thirty-seven," I said. "The sun sets around seven thirty."

"Hold it," Aly said. She pointed upward into the canopy of a tree. There, a small camera sat on a branch.

She quickly climbed to the branch, then pulled a nail file and a paper clip from her pocket. Prying open the back of the device, she tinkered with it and climbed down. "We're safe."

As if in response, an explosion of animal shrieks echoed back at us.

Cass jumped. "Who invited them?"

"They sound scared," I said. "Which means maybe we should be, too."

A sudden roar erupted from our right. The animal shrieks became panicked squeals. I could hear a thrashing of leaves not far away.

"Follow me!" Cass shouted. He raced away to the left. I grabbed Aly's arm and pulled her after him. There were no paths here, not even enough room for Aly and me to walk abreast. It took only a moment to lose Cass in tree cover. "Cass, where are you?" Aly cried out.

"Thirteen degrees southwest!" Cass yelled back.

"In human terms, please!" she shouted.

"Just follow my voice!"

I tried to keep up. My sandals caught on vines and roots. I whacked my head against a low-hanging branch. Visibility was about three feet, tops.

I lost sight of Cass first, and then Aly. "Guys?" I called out. *"Guys, don't get too far ahead of me!"*

No answer. The trees were so thick even sound didn't travel far.

By now I could smell the faint saltiness of sea air. That

meant we weren't too far from the beach. As I hauled myself around a fallen tree, I stopped to take a breath. A monkey swung overhead, and I felt a tiny nut bop the top of my head. "Thanks a lot," I grumbled.

Eeeee! cried the monkey. It was standing upright on a branch, gesturing deeper into the woods. *Eeee! Eeee!*

It looked a lot like Wilbur the extremely smart chimp, Torquin's friend, who had given his life for us. These island monkeys were not normal. This one seemed to be warning me.

"What?" I strained to see into the jungle but nothing seemed unusual.

Eeee!

"Thanks, that makes it clearer," I said.

There.

A flash of black.

I squinted. Something moved in the distance, from one tree to the next. As I instinctively jumped back, the monkey pounded its own chest as if to say *See? What did I tell you?* Then it swung away and out of sight.

"Hello?" I called out.

More than anything I wanted to hear Fiddle's voice or Nirvana's. But I got no response. I waited a few minutes, then picked up a rock and threw it in that direction.

With a hollow thump, it bounced off a tree and fell to the ground.

I looked back toward the direction Cass and Aly had

disappeared. They would be noticing my absence now. But if they tried to find me in these woods, they might get lost. Even with Cass's help.

"*FI-I-I-DL-L-LE!*" I shouted. Then, "*CA-A-A-ASS! A-A-A-L-Y!*"

My voice echoed briefly into the canopies then faded quickly, answered only by a few curious bird calls. I began thrashing my way after Cass's path.

At least I hoped it was Cass's path.

The ocean smell came and went. I was sniffing up the sweat that poured down my face in torrents. Neither Cass nor Aly had left footprints in the thick piles of decaying leaves. My ankles were crosshatched with tiny lashes and swollen with bug bites. The trees seemed to be growing closer, threatening to strangle me. I knew it was the dead of afternoon, but the skies seemed to be darkening.

I heard a rustling sound and paused. *The sea?*

No. It was behind me. In the trees.

At the sharp, pistol-like snap of a branch, I spun around. The shape was closer, ducking behind a tree. I saw a flash of a black boot and knew it was human.

Not a rebel, I figured. They knew who I was, and they would come out of hiding to meet me. Then who? A Massa spy? "Hello? Hey, I see you. We were told we had until darkness!"

No response.

218

I turned and ran away as fast as I could. In about twenty yards I came to a dense copse off to the left and dived into the brush. My breaths came in loud, ragged gasps, but I tried to control the noise.

I heard footsteps. The figure was coming closer now. I could wait till he passed. Or jump him.

The steps crashed through the underbrush and then abruptly stopped. I held my breath. A mosquito buzz-bombed my ear and I swatted it.

Carefully I pushed aside the branches of the bush and peered into the pathway, where I'd last heard the steps.

It was empty.

I felt a hand grab my arm, and another jam against my mouth. A scream caught in my throat as I turned, staring into the fabric of a black hooded mask.

I struggled to get free. My attacker was trim and barely taller than me, but his strength was awesome. There aren't too many things more awkward than being dragged through a jungle by your arm. I stumbled in the brush and nearly fell three times.

He came to a stop near a fallen tree, set me against it, and whispered, "Speak softly."

It was not a *he* voice at all. I watched in disbelief as my assailant removed the black mask. My throat dried instantly, and I had to swallow to speak.

"Mom?"

219

CHAPTER THIRTY-TWO

REUNION

MOM'S HAIR WAS close-cropped, almost like a boy's haircut, but nothing could hide her humongous smile. "I am so, so sorry, Jack," she said softly, "but that place where I found you . . . it had cameras."

"It's o—" I said, but her arms were wrapped around me before I could get to the "kay."

I didn't think about cameras. Or about the island at all, or my body's time clock or the fact that my friends were nowhere to be seen. In that moment, seven years disappeared and I was a little kid again. I smelled mac and cheese bubbling on the stove, and a blast of chilly air through the kitchen door. I remembered the curve of her arms and her sweet smell and even her little, barely audible sob.

"I don't mean to smother you," she said. "I have been waiting to do this for years."

Smothering was okay. I gripped her as hard as I could. There was so much I wanted to say. A geyser of thoughts rose up inside me—angry and giddy, desperate and confused, all tripping over each other to get to my mouth. "How could you . . . why didn't you . . . Dad and me . . . all this time—"

"Shhhh," Mom said, placing her fingers on my lips. "Not so loud, Jack. There's so much I need to tell you. You're right to be upset. I never meant to abandon you and your dad, you have to know that."

"I do know," I said. "The Omphalos put a contract on your life. Number One told us."

"Yes," she said, tears gathering at the corners of her eyes. "I had no chance against him, Jack. If I hadn't carried out my plan in Antarctica, I would be dead now. And then I would have no chance to find a cure. No way to save you. I wanted to tell you and Dad, but it all happened so fast."

"But *why?*" I said. "Why would someone want to kill my mom?"

"Because I was hopelessly naive," Mom replied. "All I wanted was to find the cure, and I thought the Massa and Karai wanted that, too. But like the princes they were descended from, they couldn't agree. They worked in secret from one another, while kids all over the world were dying.

You were going to die. I decided to force them to work together. So when I began to unravel the G7W gene, I declared I'd give my findings to the Massa as well, so that our chances of finding a cure would be doubled. I asked the Omphalos to reach out to Aliyah. Instead, he ordered his people to kill me and take my work. I had no choice but to turn to the Massa. They took me in, no questions asked. They accepted my findings. Valued my work. But to be safe, I created a new identity so they wouldn't connect me to you."

I nodded. "So it's true. The Karai are the bad guys."

"No, no, it's not so simple." Mom shook her head, wiping her cheek. "You must understand, Jack, Professor Bhegad would never have wanted anyone to harm me. He was a mentor and a good, kind man, even if he didn't always show it. And I see now that the Omphalos only wanted to make sure the information didn't fall into the wrong hands. He saw that raising Atlantis would bring devastation. So their work is *good*, Jack."

"But their leader was ruthless . . ." I said.

"*Is*," Mom murmured.

She began to cry, and I couldn't help myself either. We both rocked back and forth in each other's arms. "I wish we could both go home," I said. "I wish we were all normal again."

Mom nodded, gently pulling back and looking me in

the eye. "We'll get through this, Jack. We'll get the Loculi and save your life. I swear it."

"Mom, Number One is threatening us," I said. "She thinks we stole the Massa's Loculus shards. But someone else did—"

I stopped short of mentioning the rebels. But Mom touched her finger to my lips, as if to shush me. "Of course you didn't. No one did. The shards are where they have always been since we got back to the island, in a secure hiding place very close to Aliyah."

"Wait. *What?*" I exclaimed. "So she lied to us? Why?"

"The same reason she lied about the xylokrikos and the electrified trap that wasn't."

Mom's raised eyebrow told a complete story. *Of course.* How could I have been so thickheaded?

"She's manipulating us," I said. "She knows we'd assume the rebels stole the shards. And that we'd go after them. So she's using us to flush them out of hiding. To do the work she can't do."

Mom nodded. "That is how the Massa work."

"Okay, we have to tell Cass and Aly," I said, looking over my shoulder. "Last I saw, they were headed to the beach."

Stiffening, Mom reached out and grabbed my arm. "Don't . . . move . . ." she whispered.

Directly ahead of us was a thrashing sound. Mom crouched behind the bush, pulling me with her. "With the opening of the rift," she whispered, "there are all manner of beasts in the jungle."

"If it's a vromaski . . . ?" I said.

Mom gulped. "We run."

As we tensed for action, I heard another rustling noise—this time, behind us. I spun around in time to see Cass and Aly burst through the trees.

I put my fingers to my lips, and they fell silent. Mom was focused on the sound ahead of us, pointing a small gun. Through the trees emerged a massive figure with no hair; blackened skin; and filthy, ripped clothing. As his green eyes focused on us, Mom pulled her trigger.

"No!" screamed Aly. *"Don't you know who that is?"*

The giant attacker put a hand to his neck and fell to his knees. It was only by the sound of his roar and the scar on his cheek that I knew who he was.

CHAPTER THIRTY-THREE

PREPOSSEROUS

MOM TOOK AIM again, but I knocked the gun from her hand. *"Stop! You just shot Torquin!"*

As Aly ran toward the giant, Mom's mouth fell open. "But his face! I didn't recognize him."

"He was in an explosion," I said. "He—he should be dead."

"Now he is," Aly called out.

"No!" Mom said. "It's a tranquilizer bullet."

With a grunt, Torquin glanced at Aly, confusion dancing across his slitted eyes. His face was swollen and mottled with angry orange-red blotches. The lashes and brows had been scorched off. His unruly thick red mane was gone, leaving only a few ragged tufts of blackened hair.

I ran to him as fast as I could. Aly, Cass, and I tried to lift him to his feet, but it was no use. At nearly seven feet tall and three hundred pounds, Torquin was either going to fall or stand on his own.

Mom came toward us, frantically rummaging in a leather pouch. "He'll need an antidote. That dosage was enough to take down a rhinoceros."

"Pre . . . posserous," Torquin mumbled, his eyes crossing.

"Hold out his arm!" Mom pulled out a small vial and quickly yanked the cap off a hypodermic needle.

Torquin was swaying back and forth groggily, singing a song from *The Little Mermaid*. Lifting his arm was like trying to grab a tree trunk on a moving lumber truck. Mom broke three needles on his thick skin before she could administer the antidote. She sat with him, snapping her fingers in his eyes and slapping his cheeks to keep him awake.

In a moment Torquin's eyes fluttered. He lowered his chin and let out a belch that rocked his entire body.

"I think he's feeling better," Cass said.

Aly gave him a gentle hug. "I'm so glad you're alive."

I leaned close. "Torquin . . . it's Jack, Cass, and Aly. How did you survive that explosion?"

"Barely," Torquin grumbled, eyeing Mom warily.

"It's okay, she's on our side," I said. "She's my mom."

Torquin's eyes went from slits to saucers.

"I submit to no group," Mom said. "I am a free agent representing the interests of my son and the Select. I will keep your secrets and help you in any way."

"Saw explosion coming . . . ran . . . too late . . ." Torquin said. "Blew me into bushes. Woke up and walked to street, flagged taxi . . ."

"You got a taxi?" Cass said. "I wonder if it was the Massa spy?"

"No spy," Torquin said. "Driver saw me and ran away. Torquin drove cab to airport."

"So you got here with Slippy!" Aly said. "You slipped under the detection."

Torquin nodded, glancing around the woods. "And you found rebels?"

"Not yet," I said.

"They're here somewhere, Torquin," Mom said softly. "They operate at night with tiny acts of sabotage—setting fires, stealing food and equipment, disabling security. I don't know how they are surviving or how many there are. The Massa have not mounted a full-scale search for them yet, but it will happen soon, now that Dimitrios is back on the island. He suspects they're somewhere near Mount Onyx. But the place is surrounded by video feeds and nothing has ever been detected."

"We have to find them, Mom," I said. "And we have to get those shards. We have the missing piece, and it will fuse with the others. We can make that happen."

"The Massa have the Loculi of Invisibility and Flight, too," Aly said. "If we can get them, we'll have three."

"There's a fourth Loculus, too," Cass said warily, "but a god ran off with it. Long story."

"Can you get them for us, Mom?" I said. "The two Loculi and the shards of the third one? We need to get them and meet up with the rebels, and we have to do it all before darkness. If we're not back by then, they'll start coming for us."

Mom exhaled, looking back toward the compound. "It won't be easy. If they catch me, it will change everything. They will kill me."

"They can't catch you," I said. "Not after all these years, Mom. Promise me, please. Promise me they won't catch you?"

Mom met my glance levelly. She looked as if she'd aged just in the last few minutes. "I guess I need to make up for lost time, don't I? I promise, Jack. I have gotten very good at avoiding detection."

I nodded, but I felt as if someone had turned me inside out.

Torquin turned and blew his nose, sounding like the horn of an eighteen-wheeler.

"I will return to this spot as quickly as I can and give this signal—" Mom stuck two fingers into her mouth and let out a raucous, three-note whistle. "Torquin, I will need you to come with me. There's one person I have to extract—someone the Massa may use as a hostage. She's a bit of a handful, but we can't leave her behind."

"Who is person?" Torquin said dubiously.

"Her name is Eloise," Mom said.

"What?" Aly blurted out.

Cass's face drained of color. "No. Absolutely not. Number one, she's disgusting. Number two, she's bratty. Number three, she's obnoxious and gross—"

"Number four, Cass," Mom said with a sigh, "she's your sister."

CHAPTER THIRTY-FOUR

My Sister the Monster

AFTER CASS FINISHED cackling, he picked himself off the ground and wiped off clumps of jungle leaves. "Oh, thanks," he said. "That is hilarious. I like your mom, Jack. She doesn't take life too seriously, even at times like this. *My sister! Ha!*"

Mom's expression was dead steady. "Cass, I need your cooperation on this."

A laugh caught in Cass's throat. "Hrm. So you—I mean, this is a—you can't . . . um, Mrs. McKinley, you don't know me, but I can assure you I don't have a sister. I'm an only child."

"And I'm a geneticist," Mom said. "Your parents gave birth to a girl when you were four years old. At the time, you were in foster care. Like you, she became a ward of the state."

Cass nodded. "I was with the Hendersons."

"They called you Li'l Runt," Mom said. "You slept in a room by the laundry machine. There were four other children."

"You didn't have to remind me of that," Cass said.

"G7W runs in families, Cass," Mom said. "It's not so surprising she has it."

"She does look like you," Aly volunteered.

"She speaks Backwardish," I added.

Cass put his head in his hands. "Won em toohs."

* * *

As we walked toward Mount Onyx in search of the rebels, my head throbbed and my ankles looked like the surface of a pizza. I felt like we'd walked into a flash mob of mosquitoes. I'd slapped my own face so much I nearly dislocated my jaw. Above us a team of monkeys took turns dropping nuts on us and screeching with hilarity.

"Ow!" Cass flinched. "Why is it they always seem to hit *me?*"

"Shhh," Aly said. "We have to hear Jack's mom's whistle."

"Tell that to the monkeys!" Cass said.

I looked at my watch. 4:43. "We have to be patient."

"Right. She and Torquin have to deal with my sister the monster," Cass said, as another fistful of nuts rained around him. "Maybe she's actually up there with her look-alikes."

231

A high-pitched whine sounded in the distance, and we stopped. It grew louder like a police siren. "An alarm," Aly said. "You mom mentioned there were—"

She was interrupted by the crack of a gunshot. Shrieking, the monkeys almost instantly disappeared.

"Th-that was from the direction of the compound," Cass said.

The blood rushed from my head. *If they catch me, it will change everything,* Mom had said. *They will kill me.*

I began running toward the noise. "Mom!"

"Jack, what are you doing?" Aly shouted. "Come back here!"

I ignored her, racing through the jungle. My bug-swollen ankles scraped against thorns and branches. The sun was beginning to set below the tops of the trees, darkening the path. In a moment I could hear Cass and Aly running behind me, shouting.

Another shot rang out. I was off course. Too far to the north. As I shifted my path, I could hear a thrashing in the woods.

A shrill, three-note whistle pierced the air.

Mom.

"Over here!" I bellowed.

A shadow materialized between two trees, and in a moment, I saw Mom's face. At first it looked like she was wearing a half mask, like the Phantom of the Opera, but when I got close I realized the left side of her face was coated with blood. *"Mom! What happened?"*

She held up her left hand, which was wrapped in a bloody towel. "The safe . . . was booby-trapped," she said, gulping for breath. "My hand got stuck . . . I wiped it on my cheek. Face is fine, but the hand will need some TLC. I'll be okay, Jack."

"Did they see you?" Cass asked.

"I don't think so," Mom replied. "I wore gloves. No prints. But I can't be sure."

As Cass and Aly ran up behind me, I realized Mom had a giant sack slung over her shoulder. She swung it around, letting it thump heavily on the ground. "There are three steel boxes inside," she said, "with the two Loculi and the shards. Each box is secured with an encrypted electronic lock. We will have to worry about that later."

"You're the best, Mom," I said. "But I'm worried about you."

"Don't be," she said. "You guys don't have the time to—"

YEEAAAAARRGHH!

A roar like an angry lion blasted through the jungle. As we all spun toward it, a different voice wailed, high-pitched and nasal: *"Ew, ew, ew, ew, ew—that tastes disgusting!"*

Torquin crashed through the underbrush, stepping into the clearing. His browless eyes were scrunched with pain and even in the dim light I could see a crescent-shaped

233

red mark on his right arm. Yanking his arm forward, he dragged Eloise into sight. "She bit me," he said.

Cass looked at Mom's belt pouches. "You have a rabies shot in there, by any chance?"

"*Rrrrrraaachhh, ptui!* When was the last time you took a bath, Hulk?" As Eloise spotted Mom, then us, the agony on her face vanished. "Sister Nancy? What's going on?"

Mom took Eloise by the arm and brought her forward. "Eloise, dear, come meet your brother."

"I don't have a brother," she said.

"Sweetheart, you do," Mom said. "This is Cass."

Eloise's face fell. "The dorky one?"

Cass waggled his fingers. "Sorry."

"I feel sick all over again," Eloise said.

"Well, that's a touching reunion," Aly said.

Mom knelt by Cass's sister, looking her in the eye. "Eloise, the Massa took you from your foster home and told you a lot of things—"

"They said *you* picked me!" Eloise replied. "They told me I had no mom and dad."

Mom nodded sadly. "The Massa have forced both of us to do things we never should have done. They are keeping many truths from you. Before they brought you here, they did some horrible things to the Karai Institute, the people who first settled this place."

"Those were the rebels, the bad guys . . ." Realization

234

flashed across Eloise's face. "Sister Nancy . . . you're a spy?"

"Do you trust me, Eloise?" Mom asked.

"Yes! You're—you're amazing," Eloise replied. "You're the only one who's nice to me, but—"

"Do you believe I'm telling you the truth?" Mom pressed.

Eloise nodded silently.

"It's a long story, dear," Mom said, "and there will be time to tell it someday soon. Jack is my son. I was forced to leave him, too. Please, stay with him and your brother. These people have your best interests at heart. Not the Massa."

Eloise stared at her feet for a few seconds. Cass moved toward her. He looked like he wanted to put his arm around her, but finally he just stood by her side.

When Eloise spoke, her voice was barely audible. "Okay," she said. "I believe you, Sister Nancy. But—I did something really dumb." She glanced up at Torquin. "When this guy came to take me, I set off the alarms all by myself."

"Wait—*you* set those off?" Mom said.

"I'm sorry!" Eloise looked like she was going to cry.

"No, no, that's all right, dear," Mom said.

She looked at me, and I knew exactly what she was thinking. If the alarms hadn't been tripped by Mom—if they were focused on another area of the compound—then maybe she hadn't been seen after all. A smile flashed across her face. "I can't hang around. But promise me you'll stay with your brother?"

235

"Where will you go, Sister Nancy?" Eloise asked.

"Back to the Massa. But I'll be watching, from a safe place," Mom replied. "As much as I can."

The words hit me hard. "Come with us, Mom."

"I—I wish I could," Mom said. "But the Omphalos does not forget or forgive. If I joined you I wouldn't last long, Jack. As for the Massa . . ." She let out a long sigh. "I'm hoping they don't suspect me. If they do, I'll need to go into hiding."

"No!" I blurted out. My face was boiling hot. I could barely see Mom through a surge of tears, as if she were already beginning another slow fade into memory.

She touched my chin with her bandaged hand. "You're beginning to look so much like your father."

"He misses you, too, Mom," I said. "A lot. Just as much as I do. What if we never see each other again? If the Massa catch you . . . or the continent is raised and floods the coasts? What happens if I turn fourteen before—"

Mom wrapped me in a hug and whispered into my ear. "I failed you, Jack. I was going to find the cure, but I didn't. Now it's your turn. You'll have to figure it out. You and your friends are the only ones who can. Take care of the Loculi."

With that, she released me and ran off into the jungle.

I watched as the darkness swallowed her up.

GOON NUMBER SEVEN

MY WATCH CLICKED from 6:36 to 6:37.

The jungle was nearly dark. We could just barely see the contours of the trees. I'd strapped my flashlight to my head. Cass was in front, but the going had been slow. Right now we were standing still in a clearing, waiting for Aly to rewire a camera in a tree. It was the fifth one she'd found.

"Can't you do that faster?" Cass hissed.

"Done," Aly said, hopping down. "Next time *you* do it, Mr. Jitters."

"Did you just call me *Mr. Jitters?*" Cass shot back. "This isn't a stroll in the woods, Aly. They told us we had till darkness. Look up!"

"Cass, the sun hasn't completely set yet," I said. "It just

looks dark because we're in a jungle! Aly's trying to keep us safe."

Cass took a deep breath. "Right . . ." he said, turning back toward the mountain. "Right . . ."

"Are you sure we're related?" Eloise asked.

We began trudging again. With each step, the sack of Loculi grew heavier and heavier around my shoulder. "Guys, I really need to rest," I said.

"No!" said Cass.

"Yes!" said Eloise and Aly at the same time.

I stopped walking and let the sack drop. Eloise sighed deeply, leaning against a tree. I looked back into the blackness, expecting Torquin to lumber up to us, but he wasn't there. "You okay, Tork?" I called out.

Cass came up beside me. "Maybe he caught a vromaski in his bare hands and decided to eat it."

"*Torquin!*" I shouted, walking back the way we came, shining my flashlight around.

"Yo, Tork!" Aly said.

As we reached the clearing where Aly had rewired the last camera, I stopped.

My flashlight focused on a massive lump at the edge of the clearing—Torquin, lying on his side with his eyes closed and mouth wide open.

"Is he sleeping?" Eloise asked.

I raced toward him and knelt by his side. His chest was

moving. I grabbed his shoulders and tried to shake him. "Torquin!" I said. "Get up! We're almost there!"

"That's good to know," came a voice from the darkness.

Eloise screamed. I stood up quickly, my flashlight tracing the contour of a long black robe until it reached the bearded face of Brother Dimitrios.

"That's a bit bright," he said, shielding his eyes with a hand that was clutching a truncheon. "But alas, your overgrown Karai thug is not. Although I give him credit for getting here. We certainly didn't expect to find him."

"You cheated!" Eloise said. "You told them you were going to come in darkness. Liars!"

Dimitrios's eyes widened. "That was before you tripped off the alarms, young lady. Oh, yes, we saw that. That is your gratitude for all we've done? You connive with these hoodlums to steal the two Loculi and the Loculus shards, and then try to take them to the rebels? I'm sorry, children, this game is over. We can no longer trust you."

"Oh blah-blah, fumfy-fumf, look at me, I am soooo important." Eloise folded her arms.

"Trust *us*?" I said. "You were the ones who lied. You accused us of stealing the shards when you were really hiding them. You were using us—trying to get us to flush out the rebels!"

"I must say I admire your cleverness and your cheek," Dimitrios said, rubbing his forehead. "I don't know how

239

you discovered our little plan, much less how you found the shards' location. But I'm disappointed that you needed to twist young Eloise's impressionable mind, convincing her to do your dirty work—"

"I can think for myself, Brother Dimhead," Eloise said. "Leave us alone."

"I was given clear instructions, princess—shards, Loculi, and Select. Immediately. Number One would like to talk to you." Brother Dimitrios exhaled, looking down at Torquin. "By the ghost of Massarym, she will not be pleased to see this one."

I glanced nervously back into the jungle. The Loculi and the shards were sitting in my backpack, just beyond the clearing. I couldn't see the backpack now, but it would be easy to find. We had to get rid of this guy. "Sorry, Brother D," I said. "We don't have the Loculi and the shards. And we won't tell you where they are. So *you* go back and tell that to Number One."

"Yeah!" Eloise said, sticking out her chin.

"I don't believe I offered no as an option." Brother Dimitrios reached into his pocket and took out a gun.

"He's going to shoot me?" Eloise said.

"Over my dead body," Cass said, stepping in front of her. Then he flinched. "Oh wow, did I really just say that?"

Brother Dimitrios snapped his fingers. Behind him, out of the shadows, stepped a team of Massa—Cyclops, Yiorgos, Mustafa, and two others I didn't recognize. "You know most of these gentlemen," Dimitrios said. "May I introduce two of our most accomplished security staff, Mr. Christos and Mr. Yianni."

Christos had the build of a sumo wrestler and Yianni looked like he'd stepped off the Russian Olympic basketball team. Mustafa was flexing his arms, and the bruises from the minivan window looked like dancing tattoos.

"There are *six* of you?" Aly said.

"Actually, seven," Dimitrios said, glancing over his shoulder for his missing goon. "Like the Loculi."

"And the Wonders," Yiorgos said. "It is a lucky number."

Now I could make out a seventh massive silhouette behind the rest, his face shielded by a hood. This group was practically a squadron.

And our plan was dead.

Dimitrios's goons fanned out on either side of him, as if to impress us—first Mustafa, then Yiorgos and Cyclops, and then the two new guys.

"Any more protests, children? Good. Now, let's move quickly. We need to get Mr. Torquin to our hospital." Dimitrios pointed to the hooded goon. "You will keep Jack company while he fetches the Loculi. Move!"

The seventh Massa stepped forward. As I turned to him, my flashlight beamed smack into his eyes.

He flinched away, but not before I got a clear view of Marco Ramsay.

CHAPTER THIRTY-SIX

PULL MY FINGER

ALY LUNGED FORWARD and slapped him.

"Ow!" Marco said.

"*Et tu*, Marco?" she said through gritted teeth.

"Dude, I didn't study French," Marco said. "Look, no one told me Brother D was packing. I thought I was just coming to pick you guys up."

"It happens to be Latin," Aly said, "and it means, 'And you?' From *Julius Caesar*—who said it to his trusted friend Brutus right before Brutus stabbed him."

Marco grinned. "You and old movies. Dang. Gotta rent that one. But listen, Als, I'm not like that—"

"You two may continue your love spat at another time," Brother Dimitrios snapped. "Marco is a soldier, and a soldier takes orders."

"I can't believe this," Cass said. "That's what *Soldier* means to you now, Marco? If Dimitrios told you to kill us, would you do that? Or maybe trap the rebels and bring them back to be tortured—your *friends*? Huh?"

"You're delaying us, Cass," Dimitrios said. "We have no incentive to harm these rebels. We shall restore them to health. Reason with them. Make them see that our interests are the same—"

"How's that working with the group we saw *in chains*?" Cass's face was red. Veins bulged from his neck as he walked straight up to Marco. "How does it feel to be a soldier for *liars and murderers*?"

"Dude, whoa," Marco said. "The pharmacy here has some good herbal anxiety remedies—"

"And the way you talk is idiotic," Cass spat back. "What happened to that promise to make you Massa king? You're a Massa nanny! A punching bag for little rug rats. What happens when you finally have an episode—or do you still think you're immortal?"

Mustafa lumbered forward. "Let me take care of that one."

"Chill, Moose Taffy," Marco said, then turned back to Cass. "Dude, I *had* an episode. They thought I was going to die. But the scientists here? They're off the charts, Brother Cass. One of them brought out the shards. He figured he

243

would put the Loculus of Healing together for me. He couldn't, but just being near those suckers—they made me feel better." He smiled. "They saved my life. And they'll do the same for you. So give Brother D a chance, dude!"

"*Aaaaauuuurrrrrgh!*" With a scream that seemed to come from somewhere in Cass's solar plexus, he ran for Marco at full tilt.

Marco's eyes shot open wide with shock. Cass swung at his face with the flashlight, but Marco caught his arm easily. "Easy, little brother," Marco said with a baffled laugh.

Cass spun around, ducked, and head-butted Marco in the belly. Marco staggered backward, more surprised than hurt.

"Seize him!" Brother Dimitrios cried out.

"*I HATE YOUUUUUU . . .*" Cass's voice was a distorted scream. He was in an out-of-control windmilling frenzy, all arms and legs, like some berserker at a mosh pit. He clipped Brother Yiorgos in the eye with a flying finger and kicked Brother Christos in the groin.

Or maybe it was Brother Yianni.

Christos-or-Yianni folded, groaning. But the other four Massa moved fast, surrounding Cass. Aly and I tried to pull them away, but their backs were like a thick wall. In about two seconds, we could no longer see Cass's whirling-dervish arms. In about three, we stopped hearing his voice.

"*Get away from him!*" Aly shouted, finally managing to

plow through the Massa guards.

In the center, Cass was crumpled up in the dirt.

"Nerve pinch in the neck," Brother Yiorgos said. "Painless. He will be fine."

"I could finish the job," Mustafa said.

Dimitrios scowled at him. "We are not barbarians."

"Could have fooled me," said Eloise, kneeling by her brother.

"Whoa, me, too, little sister." Marco stepped forward, then fell to his knees next to Eloise. He reached down to Cass, straightening out his head, which had become twisted to the side. "That was pretty harsh, Brother D."

"It is a pity that he attacked us," Dimitrios said.

Marco turned to him. "Dude, did you ever think—hey, is this any way to treat one of our future bosses?" he said. "Because you know Brother Cass is going to be pretty powerful in the kingdom of His Jackness."

He glanced over to me and flipped a thumbs-up.

I gulped. He knew about the prophecy!

"Jack . . ." Aly said. "What is he talking about?"

"You don't know?" Marco said, as he sat Cass up against a tree. "Old Jacko is going to be our king—not me, like they first thought. Seventh Prophecy says it's a win for McKinley!"

Eloise's face lit up. "Does he get a crown?"

"A big one, with jewels, I hope," Marco said.

"So that's why Dimitrios was acting nice to us all along." Aly shot me a sharp, assessing glance. "And it's why he pulled Jack away from us, yesterday morning . . ."

"Hey, maybe you also noticed how he was treating your pal Marco?" Marco said. "One minute a hero, the next—*bam!*—a slave. Because that's that way Dimo rolls: butter up the superiors, spit on everyone else. So I gotta say, D, the boss lady's not going to be happy about the way you're treating Jacko the Future King. In the new world order, you're gonna be like a sewer inspector. Or a vromaski catcher."

"We have no time for chatting," Brother Dimitrios barked. "All of you—take Torquin and the boy, and let's go!"

From below, Cass groaned in pain. As his eyes fluttered open, Marco knelt over him. "Good morning."

Cass hocked a glob of spit into Marco's face. *"Traitor!"*

"Auuuccchh, did you have to do that?" Marco said, staggering backward.

Christos reached down and grabbed Cass's arm. "Get up."

"Leave him alone!" Eloise shouted, kicking the goon in the shin.

Yianni grabbed the back of her T-shirt and lifted her high. "Little mosquito," he said with a grin.

With superquick reflexes, Marco snatched her away and set her down gently. He turned to Yianni and stuck a finger in his chest. "Back off, baklava breath."

"Marco . . ." Brother Dimitrios growled. "Remember whose side you're on."

"Yeah, didn't mean to diss you, Yianni, your breath is more like moussaka. With extra garlic. Peace out." He stuck out his hand toward the Massa goon. With a reluctant grunt, Yianni reached out to shake it—but Marco yanked back his hand, holding up one finger. "Pull my finger."

Yianni looked at him, slack-jawed.

"Do I need to speak Greek?" Marco said. "Pullus fin-geropoulos. Aly? Cass? Dimitrios? Christos? Yiorgos?"

"*HAW!*" Brother Cyclops broke into a deep belly laugh. "I love this kind of joking!"

"Jack?" Marco said. "Et tu?"

"Have you all lost your minds? Let's go!"

Dimitrios was shouting, but the other men were hesitating. Marco may have been demoted, but those goons knew what he could do, and they were afraid.

I wasn't. Marco was holding up his finger to me, a crazy look in his eye. And I was in no mood for games.

"Sorry, Marco," I said. "No."

Marco looked chagrined. "No? Do you know what that means, Brother Jack? How about you, Brother D? *Do you know what this means?*"

"Number One will get a report on each of you if you don't act now!" Dimitrios snapped his fingers, and the other five goons all stepped toward Marco.

"It means . . . *escape valve not activated.*" Marco began spinning around wildly, finger in the air. "Aaaaaahhhhh!"

"*Grab him!*" Brother Dimitrios shouted.

"*Losing controlllllll!*" Marco took one step toward Cyclops, leaped high, and landed a kick on the man's jaw. The big man jolted back and fell to the ground in a heap.

Dimitrios lifted his gun to Marco's face.

"Don't!" Aly screamed.

Marco crouched into a football stance. "Brother D, I have wanted to do this for a long time."

Dimitrios pulled the trigger. The bullet winged over Marco as he hit the monk headfirst with a flying tackle, driving him into a tree. With a helpless cry, Dimitrios lost consciousness and crumpled to the ground.

Marco sprang to his feet as the other Massa rushed toward him.

"*Don't just stand there, Jack!*" Marco shouted. "Be a king!"

CHAPTER THIRTY-SEVEN

THE MEATHEAD STARTS OVER

NO TIME TO think. I leaped toward Brother Yiorgos's legs and tackled him to the ground. His head hit the side of a tree with a thud.

Aly was right behind me. She'd grabbed my backpack from the shadows and removed the sack containing the three boxes full of Loculi. With a grunt, she swung them at Brother Christos. He tried to duck, but she connected squarely with the side of his head, and he collapsed in pain.

"*Kcatta!*" Cass jumped onto Christos's back. The goon straightened up and twirled him like a backpack.

"I'll take over from here," Marco said, lifting Cass away. As Christos faced him, Marco took him out with an upper-cut to the jaw. "Three down. Two to—"

249

As he turned to me, a pair of hands reached around and grabbed my throat. Marco darted toward me but stopped short as Brother Yianni pulled out a knife and held it to my throat. "Party over," he growled into my ear.

Marco, Cass, and Aly stood paralyzed, staring at me in dismay, their breaths coming in gulps.

"Let him go, Yianni," Marco said.

"Where is Mustafa?" the man replied.

"He was here a minute ago," Marco said, his eyes darting from side to side.

Christos tightened his grip. *Mustafa! Where are you?"*

At the edge of the clearing, a tall, rangy silhouette staggered forward. "Here," Mustafa said, barely audible.

As he got closer, it was clear that his eyes were closed, his head lolling to one side. "Acchhh, *vre*, Mustafa, drinking *now?*" Yianni said with disgust.

As Mustafa slouched forward, I could see a set of thick fingers gripping either side of him, holding him upright from behind.

He stopped moving and fell to the ground in a limp heap. Torquin, burned and smiling, stood over him. "Surprise."

It was all the distraction I needed. I shoved my elbow back into Yianni's midsection. As he let out a grunt of surprise, his hands loosened around my neck.

I dropped to the ground and rolled away. Marco and

Torquin were running toward me, but there wouldn't be enough time. Yianni whipped his arm around, the knife slashing through the air toward my face. All I could think to do was kick his knee. Hard.

With a scream, Yianni fell back. The knife flew out of his hand. Before he hit the ground, Marco was on top of him, delivering a punch to the face.

As he went still, the jungle was quiet again. Even the birds seemed to have backed off.

Marco stood up, wiping his brow. "I could go for some ice cream."

Cass was staring at him in awe. "That was gnizama."

"And soooo scary!" Aly cried out, nearly tackling me with a hug.

It hurt. My whole body hurt. But I didn't push her away. Somehow the pain was, for that moment, tolerable.

Torquin was stepping toward Marco, clenching and unclenching his fists. His face, already burned, was turning redder.

"Whoa, is that Torko the Terrifying?" Marco exclaimed. "Dude, nice haircut!"

"Torquin clobber Marco the Meathead," the big guy growled.

"*No,*" I said. "Leave him, Torquin! He saved us. He did . . . all this."

Torquin looked around at the unconscious Massa.

251

"But—Marco is—"

We were all looking at Marco now. "Explain yourself," Aly said softly. "Because right now, to me, you are a big enigma."

Marco scratched his head. "I'm a ship?"

"*Enigma* means 'mystery,'" Aly said with a groan. "Herman Wenders just gave that name to his ship!"

"Marco, why did you turn on the Massa like that?" I asked.

Marco shrugged. "You didn't pull my finger."

"Not funny." Torquin lunged at Marco, grabbing his tunic collar and raising a fist. "I have message. From Professor Bhegad."

"Whoa, back off, Kong! Chill," Marco said, wriggling loose from Torquin's grip. "No more joking. I promise. Look, I messed up. Totally. I've been thinking about this a lot. I mean, okay, back at the beginning? Brother D is all, behold His Highness Marco the Magnificent, woo-hoo! At first I'm skeptical, because I don't want to leave you guys— but they're all, hey, no worries, your pals will come over. So I listen to their side of the story and it makes sense. Plus, I get to fight beasts and learn leaps and other stuff while I'm waiting for you guys to change your mind and go Massa."

"You really thought we'd do that?" Aly asked.

Marco nodded. "I hoped you would. They treated me really well. Until one day it's like, *meeeeeaaaaah*, you missed the daily double, sorry, we changed our minds. I start having to train these bratty kids and people are ordering me around like I'm just another goon. No one says why, so I start really listening to their conversations and they're all about raising the continent, and death counts, and body disposals—and suddenly Brother D is talking about the *Destroyer* and *Loculus shards*, and I'm like *what?* Then one day, bang, you guys are here. No warning, nothing. I see how they're treating Jack, and I start putting two and two together—but slowly, because math is not my strong point . . ."

His voice trailed off. I didn't recognize the expression on his face, because I'd never seen it before.

I was guessing vulnerability.

Aly stepped closer to him, but he turned away. "So, yeah," he said. "I was a traitor. You guys can be haters, I understand that. But it's over with the Massa and me. Sorry for being such a dork. You, too, Tork." A tiny smile grew across his face. "Traitor, hater. Dork, Tork. I'm a poet and I don't know it."

Torquin turned to us. "This is English?"

"I understood it," Aly said. She reached out and put a hand on Marco's arm. "I want to believe you. But you really hurt us, Marco. How can we trust you?"

"Don't you?" Marco swallowed. "I mean, we're family, remember?"

No one answered.

253

"Professor Bhegad always said trust had to be earned," I said quietly.

Marco nodded. He looked us each in the eye. I was afraid he'd make some lame joke, but he looked more serious than I'd ever seen him. "So I guess I start now."

He reached out with open arms. Eloise, who had been standing silently the whole time, flew into them. He lifted her off the ground.

Aly was next, then Cass, and finally I gave in, too. He lifted us all, and it felt really good to have him back.

"Marco, I'm curious about one thing," I said as he let us down. "What would you have done if I *had* pulled your finger?"

"Farted," Marco said.

Aly grimaced. "Maybe we don't want you back."

But Marco didn't answer. His eyes were focused into the woods, and he swallowed hard. "Dudes," he whispered, "they're coming in quick. We are toast unless we move now."

"You can see that?" Cass said.

"A night-vision thing," Marco said. "G7W works in mysterious ways. Get down! Now! *DOWN!*"

We all hit the ground. I heard whistling noises, followed by thuds.

A few feet away, Brother Yianni's body jerked, an arrow jutting up from him.

CHAPTER THIRTY-EIGHT

AMBUSH

ARROWS WHISTLED PAST us. A monkey fell from a tree with an agonized howl. I ducked behind Brother Dimitrios's motionless body. The sack that contained the Loculi was just to my left, lying next to my backpack. I gathered them both up and held them close.

Aly stared at the arrow stuck in Yianni's chest. "They're hitting their own people!"

"What do we do now, your majesty?" Marco called out.

Don't run if you don't know where the enemy is.

I took a deep breath and fought back panic. I didn't want to lead us into ambush. Peering up from behind Brother Dimitrios, I watched the arcs of the arrows as they dropped into the clearing—all from one place, directly opposite us.

Cass was the one who could guide us to the volcano. But he was still shaking. I was worried about him. We would need him to focus on his own skills, but he was a basket case right now.

I grabbed a knife, a gun, and a flashlight from the belt of Brother Dimitrios. "They're all clumped together," I said. "We need to get out of the arrows' pathway. It's dark, but I think I can get us clear. Cass, when I give the word, can you put us back on the path to Mount Onyx?"

"Yeah, but—" Cass said.

"Good!" I shot back. "Follow me! *Now!*"

I hooked the backpack over my shoulder. Crouching as low as I could, I ran. I used my flashlight to guide the way in the darkness and Dimitrios's knife to bushwhack a path through the vines and branches.

I was nearly out of breath when the trees gave way to a swamp. I paused by the edge. My flashlight beam was starting to dim and I shut it off. The only sounds I could hear now were my own breaths and the buzz of mosquitoes hovering over the muck. "Hold up!" I said, as Aly, Marco, and Torquin ran up beside me.

I waited for two other sets of footsteps.

"Um, where's Cass?" I said.

A distant, high-pitched shriek was my answer. *"Eloise!"* Aly said. "Something happened to her."

She and I jumped toward the sound, but Torquin

grabbed both our arms. "Getting Cass not safe."

"Leaving Cass not sane," Marco said, sprinting into the jungle.

"Don't!" Aly cried out, but he was out of sight.

As Torquin roared his disapproval, I pulled loose of the big guy's grip.

"Don't you dare go after them and leave me alone," Aly said.

"I have a gun," I said. "If we circle around carefully, we can surprise the attackers."

"You're going to *shoot* them?" Aly said. "When have you ever shot anything?"

"I went duck hunting with my dad," I said. "Once."

"Did you hit any of them?" she asked.

"I missed on purpose," I said. "Come on!"

Without waiting for a reply, I dropped the backpack on the ground, flicked on my flashlight, and began to run. I beat a path parallel to the one we'd taken, keeping Eloise's screams to my left. The attackers would be following her screams, too. If they got to her first, we needed to be in a position to ambush.

At the distant sound of rumbling voices, I stopped. Aly and Torquin came up behind me. I put my finger to my lips and clicked off the flashlight.

The attackers were directly ahead. I heard a moan, and some frantic-sounding whispers. As we tiptoed closer, branches cracked beneath our feet, but no one seemed to hear us.

There.

About twenty yards in front of us, a dim light flickered. I fell to my chest and crawled forward, until I could make out a group of silhouettes gathered around a fire—not many, maybe three or four. As Aly and Torquin crawled up beside me, I took aim with the gun. My hands shook.

"What are you doing?" Aly said. "What if you hit Eloise or Cass?"

"I don't see them," I said.

"Time to squash Massa," Torquin said, crouching as if to pounce.

The voices fell silent. Torquin fell to his stomach, and we all held our breath.

A moment later, I heard the click of a cocked pistol from behind us.

Aly smacked my arm. "Stop it. This king stuff is going to your head."

"It wasn't me!" I protested.

"What?" Aly shot back. "Then who—?"

I whirled around, gun in hand.

"Drop it, cowboy," a female voice said.

I let the gun fall. Rising to my knees, I put my hands in the air. Together, Aly, Torquin, and I stood and turned.

A dark figure stood before us, holding a flashlight. Slowly she pointed it toward herself, chest high, shining it upward until her own face was revealed.

"Why didn't you lame-os tell us it was you?" said Nirvana.

CHAPTER THIRTY-NINE

FIDDLE AND BONES

THE BLACK LIPSTICK was gone.

That was the first thing I noticed. Her jet-black hair was growing in sandy blond, her cheekbones were sharper, and her skin was deeply tanned. But there was no mistaking Nirvana's lopsided, ironic smile. "You . . . scared me . . ." was all I could think to say.

"Be glad I'm not wearing my goth makeup. You'd have a heart attack." She holstered her gun and held open her arms, her smile growing into a wide grin. "Oh, by Qalani's eyelashes, *is it good to see yooooooou!*"

Aly and I flew into her embrace and hugged her tight. Torquin shifted from side to side in an elephant-like way and cocked his head curiously, which was about as close as he got to cuddly. It took Nirvana a moment to recognize him. "Whoa, is that Torkissimo? What happened, dude— someone stick your face in a jet engine?"

"Um . . ."

As the big guy formulated an answer, Aly shook her head sadly, looking at our friend's gaunt figure. "I could feel the bones through your shirt, Nirvana."

"So we gave up fine dining for the cause," Nirvana said with a laugh. "Girl, I can't believe this! How on earth did you guys get here? How did you take out those Massa? *Oh who cares, I am so happy to see you!*" She turned and called over her shoulder, *"Guys! It's Aly and Jack! And a radically reimagined Torquin!"*

A chorus of screams echoed through the woods again, but this time it wasn't monkeys. I saw Fritz the mechanic, Hiro the martial arts guy, Brutus the chef, and an architect I'd once met whose name was Lisa. Their smiles beamed through sunken, grime-covered faces. They mobbed us, high-fiving and whooping at the top of their lungs.

Behind them were Eloise and Cass. "Where were you?" I called out.

"They ambushed us, thinking we were Massa," Cass said. "Eloise screamed."

"*You* screamed!" Eloise said.

But Cass had recognized Nirvana and was running into her arms, shrieking with joy.

"Pile up!" boomed Marco.

As he jumped into the group, nearly knocking us all over, Nirvana shot Cass and me a nervous glance.

"Marco's one of us again," Cass explained.

"Are you sure?" she asked.

I shrugged. "Can we be sure of anything?"

"Word." Nirvana, Cass, and I silently looked at the small, ragged group. Everyone seemed so happy. But the ripped clothing and haggard bodies made it clear that the rebels had been through some tough times.

One of them, I noticed, was missing. "Where's Fiddle?" I asked.

Nirvana's eyes darted back in the direction they'd come. "Come on. He'll want to see you."

As she pulled me through the rejoicing crowd, I called out for Aly, Cass, and Marco. Together we ran to the fire, which was in a small clearing. One of the Karai medical staff was hunched over Fiddle's body—someone I vaguely remembered seeing at the hospital back in the Karai days. "How's he doing, Bones?" Nirvana asked.

"The fever spiked again," the doctor replied, her face drawn and hollow. "One hundred four and rising."

Nirvana squeezed her eyes shut. "He insisted on coming with us. I knew he was too sick. I shouldn't have let him."

By now my two friends were kneeling by our side.

Three friends. I had to include Marco now.

"What happened to him?" Aly asked.

Bones sighed. "It's the jungle. There are disease-carrying insects, birds, mammals, poisonous berries. It could be any of those things. I wish I could diagnose him properly, but we're nowhere near any equipment or medical supplies. He's been like this for a while. Coming out with us was not a good idea."

"Will he be okay?" Aly said, smoothing out Fiddle's hair across his forehead. "Hey, buddy, can you hear me? What can we do for you?"

"I could use"—Fiddle struggled for words, his eyes blinking—"a burrito."

Aly smiled. "We're out of chicken. Will monkey meat be okay?"

Fiddle's glance moved from her to Marco to Cass to me. "Okay, tacos . . . instead."

"It's us, Fiddle!" I said. "Jack, Aly, Cass, Marco, and Torquin."

His eyes seemed to flash with recognition. "Can't . . . believe this . . ." he rasped. "The fearsome fivesome . . ."

He laughed, but the laugh made him cough. The cough quickly grew until his body was spasming and his soot-darkened face began turning red. Nirvana quickly reached into a weather-beaten sack, pulled out some kind of animal bladder, and began squeezing water into his mouth. "You're going to make it," she said.

263

He moved his mouth as if to respond, but he gagged. His head jerked upward and his arms and legs twitched. I could see Dr. Bones racing over as his body went limp and his eyes rolled back into his head.

"Fiddle? *Fiddle, do you hear me?*" Dr. Bones slapped his face, then grabbed his wrist briefly to feel for a pulse. Almost immediately she let go and leaned hard into his chest, pumping it three times, and then three times again.

"Yo, let's bring him to the waterfall!" Marco blurted out, reaching for Fiddle's shoulders. "That thing put me back together again."

"No, Marco, it won't work for him—you're a *Select*," Aly said. "It works for us, not for normal people."

"Cass," I said. "The shard!"

Cass swallowed. "I don't know, Jack . . ."

"Just give it to me!"

Cass reached into his pocket and pulled out a small plastic pouch that contained the fused, pebble-sized shard. I spilled it into my palm and ran around to the opposite side of Fiddle's body from Dr. Bones. Falling to my knees, I pressed the shard to his abdomen. I could feel the little remnant begin to shrink again. "Come on . . ." I murmured. "Come on, Fiddle . . ."

"Works for Select only," Torquin said, "like waterfall?"

Aly shook her head. "No, Loculi are different. The touch of a Select lets the power of the Loculus flow through. But

264

this one's wasting away. We need the other pieces. *Where are the other pieces? Where's the sack?*"

"I left the backpack by the swamp," I said.

"I'll get it!" Cass said.

As he ran back, I kept pressing the shard until I felt nothing. The doctor, still holding on to Fiddle's wrist, placed his arm down on the ground and shook her head.

I pulled away and sat back. Overhead the monkeys fell silent. As if they knew. Fiddle's mouth was open, his eyes staring upward and his brow beetled as if he'd noticed the silence, too.

Something the size of a seat cushion landed softly on my shoulder, and I knew it was Torquin's hand. "Good try, Jack," he said softly.

All around me, heads bowed and tears ran runnels through dirt-stained faces.

I opened my palm. At the center was a small, colorless dot, about the size of a sesame seed.

CHAPTER FORTY

THE LABYRINTH AND THE TAPESTRY

"HERE IT IS!" Cass shouted, running toward me with the sack containing the shards. When he saw Fiddle, he stopped short. "Is he . . . ?"

"I'm sorry . . ." I murmured, both to Fiddle and to my friends. "I'm so sorry."

Eloise burst into tears. "I never saw a dead person before . . ."

Cass put an awkward arm around her shoulder. As the KI people gathered around the body, one of them held some kind of makeshift torch. Fiddle's features seemed to flutter in the light of the flame.

"My best friend on the whole island . . ." Nirvana said, swallowing a sob. "I was such a brat when I got here. He schooled me."

"I don't know why the shard didn't work," I said. "It worked with Aly . . ."

"Maybe too small," Torquin suggested.

I stared at the tiny, freckle-sized dot in my palm. "I could have run for the other shards sooner. What was I thinking? I killed him . . ."

"The shards are locked in a box, Jack," Cass said. "It's not your fault he died."

"If it's anyone's fault, it's mine," Marco said. "I never should have left you guys in the first place."

"Stop it," Aly said. "It's done. We can't just stay here. How long till Dimitrios wakes up, or till the Massa back at camp come after the missing goons—"

"Or come after the missing Loculi," Cass added.

Nirvana stood. "We'll take Fiddle into the headquarters and bury him there. Let's move."

Marco crouched down and lifted up Fiddle's shoulders. "Help me lift him, Tork."

"I'll grab some flashlights from the Massa," I said.

Fritz nodded grimly. "I'll get their weapons."

* * *

Grieving would have to wait. Speed and silence were crucial.

We hit the path with only a few flashlights as guides, to conserve batteries. Mine was already almost dead. The walk was silent and steady. Marco held Fiddle's arms and Torquin his legs. Aly and I stayed together, while behind us Cass and Eloise walked single file among the other Karai.

I could not shake the image of Fiddle's body going slack.

"Penny for your thoughts," Aly said.

I smiled and shook my head, concentrating on the narrow path.

"Okay, a dollar." I felt her slipping her fingers into mine. "Hey. Mr. Moody Broody. It's not your fault."

"Right." I took a deep breath. "We . . . we have to look on the bright side."

"Yes," Aly said.

"We found the rebels," I said.

"And got Marco back again," Aly added.

I nodded. "Also, my mom turned out not to be evil after all."

"Exactly!" Aly said. "Plus we have the two Loculi back, *and* all the shards."

"And I guess I'll be king soon," I added, forcing a smile.

"Heaven help us all," Aly muttered.

We were at the base of Mount Onyx now. The volcano's peak rose pitch-black against the star-freckled sky. Nirvana's flashlight beam strafed the vines and bushes lining the sides. When the vegetation gave way to an expanse of silver-gray rock, we stopped. Above us, a deep crevice in the rock formed a giant seven. The bottom of the seven's diagonal pointed to a small bush that seemed to have grown into the wall, about eye level.

I knew immediately that the bush must have been fake. Under it was a carving of a griffin's head, which was actually a secret keyhole into the volcano's inner labyrinth.

Aly looked around nervously. "No cameras?"

Nirvana eyed the trees. "One," she said. "But we moved it."

She reached into her shoulder bag and pulled out a familiar-looking rock that contained a code left by Herman Wenders, the discoverer of the island. "Can I do the honors?" I said.

"Quickly," Nirvana said, shoving the black stone into my hand.

I inserted the stone into the carving. With a deep scraping noise, the entrance slowly slid open.

As the black triangle opened into the thick inner wall of the mountain, a gust of cool, vaguely rotten-smelling air blasted out. Nirvana looked nervously over her shoulder. "It's a miracle the Massa haven't found this yet."

She went in first, followed by Marco and Torquin with Fiddle's body, then the other Karai rebels.

Cass, Aly, and I hung for a moment at the dark entrance. "I hate this place," Cass said, gazing in at the dark, mossy-walled corridor of the labyrinth. "I almost died in here."

Aly nodded. "Marco *did* die."

The memories flooded out like ghosts in the rock: Cass on fire, screaming with pain. Marco's body, limp and crushed after a fall into the volcano. The waterfall that miraculously healed them both. Back then the journey was baffling, with the promise of death at every wrong turn.

But now, as we finally entered, we were following a group who had walked the path a hundred times. "Welcome back," I said.

The air quickly grew stale in the narrow passage. I avoided stepping into the crevice where Aly had long ago dropped her flashlight. I caught the acrid smell of roasted bat guano, from the wrong turn that had led to Cass's accident. In one of the other intersecting paths, I saw the skeleton of a horse-sized animal. Yet another contained a set of manacles bolted into the wall. "Ch-ch-cheery, huh?" Cass said.

I kept a quick pace, but I had to slow down at the entrance to one of the side tunnels. Just inside it hung a large, faded, ancient tapestry. We'd seen a work like this before, but it had burned in the guano fire. This one was different. It depicted a fierce argument between the king and queen. Qalani was standing regally behind the Heptakiklos, which was filled with seven glowing Loculi of different, rich colors. Beside her was Massarym, kneeling before the creation, with an expression of awe. In the foreground, King Uhla'ar pointed at them with furious accusation. His face was stern and sharp boned, his eyebrows arched and his hair thickly curled.

There was something familiar about the face, but I couldn't put my finger on it.

"Jack! What are you doing?" Aly cried out.

"I'm looking . . ." I said, tilting my head toward the tapestry. "Why do I think I've seen this guy before?"

"Because, duh, it's Uhla'ar, and you've been dreaming about him since Bodrum," she said, grabbing my arm. "Now come on. We'll do the museum tour later."

She pulled me away, but the face was stuck in my head. The dream had been vivid; Aly was right about that. But I wasn't sure that was it. I felt like I'd met this guy.

We caught up with the others and trudged over cold stone toward the center. I'd forgotten how long the path was. Even with people who knew the way, it seemed to take forever.

I knew we were close to the center when I felt a prickling sensation in my brain that grew to a steady hum.

Aly gave me a look. "You've got that Song-of-the-Heptakiklos expression on your face. Either that or diarrhea."

"Don't you hear it, too?" I asked.

Aly shrugged. "Cass, Marco, and I—not being king material—we have to be right on top of it to hear it. You go ahead of me."

I walked forward. The sound seeped into me, like little

gremlins twanging the nerves of my brain.

Soon the Song was mixed with the whoosh of falling water. Just ahead, Marco and Torquin had stopped by the edge of the waterfall's pool. Marco was holding Fiddle's wrists with one hand now, and with the other he stooped to splash water onto Fiddle's face. "I know, I know, you said it won't work," he said. "But I had to try."

"Okay," Torquin said quietly, "but we go."

He and Marco continued onward with Fiddle's body, into the caldera.

I had to adjust to the eerie glow. It was the dead of night, but the moon seemed to be concentrating its rays here, making the whole place glow green-gold as if the walls themselves held light.

"Did you ever try to imagine what this must have been like?" Cass whispered. "I mean, back when it was the center of a whole continent?"

"It was a valley . . ." I said. "Beautiful, too, with tall trees ringing the top, and a carpet of flowers . . ."

My early dreams of Atlantis were so vivid I felt like I'd been there. I would always be running through that valley toward my own death. Talking about it scared me.

But I had no fear right now. I had work to do.

Marco and Torquin settled Fiddle down by the vast, rounded wall. Lisa and Fritz began digging a grave, using a shovel and a pickax.

Nirvana looked away, her lip quivering. "Well," she said, trying to be cheerful, "shall we show you around our vast complex?"

She and Hiro began lighting torches that were made of dried thatch set on tripods of tree branches. A motley collection of tools had been propped up against the caldera walls, along with a few pots and some canvas bags.

"These contain dried food—hardtack, pemmican," Nirvana explained. "The stuff is pretty foul but edible. Way back when, Professor Bhegad and the old-timers made sure to hide emergency supplies in some undisclosed locations. Fiddle was the only one who knew how to get to those places. We have some communications, but it's all pretty basic."

I followed her to a table made of three flat rocks. On it was an old laptop connected to a set of wires, a heavy-duty battery, and an antenna made of wire hangers and tinfoil. Next to the table were three other spare batteries. "Needless to say, no internet," Nirvana went on. "But we use walkie-talkies to keep in touch on recon operations. Two of our best people, Bird Eye and Squawker, are out in the field now. They're keeping an eye on Dimitrios and the sleeping beauties. If anything bad happens, we'll know. Unfortunately, we have to be careful about energy—everything's shut off most of the time, except for extreme emergencies."

"Wow . . ." Aly said. "Stone Age living."

Nirvana laughed. "That's me, Wilma Flintstone."

As they went back to talking tech, I walked toward the shadows at the rear of the caldera. The Song was deafening, drawing me to its source. A strange mist rose from the shadows, disappearing upward in swirling wisps. I hadn't seen the Heptakiklos since our last visit, and I had no real reason to see it now. But I couldn't help wanting to.

As I got closer, the mist cleared. I saw the outline of the round temple, sunken into the rock floor. It seemed to glow from a light source below the surface of the earth.

It was the place where Queen Qalani had first harnessed the energy of Atlantis into the seven Loculi. And it had sat empty ever since Massarym had stolen them away.

I knew not to touch the shaft. I'd pulled the whole thing out once before. It had opened the rift and allowed the griffin to fly through. Professor Bhegad called this a space-time flux point—yet another wonderful horrible thing that only Select could access.

This time we had two Loculi. Three, if we could put together the Loculus of Healing. Once we got the boxes open and reconstructed the Loculus of Healing—*if* that was still possible—we could insert them in their places. I was dying to do that ASAP.

Three Loculi was three-sevenths of the way to completion. Or .428571. Forty-three percent.

Almost half.

"Jack?" Marco's voice called out. "You let a griffin loose and I will personally pound your head into oatmeal."

I began to back away. From behind me came the sharp chink . . . chink . . . chink . . . of the digging. Marco was waiting nervously. "Let's see if we can put together Number Three," I called out.

Aly crouched by the wall, opening the canvas bag to reveal the three boxes. Each was sealed by a thick brass latch with a metal LCD plate. Under each plate was a number keypad. "What the—?"

"I know the codes." Nirvana ran over. She began tapping out numbers on the pad, and finally let out a big groan. "Great. First they steal these lockboxes from us, and then go and reprogram the locks! That's military-grade encryption. We'll never get it."

Aly nodded thoughtfully. "Give me a few minutes."

She pulled back a chair and sat at the table, jiggling the laptop's mouse. Numbers began flowing down the screen like a weird digital rainstorm.

"That'll take days," Nirvana said, "even with our encryption software."

"Not if I improve the software," Aly said, her fingers clattering on the keyboard.

"I have a better idea." Marco shoved the boxes back into the sack, strapped it to his belt, and began climbing the caldera wall. "Bet you I can get to the top and drop these babies before you finish. That'll open them."

"Whoa, Marco, no!" I shouted.

Cass and I ran to the wall. But Marco was quicker by far. He dug his hands and feet into the crevices and jutting roots, as if he were climbing a ladder.

Aly looked up from the desk. My heart was quickening, and I had a realization—something I hadn't wanted to admit till now. "I'm still not sure I trust him," I whispered. "What if he escapes?"

I expected them to argue. Aly had a crush on Marco,

that much I knew. Cass idolized him. But neither of them disagreed. There wasn't much we could do. None of us could possibly follow him.

As we all watched him, I tried to mentally block the Song of the Heptakiklos, which was giving me a headache. But now another sound was almost drowning it out—a distant, steady rumbling from above.

"What the heck is that?" Cass murmured.

"A plane?" Nirvana said.

Nirvana's walkie-talkie squawked, and she picked it up. "Base."

A tinny reply echoed through the caldera. "Bird Eye. Unknown craft in island airspace. Repeat . . . aircraft overhead!"

Nirvana frowned. "Copy. Is the craft Massa, Bird Eye?"

"Negative," the voice crackled in response. "It looks . . . military? Maybe trying for a beach landing?"

"*Military?*" Nirvana said.

"Greek."

"That's impossible."

A tremendous boom shook the mountain, nearly knocking me off my feet. Above us, Marco screamed in surprise. Rocks and soil tumbled down the side of the caldera, landing in clouds of dust.

Nirvana dropped the walkie-talkie. "*I don't think it's a beach landing!*" she cried out. "*It just crashed!*"

277

CHAPTER FORTY-ONE

IS NOT GORILLA

"MARCO!" ALY SCREAMED up into the caldera.

Nirvana shone her flashlight upward, pinning Marco in its beam. The crash had shaken him away from the wall. He swayed back and forth in the air, gripping a tree root. The bag of Loculi came crashing down, landing on the ground with a sharp clatter. *They couldn't use the airport?* he called down.

"Marco, get down now!" I said.

"Yeah, I was thinking the same thing!" Marco managed to grab a sturdier root with his free hand, then dig his feet into the wall. In a few seconds, he was heading steadily downward.

Aly turned back to her screen. "Okay, good news, guys.

278

The Massa have a limited-range VPN, which means probably some sort of satellite rig accessing a small part of the broadband spectrum. If I use command-line code to avoid the GUI, I think I can exploit security holes in the back end and avoid detection, at least temporarily."

Cass and I looked over her shoulder. "And the English translation?" Cass said.

"I'm able to hack into their system," Aly said, typing lines of code into a black screen, "including the surveillance network. I'm trying to locate the video feeds from those cameras they planted in the jungle. Maybe one of them will let us see our location. And we'll identify what just happened. The problem is, everything's labeled randomly. Hang on, I'll scroll through them . . ."

The lines of code vanished, and eight small images appeared. All of them were practically pitch-black—except for the scene in the lower left, which showed a flash of bright orange.

Aly clicked on it. The image filled the screen, showing the black cone of Mount Onyx against the gray sky—and a plume of smoke rising from flames near the top of the volcano.

She zoomed in. Flaming chunks of airplane wreckage dotted the bushes. Above them, the outline of a small tail section emerged from a cluster of trees, ringed by flame. It looked exactly like the planes I'd seen overhead while we were outside Routhouni.

I was staring so closely at the wreck, I almost didn't notice a small gray shadow moving through the nearby trees.

"Is that a person?" I asked.

"Unless a gorilla flew the plane," Aly said.

"Possible, considering the landing technique," Cass said.

Now the whole group was gathered around Aly, including the gravediggers—and Marco, covered with dirt.

"Pay attention." Aly zoomed as close as she could on the small, moving blotch. But it wasn't going downward. "It's *climbing*."

"Is not gorilla," Torquin grumbled.

"Is there a camera at the top of the volcano?" Cass asked.

Nirvana shook her head. "There were three. But we destroyed them."

"How about on the sides?" Aly began typing in more commands. "Okay. I'm picking up feeds from a couple of locations on the volcano slope . . . hang on . . ."

As Aly clicked, three completely black images showed on her laptop screen. She was about to click away from them when I thought I saw a small movement in the middle one. "Hold it. On that one. Can you adjust the brightness?"

Aly clicked on the middle image. It filled the screen. With a few more clicks, she managed to make the blackness a lot lighter, but it was extremely grainy. "This is the best I can do. The moonlight helps."

I leaned closer. A silvery figure was making its way

slowly up the side of the mountain. Definitely human. And quickly passing upward and out of the frame.

"Let me access the camera's remote motion control," Aly said. "I think I can swivel it."

The image vibrated as the camera began to turn. For a long moment everything was a blur, until the lens pointed directly up the slope.

The tree cover was sparse, the flat summit of Mount Onyx visible at the top. The moon must have been directly over the frame, because the figure was using the light to climb. There was no doubt now that it was a man.

We watched silently as he hauled himself over the rim of Mount Onyx, where he stood to full height. A leather sack, cinched with rope, was slung over his shoulders. Silhouetted by the moon, he turned in the direction of the camera, and I got a good view of a few characteristics.

Thick beard. Bare calves. Sandals.

"I don't believe this . . ." I murmured under my breath.

As the man glanced over the island below, he threw back his head and opened his mouth wide. From above us, we heard a muffled cry that echoed a fraction of a second later through the video feed:

"ATLAAANNNNTIS!"

"If I'm dreaming, someone kick me awake," Aly said. "And if not—ladies and gentlemen, meet Zeus."

"Zeus?" Nirvana said.

"How did he get here?" Cass asked.

"Wait," Marco said. "Did you say *Zeus*? Like the god of all awesomeness who never really existed but they made a statue of him at Olympia which became one of the Seven Wonders? *That* Zeus?"

"While you were babysitting rug rats, we found that statue, Marco," Aly said. "It has the fourth Loculus. Which I'm willing to bet is in his sack."

"Who are you calling a rug rat?" Eloise shouted.

"But . . . it's a statue!" Marco said. "Since when do statues fly planes?"

"Since when do statues rise out of rock piles, and ancient civilizations hang out across rivers, and zombies frolic underground?" Cass asked. "Since when do normal kids develop superpowers?"

"Good point," Marco said.

We looked closely at the bushy beard, the angular face with its straight nose and close-cropped hair. No question that it was the creature that had chased us in Routhouni.

But he was reminding me of someone else, too.

"The face in the tapestry . . ." I said.

"The who?" Marco asked.

"Back in the labyrinth," I said. "There was a portrait. It was the same face."

"A portrait of Zeus," Aly drawled. "How original."

"You don't understand," I replied. "This guy is not Zeus."

Aly and Nirvana peeled their eyes from the screen. They, Cass, Marco, and Eloise looked at me as if I'd grown antlers. "Um, Jack, if you recall, the statue moved from Olympia," Aly said. "We saw proof. It had a Loculus."

"My dream . . ." I said. "It's all making sense now. I was Massarym. The king had put a curse on me and I cursed him back."

Nirvana looked at Aly, jacking a thumb in my direction. "Has he gotten this weird just recently?"

"The statue was a big hunk of marble," I went on. "And somehow I—I mean, Massarym—was able to cast him inside it."

"Jack, what does that have to do with this?" Aly said.

I put my hand on the screen, where the man was walking to the edge of the caldera, looking down.

Looking toward us.

"Massarym imprisoned his own father in stone—turned him into a statue," I said. "That statue isn't Zeus. It's the king of Atlantis."

CHAPTER FORTY-TWO

THE TEFLON KING

"BROTHER JACK, HAVE you been inhaling too much Heptakiklos gas?" Marco asked. "I mean, the statue was official. The Statue of Zeus. So if it wasn't really him, wouldn't people see the face and wonder, hey, why is this other guy's face on the statue?"

Aly dropped her head into her hands. "Zeus is mytho-logical, Marco! No one knew what he looked like!"

"In Greece, no one knew what King Uhla'ar looked like either," I pointed out. "So Massarym could call the statue whatever he wanted."

No one said a word. On the screen, Uhla'ar was disap-pearing from the frame. Downward.

We looked up. Way at the top of the caldera, barely

visible in the moonlight, a tiny black shadow made its way toward us.

"By the blood of Karai, what does he want from us?" Nirvana added.

"How did he get hold of a plane—and fly it?" Eloise asked.

"How could he be alive at all?" Aly asked.

"So . . . is actually *Uhla'ar* statue, not Zeus statue?" Torquin said.

"Personally, I am finding this hard to follow," Marco said.

"I don't know why he's here!" I said. "All I know is that we found the statue in some cheesy village in Greece, where he spent the last few decades watching TV."

Marco spun toward me. "Okay, so the way I'm seeing it, this is great, right? You said this thing had a fourth Loculus. That's . . . ewoksapoppin'! Wait. What's the word, Cass?"

"Emosewa," Cass piped up.

"Emosewa," Marco said. "The guy is handing it to us!"

A small shower of rocks and soil fell from above, crashing to the ground in a small cloud. Nirvana shone her flashlight upward. The light barely reached the top, just enough to silhouette the king as his sandaled feet dug into the sides of the caldera.

"Yo!" Marco called up. "'Sup, King Ooh!"

"He doesn't understand!" Aly said.

"Sorry," Marco replied. "Lo! Greetings, yonder king! What a big Loculus thou hast. Canst we holdeth it?"

In response, Uhla'ar plucked a rock from the soil and flung it downward.

"King does not come in peace," Torquin said.

"By the way, Marco, there's one problem," Cass said. "It's the Loculus of Strength. Just in case you're planning to tie him up like a vromaski."

Eloise was trembling. "Maybe I could try biting him?"

The king descended slowly, the Loculus sack bouncing on his back, and I had an idea. "I don't know why he's here, but something tells me he's not going to give up that Loculus. Marco, if we get him to drop it, could you catch it?"

Marco smiled. "If it's not falling fast enough to burn in the atmosphere, yeah, it's mine."

My eyes darted toward a pile of Karai equipment against the wall, stuff the rebels had managed to salvage. I ran over, quickly rummaging through coils of wire, sections of rubber hose, tools, and metal frames.

There.

I pulled out a small Y-shaped pipe riddled with holes along each side. It looked like part of an old sprinkler. I never thought that in a tropical rain forest the Karai would have to use sprinklers.

Grabbing a length of rubber hose, I quickly tied one end to each section of the Y.

Perfect slingshot.

"David?" I said, handing it to Marco along with a baseball-sized rock.

Marco looked at it blankly for a second, then smiled. "Ohhhhh, I got it . . ." Nestling the rock into the hose, he held the contraption upward, pointing it at Uhla'ar. Then he pulled the hose back . . . back . . . "Right upside Goliath's head, Brother," he said.

As he let go, the rock hurtled into the darkness.

I could hear the dull *thwock* on the back of Uhla'ar's head. The old man let out a cry of surprise, then turned his face toward us and shouted in obvious anger. I couldn't hear what he was saying, but in Nirvana's flashlight beam I could see him swinging the sack around. He was cradling the Loculus like a football, as if he were trying to protect it. I could now see that the sack had been cut in several places, like preslashed jeans. Which meant his fingers were in contact with the object inside.

"What do you guys think you're doing?" Aly said, racing toward us. "You want to kill him?"

"The guy's Teflon," Marco said. "He survived a bazillion years."

"You're just getting him angrier!" Aly said. "What if he's here to help? What if he wants to return the Loculus to the Heptakiklos?"

Using his free hand, Uhla'ar was moving like a spider,

287

clutching tree roots with his fingers, leaping from one foothold to the other with perfect precision. Like a dancer on steroids.

Marco dropped the slingshot. "Holy mutation. He's climbing down with one hand. Who does he think he is—*me*?"

We all backed off. In a few moments, King Uhla'ar landed on the caldera floor with a solid thud. He faced Marco, his eyes red and accusing.

"'Sup, Spidey?" Marco said.

As he walked forward, his hands still tucked into the slashes of the sack, Uhla'ar glared at us silently. "What's with his eyes?" Marco said. "They're all swirly."

"He's not human!" Aly said.

"Does he understand English?" Marco asked.

"He's been watching lots of TV," I replied.

"Okay, that makes total sense," Marco said.

Aly stepped forward toward Uhla'ar. "Greetings, O Great King of Atlantis, trapped cruelly in stone and now released just in time to restore the Loculi to their rightful places. We greet thee with joyful open arms."

"Get to the point," Cass hissed.

Holding the sack tightly, the king turned slowly to Aly. His eyes were like small torches. He didn't react to her words, but instead began walking directly toward her, as if she weren't there.

She jumped away. Uhla'ar was heading straight for the center of the caldera.

For the Heptakiklos.

In my ears, the Song was like a scream now. I could see Uhla'ar shaking his head, hesitating. He must have been hearing it, too. Aly's face was creased with worry, but Cass put an arm around her. "He's putting it back," Cass said.

"I thought he was supposed to hold and protect it," Aly replied. "He killed that guy centuries ago who tried to take it. He tried to kill us."

I thought about the dream. About how the king blamed Massarym for the island's destruction. Uhla'ar wanted one thing only—to undo what his son had done. To return the Loculi to Atlantis.

"He's no dumb statue, Aly," I said. "He's Uhla'ar. He was protecting the Loculus for himself—so that one day he could bring it back to his homeland."

"Jack, this is amazing," Aly said. "He's helping us. We've been going after all these Wonders to fight for the Loculi. Now one of the Wonders is bringing a Loculus to us!"

Aly, Cass, Marco, Nirvana, and I followed Uhla'ar. Could it be? Not long ago we were as good as dead. Now we had a chance of being more than halfway to our goal.

Four Loculi.

My heart was pounding so hard, I wasn't even thinking about the Song. Uhla'ar stopped at the edge of the

Heptakiklos. The rift light surrounded him in an amber-green halo, flickering in the mist.

He set the bag down and bent over the Heptakiklos. Then, wrapping his fingers around the broken blade, he began to pull.

Marco was the first to run forward. He grabbed the king's shoulder. "Whoa, that's a nasty mistake. Trust us."

The king whirled on Marco. With his free hand, he grabbed Marco by the collar and lifted him clear off the ground. *"MAKE MY DAY."*

CHAPTER FORTY-THREE

BRAGGART, TRAITOR, DESERTER, KILLER?

TORQUIN RAN FORWARD to help, but Marco managed to shake himself loose from the king's grip. "Stay back, Red Beard! I can handle this guy."

"We need backup!" Nirvana cried out to the other rebels.

As Uhla'ar turned back to the rift, Marco grabbed him in a headlock. The king roared, but Marco held tight, pulling him back . . .

Back . . .

They were clear of the mist now, clear of the light. With a powerful thrust, Marco threw the king away from the Heptakiklos, toward the middle of the caldera. *"Just stay away!"* Marco yelled. *"What is wrong with you?"*

The king landed hard and rolled, then sprang to his feet.

291

Nirvana was holding a crankshaft now, Fritz a rusted metal pipe. The rebels were all armed with the detritus of the old headquarters.

"What are you doing?" I said.

"We need that Loculus," Nirvana replied. "We've worked hard. Our ancestors have worked hard. We don't need him to ruin everything for us."

"He's the king!" I replied.

"Not anymore," she said.

Uhla'ar's eyes scanned across the line of Karai. Marco stood solidly between the king and the Heptakiklos. *"AT . . . LANTIS . . ."* the king growled, unsheathing the dagger from his belt.

Its hilt was huge, weirdly large for a knife that size. It housed a jagged blade, twisted and sharp like a broken bottle.

"What the—?" Marco sputtered.

"Watch out!" Aly shouted.

Marco darted over toward the Karai pile and pulled out a long, hooked crowbar. Leaping between the Karai and the king, he thrust it toward Uhla'ar's head like a sword.

The king's free arm seemed to vanish for a moment as it moved to block the attack. With a sharp clank, the dagger stopped the thrust and sent Marco sprawling.

"COWABUNNNNGAAAAA!" King Uhla'ar said, charging toward Marco again.

Marco spun around, took two steps toward the wall, then leaped. His head snapped backward as he took three gravity-defying steps up the wall. With a powerful thrust, he backflipped over the head of Uhla'ar.

The king's jagged blade jammed into the dirt wall.

"Enough!" Torquin grumbled. As Marco landed, the big guy lunged for the king. He wrapped his thick arms around Uhla'ar and threw him to the ground. The king landed with a loud thud, inches from the sack he had carried here on his shoulders.

The Loculus.

I dived for it at the same time Marco did. He managed to grab the fabric first, pulling the Loculus out of the sack.

"ARRRGGGHHH!" The king's cry echoed in the caldera as he sprang to his feet, pulled his stuck dagger from the wall, and started for Marco.

Marco tucked the Loculus of Strength under his left arm. Wheeling around, he twisted away from Uhla'ar's thrust. The blade flashed. Blood sprayed from Marco's leg. Now Torquin was coming at the king again, holding aloft a long mallet with a thick metal head.

Uhla'ar turned calmly to face the big man. As Torquin's powerful blow flashed downward, the king ducked. With a swift, continuous move, he grabbed Torquin's arm and threw him against the wall. His head hit the stone with a dull thud, and he fell limply to the ground.

No.

I picked up a rock, reared back with my arm, and threw it at Uhla'ar. It connected with his shoulder, and he stumbled.

"Steee-rike, Brother Jack!" Marco said. Holding the crowbar aloft with his right hand, his leg red with blood, he lunged at the king and swung hard. With a loud clank, Marco knocked the dagger out of the king's hand.

Uhla'ar was weaponless now. His eyes were fixed in the direction of the Heptakiklos. "He's not going to cooperate," Marco said, clutching and unclutching the crowbar. "He's *obsessed* with that thing . . ."

"Please, Marco, you're losing a lot of blood!" Dr. Bones called out.

Marco blinked hard, as if trying to maintain his balance. A pool of blood gathered below his foot. "I've got the Loculus of Strength, baby, I'm good."

As the king leaped toward the Heptakiklos again, Marco blocked him. Both thumped to the ground. The crowbar went flying, but Marco held tight to the Loculus. With his right hand now free, he pinned the king by the neck to the ground. "Sorry, dude," he said. "If you're not going to cooperate, we have to take you out."

"Marco, you're choking him!" Aly yelled. *"Have you gone crazy? He was the king of Atlantis!"*

I raced toward him. As Marco pressed harder on the

neck, Uhla'ar's legs kicked like beached fish. The king began to raise his arm as if to strike out, but instead it fell to the side.

I wrapped my fingers around the Loculus. Marco wouldn't let go, but the orb's power jolted through me, too. I yanked him upward by the collar and he flew backward, tumbling toward the shadows.

"Jack . . . ?" he said in disbelief.

The king's body was slack. His chest was still.

Marco groaned, clutching his injured leg. Dr. Bones raced to his side, quickly wrapping the injury with a tourniquet.

Cass stared at the king. "Is he . . . ?"

Racing over to Uhla'ar, the doctor placed her fingers against his neck. "No pulse."

"I—I didn't know he could die . . ." Aly said.

I set the Loculus down against the wall, not far from Marco. We had it in our possession now, and that was good. But I didn't feel any sense of triumph. "He was *there*, when it happened to Atlantis," I said. "He could have told us so much. Answered so many questions."

"Professor Bhegad . . . Fiddle . . . now the king of Atlantis," Aly said. "All dead. When does it stop?"

Eloise was whimpering, standing with her fists clutched to her sides. "My second dead person ever."

All of our eyes were locked on Marco. Slumped against

the wall, he seemed to fold into himself. I wasn't sure who I was looking at anymore. He'd been a protector and friend. He'd been a braggart, a traitor, and a deserter.

But he'd never been a killer.

"I—I had to do it . . ." Marco stood slowly, backing away from the body along the wall. As he glanced at us, from face to face, we turned away. No one knew what to say.

I kept my glance focused on the body of the king. In death, the anger was gone from his face. He looked handsome, wise, and weirdly familiar.

It took awhile for me to realize he actually resembled my dad.

Behind me, the grave digging had begun again. There would be two bodies now. I figured I'd have to help.

As I got up to go, I finally turned away from the fallen king.

But not before I saw his fingers twitch.

CHAPTER FORTY-FOUR

THE SWORD AND THE RIFT

"HE'S FAKING!"

My shout rang through the caldera.

But it was too late. King Uhla'ar was on his feet, with a clear path to the Heptakiklos.

"*No-o-o-o!*" Aly was the closest. Screaming, she ran to block his way.

We all converged toward him. But Uhla'ar grabbed her by the neck, holding his dagger high. "*I . . . will . . . kill . . .*" he said.

My feet dug into the ground. All of us stopped. "Let her go," I said.

The king didn't reply. Instead, he dragged Aly with him, toward the rift. She was trying to say something, but

Uhla'ar had her tight around the neck. Her face was reddening by the second.

Out of the corner of my eye, I could see Fritz the mechanic lifting a gun. "Don't do it!" I called out. "It won't affect him, and you might hit Aly."

"We have to do something," Nirvana said.

I stepped toward Uhla'ar, reaching toward Aly. "Give her back to us, Uhla'ar. Release her and go ahead. Open the rift."

Uhla'ar smiled.

"Jack, no!" Nirvana cried out.

With a rough shove, the king threw Aly toward me. As she stumbled into my arms, he leaped toward the rift, his snaggletoothed dagger in hand. From the center rift, the mist rose like coiled fingers. The piece in the middle, the broken blade I'd idiotically pulled out when I first got here, was glowing brightly.

Slowly the king turned, pointing his broken dagger toward the blade at the center of the Heptakiklos. Two arched lines of white, like evil smiles, leaped upward from the edge of the blade. I could see now that the jagged edge of his dagger had not been designed that way. It matched exactly the pattern of the blade in the ground.

It wasn't a dagger at all. It was the missing half of a sword that had long ago been split in two.

A flare of bright white engulfed the space between the

298

blades. Uhla'ar lurched forward, nearly losing his balance. He cried out with pain but held tight to the hilt. The whiteness dissipated around him like an exploding snowball, and he stood in a blue glow.

The broken blade had pulled the dagger toward it. Now the two were fused into one long, sleek sword still stuck in the rift.

"*ISCHIS* . . ." Uhla'ar said.

Through the rift, the Song of the Heptakiklos poured out, transforming into a noise of screams and chitters and flapping wings.

I stepped toward him. "No!" I yelled. "*Whatever you do, don't pull that out!*"

Uhla'ar gave the sword a powerful yank. With a *ssshhhh-iiiiick* that echoed sharply, it came out clean.

KEEEAAAHHHH!

I knew the griffin's call. I'd hoped never to hear it again. I could smell its fetid, garbage-dump odor as it swept overhead on a gust of hot wind. As I covered my head with my arms, I heard the panicked snuffling of a hose-beaked vromaski, speeding past me for the safety of the labyrinth path.

The ground shook, knocking me off my feet. A snake with the head of a fanged rat slithered past, and a winged spider with talons climbed onto my head and launched itself upward.

"*Eeeewww! Ew! Ew! Ew!*" Eloise cried.

Though the chaos of mist and flying beasts, I saw her flinging a dark, thin, furry creature to the ground. As it landed with a screech, it spit a glob of yellow liquid straight upward.

A vizzeet. We'd had way too much experience with those nasty things.

"Get away from that—it spits poison!" I shouted.

Cass was already pulling his sister to safety. But the vizzeet didn't care about either of them. It leaped up, turned, and joined two others that were already climbing the caldera walls.

I lay flat on my stomach as flapping wings tapped the top of my head. *Aly. Where was Aly?*

Marco and Cass were huddled together in a cloud of dust kicked up by a fallen chunk of wall. Nirvana was trying to protect Fiddle's body from the flying debris and crazed beasts. The other rebels were scattered about, seeking shelter. All alive.

Moving through the center of it all was King Uhla'ar. He swung his sword against the attack of a leathery, batlike creature with a human head. In midcackle it was split in two, its twitching halves flopping downward.

He was heading back to the rift. I fought back nausea as I moved through the slavering wild beasts. The rift was shaking now, the Song of the Heptakiklos drowned beneath an unearthly rumble. It was about to blow wide open. When that happened, the barrier between then and now, between Atlantis and modern times, would shatter. Time and space would fold in on themselves, and what would happen to the world then?

"You see what you did?" I shouted. *"Plug it back up!"*

As the king stood over the rift, something hurtled through the air toward him.

Aly.

The king stumbled. The sword went flying. *"Grab it, Jack!"* she said. *"He wants to go in! Grab the sword and plug it up after he leaves!"*

"What?" I said.

"He told me, 'There's no place like home'!" she shouted. *"He's trying to get back there, through the rift! That's what he wants!"*

As I ran toward the sword, Uhla'ar grabbed Aly's arm. She lifted her leg and stomped down on his sandaled foot. Hard. The king let out a roar.

She tried to wriggle free, but he held tight. A blast of silver-blue light surrounded them both like a flame. He was dragging her with him toward the rift. Aly's eyes were enormous, her mouth open in a scream. She was looking straight at me.

"NO-O-O-O-O!" I screamed.

An explosion knocked me backward, blinding me. As I staggered to my feet, my eyes adjusted. *"Alyyyy!"* I called out.

But she and Uhla'ar had both dropped out of sight.

CHAPTER FORTY-FIVE

SOMETHING MUCH WORSE

MY KNEES BUCKLED. I fell to the ground. I didn't even notice the swarm of hideous creatures. The ground shook once . . . twice, and it was hard to stay upright, even kneeling.

I crawled toward the Heptakiklos, my fingers wrapping themselves around worms and fur. The light from the rift was spewing upward, as if the sun itself were emerging. *"ALYYYYY!"* I screamed again.

"Brother Jack, what are you doing?"

Marco. I could feel his hand on my shoulder, pulling me upward. "She's gone," I said.

"Dude, we have to close the rift!" he said. "Where's the sword?"

He didn't know. He had no idea what had just happened.

"Got it!"

That was Cass. Now I could see him racing by. He had the sword in his hand, a confused, rodentlike creature hanging onto the tip.

He and Marco, together, held the sword over the rift. With a sickening *crrrack*, it ripped open another eight or so inches. Maybe a foot. A greenish-black beast began to rise from below. It was something I'd never seen before, its head a glob of shifting shapes—eyes morphing into mouths morphing into gelatinous black pools.

I ran toward them. *"Don't do it!"*

"Don't do what?" Marco said.

"Close the rift!" I reached for the sword, but Marco pushed me away. He plunged the sword into the beast's pulsating crown. Its cry was a physical thing, shaking the ground beneath us. As I scrambled to my feet, the swirling mists began to gather. They were changing course, sucking back into the hole as if by a giant vacuum cleaner. The ground began to thrust upward, reversing its motion. The beast seemed to dissolve but the sword was holding fast.

With a snap, the rock closed around the blade like a fist.

"NO-O-O-O!" I cried out.

The Song was deafening again. The Heptakiklos was no longer oozing light but nearly blinding me with its brightness. Its faded, ancient edges seemed brand-new.

303

I grabbed the sword again, but Marco took my wrist. "What has gotten into you, Jack?" he pleaded.

"Aly's gone!" I said. "He took her with him!"

Cass and Marco both went pale. Marco let go of my hand.

I didn't care if the rift opened. I didn't care what kind of beast came through. We could not leave her.

As I gripped the sword, the ground juddered beneath us. My hands slipped and my legs gave way.

We all hit the floor, Torquin landing with a dusty thump. "Earthquake?" he mumbled.

I felt hands grabbing my arms. The rebels had surrounded me. Nirvana's face was bone white. "Jack, you can't open that rift again," she said. "This is not an earthquake."

"Then what is it?" Marco said.

A pine tree, dislodged from the top of the volcano, came crashing down behind us.

"It's something much worse!" Nirvana said. "Out of here—now—before the whole thing collapses!"

EPILOGUE

WHEN WE GOT to the shore, Mom was there. She stood shoulder to shoulder with Number One. Brother Dimitrios sat by the edge of the jungle along with his cronies, attended to by Massa health workers.

When Mom saw me, she came running. "We lost Aly . . ." I said.

I think she already knew. I felt her arm around my shoulder, but I was numb.

A thousand different scenarios raced through my brain. I could have pulled Aly away from Uhla'ar. I could have used the Loculus of Strength. Plugged up the rift before he got to it.

"It's not your fault . . ." Mom said, as if she were reading my mind.

I looked around. I knew this looked odd. I wasn't supposed to know Sister Nancy. Her putting her arm around me was risky. But no one seemed to be noticing. Their eyes were fixed toward the sea.

The once-narrow beach was now a vast expanse of sand, littered with ancient driftwood planks and black clumps of seaweed. It extended at least fifty yards to surf that was now far away. Its waves crashed violently against the shore, but at that distance it was barely audible. Beyond it, the black sea formed mountains that undulated, slowly rising and sinking. A small whale flopped helplessly, trying to return to the sea.

At the edge of the receding surf, battered by the waves, was the tilted frame of a barnacle-covered ship. Its masts had broken off and its hull had mostly given way to rot.

But the wood that remained was sturdy and thick, its bow slathered with seaweed. Except for one section, where the vegetation had been pulled away by the movement of the rising land.

As I stared at it, I felt my entire body sink.

It's something much worse, Nirvana had said. Now I saw what she meant.

It had started.

The continent was rising.

THE ADVENTURE OF A
LIFETIME AWAITS.

4 Friends.

12 Relics.

**A Race to
Save the
Fate of the
World.**

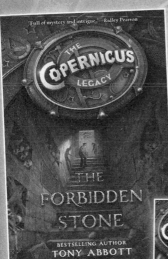

SEVEN WONDERS

FOLLOW THE ADVENTURES OF

Jack McKinley in the mysterious, action-packed series that takes place throughout the Seven Wonders of the Ancient World.

For teaching guides, an interactive map, and videos, visit www.sevenwondersbooks.com

DISCOVER THE HISTORY BEHIND THE MYSTERY!

HARPER
An Imprint of HarperCollinsPublishers

In His Arms

ALSO AVAILABLE IN BEELER LARGE PRINT BY
ROBIN LEE HATCHER

PATTERNS OF LOVE

In His Arms

ROBIN LEE HATCHER

BEELER LARGE PRINT

Hampton Falls, New Hampshire, 2000

Library of Congress Cataloging-in-Publication Data

Hatcher, Robin Lee.
  In his arms / Robin Lee Hatcher
  p.   cm.
  ISBN 1-57490-279-2 (alk. paper)
  1. Armagh (Northern Ireland : County)—Fiction. 2. Large
type books. I. Title.

PS3558.A73575 I5 2000
813'.54—dc21   00-039849

Published in Large Print by arrangement with
HarperPaperbacks, a division of HarperCollins *Publishers*

BEELER LARGE PRINT
is published by
Thomas T. Beeler, *Publisher*
Post Office Box 659
Hampton Falls, New Hampshire 03844

Typeset in 16 point Adobe Caslon type.
Printed on acid-free paper and bound by
Sheridan Books in Chelsea, Michigan

Acknowledgements

No book is truly written alone. Everything that touches a writer affects her work in some way. Recognizing the truth of that, I am grateful for the love of my husband, daughters, mother, and all the rest of my wonderful extended family. I am thankful for the members of the LoveKnot who have sustained me with their prayers and inspired me to reach ever higher, both in my writing and in my life. I appreciate the continuing support of the members of the *Coeur du Bois* Chapter of Romance Writers of America and my many writer friends everywhere.

Above all, I want to thank my faithful readers. This book is my twenty-fifth, a milestone in what I hope will be just one of many milestones to come. I appreciate all the letters I receive and feel blessed when a reader shares how one of my stories has touched a heart in some way. Thank you for sharing yourselves with me.

For all of you, I pray that this old Irish blessing will come true:

May the road rise to meet you.
May the wind be always at your back.
May the sun shine warm upon your face,
And the rains fall soft upon your fields.
And until we meet again,
May God hold you in the palm of his hand.

To my cousin, Connie Burke Bunch, who loves all things Irish. And to Mom, who told me I should use my great-grandmother's name in a book some day. So here is my story about Mary Emeline Malone from County Armagh, Ireland. I'm hoping you find her perfect altogether.

Prologue

Ellis Island, New York Harbor
April 1897

WITH HER HEART HAMMERING IN ANTICIPATION, Mary Emeline Malone searched for her belongings in the ground-floor baggage room of the federal depot. The immigration process had been no worse than she'd expected and no better either. Long and stressful, to be sure, but bearable. Even though she was a woman traveling unescorted, Mary's admission to America had been granted with surprisingly little fuss. Of course, she had lied through her teeth on any number of questions—especially the one about her husband waiting for her—but she wasn't about to consider the right or the wrong of those lies now.

By some small miracle, she found her valise and satchel without undue delay. Then, with them safely in hand, she hurried outside into the fresh air, joining the flow of immigrants on their way to the ferry slips.

She looked about her for a glimpse of her friends, Beth Wellington and Inga Linberg. She'd become separated from them many hours ago, but still she had hoped to be able to see them one last time, if only to say a proper good-bye. Later today, if all had gone well for them inside, Beth would be taking the train to Montana, and Inga, her parents, and sisters would be leaving for Iowa. Only Mary would remain in New York.

A fearsome city, that.

She stared across the choppy waters of the harbor.

Somewhere in that sprawling mass of humanity known as New York City, she would find Seamus Maguire, her fiancé and the father of her unborn child. When she found him, they would be married, just as they'd planned before he left England. Seamus hadn't expected her to join him this soon, but he would be glad to see her. He loved her, Seamus did.

Mary reached into her pocket, felt the scrap of paper with Ryan Maguire's address written on it. That's where Seamus had said he would stay until he found work, with his cousin Ryan. It was where she had sent her letters to Seamus in the few months they'd been apart. Now it was where she would find him.

Faith, if she didn't believe her new life in America was going to be perfect altogether.

One

New York City, July 1898

THE DOOR TO THE MASTER'S STUDY SWUNG SHUT behind Mary, causing her to gasp in surprise. But it was Winston Kenrick's soft chuckle that made her whirl about and her pulse to quicken in dread.

"I wondered how soon you would get to cleaning this room, Mary."

"If 'tis a bad time, Master Kenrick, I could be coming back later. When you're not so busy and all."

He smiled, but the look was more feral than comforting. "I wouldn't think of causing you the trouble. Come in and be about your business."

Mary tried to disregard the ominous feeling in her chest. In the months she had worked for the Kenricks,

2

nothing untoward had happened to her. Yet it seemed the master was always watching her. It seemed he was around every corner, in every room, waiting, observing, smiling. The truth be told, she didn't like him much.

"I'll be trying not to disturb you, sir," she said as she set down her bucket of soapy wash water. She pulled the feather duster from her waistband and walked to the bookcase where she set to work, ignoring the man behind her.

The master chuckled again. "But don't you know, my dear girl? You *always* disturb me. You can't help it."

"I'm thinking I don't know what you mean," she replied without looking at him. But she was more than sure she did know what he meant.

Winston moved closer. "How is that little boy of yours, Mary Malone?"

Her heart nearly stopped. Her hand stilled, the feather duster resting on the spine of a book. "Me boy?" she whispered. She'd never told anyone in the Kenrick household about Keary. How did Master Kenrick know about him?

"It must be difficult, raising an infant on your own. What is he? Almost a year old now?"

She remained stubbornly silent.

"I could make it easier for you, Mary." His voice was low, intimate.

"I'm having no complaints as things are now."

His hands alighted on her shoulders. Slowly, he turned her to face him.

Winston Kenrick was a handsome man in his midforties. His hair was silver gray, but rather than making him look old, it only added to his distinguished appearance. He had enormous power and influence among the wealthy members of New York society. He

3

watched Mary now with eyes that said he knew exactly how to use his power and influence to get what he wanted.

"My dear girl," he continued in a husky voice, "you have no idea what I'm offering to do for you."

Mary's infamous temper flared. Discretion fled. "But I'm thinking I do know, sir, and I'll be having you know I've got no interest in lying on me backside for the likes o' you. Not for any amount of your charm or your money."

His eyes narrowed. "Don't play the innocent with me."

"Oh, I'll not be pretending innocence, sir. You already know I'm not married and I have me a son, so there'd be no use to it. But I learned me lesson well with Seamus Maguire, I did. I've been betrayed, but I'll not be used. Not by you nor any other man."

She tried to push him away, but his grip on her arms only tightened.

Winston grinned. "I think I can change your mind." Then he kissed her.

For a moment, she didn't fight him, too stunned to move. But then he eased her back against the bookshelf, pressing his body up close to hers, and he chuckled low in his throat, pleased with himself and with what he was doing.

Her anger flared hotter. She bit his lip. Hard.

He howled as he stepped back from her. Mary used the opportunity to slip away, dashing to the opposite side of the master's enormous cherry wood desk. Winston, in turn, positioned himself between her and the door.

He touched his lip with his fingertips, then looked at them, as if checking for blood. "You Irish witch," he said softly. The words would have seemed less terrifying if he'd shouted them at her.

"Just let me go, Master Kenrick. I'll collect me pay and be gone from here."

He acted as if she hadn't spoken. "You know, Mary, I have never had to take a woman unwillingly. I don't intend to begin with you."

Relief flooded her. He wasn't going to force himself upon her as she'd feared. Perhaps it was going to be all right, then.

But her relief was momentary.

"Are you aware that the authorities could deport you because you lied to get into the country? You told them you were married. They could send you back to Ireland." He paused a heartbeat, then added, "Without your son."

"They'd never do that." Fear made her mouth dry, her tongue thick. "They'd never do that."

He smiled. "Do you dare take that chance?"

She shook her head, whether in disbelief or in answer to his question, she didn't know.

"I promise you, Mary, you would not regret our time together. I know how to please a woman. And you wouldn't find me ungenerous. We would both benefit from the arrangement."

"I couldn't betray Mrs. Kenrick nor meself in such a way."

He moved toward the door. "I have very powerful friends. Police officers. Judges. I can make certain you never see your son again. Never. Is that what you want?" With a click, he turned the key, locking the door. Then he turned to look at her again. "Be very careful what you decide to do, my dear. Be very careful. Your son's future is entirely up to you."

Keary. Me darlin' Keary.

Winston moved to the center of the room, then crooked his finger at her. With heart pounding, she came around from behind the desk. She told herself she could do this for her son. She told herself it wouldn't matter when it was over. She would take Keary and go away. Far away. And she would forget Winston Kenrick. A few minutes in the master's study wouldn't destroy her. She had lived through worse and survived.

"That's a good girl," he said, his voice husky and self-satisfied. "Now, let's have a look at that beautiful body of yours, shall we?"

He stepped toward her. She stepped backward. He grinned, enjoying the game. Mary's buttocks bumped up against the desk, stopping her retreat.

Winston laughed aloud. "Still playing it coy, Miss Malone?"

"Don't do this, sir," she whispered. "Just let me go, and I'll be no more trouble to you."

"You're no trouble now." He reached to unbutton her blouse. He moistened his lower lip with the tip of his tongue. Desire smoldered in his eyes. "No trouble at all."

For Keary, she reminded herself. To protect Keary she could bear anything. For her beloved son, she could do anything.

Winston's hand slipped inside her blouse, cupping her breast. Panic surged, and she instinctively tried to push him away.

"No!" she cried.

Irritation flashed in his eyes, and with unexpected swiftness, he rent the front of her blouse. "Let's be done with this silliness. I find myself more than a little eager for you."

6

"Leave me be!"

He pressed his body, hard and ready, against her, causing her to bend backward over the desk. She tried to brace herself with her hands, hoping for enough leverage to shove him away.

"Maybe taking an unwilling woman wouldn't be so bad," he panted, then laved her exposed throat with his tongue. When he raised up to look her in the eyes, he added, "And taking a housemaid on my desk will be a new experience, too. You'll like it. I promise."

Mary's anger flared again, and she began to struggle. Then her right hand closed around something large, cool, and hard on the desk. "You'll not be taking this housemaid on your bloody desk!"

She swung her arm with all her might. The second after she hit Winston on the side of his head with the object in her hand, she saw a look of disbelief in his eyes. He stumbled backward a few steps, teetered drunkenly, and crumpled to the floor, lying in an awkward position on the Oriental rug.

Breathing hard, Mary took a step toward her employer. She nudged him with the toe of her shoe, but he didn't move. He made no sound. And then she saw the red stain spreading near his head across the elegant fibers of the carpet.

"Faith and begorra!" she whispered, her eyes widening. "Have I killed him, then?"

The answer lay before her, still and unmoving.

She would swing for this, see if she wouldn't. And then what would become of her wee Keary? She would have to get her son and run away before the master's body was found. She had little time to think about where she would go. She simply knew she must do it quickly.

She felt light-headed and out of breath as she hurried across the room. It wasn't until she reached for the key that she realized she still held the weapon she had used against Winston Kenrick. She looked at the ornate box. It was real silver, she'd wager, and valuable. It was better if she took it with her, she decided hastily. Perhaps the police would think the house had been burglarized. Maybe they wouldn't even notice the absence of one of the housemaids if they were looking for a thief instead.

Turning the key, Mary unlocked the study door, then turned the knob. She trembled as she looked out into the hallway. If one of the other servants were to see her . . .

The hall was empty. Now if she could just get out of the house without being seen.

She remembered her bodice was torn down the front and knew she couldn't go running through the streets of New York, down Madison Avenue itself, looking like this. People would take one look and know she was guilty of something. They would summon the police and have her arrested. All would be lost.

Panic threatened to overwhelm her.

Use your head, Mary, me darlin' girl, her da's voice whispered in her head. One hapless act may undo you, but one timely one will put all to right. Think, now.

Mary forced herself to be calm and work things through in her mind. She knew Mrs. Norris, the cook, always kept a spare apron hanging near the rear kitchen door. If Mary was to put it on, it would hide her ripped bodice. And her hat . . . She would need to get her hat. She had to look like any other young servant girl, out running errands for her mistress.

She glanced over her shoulder at the body of Winston Kenrick and a shiver ran through her. He'd been an evil

8

man, he had, but she would always be sorry she'd killed him. Because of it, she was certain she would never know a moment's peace for the rest of her miserable life.

Blanche Loraine was going home to die. She'd seen all the fancy doctors her considerable wealth could afford—which meant, in her humble opinion, far too many of the educated idiots. She'd listened to their collective advice. And now she was going back to Idaho to spend what time she had left with the people she knew best. Not that she expected any of them to mourn her passing.

Her lap dog, Nugget, whimpered for attention.

"I know, boy," Blanche said as she stroked his silky coat. "I'm not looking forward to the trip either. But won't we be glad to get the hell outta New York City."

Nugget licked her gloved hand.

A sudden coughing jag gripped Blanche. She covered her mouth with her handkerchief and tried to subdue the wretched hacking that seemed ready to rip her lungs right out of her body. Even as she fought for control, she noticed the couple opposite her get up from the seat and move to another part of the passenger car. She thought of a few choice—and most unladylike—things the strangers could do to themselves. Of course, Blanche Loraine was no lady and had never pretended to be.

As she folded the handkerchief, she noticed the red stains on the white cloth.

"Miss Loraine," one of the doctors had said to her only yesterday, "you should not undertake such an arduous journey at this time."

Idiot, she remembered thinking. He'd just finished telling her that her condition wasn't likely to improve.

So exactly when was it she was supposed to travel home?

"Excuse me, mum. Would you be allowing us to sit here?"

Drawn from her musings, Blanche looked up at the prettiest face she'd seen in all her born days. And in her line of work, Blanche had more than a passing knowledge of what made a woman beautiful. "Of course," she said, waving toward the seat opposite her. "Sit yourself right down."

The young woman—in her late twenties, Blanche guessed—set her small child on the indicated seat, then, standing on tiptoe, managed to shove her satchels onto the rack overhead. As she sat beside the toddler, she adjusted her straw hat, which had been knocked slightly askew during her efforts with the luggage. Her ink black hair was thick and curly, and long wisps had escaped her hairpins to coil at her nape. She had a heart-shaped face with a milky complexion that was absolutely flawless. Her eyes were dark brown, fringed in thick black lashes, and there was the look of a trapped animal in those eyes that intrigued Blanche.

"You going far?" she asked.

The young mother shook her head, shrugged, then quickly looked out the window, as if wanting to avoid the question.

"My name is Blanche Loraine."

After a long moment, she met Blanche's gaze again. "Mary Emeline Malone." Suddenly her eyes grew round, and she pressed her lips together tightly.

She's in trouble and didn't mean to tell me her name. But what kind of trouble? Aloud, she said, "Well, Mary, it's a pleasure to meet you. And who is this little man you've got with you?"

Again she was silent a spell before answering. "Me

10

son, Keary Malone."

The boy bore more than a slight resemblance to his mother. He had the same wavy black hair and the same large brown eyes. But he knew how to smile, something Blanche suspected his mother hadn't done freely in quite some time.

Keary leaned forward, his chocolate-colored eyes staring at Nugget, his arms outstretched.

"Oh, I see you like dogs." Blanche lifted her pet off her lap. "Do you want to pet him? This is Nugget."

The child laughed and bounced his pudgy hands off the dog's back.

"Be careful, Keary," his mother said softly. Then she looked over her son's head, staring out the window with an anxious gaze. "I'm thinking we should be under way by now. Could there be trouble?"

"Trains hardly ever leave on time."

Mary worried her lower lip with her teeth. Fear was stamped on her pretty features as clearly as anything Blanche had ever seen. Oddly enough, it bothered her.

Blanche Loraine was not a charitable woman by nature. She knew the value of a dollar, and she didn't squander her money on anything she didn't believe might bring her a profit. Still, there was something about Mary Emeline Malone that tugged at her life-hardened heart.

"Tickets," a man called from the rear of the car. "Tickets, please."

Mary started as if she'd been pinched. Fear was replaced by an expression of near-panic as the conductor drew closer.

Blanche reached forward and squeezed Mary's knee, drawing her gaze. "Sit still and say nothing," she warned. "Do you hear me?"

Mary nodded.

"Give me your passenger ticket." She held out her hand. After Mary obeyed, Blanche continued, "Now, take that boy in your arms and turn toward the window. Rock him as if you're trying to get him to sleep. That way your face won't be seen, and no one will remember you were even here."

By the time the conductor reached their seats, Blanche was ready for him. With one hand, she stroked Nugget. In her other hand, she held their tickets. "My good man," she said in her most authoritative voice, "someone has sold my niece the wrong ticket. As you can plainly see from mine, we are on our way to Whistle Creek, but she has been given one only to Omaha."

The conductor frowned as he took the tickets from her. "She shoulda said something 'fore now."

"Well, don't you think she would have if she'd noticed? She thought she was dealing with competent people. Goodness, it isn't easy, traveling with a child and an irascible aunt. Now see that her ticket is exchanged for one to match my own. There'll be a handsome reward in it for you if you can do it quickly."

"I'll see to it, ma'am. Don't you worry."

As soon as the conductor was gone, Mary Malone turned from the window. "I'm wondering why you did that altogether, Mrs. Loraine."

"There's no missus in front of my name. Folks back in Whistle Creek call me Miss Blanche. You can, too." She cocked one eyebrow. "And to tell you the truth, I'm not sure why I did it. I suppose because there's a look about you."

"A look, mum? What do you mean?"

"Nothing really." Blanche lowered her voice so as not to be overheard. "Where in Ireland are you from?"

12

Mary's reply came softly, "I was born in County Armagh."

"And how long have you been in America?"

"More than a year, just." She held her son more closely. "But you've not answered me question. Why did you do what you did? I can't be paying you back." She tilted her head, thrusting her chin slightly forward, the gesture filled with pride and a bit of bravado.

Blanche waved her hand. "I'm not asking you to pay me back, girl." Her own retort surprised her, and she wondered if she spoke the truth. She frowned as she sought a believable explanation for it. "I am not a well woman, Mary. I came to New York to seek the advice of medical experts." She laughed sharply. *Experts. Ha!* "Now I'm headed home, and I find I need a companion to make the journey more enjoyable and to help me should my health worsen."

"But you know nothing about me."

"I know you're in some sort of trouble."

Mary paled.

Perhaps that was why she was helping her. Because Blanche remembered a time, many years ago, when she had been in trouble and afraid, and there had been no one in the world who would help her. No one who'd cared. She'd fought for everything she'd ever had in this life. No one had given a damn about her, about whether she lived or died. Maybe she didn't want to leave this world without helping some other poor girl avoid what she'd been through.

"Where is your husband?"

A pause, then, "Me son's father is dead and buried these many months."

Ah, so he'd never married her, the blackguard. She'd seen it often in her lifetime.

Blanche's gaze dropped to the toddler in Mary's lap. The boy had fallen asleep. He looked cherubic. He was plump and well cared for. Loved, the way a child ought to be loved.

She looked at his mother again. "Let me help you, Mary Malone. If you decide you want to get off the train at any time, you're free to do so. You'll owe me nothing. But if you want to come all the way to Idaho with me, then you'll be welcome."

"Idaho?"

"Yes, that's where I live. Whistle Creek, Idaho."

Mary was silent for a long time, her dark gaze searching Blanche's face. Finally, she gave the smallest of nods. "I'll come and be glad of your help. May God bless you, mum."

Later that night, Mary lay on the top bunk in the sleeper car, staring at the ceiling that was hardly a foot from the tip of her nose. Beside her, Keary slept on his stomach, his tiny bottom stuck up in the air.

She wondered where they were now. It was well past midnight. How many miles away from New York City had they traveled? Was it far enough?

Every time the train came to a stop that day, she'd feared the authorities would swarm into the passenger car and drag her away. Every time the train pulled away from a station, she'd breathed a fresh sigh of relief.

She closed her eyes and commanded her breathing to slow. Worrying would not help. She had locked the master's study from the outside, then slipped out of the house without seeing another person. She'd worn the cook's spare apron to cover her ripped blouse. She had forced herself to walk with unhurried steps along the sidewalks of Madison Avenue. No one could have guessed by looking at her that she'd just killed a man. Besides, the wealthy never paid any attention to servants on the street. It would have been beneath them.

No, she was worrying needlessly. And even if the police wanted to question the missing housemaid, they wouldn't know where to look for her. In the few months she'd worked for the Kenricks, she'd never told anyone where she lived. She'd kept to herself, doing her work and then going back to the Dougals' apartment and her adorable baby son. She supposed most of the servants thought her unfriendly. Now she could only be thankful they knew nothing about her.

A wave of something akin to seasickness swept over her. Sweat beaded on her forehead. She'd killed a man.

May God forgive me.

She hadn't meant to kill Winston Kenrick. She'd hated him for what he'd been trying to do. She'd wanted to stop him. But she hadn't meant to kill him.

Truth be told, she hadn't meant for many things in her past to happen. She hadn't meant to bed down with a man who wasn't her husband, a man who was destined to betray her, fool that she was. She hadn't meant to bear a child out of wedlock, although she loved her Keary more than anything. She hadn't meant to find herself a penniless immigrant, dependent upon the charity of strangers. But that's what had happened, and there'd be no changing any of it.

In the berth beneath her, Blanche Loraine suffered another coughing spell. Mary had seen the flecks of blood on the woman's handkerchief, listened to her labored gasps for breath. She knew the signs of a dying woman when she saw them. She was sorry for her, to be sure, and she was thankful besides.

Idaho. Sure and it was nothing short of a miracle.

15

What else but the hand of the Almighty could have sat her down with a woman from Idaho, then caused the stranger to take Mary with her?

Aye, a miracle, for her brother Quaid could be somewhere in that state. She'd not heard from him in many a year. She'd still been in service near Belfast, before leaving for England, when the last letter from Quaid had come. He was working in a mine in a place called Idaho, he'd written. True, he might not still be there. He might even be dead like Seamus Maguire for all she knew.

But she'd not believe Quaid was dead. Not when the good Lord had seen fit to send her to Idaho to find him. Though why God was helping the likes of her—a fallen woman and a murderess besides—was beyond her. Still she wasn't one to spit into the wind.

It was to be Idaho, then. Mary had no idea where exactly that was, but she was given to understand it was far from New York City.

And that made it a good place altogether.

Two

"SHERIFF! YOUNG TODD STOVER, THE BLACKSMITH'S son, burst through the front door of the jail house. "There's trouble over at the Painted Lady."

Carson Barclay set the blue-and-white speckled coffeepot back on the woodstove. "Already? It isn't even noon yet." He reached for his hat. "What happened?"

"I don't rightly know. Pa just said there was trouble and sent me after you."

Carson strode toward the front door, moving swiftly and with purpose. When there was trouble at the

16

Painted Lady Saloon—as there was on a fairly regular basis—it could quickly escalate into gunplay. And if there was one thing Sheriff Carson Barclay hated, it was folks getting shot up in his town. They could blow themselves to pieces elsewhere for all he cared, but not in his town.

The narrow main street of Whistle Creek, Idaho, was quiet this time of the day. The men from the Lucky Lady Mine's night shift were at home in their beds. The day shift was down in the bowels of the earth, chipping away at walls of rock, looking for the black-coated silver ore. As for the townsfolk, they were going about their own business indoors, it seemed. Other than a couple of horses tethered outside the boardinghouse, a wagon and team standing in front of the mercantile, and Abe Stover's motley wolfhound lounging in one of its favorite spots, Main Street was empty.

Everything was quiet, just as Carson liked it.

Except at the Painted Lady.

The saloon was the fanciest business establishment between Spokane and Missoula, and with the exception of the cavernlike buildings out at the mine, it was the largest, too. It boasted brass fixtures and spittoons, red velvet upholstery, and elaborate oil paintings of large-breasted, half-naked women. Three stories tall, with plenty of upstairs parlors for private entertaining, the Painted Lady was home to twenty females, most of them young and all of them pretty, who, for a portion of any poor fool's hard-earned money, would give him his ease.

Carson frowned as he drew closer to the saloon. He had more than a passing acquaintance with enterprises like the Painted Lady, and he didn't figure anything good ever came out of them. He wasn't a puritan. He'd

17

done his own share of drinking, carousing, and womanizing in his younger days, before he'd had some good sense knocked into him. But liquor and loose women meant trouble, and Carson hated trouble in his town.

It would have made his life a whole heck of a lot easier if Blanche Loraine would take her business and her girls elsewhere. That wasn't going to happen. The Painted Lady was as much a part of Whistle Creek as the mine and the stamp mill, the mercantile, the livery, and the Northern Pacific Rail Road line that ran between Mullan and Spokane.

The sound of shattering glass greeted him as he stepped through the swinging doors of the saloon. He saw Mac MacDonald, the card dealer, duck just in time to miss a flying beer mug as it hurtled toward him.

"Cheated me agin!" John Tyrell shouted, his words slurred. "By darn, ya cheated me agin, Mac!"

"That's enough, John," Carson said.

The young man spun, staggered, nearly fell before catching himself against the bar. "He cheated me, Sheriff. Dadburned thievin' cardsharp. He cheated me agin."

"I don't hardly doubt that." Carson smiled goodnaturedly at the dealer, a look that said *no hard feelings*. Then he approached John. "But I guess if you thought he'd cheated you before, you shouldn't've come in here again, now should you? Doesn't seem to me you've got money enough you can afford to throw it away playing poker."

John blinked his eyes as he leaned dangerously to one side.

"I'm afraid I don't have much sympathy for you, John. Nobody forced that liquor down your gullet, and

18

nobody made you sit down at Mac's table either." He eyed the broken mirror behind the bar. "I reckon Miss Blanche isn't going to be none too pleased with what you did here this morning."

"But I'm tellin' you, Sheriff—"

"Yeah, I know." He took hold of John's good arm. "Let's get you over to the jail so you can sleep it off." He looked at Lloyd Perkins, the bartender. "I heard Miss Blanche is finally coming back."

"Yup. Matter of fact, she left New York at the first of the week. I expect her on the afternoon train."

Carson nodded, then led his prisoner out of the saloon. John struggled to keep up, stumbling along beside him, muttering about being cheated.

Carson didn't think John Tyrell had drawn a sober breath in a full three years. Not since the blasting accident down in the mines that had left him, at the age of nineteen, with his face scarred and his right arm useless. No longer able to work in the mines and forced to live with his older brother, sister-in-law, and three nephews, John had taken to drink like an infant takes to its mama's breast.

"When are you gonna dry out, John?" Carson asked, a note of frustration in his words. "You're not the first man to be hurt in the mines. And you're sure as heck not being fair to Wade and Dora and the kids."

John cursed in reply.

"Wade's money's hard enough to come by without you throwing it away in that saloon."

John remained stubbornly silent.

Carson shook his head as he opened the door to the sheriff's office and led his prisoner to the back room that held the jail cells. "It wouldn't hurt for you to think of someone besides yourself for a change." He unlocked the nearest cell and gave John a little push toward the cot. "Sleep on that thought for a while."

He didn't wait to see what the drunken man did. Instead, he turned, walked out of the back room, and headed for the stove and that cup of coffee he'd been wanting. As he took his first sip of the dark brew, he thought about the broken mirror over at the saloon. Wade wasn't going to have the kind of money it would take to replace it. That spelled real trouble for John.

Carson crossed to his office window and looked outside. Clanging sounds came from the interior of the livery. Abe Stover was probably shaping a horseshoe to fit or repairing a wagon wheel. Next door at the mercantile, Chuck Adams washed the dust off the shop windows while old Dooby Jones reclined on a nearby bench, smoking a pipe and, no doubt, reminiscing about the first gold strikes in Idaho and how he'd been there when it all began. Farther down the street was the small, whitewashed Whistle Creek Community Church, empty now on a Friday.

Carson glanced in the opposite direction, toward the Painted Lady. Blanche Loraine was due back in Whistle Creek today. She would want reimbursement for that mirror. Lloyd Perkins, who'd been running the place in her absence, would have probably agreed to let John work off the debt. Blanche was another story. She was a tough businesswoman who never wasted a red cent. She reminded him a little of Aldora Barclay in that regard.

Breaking off the uncomfortable direction of that thought, Carson set his jaw and turned from the window. He'd better get out to the Tyrell place and let them know John was in jail. Standing here wasn't doing anyone any good.

Mary stared through the soot-smudged window of the train. In the past four days and nights, she'd seen more changing landscapes than she'd have thought possible in one country. She'd seen a few big cities and many small towns that were not much more than the train depot. She'd seen prairies that stretched as far as the eye could see and mountains that touched heaven itself. She'd seen deserts and forests, antelope and rabbits, purple sagebrush and wide, muddy rivers.

For quite some time, the train had been winding through what seemed to be one long, continuous valley, mountains rising on both sides. Sometimes the valley narrowed to allow hardly more than the tracks and the river that ran alongside them. Other times it widened into lush meadows, occasionally dotted with a farmhouse or two. Since departing Tekoa that morning, they'd made stops in several towns with names like St. Joe, Kellogg, and Osburn.

"We'll be in Whistle Creek soon," Blanche said, drawing Mary's attention from the window and the scenery beyond.

Mary knew a great deal more about her benefactress now than she had four days ago. She knew Blanche Loraine owned a saloon, and Mary suspected she knew exactly what sort of women worked for Blanche inside that saloon. She'd guessed that they served up more than ale for their customers.

But Mary had also discovered during the journey that she liked the no-nonsense woman who had befriended her, no matter how she made her living. Blanche had a way of speaking her mind that was refreshing. She didn't put on airs even if she did have plenty of money. Nor did she seem to feel sorry for herself, even though she was obviously quite ill.

21

"Here. Let me have the boy." Blanche held out her arms to take Keary, who was fast asleep in Mary's arms. "You look plum tuckered out."

Mary nodded. She *was* tired. Keeping an active toddler entertained in such a confined space for so many days hadn't been an easy task. Keary was a good baby most of the time, but even he was cranky and tired of train travel by now. Add to that the summer heat, making the rail car stuffy and close, and it was no wonder Mary was exhausted.

She handed Keary to Blanche. "Thank you."

"Nothing to thank me for. I enjoy holding him when he's asleep." Her expression softened. "You're a good mother, Mary."

She stared at her son and felt her chest tighten. "He's everything to me. I'd do anything for him."

"Mary?" Blanche's tone was thoughtful.

She looked up to meet the other woman's gaze.

"Seems to me you've got a real good head on your shoulders. I'd like you to come to work in my saloon."

Mary shook her head emphatically. "I couldn't be doing that."

"Oh, I don't mean as one of my girls." Blanche chuckled. "Although you'd no doubt make me even richer than I am now if you did." Her smile vanished. "No, I mean I'd like you to try your hand at managing the business. I don't know how long I'll be able to do it myself. I'd like to know I've got someone I can depend on helping me run things."

Mary was stunned. Manage a saloon?

"Lloyd's been looking after things for me while I was in New York. He's my bartender. But he's not exactly the brightest of men. It's been an enormous responsibility for him. I think I could trust you, Mary,

22

to handle things as they should be."

Mary thought of Winston Kenrick, lying dead on the floor of his study. "I don't know why you'd say such a thing," she whispered. "You've no reason to trust me."

"I say it because I'm a keen judge of character." Blanche's eyes narrowed. "And besides, I like you, Mary Emeline Malone."

She smiled. "I like you, too, Miss Blanche. You've a kind heart, you have."

The other woman hooted a loud laugh. "That's not something I've heard said about me before, and I'd just as soon you keep it to yourself. It wouldn't do for my reputation to be gussied up."

Mary wasn't certain she understood what Blanche meant. Still, she nodded in agreement.

"Now, back to my proposition. You need some way to make a living to support you and this boy here, and I'm going to need someone to keep my place running the way I want it to. You're not going to find any folks needing a maid in Whistle Creek. None of the wealthy mine owners live there. And I could use you for better things than dusting the furniture. Are you willing to give it a try?"

"Me ma would turn over her in grave," Mary muttered to herself.

Blanche heard her and chuckled. "I expect so. But will you do it anyway?"

"Aye," she answered quickly, before she could think better of it. "I'll do it, Miss Blanche. Sure, and I'll be doing me very best, too."

"I know. I wouldn't have asked otherwise."

The train whistle echoed up the valley, announcing the arrival of the three-fifteen. And it was only a half an

23

hour behind schedule, according to Carson's pocketwatch.

Giving the brim of his Stetson a tug, he bid good afternoon to the gentlemen lounging outside of the mercantile and set off toward the depot. He'd promised Wade Tyrell he'd have a word with Blanche about the broken bar mirror. Not that Carson thought the madam would be any more sympathetic with the words coming from him. Nobody knew better than he did that the myth about the whore with a heart of gold was pure bunk. But he and Blanche did have a sort of mutual understanding. She didn't have much use for the law. He didn't have much use for prostitutes. And they both knew the other wasn't going away.

He arrived at the depot just as the Northern Pacific rolled to a stop amid the hiss of steam and the squeak of brakes.

"Whistle Creek," he heard the conductor shout. "Next stops, Wallace and Mullan."

Carson saw movement inside the passenger car. He headed toward the rear exit.

His first glimpse of Blanche Loraine in six months told him everything he needed to know about her health. She must have lost forty pounds while she was gone, and there were dark circles beneath her expressive green eyes. She'd always been a handsome woman, but her sickness was destroying her looks as well as her lungs.

"Well, as I live and breathe. Sheriff Barclay." She flashed him one of her coquettish smiles. "Have you come to meet me at the train to welcome me home?"

"As a matter of fact, Miss Blanche, I have. In a roundabout way."

"Will wonders never cease."

He stepped toward her. "I reckon not."

He held out his hand to help her down to the platform. Instead of taking it, she handed him that silly lapdog of hers, then descended unaided. Once down, Blanche turned and looked behind her. Carson followed the direction of her gaze.

A young woman, toddler in arms, appeared on the train's steps. A young woman prettier than any he'd ever laid eyes on—and that was saying something.

Angelic.

Heavenly.

A natural beauty, unspoiled by artificial adornment of any kind.

His mouth went dry. His pulse quickened.

"Sheriff Barclay, I'd like you to meet my friend, Mrs. Mary Malone, and her son, Keary. Mrs. Malone lost her husband a year or so ago. They're going to be staying at the Painted Lady while she manages the saloon for me."

His gaze swung to the madam. "They're going to *what?*"

"Yes, I agree, it is a shame to waste such a beauty on my books and ledgers."

He looked at Mary Malone again. She didn't appear quite so angelic or heavenly to him now. And from the expression on her face, he didn't look too good to her either.

"Ma'am," he said stiffly.

"Sheriff," she whispered.

He showed the woman his back, then said to Blanche, "I need to talk to you."

"So I gathered. Well, walk along with us if you like. I've already asked the porter to see that our things are sent to the saloon." She held out her arms. "Here. Give Nugget to me. You're holding him all wrong."

Carson obeyed, glad to be rid of the animal. Then he fell into step beside Blanche, adjusting his stride to hers. He guessed Mary Malone followed behind them, but he refused to give into the urge to look.

"I take it there was some trouble at the Painted Lady," Blanche said, her tone all business.

"John Tyrell."

"Ah."

"He busted the mirror behind the bar."

Blanche frowned. "Damn the young fool. Even when he was working for the mine, he couldn't make in a month what that mirror cost me."

"Look, I've got him in jail right now, but I was hoping you'd let him work it off. He doesn't have the money to pay for it, and neither does his brother."

"He'd probably just break into the liquor and get stinking drunk."

Carson couldn't argue with her. That was more than a slight possibility.

"I'm dying, Sheriff," Blanche suddenly said, her voice low. She stopped walking, looked at him, her expression grave. "But then, I guess you've already figured that out."

He didn't deny it.

"I turned forty last month. No spring chicken, I admit, but still plenty of years left that should've been mine."

He almost felt sorry for her.

As abruptly as she'd stopped, she started walking again. "All right, I'll let him work it off. But the first time he gets drunk on my time or my liquor, he goes right back to jail. Agreed?"

For a moment, Carson couldn't answer. He'd never actually expected Blanche to consent to his plan. He hadn't thought she had a compassionate bone in her body. Especially for the town drunk.

"Is that agreed?" she persisted.

"Agreed."

Blanche slowed her pace while turning her head to look at him. "Believe it or not, I've missed you, Sheriff Barclay."

Once again she'd stunned Carson into silence. He couldn't do anything more than just stare at her.

She smiled, and the humor returned to her green eyes. "Now if you'll excuse us, Sheriff, I need to get Mary and her little boy settled in, and then see just how much money Lloyd's laziness has cost me in the months I was gone."

Carson stepped off the boardwalk and let Mary Malone pass him by.

Blanche had *missed* him? Blanche Loraine? What sort of thing was that for her to say? Her sickness must be eating away at her brain, too. That's the only reason he could think of for her passing comment.

As he stared after them, the younger of the two women glanced back over her shoulder. For just a moment, Mary Malone's gaze locked with Carson's. He felt a kick of desire so strong it stole his breath away.

Dang!

She was going to mean trouble for sure, and just as always, Carson hated trouble in his town.

Three

A HALF HOUR LATER, BLANCHE BACKED OUT THE doorway of Mary's room, saying, "You just get yourself settled in. I'll have your supper sent up to you in an hour

27

or so. Tomorrow will be soon enough for us to start work."

The moment the door closed, Mary sank onto the bed and released a deep sigh. She didn't realize how closely she was hugging Keary to her chest until he objected.

"Sorry, love," she whispered, then set him on the floor and watched him toddle across the room, investigating their new surroundings.

Dread had sapped any reserved strength Mary had. The moment she'd seen the sheriff standing on the train platform, waiting for them, she'd been overtaken by fear. Even after she'd realized he wasn't there because of her, she hadn't been able to rid herself of the oppressing sense of doom. Just the idea of being introduced to the sheriff made her sick inside. Now he knew her name. If he should learn the authorities in New York were looking for a Mary Malone . . .

She should have taken a different identity. She should have lied about her name when Blanche asked what it was. But she hadn't been thinking when she answered the question. After that, there'd seemed no going back.

Maybe there wasn't reason to worry, she tried reassuring herself. Maybe no one was looking for her. At least the sheriff thought she was a married woman. Maybe he wouldn't put two and two together, even if . . .

The washstand wobbled, Keary's hands gripping its spindly legs. The porcelain pitcher and bowl atop it started to slide toward the edge. Mary jumped up quickly, just in time to save everything from crashing down on her son's head. Once the table was steady, she lifted him into her arms.

"Lord, what is it we're doing here?" she whispered, her cheek pressed against Keary's down-soft hair. "'Tis a

28

bawdy house, to be sure, and me with a wee son t' look after. 'Tis no place for us."

A knock on the door interrupted her search for answers. She went to it, cracking it open an inch or two.

"Hello." The girl on the opposite side of the door was no more than sixteen or seventeen years old. Her appearance was at once innocent and carnal. "You must be Mrs. Malone."

"Aye." Mary opened the door a little farther.

"I'm Edith."

"Hello, Edith." She opened the door the rest of the way.

Edith's blue eyes, lined with black, turned toward Keary. "And this must be your son?"

"Aye."

She smiled. "I love babies. May I hold him?"

Mary hesitated, uncertain what to do. Although it was not yet five in the afternoon, Edith was dressed as if for bed, wearing a gauzy robe over what looked like a low-cut satin nightgown. Her hair, a lovely shade of gold, was pulled back from her face but hung loosely down her back in a cluster of ringlets. Her mouth was stained ruby red, and there were jeweled rings on several of her fingers.

"Please?" she said, meeting Mary's gaze again. "I won't hurt him. I've got six brothers and sisters of my own. All younger. I'll just hold him while you get unpacked. That way, he won't be underfoot."

There was something touchingly painful about the girl and her plea, and Mary was unable to resist it. Wordlessly, she nodded.

Edith held out her arms to take Keary, smiling now. "I reckon you must be mighty tired after comin' all the way from New York City." She crossed the bedroom,

29

carrying Mary's son with her, and settled on a straight-backed chair near the window. "This is one of Miss Blanche's best rooms, outside of her own, of course. Hers is almost like a house, all by itself. She's even got a private bathing room in there."

Edith paused talking long enough to lift Keary over her head. He giggled as she lowered him quickly, then raised him up again, arms straight, elbows locked.

"You're gonna like workin' for Miss Blanche," she continued after a while. "She's got strict rules, but she's fair."

Mary frowned. "I'm thinking I'd like to know how long you've worked here."

"It'll be two years come July." The girl's pretty smile disappeared as she lowered Keary to her lap. "I had me a fella I was gonna marry. His name was Jack. But Pa didn't think much of him, and he told him to take his no-account self off our farm. Over in Montana, it was. Then I come up expectin'-like, so Pa told me to get out, too. Jack said he was gonna find work over in the Idaho mines, so I came lookin'. Never did find him."

"And your baby?" Mary asked softly.

"She was stillborn."

"Faith, but 'tis sorry I am, Edith."

"I named her Ruth 'fore I buried her up on the hill there." The girl blinked away her tears and smiled at Keary once again. "I don't reckon it hurts so much now. Miss Blanche, she took me in, and she had the doctor to see to me when the baby was comin'. He did everything he rightly could, but I don't guess she was meant to live. I couldn't've taken proper care of her, things being as they were."

Mary sat on the edge of the bed, anxiety forming a tight fist in her belly. The story sounded all too familiar.

30

If circumstances had been a little different, her fate could have been the same as Edith's. "Did she . . . did Miss Blanche *force* you go to work for her?"

"Glory, no!" Edith answered. "Miss Blanche never asked nothing of me."

"Then why. . ." She let her voice trail into silence.

"Why do I sell myself, you mean?" There was a hard edge in her voice that made her sound old beyond her years. "'Cause there ain't nothing else a girl like me can do to keep herself from starvin', that's why. I made a mistake. The kind there's no forgivin'. And then my own pa threw me out. Just who else was gonna take me in? Men're gonna look at me as soiled goods whether I'm here or not, and respectable folks wouldn't give me the time of day, let alone give me work. Least this-wise I can decide who I want pawing me. You know what I mean?"

Mary thought of Master Kenrick. Somehow, he had found out about Keary, the son she'd borne out of wedlock. He'd thought that made his housemaid fair game. He'd thought Mary was *soiled goods*, as Edith had put it. "Aye," she whispered. "I understand altogether."

"Miss Blanche, she's got real strict rules, just like I said. Anybody gets rough with her girls, she makes sure they never come here again. She's even had a fella or two arrested. And she don't hold the girls if they ever want to leave. Last year, Kitty got married to a farmer over near Spokane."

Mary rose from the bed and busied herself with unpacking her few belongings. Edith continued to chatter about the other girls and women who lived and worked at the Painted Lady, and about Lloyd the bartender, Mac the dealer, and Hank the hired man.

"Now, looky here. Ain't this pretty?"

31

Mary glanced over her shoulder. She felt the blood drain from her face when she saw what Edith held in her hand.

"Is it from Ireland?" the girl asked as she fingered the silver filigrees on the fancy box from Master Kenrick's study. "Is it a jewelry box?"

"No," Mary answered, sounding breathless. She reached out and took it from Edith. "No, 'tis not from Ireland and 'tis not for jewels." Quickly, she tucked the offensive item in the back of a drawer.

Edith gave her a strange look, then continued with her prattle as if she'd never interrupted herself. "Can't say I know hardly any other folks in town. 'Cept some of the men, of course, and most of 'em that come in here work for the mines and don't have families to go home to." She shrugged. "We pretty much keep to ourselves at the Painted Lady. Let others come to us if they've a mind to."

Mary liked the idea of keeping to herself. It sounded safe.

Edith stood, balancing Keary on her hip as she stepped over close to the window, her gaze directed toward the street below. A smile curved her mouth. "Now if there was somebody in Whistle Creek I'd like to get to know better, that's him there." She almost purred the words, sounding much more like an experienced woman than a girl in her teens.

Curiosity drew Mary to the window. Sheriff Barclay stood on the sidewalk opposite the saloon, talking to a man on horseback.

"I've never seen anybody more handsome than the sheriff," Edith concluded with a sigh. "Not even Jack."

Handsome? Mary hadn't noticed. She'd been too afraid to really look at him.

"He's got the bluest eyes I ever seen in all my born days," Edith went on, her tone almost worshipful.

The sheriff's face was shadowed by his black Stetson, but Mary remembered from the depot that he was a tall man, tall and lean and, she suspected, strong. He wore a set of pistols strapped to his thighs, like a gunslinger in a dime novel. She wondered how many men he'd shot.

"How often does he come to the Painted Lady?" she asked, afraid of the answer.

"Him?" Edith set Keary on his feet, then followed behind him as he toddled away. "Sheriff Barclay hardly ever comes here, and then only for a drink at the bar. Never visits the ladies. Never gambles." She laughed. "Well, he does have to come when there's trouble, so I guess he's here more'n a few times a week."

The man on horseback rode away. Afterward, the sheriff tilted his head and looked straight toward Mary's window. Her breath caught in her throat, and a shiver ran through her. She took a step backward, hoping he hadn't seen her watching him. She didn't want to be noticed. Especially by the law.

"Something wrong, Mary?"

She turned, pretending a calm she didn't feel. "No. Nothing's wrong. But I am tired altogether. I'm thinking I'd like to lie down with Keary and see if we might sleep a wee bit before supper."

"'Course. I should've guessed. I'll leave you be." Edith moved toward the door. When she reached it, she glanced behind her. "But I hope you won't mind if I come to see Keary every now and again. It was real nice to hold him."

Mary nodded. "He'd like that, Edith. And I'm thinking so would I."

Carson saw someone move away from a third-floor window, and instinctively, he knew it was the Malone woman. But it was the lingering images of Aldora Barclay—not those of Mary Malone—that made anger boil up in his chest, sudden and furious.

He turned on his heel and started walking toward his office.

He didn't like remembering Aldora. His mother.

Mother? In a pig's eye. Even she hadn't let him call her that. She had always been Aldora.

Carson's earliest memory was of falling down the back stairway of the Golden Eagle Dance Hall in Idaho City. He'd been not quite four at the time. He still bore the scar from that fall. He touched the hairless spot in the center of his left eyebrow. He remembered one of the saloon girls, smelling of whiskey and cheap perfume, lifting him and carrying him upstairs to Aldora's room. He'd been crying. He remembered that, too, because it had made Aldora real mad. She'd hated to be interrupted when she was working. Especially by the child she'd never wanted. She'd scolded him for crying, for not staying in his room, then she'd hauled him up another flight of stairs.

That was the first time Carson had been locked in the attic. It hadn't been the last.

He gave his head a brief shake, driving off the unwelcome memories as he opened the door to the sheriff's office. He walked through to the jail cells.

"John?"

His prisoner was lying on his right side, his back toward the cell door.

"John," Carson said, louder this time.

He groaned. "What?"

"I've got some good news for you."

34

"Leave me be, Sheriff." John brought his left arm up, covering his ear and the top of his head. "Don't care about no good news."

"But you should." Carson put the key in the lock, turned it, and opened the door. "You're not going to have to stay in jail."

Slowly, John rolled over. He opened his eyes a fraction.

"You've got a job."

John groaned again. "A job?" He closed his eyes, as if the light of day hurt them. "What sorta job?"

"Whatever Miss Blanche wants you to do, I reckon. You're going to be working over at the Painted Lady to pay off that mirror you busted. But first you need a bath and some fresh clothes. I'm going to take you out to Wade's place so you can clean up."

"I'm not feelin' up to movin', Sheriff." He rolled onto his side again. "Maybe tomorrow."

Carson poked John in the ribs with an index finger. "Get up." When the young man didn't move, Carson took him by his left arm and gave a steady, firm pull. "Up, I said. Time's a-wastin'."

"You don't have no pity, Barclay."

"Yeah, well, you haven't got much sense."

John swore softly, but he didn't put up any more resistance. He allowed Carson to lead him from the cell and out through the office to the sidewalk. An hour ago, Carson had asked Abe Stover to hitch up a wagon so he could take John out to his brother's farm. He found the buckboard waiting for them in the street.

"Get in," he told his prisoner. He waited behind him, just in case John fell over backward while trying to maneuver himself onto the seat. When the young man was safely in place, Carson went around to the other side and climbed aboard. As he picked up the reins, he said, "Listen close, John. If you don't work off this debt to Miss Blanche, you're going to find yourself doing some serious time in jail. You've been in trouble before. But this time you could be sent down to the penitentiary in Boise."

John mumbled a nonsensical response.

Carson slapped the reins, and the buckboard jerked forward as the horse stepped out. "She's serious this time. You mess up, you dip into her liquor, you take something that's not yours, she'll have you locked up again in no time. How'd you like to be in one of those cells for years?"

There was a lengthy pause before John answered, "Wouldn't like it none."

"No, you wouldn't."

They traveled in silence for about fifteen minutes before the younger man spoke again. "How come you're so all-fired bent on helpin' me, Sheriff?"

"How old are you?" Carson asked, answering a question with a question.

"Twenty-two . . . I think. What year is it?"

Carson smiled without humor. "You're headed for real trouble, John. So was I once. But somebody stepped in and turned things around for me. Let's just say I'd like to do the same for you."

"Well, ain't that real charitable of you." The words dripped with sarcasm. "Helpin' the cripple. You shoulda been a preacher man."

"You asked why I was doing it. I told you the truth."

"I need a drink."

Carson sighed. How was he supposed to get through to John?

He wondered if David Hailey had felt the same

frustration over him, all those years ago. Carson had been a smart-mouthed kid, just spoiling for a fight, just looking for mischief, just daring somebody—anybody—to do something nice for him.

A lot like John Tyrell, he reckoned.

As if reading Carson's thoughts, John said, "I don't want your help, y' know, Sheriff."

"Yeah, I know. But I guess you're going to get it, like it or not."

Four

BLANCHE FROWNED AS SHE STUDIED THE LEDGERS in front of her. The story they told was worse than she'd expected. The saloon had lost a considerable sum of money in the months she'd been back East. Could it be more than mere incompetence as a manager on Lloyd's part? She hated to think so. Lloyd Perkins had been with her for ten years. At one time, he had been far more to her than just a bartender in her saloon.

A soft rap on her office door broke into her thoughts. "Come in," she said, looking up.

"Am I too early?" Mary asked when the door was open. She carried her son in her arms.

Blanche motioned her in. "'Course not. You're right on time. Close the door behind you." She waited until Mary had taken a chair on the opposite side of the desk, then asked, "Did you have breakfast?"

"Aye. Greta made us . . ." She frowned. "Now what was it she was calling them?"

"Flapjacks," Blanche offered with a chuckle. "They're what she does best. Greta's not a fancy cook, but she takes good care of the girls and me. Makes sure none of us go hungry, at any rate." She glanced at Keary. "How'd you and the boy sleep?"

"'Twas a wee bit noisy, don't ya know," Mary answered honestly.

Blanche smiled. "You'll get used to it. Everyone does eventually. Late hours come with the territory in the saloon business."

There was no return smile as Mary replied, "I'm thinking a body can get used to many things when forced to. Often as not, there's little enough choice in the matter."

Blanche leaned back in her chair, wondering about Mary's cryptic words. She had learned surprisingly few facts about the young Irishwoman in their days of travel together, other than that Mary was bright and had received some schooling, enough to read and write and do sums. Yet Blanche believed she understood things about the younger woman that were far more important. Mary had walked side by side with trouble, Blanche was sure of it, yet she hadn't given into despair. She'd kept her pride and dignity. Perhaps most telling of all was the way Mary was devoted to her son.

"Mary . . ." Blanche began slowly, "I figure you know that I'm dying."

"Aye."

She rose from her chair and walked to the window. "I don't want the girls here to know. Not yet anyway. They'll guess soon enough."

"Aye."

Blanche's first-floor office at the rear comer of the saloon had a view of the railroad tracks, set about a hundred feet away. Beyond the tracks flowed the South Fork of the Coeur d'Alene River, and beyond the river were the mountains, their slopes garbed in pines and

38

aspens. Lord love it, this country was a whole sight prettier than New York City with its millions of people and tall buildings.

"I was right attractive when I was young like you," she said without looking behind her, feeling the need to talk, to explain, to be understood. "Even had me a fella of my own once. I was mighty bitter when he up and married someone else. A woman with more money and more class. I swore than that I'd never marry, and I didn't. And I swore I'd never trust another man, not as long as I lived. Guess I kept that oath, too." She turned, waved her arm in an arc. "I built the Painted Lady, built this business, to take back from men what I thought they'd taken from me. But now that my time's short, I'm finding bitterness is cold company. I'm all alone."

"Sure and you're not alone. You have everyone here—"

"Honey, they aren't here because they love me." She said it flippantly, but Blanche was surprised by how much it hurt to admit it. The urge to open up to Mary vanished. She returned to her desk and shoved the ledgers toward her newest employee. "I want you to look these over. We've been losing money pretty fast while I was away. I want to know why. I have my own suspicions, but I want to know what you think. Can you do that?"

"Aye, I'll be doing me best."

"Good." Jerking her head toward Keary, she added, "You can fix a little play area for him in the corner if you want. Put some toys in here and whatever."

"Thank you."

"I'll leave you to your work." She picked up Nugget, who'd been lying in his bed beside the desk, and headed for the office door.

"Miss Blanche?"

She stopped, turned, met Mary's gaze.

"I'm hoping you know I mean that altogether.

Me thanks, that is. For more than just saying I can bring toys into your office here. I fancy others have known your kindness, too, and are grateful for it. But none more than me." She offered a hesitant smile. "I'll be proving it the best I can."

Blanche had the awful feeling she was about to cry. "Just find out why I'm not making money the way I usually do. That's all the thanks I want from you."

With her dignity wrapped around her like a protective robe, she left the office.

Carson ate his breakfast at the Whistler Café, just as he did every day of the week except Sundays, when the restaurant was closed. Nobody rustled up eggs and bacon quite like Zeb Brewer, both chef and owner of the café, and his flapjacks were lighter than air.

The dining room was busy, filled with the usual breakfast crowd. Quite a few of the miners came here to eat on their days off. The Lucky Lady Mine employed over three hundred men. Most of them lived in the shacks the company had thrown up years ago. During their work week, they ate at the company restaurant when they didn't cook for themselves, and they bought their supplies at the company store. But on their days off, you could count on quite a few of them making their way into town. They ate at the Whistler Café and shopped at Chuck's Mercantile, and they gambled and caroused at the Painted Lady. Without the miners and their hard-earned wages, Whistle Creek would dry up and become just another ghost town.

Carson only half listened to the conversations going

on around him. His thoughts were elsewhere. He was thinking about John Tyrell, wondering how the angry young man was doing. John had been in a dour mood yesterday when Carson left him in Blanche's office. For all he knew, John had bolted and wasn't even there. There was no telling what bitterness, anger, and the want of drink might cause a fellow to do.

Carson pushed his empty plate back from the edge of the table, rose from his chair, and reached into his pocket for some money. He dropped the necessary coins beside his plate. "Thanks, Zeb."

"Sure thing, Sheriff," the chef replied without looking up from his cooking. "See ya later."

At the door, Carson retrieved his black Stetson from one of the pegs on the wall. Once outside, he turned left and followed the sidewalk past the boardinghouse and to the door of the sheriff's office. He paused there, as if to go inside, then changed his mind. He'd better check on John, or he'd just go on wondering about him the rest of the morning.

A few minutes later, he stepped through the front entrance of the Painted Lady. Lloyd was alone in the saloon, wiping the bar with a damp cloth. There was no sign of John. Mac, of course, would be sleeping in; card dealers, like the girls who lived upstairs, did most of their work at night.

"Mornin', Sheriff," Lloyd called to him.

"Mornin', Lloyd. Miss Blanche around?"

"In her office. Go on back. You know how to find it."

"Thanks."

Carson wound his way through the card tables that cluttered the spacious room and past the sweeping staircase with its plush red carpet and the small stage where some of the girls sang and danced nightly for the

41

customers. In the center of the back wall was a door, camouflaged with red and black wallpaper. Even the latch was inconspicuous, but Carson knew where it was. He lifted it and opened the door.

The hallway was narrow and dark, but he didn't need any light to find the way. He'd had more than a few meetings with Blanche Loraine in her office since he'd become sheriff of Whistle Creek back in ninety-two.

Blanche's office was located near the back stairs.

Unlike the grand staircase in the main saloon, there was nothing sweeping about the narrow flight of steps used by the owner and residents of the Painted Lady.

Carson rapped on the door with his right hand while already opening it with his left. "Miss Blanche, I—" He stopped suddenly as Mary Malone shot up from the chair behind the desk.

Her eyes—dark as ground coffee beans—were wide with alarm as she stared at him. Then she glanced over her left shoulder toward the corner where her little boy was playing with some blocks of wood. As her gaze returned to Carson, she stepped sideways until she stood between him and the child.

"You'll not be finding Miss Blanche here," she said. There was a slight quiver in her voice, but there was also a hint of defiance in the way she held herself.

"Do you know where she is?"

"Sure and I couldn't be saying."

Carson had never before found an Irish accent so appealing. The lilt in her words seemed musical to his ears. Unconsciously, he took a step closer to her. Mary let out a soft gasp and took a corresponding step backward.

He frowned, wondering if she was hiding something. He glanced toward the desk. "What are you doing in

42

here anyway?"

She didn't answer.

He looked at her again, and he felt that unsettling pull of desire. Even dressed as simply as she was in a gray muslin gown, her face devoid of any rouge or powder, her thick hair swept into a smooth bun at the nape, she had a natural, earthy appeal that transcended mere beauty. It was almost perfection.

He pulled his thoughts up short, then forced himself to remember who and what she was. Perfection? No, she was just another whore raising an unwanted child in a saloon, and he should remember that.

"I asked what you're doing in here," he said, his voice harsh as he shoved away unwelcome memories from his own childhood.

He could see she was afraid of him, but she didn't back down. She stood her ground. He had to give her that.

"I'll be doing the work Miss Blanche gave me to do." Her chin lifted a notch. "If it be any concern of yours, sir."

"Mary is right, Sheriff," Blanche said from the doorway. "It *isn't* any of your concern."

He turned around.

"Is this what you do in your spare time?" the madam asked with a raised eyebrow. "Badger my employees?"

"I just thought—.,

"I'm sure I know what you thought," she interrupted.

From the look in her eye, he was afraid she *did* know what he'd been thinking, and not about what Mary was doing in this office either. He was afraid Blanche knew the more carnal thoughts he'd been entertaining about the Irish miss. And he didn't much like her knowing it either.

"Well, if it *was* any of your business, Sheriff, I'd remind you I've employed Mrs. Malone to see to my bookkeeping."

"Your bookkeeping?" Carson couldn't help the tone of disbelief in those words as he turned toward Mary once again.

She blushed scarlet, but there was real anger in her eyes, her fear of him apparently forgotten. "And you'd be thinking I'm not smart enough for bookkeeping, would ya now?"

"No I—"

"Is it because I'm Irish that you feel this way, or just because I'm a woman? I'm thinking that either reason would make you a fool, Sheriff Barclay."

Carson was saved from the need to reply by the child's sudden wail, brought on, no doubt, by his mother's raised voice. Mary immediately turned and whisked the little boy into her arms, murmuring words of comfort while keeping her back toward Carson and Blanche.

The madam chuckled as she entered the office and walked over to her desk. When she looked at him again, she smiled and said, "I think Mrs. Malone put that quite well. Don't you, Sheriff Barclay?"

For her part, Mary thought she'd said far too much. She couldn't believe she'd actually challenged the sheriff. Whatever had possessed her to shout at him? The law, of all men.

Sure and it was her temper that had always been her undoing.

What am I goin' t' do with you, Mary Emeline? It was like she could still hear her dear departed mother's gentle scolding. Will ya be fightin' like your fool brothers all your life, then? Why don't you use the sense

44

God gave you instead? I'm thinkin' that'd be the better way altogether.

Mary realized Keary had stopped his fussing and the room had grown silent. Drawing a deep breath, she turned toward Blanche and Carson Barclay.

The sheriff removed his hat, then with one hand smoothed back his thick brown hair, hair that was streaked with gold, as if kissed by the sun. "I owe you an apology, Mrs. Malone."

Edith was right. He *did* have the bluest eyes Mary had ever seen. Strange that she hadn't noticed them before. And those blue eyes seemed capable of staring right into her most secret thoughts.

"'Tis sorry I am, too," she whispered.

For a breathless moment, their gazes held. Mary couldn't have looked away to save her soul. As the seconds passed, she felt a shiver—something akin to fear but very different at the same time—run up her spine.

It was the sheriff who broke the glance. "Miss Blanche, I came to ask about John."

Mary drew a breath at last, the odd spell broken. Without a word, she headed for the door, desperate to escape.

Blanche's voice stopped her. "You needn't go, Mary."

She sighed inwardly, then turned. She avoided looking at Carson. "'Tis a bit of fresh air we'd be needing, mum. I'm thinking the lad might sleep a wee bit after."

"All right. Come back here when you're finished with your walk. Keary can nap on my sofa. And Mary, stay within sight of the saloon. You're still a stranger here. This town's got a few bad apples like any other."

Mary nodded, then left the office. She was reminded of the forced composure she'd worn as she'd fled the

45

Kenrick mansion. She'd felt anything *but* serene then, and it was the same now.

Sheriff Barclay was a threat to everything she held dear—her son, her very freedom. He didn't like her, didn't trust her. For that alone, he would watch her more closely. But there was something else about the way he looked at her, something about the way she responded inside herself to that look, that disturbed her most of all.

Mary followed a path to the river and made her way across on the bridge. Once on the opposite side, she carried Keary a safe distance from the water, then put the boy down in the long yellowgreen grass. He giggled in delight.

"Oh, Keary," she whispered as she sank to the ground beside him. "Whatever will become of you if I'm found out? I swore I'd give you the life you deserve, and see what it is I've done, then."

She thought of the sheriff's blue eyes, of the way they'd held her captive. What if he *could* see into her soul? What if he guessed what she'd done? She would hang for it, and then what would become of Keary?

'Tis a man who is his own ruin, Fagan Malone used to say to his sons and daughter. 'Tis a wedge from itself that splits the oak tree.

"Aye, Da," she replied, as if he'd spoken to her now, "I'll be keeping meself far from the sheriff. That I will."

Portia Pendergast Kenrick was not a foolish woman. She knew her husband did not love her. She did not pretend he had ever loved her. She knew Winston had married the plain, plump spinster for the Pendergast fortune just as Portia had married a feckless man ten years younger than herself for his good looks and the

46

society doors the Kenrick name could open for her.

She also knew Winston had never been a faithful husband. His conquests had ranged from other society matrons to scullery maids in her and Winston's several residences. But, to his credit, he'd had the good sense to be discreet in his many dalliances. He had certainly never flaunted them before his wife. Of course, Portia was wise enough to have kept Winston on a rather short leash all these years, an easy enough task when she and she alone controlled the purse strings to the wealth of Pendergast Industries. Knowing his wife could cut him off without a penny had kept Winston from being careless, Portia was sure.

Twenty-four years after Portia and Winston had wed, she thought her husband was still a handsome man. As he'd aged, he seemed to grow even more distinguished in appearance. She rather liked the tiny lines at the corners of his eyes and mouth. She approved of the mustache he'd grown more than fifteen years before, and she was especially fond of his silver gray hair.

But she couldn't see his silver hair now. Not with his head wrapped in white bandages.

"I still believe we should allow the police to handle the matter, Winston." She was seated on a chair beside his bed, watching him as he sipped tea from one of Portia's prized china cups.

"No!" He winced, jostling tea into the saucer, then closed his eyes. More softly, he continued, "This is a matter of pride, my dear. The girl didn't just strike me. She stole the only thing of sentimental value I have from my father."

Portia raised an eyebrow. Winston was not, nor had he ever been, a sentimental man. However, the ornate cigar box, finely crafted in silver, had sat on his desk

47

throughout their marriage. She supposed there could be a grain of truth in what he said.

"I have hired a private investigator to help in the search," Winston continued, teeth clenched. "I *will* find the girl, and she *will* pay for this."

Portia sighed. "I rather liked Mary. She always worked hard, and she never caused a moment of trouble."

"I told you we shouldn't ever hire Irish. You can't trust them. They're all thieves."

"Yes, you have said that, Winston." She rose from the chair, leaned over, and kissed his forehead. "But we would have less trouble with our Irish housemaids if you weren't so intent on getting into their skirts."

She smiled as she took the teacup and saucer from his hands, then left his bedchamber without another word.

Five

Sunday, 24 July 1898
Whistle Creek, Idaho

Dear Inga,
As you will be seeing from this post, Keary and I have left New York, and there is no sorrow in the telling of it. We traveled far across the country to Idaho, and I have found employment with a woman named Blanche Loraine. Miss Blanche, as she is known, has enjoyed much success, but I cannot say everyone in this town is holding her in as high regard as I do.

It is not within me to be telling you the reason for our leaving New York City. I can only say it

48

was a dark day that forced our going. My da always said it is well misfortunes come one by one and not all together, and to that, I would add my own amen.

But be that as it may, Keary and I are here, and I am thinking I will do well in Whistle Creek. And for that I owe thanks to my mother's insistence that I study my numbers and letters. The truth is, I am not working as a housemaid as I have always been doing in the past. It is a bookkeeper I am. Fancy that, would you now.

Keary and I attended the local church this morning. It was nothing like our long Presbyterian services in Ireland nor much like those in New York City, for that matter. The minister comes to Whistle Creek but once a month, this being only one of the churches he ministers to. Today it was the gentleman who owns the mercantile, Mr. Adams, who led the worship service. I cannot say I was sorry when it was over. Mr. Adams is not what I would call a stirring speaker.

Until this morning, I had met only the men and women who work for Miss Blanche in her business. Oh, and the sheriff of Whistle Creek. I have made his acquaintance, too. Sheriff Barclay is a handsome man, much taller than Seamus Maguire, but none too friendly. Which is not of great concern to me as I am content to keep to myself and have no interest in him at all.

It is the letters I receive from you and Beth, my dearest friends, that mean the most to me, so I beg you to write to me here in Idaho. I have kept all the letters you both have written to me since we

*arrived in America. I often take them out and read
them again, trying to picture your life with Mr.
Bridger and Beth's with Mr. Steele.*

*Today being the Sabbath and my day of rest, I
have decided to take Keary on a picnic. The town
is surrounded by beautiful mountains, and today I
mean to be doing some exploring in them.*

From your affectionate friend,
Mary Emeline Malone

Carson let the dun gelding have his head. Cinnabar
knew his way up the narrow trail. The two of them
traveled it every Sunday afternoon during good weather.
A quarter mile or so up the trail was Carson's cabin. He
hadn't lived in it for several years, preferring to stay in
the room above the jail so he would be close when
needed in town. Still, he liked knowing the log house
was there.

But he wasn't thinking about his destination as he
rode. He was thinking about Mary Malone.

She'd come to Sunday services this morning. Carson
couldn't remember ever feeling so much tension in
church before. Heads craning. Furtive whispers.
Unspoken indignation.

Gossip traveled fast in a small town. Everyone knew
the Malone woman had come to Whistle Creek with
the infamous madam, that Mary and her baby were
living at the Painted Lady, that Mary was *working* there.
And the good people who attended the community
church knew just what sort of *work* went on in that den
of iniquity.

Carson figured it was only because they'd all been so
shocked that no one had gone over and demanded Mary
leave. No, not just shocked. Aghast and appalled might

50

be better words to describe their feelings. After all, none of Miss Blanche's girls had ever before entered the Whistle Creek Community Church, let alone sat down and participated in the worship service.

Carson hadn't paid much attention to Chuck Adams's dull preaching. He'd been too aware of Mary, sitting two pews behind him, and of the growing outrage of the other parishioners. He'd felt the urge to tell them that she was just the bookkeeper at the Painted Lady, but even if he had, no one would have believed it. Shoot! He wasn't sure he believed it. Beside, even if it was true, she still lived in that saloon, she still exposed her son to everything that went on there. What sort of mother did that?

His jaw tightened reflexively at the thought. He knew what sort of mother did that.

Ain't he cute, Harrison? He may be just a little bastard, but even I've got to admit, he's cute. All right, Car. Get on outta here now. You can see Aldora's got company. Find yourself something to do and stay outta trouble.

Stay out of trouble . . .

That hadn't been easy for a kid who didn't have a father, a kid who didn't have a last name to call his own, a kid who lived in a saloon instead of a house like all the other kids. When Carson was in school, he'd gotten into a fight with somebody at least once a week. Aldora hadn't cared about the fighting, as long as he didn't come home sniveling or bleeding all over her nice things. What she'd meant was for him to stay out of her way, for him not to cause *her* any trouble.

He shook off the disturbing memories just as the trail suddenly spilled into a small round valley. Near the clear-running stream cutting through the heart of the

51

meadowland stood the log cabin Carson had built with his own hands back in the fall of ninety-two, before the first snows fell.

And seated on the grassy bank of the stream, not far from the house, was Mary Malone, nursing her son. Her head was tipped to one side and forward as she stared down at Keary. Even from this distance, Carson could see the look of tender devotion on her face.

He reined in, stopping his gelding. At the same moment, Mary noticed him. She quickly grabbed a small blanket and tossed it over both the child and her shoulder, but not before Carson caught a glimpse of her exposed breast.

It wasn't lust he felt at the sight. It was something quite different. There was a poignancy about the scene that went straight to his typically cynical heart.

He clucked at his horse and rode toward the woman who had intruded on his private valley.

Her face was flushed, her eyes downcast. As he drew closer, he could sense her discomfort. Perversely, he was pleased if he'd caused her to be flustered. It was nothing less than what she'd done to him ever since her arrival in Whistle Creek.

"Afternoon, Mrs. Malone," he said as he stopped his horse a second time.

She didn't look up. "Good afternoon, sir." She barely whispered the greeting as even more heat flared in her cheeks.

"What brings you to my little valley?"

"'Tis yours?"

"Yeah." He dismounted, then stood near the dun's head. "I built that cabin when I first came to Whistle Creek."

"'Tis a fine house. But I did not go in." Finally, she

lifted her eyes to meet his. "I swear to you, on me ma's grave, that I was not trespassing in your house."

Carson experienced a twinge of guilt. "Wouldn't have mattered if you did. Nothing much there." Keary shoved at the blanket covering him, and Mary quickly turned her back toward Carson. A moment later, while his mother was closing the buttons of her bodice, the toddler made his way toward Carson, his steps uncertain on the uneven turf. His eyes were wide with curiosity, and he was grinning.

"Faith and begorra," Mary muttered as she started to rise but was impeded by her tangle of skirts and petticoats. "Keary, come back here."

Instead of stopping at his mother's command, the little boy giggled and tried to walk faster. He stumbled and pitched forward at Carson's feet. Instinctively, Carson reached for him.

"Hello there, little man. Moving too fast for your legs, huh?"

Keary's grin disappeared, but he didn't seem to be afraid of the stranger holding him. Instead, the boy studied the man with solemn brown eyes, as if not quite sure what to make of him.

"Here," Mary said as she hurried toward Carson. "Here. I'll be taking him now."

Carson frowned as he moved his gaze from son to mother. "I wasn't going to hurt him."

"Please, sir." Her voice was fearful. Her eyes beseeched him. She held out her arms in an almost desperate gesture. "Let me be having me son, and we'll be on our way. I was never meaning to trespass on your land."

Keary patted Carson's cheek with his right hand and giggled again. Carson glanced at the tyke and felt himself smiling in response to the boy's grin.

"Please, sir. I'm begging you."

"You don't have to beg, Mrs. Malone," he answered sharply, irritated by her choice of words. He passed the child into her waiting arms.

But his irritation vanished when he saw the stark relief on her lovely face. There was no doubting that she loved her son. Whatever else he might think about her, he couldn't charge her with lack of motherly love.

He took a deep breath, then said, "You don't have to run off either. You weren't trespassing." He noticed the basket and the food set on a cloth. "Looks like you were having a picnic."

"Aye."

"Then maybe you'd let me join you, Mrs. Malone?"

"I'm thinking you shouldn't be seen with the likes o' me. 'Twould only cause more talk." She turned and walked toward her basket and picnic lunch.

So, she hadn't been oblivious to the stares and whispers in church.

"Mrs. Malone, now I'm inviting you. Please stay. I wouldn't mind some company. And, if you've got any to spare, I'd like some of that cheese and bread I see there."

He figured she couldn't be any more surprised by his words than he was. He didn't know why he wanted her to stay. He just knew that he did.

Mary pondered the sheriff's request. It would be a foolish thing to do, and she knew it. The law could even now be looking for her. Even with three thousand miles between her and the Kenrick home, she knew she wasn't completely safe. Not when the man she'd killed was as wealthy and powerful as Winston Kenrick. She should stay as far away from this man as she could possibly get. The less she was known, the less she was seen, then the less likely she was to be discovered.

She turned to face him, intending to bid him a polite but firm good afternoon before taking her leave. But for some reason, the words died in her throat.

Carson had removed his hat and was watching her with those startling blue eyes of his. She felt the uncomfortable urge to touch his cheek just as her son had done moments before, if only to see if it was rough or smooth.

"I'm supposing it wouldn't hurt to share a bite to eat with you, Sheriff," she said softly.

"Thank you." He led his horse to a nearby maple and looped the reins over a limb.

Keary squirmed in her arms, eager to be on the ground and exploring. Mary obliged.

It amazed her, watching her son as he tottered on his chubby little legs, how quickly he had gone from crawling to walking. But then he was always growing and changing. It seemed only yesterday that he'd been a wee babe in her arms, just under five pounds and the doctor thinking he wouldn't live out the week. Now he was getting too heavy to carry for long, and a healthier lad Mary couldn't imagine.

"How old is he?" Carson asked as he stepped up beside her.

"Almost a year, just," she answered, her gaze still on her adventurous son. Keary was giving a yellow wildflower a close inspection.

"He looks like you, Mrs. Malone."

"Aye, there's little of his father in him." *And thanks be to God for that small blessing*, she thought.

"When did you lose your husband?"

My husband. She glanced sideways at the sheriff. To him and everyone else in Whistle Creek, she was Mrs.

55

Malone. She supposed it wasn't such a terrible lie, as lies went, although she tried not to add to it. "His da was killed in the coal mines of Virginia." That, at least, was the truth.

"I'm sorry."

She acknowledged his sympathy with a nod. "The worst of the hurt is over, and 'twould change nothing to dwell on it."

It was true. The worst was over. And besides, the pain of Seamus Maguire's death had been nothing compared to learning of his death from his American wife. Seamus had lain with Mary in his quarters above the stables of the Wellington estate. He'd convinced her that to marry in America would be better but that to wait to share the warmth and comfort of each other's bodies was unnecessary. Aye, he'd been a smooth talker, was Seamus Maguire. So he'd taken her to his bed and he'd planted his seed in her womb while promising her a better life in America. Then he'd sailed away with never any intention of sending for her, although she knew it not. If Seamus hadn't left her pregnant, Mary would still be in England, wondering why she'd never heard from him again. She wouldn't have known he'd played her for the fool she was and betrayed her heart in the bargain.

"You're lucky to have your son."

Mary smiled for there was no arguing with the truth. "Aye, I am that."

She went after Keary as he toddled closer to the gurgling brook. When she turned around, she found that Carson was reclining on the grass near her basket, his long legs stretched out before him, his elbows supporting his torso. His black felt hat lay on the ground near his feet. He made an altogether disturbing picture. Too relaxed. Too handsome. Too male. Too . . . virile.

As if she'd ever again be fool enough to fall for a man's charms!

"Mind if I just help myself?" he asked.

"No, sir."

Carson sat up, then cut off a chunk of cheese with a knife she'd brought with her. "I sure wish you'd quit calling me sir. Makes me feel like an old man."

He looked anything *but* old, she thought before asking, "What would you have me be calling you, then?"

"How about Carson?"

She stiffened. "I'm thinking that would be too familiar altogether, sir."

He smiled as he shook his head. "Then I suppose Sheriff Barclay will have to do."

Mary didn't think she was going to like that much better. It would be a constant reminder of his office and what it could mean to her freedom. Still, there seemed nothing else to do except agree with him. "Aye, that will do."

"Tell me, Mrs. Malone, why'd you come to Whistle Creek? I mean, besides because Miss Blanche offered you a job at the Painted Lady."

She almost told him she hoped to find her brother here, then came to her senses before she spoke. The less Sheriff Barclay knew about her, she realized, the better it would be. The better and the safer.

She gave her shoulders a careless shrug. "Fate, I'm thinking. Nothing more."

He didn't reply. In fact, he seemed to be waiting for her to continue. There was something about the way his eyes watched her that made it difficult not to tell him whatever he wanted to know.

In order to resist the urge, she said, "Tell me something about the mine. Are there many who work there?"

"Yeah." He cut himself another chunk of cheese. "The Lucky Lady's got about three hundred or so miners. 'Course, there's bigger operations up here in the Panhandle. These hills are full of gold and silver and other ores. There must be thousands of miners in these parts."

Thousands? How was she to find Quaid when she was afraid to ask help of anyone?

Carson continued, "I guess if your husband was a coal miner, you've lived around mines before."

"No. In England, me husband"—the lie was becoming easier to tell—"worked in the stables, though he'd done some mining before I left Ireland and joined him there."

She was distracted by Keary again, this time as he scurried toward the sheriff's horse, arms flapping at his sides for balance. She ran after him, catching him up beneath his arms and whirling him around in the air.

"Sure and 'tis into mischief you are, Keary Maguire Malone."

After she stopped and put him back on his feet, facing away from the horse, she glanced in Carson's direction. He was standing again. Standing and watching her with that piercing gaze of his. She was held captive by the look, afraid to move or even to breathe.

Finally, he said, "You're a riddle, Mrs. Malone."

"I wouldn't be knowing what you mean, sir."

He stepped toward her, hat in hand. "I mean, you're not the sort of woman who should be working in a place like the Painted Lady. That's not the proper place to

58

raise a child, and you must know it."

Her temper flared. "Would you be saying I'm not a good mother, then? For I'll have you know there's nothing I wouldn't do for me Keary." *Even murder*, she finished silently.

"No," he said, his voice deep and low, "that's not what I'm saying. I can see you're a good mother. And that's why I said you're a riddle."

Her heart was racing. She felt starved for air. Fear tangled with anger. She didn't know what to say to him. He frightened her, yet there was something that made her want to draw closer to him, made her want . . . made her want . . .

"I'm thinking I'd better be getting back to town. Good day to you, Sheriff."

Mary grabbed her son, balancing him on one hip while she hastily retrieved the remainder of her picnic, dropping food and cloth into the basket. Then, without another glance in the sheriff's direction, she walked away with as much dignity as she could muster.

Six

THERE WERE TIMES MARY THOUGHT God—in devising her miraculous escape from New York and sending her to Idaho to find Quaid—had made one grievous error. She was *not* meant to be a bookkeeper.

No matter what she tried, Mary could *not* make the figures in the Painted Lady ledgers add up. Her da had often said his only daughter had more brains and good sense than all his sons put together. She'd taken enormous pride in the compliment. But at the moment she felt nothing short of daft.

She rose and arched her back, stretching the taut muscles in her shoulders and neck. Then she glanced toward the corner where, moments before, Keary had been playing with pots from the kitchen. Only now he was fast asleep on the floor.

"And isn't that always the way of it?" Mary whispered, thinking how wonderful it must be to fall asleep so easily. But Keary was a mere infant, free from guilt, while Mary had much to feel guilty about.

Last night before bed, feeling lost and more than a little lonely, she'd searched through her meager belongings for an old photograph of her parents and brothers. She'd needed a glimpse of a happier time, a time when she was still innocent and carefree. But instead of the photograph, her fingers had touched the ornate silver box she'd taken from Winston Kenrick's office.

Why did I keep it *all* this time? she wondered now.

She walked over to the window and stared through the glass without really seeing.

Why don't I just throw it away?

She'd awakened twice in the night, her nightgown damp with perspiration, her nightmares lingering even in wakefulness. She'd been tormented by the images from her dreams. She was tormented still.

Laughter filtered through the window and into her dark thoughts, bringing her back to the present. A moment later, Edith came into view, soon followed by John.

Youthful joy brightened Edith's face as she turned to face her pursuer. She said something to John. He blushed scarlet. She touched his useless right arm, her expression suddenly sober. He flinched as if she'd

60

slapped him, but she didn't let him pull away. Instead, she stepped closer, rose on tiptoe, and kissed him full on the mouth. John stood as stiff as a board.

Even from here, Mary could feel the young man's pain. She thought she understood the shame he felt. Her heart ached for him, but she also hoped he would discover happiness. Perhaps Edith could help him find it.

She turned from the window. It felt wrong to be watching the two young people, even unobtrusively.

As she returned to the desk, Mary thought of Sheriff Barclay. He had cared enough about John to try to help him. It would seem the sheriff was a kind man, not given to abusing the authority he had by virtue of his badge.

But the image that came suddenly to mind was of the Carson she'd seen yesterday. She pictured him in that meadow near the stream and the log house. She pictured him reclining on the grassy ground, leaning on his elbows, his legs stretched out before him, his head bare and his hair mussed from the black hat he usually wore.

That memory was more disturbing than her nightmares had been.

Just as she regained her seat behind the desk, the office door opened and Blanche stepped into the room, carrying an armload of colorful gowns. She smiled as their gazes met.

"I've a surprise for you, Mary."

"A surprise?"

"Yes. I've decided to take stock of all of my possessions, and it seems I have more gowns than any ten women could possibly use. I thought some of these might do well for you. They would have to be altered, of course." Blanche laid them, one by one, over the back of the sofa.

Mary stared at the gowns—made from silk, satin, linen, crepe de chine, and velvet—and shook her head. "Faith but I'd never be able to wear anything so fine as those."

"Why not?"

"Because I . . . Well, I just couldn't, mum."

"Aha. It's because you don't think you're good enough. Is that it? It certainly isn't because they're not appropriately modest. Look at these high necklines. No, you think because you were a maid, always taking care of some English lady and her fancy clothes, that you're not good enough to wear the same things." Blanche picked up a deep blue satin gown with puffed sleeves and all sorts of draping around the skirt. "Well, you can just put such nonsense out of that pretty little head of yours. It's . . . what do the Irish call it?"

"Blarney?"

Blanche grinned. "That's it! It's blarney."

Mary couldn't help smiling in return. "'Tis kind you are to me altogether, Miss Blanche, and I thank you for the offer. But I'm thinking I shouldn't be taking your gowns. They're too fine to be worn while I sit in this office, scribbling in your books. Who's to see what I'm wearing but me son? And he cares not at all."

"Where is it written you can't look nice while you do the most wearisome tasks?" Blanche's smile vanished. "You're pretty and you're young, Mary. Grab every minute you can. You don't know how many days are left to you. None of us do."

The last of Mary's objections died unspoken. She hadn't the heart to refuse. The woman had been too kind for Mary not to repay her in any way she could.

"If it means so much to you, mum," she replied as she took the shimmery blue gown from Blanche's hands.

"Try it on and let's see how much it'll have to be taken in. I used to weigh a good deal more than I do now, and I'm at least three inches taller than you. But Mrs. Wooster is an excellent seamstress. She's got the dress and millinery shop next door to the mercantile. I expect you met her at church. She'll be able to make it fit in no time."

Mary ran the fingers of one hand lightly over the fabric, feeling the rich texture of it. "'Tis truly too fine."

Blanche cupped Mary's chin in her right hand, tilting her face upward so their gazes would meet again. "My dear Mary Malone, let me tell you how different things appear when you're looking back on life instead of forward. The world is great for trying to make some folks feel better about themselves than those they're trying to keep down. Don't believe it, honey." She paused and lowered her hand, then gave her head a slow shake. "You've got just as much right to wear fancy clothes as the next woman. No more and no less."

As if disturbed by her torrent of words, Blanche moved away from Mary. She pretended to look through the other dresses on the sofa.

Mary heard a sound that was suspiciously similar to a sniff. She decided it would be best to talk about something else. "Would you be ready to hear what I've found in your books I've been going through?"

Blanche sniffed again, then faced Mary. "Naturally."

"I'd have you be knowing I'm not sure there's been any wrongdoing, but it seems to me the entries are not altogether honest in the writing of them."

"Show me."

Mary carefully laid the satin gown aside, and the two

women turned their attention to ledger entries made by Lloyd Perkins.

The chair squeaked noisily as Carson leaned back and put his feet up on his desk. Showing a nonchalance he didn't feel, he laced his fingers together behind his head. "What brings you over from Spokane, Halligan?" He knew the answer wouldn't be good.

Standing in front of the sheriff's desk, Bryan Halligan looked every inch the wealthy mine owner, from the cut of his expensive suit to the gold watch and fob in his vest. He was as tall as Carson, but he weighed forty or fifty pounds more. A man in his thirties, Halligan sported a close-trimmed beard and mustache, sprinkled with gray now, like what was left of the hair on his head.

"There have been rumors of trouble out at the mine," he answered. "I'd like you to look into it."

"Seems to me last time there was trouble out at the Lucky Lady, you told me to stay out of it."

Halligan cleared his throat. "Perhaps I was a bit hasty. But we *did* handle that. This is different."

"Different how?" Carson slid his feet off the desk and sat up straight, ready to take the matter seriously.

"There have been threats to blow up some of the tunnels."

"Why?"

Halligan waved his hand in dismissal. "The usual complaints. Equipment. Wages. Work hours. You know these miners. They'll grumble about anything. Most of them are immigrants. Irish. Swedes. You know."

Yeah, he knew. He knew that Halligan kept as much money as he could for himself and his partners and put little of the profits back into mine safety, let alone into

64

decent wages or decent equipment or decent housing.

"I was hoping you might visit the mine, talk with the men there, see if you can figure out what they're planning. You've got a good reputation with them. They trust you. They treat you like you're almost one of them."

Carson briefly recalled the one time he'd gone down in a mine. That had been in Silver City many years ago. He remembered all too well the unbelievable heat. The lower he'd gone, the hotter it got, and he'd understood why hard rock miners stripped to their trousers and boots before riding the elevator cage down at the start of their shifts.

There had been nothing good about that experience. Only absolute darkness such as he'd never seen before or since and an endless maze of narrow tunnels and stopes. It had been his worst nightmare come true—ten times worse than Aldora's attic—and Carson had sworn he would never go down in a mine again. Not for any reason. Not even to save his soul. He'd kept that oath to this day.

Meeting Halligan's gaze once more, he said, "I don't plan on ruining their trust by spying on them." He rose to his feet. "But I'll do what it takes to maintain order in this town. I'll find out what I can."

"I knew I could count on you, Sheriff Barclay. I don't need to tell you what that mine means to the people of Whistle Creek. Without it, this place wouldn't exist."

It was a threat of sorts, and Carson didn't take to threats, especially from Halligan. He was about to say so when the door opened, and Blanche Loraine swept into the office, bringing a reluctant-looking Mary along with her. They came to an abrupt halt when Blanche saw Halligan.

"Afternoon, Miss Blanche," Carson said even as he took note of the way her eyes narrowed in dislike at the sight of the mine owner.

Halligan, on the other hand, was wearing a much different sort of expression as he stared at Mary. "Yes, good day, Miss Blanche." A blind man could have seen he was waiting for an introduction.

Blanche ignored him. "Sheriff Barclay, I must speak with you about a matter of some importance. But I can come back when you're free."

"It's all right," he replied. "Mr. Halligan was just leaving. Our business is finished."

Halligan stepped toward the door—and Mary. "Yes, I was leaving. But I cannot do so until I meet this charming young woman."

"This is *Mrs.* Malone, my bookkeeper."

"Your bookkeeper?" Halligan took hold of Mary's hand and raised it to his lips. "Well, *Mrs.* Malone, I'm delighted to meet you."

Carson decided it would be a poor example of keeping the peace if he were to knock Halligan's head against the wall a half dozen times.

"And since no one seems inclined to make the proper introductions for us," the man continued, leaning closer to Mary, "I am Bryan Halligan, one of the owners of the Lucky Lady Mine. Does your husband work there, Mrs. Malone?"

"'Tis just me and me son, Mr. Halligan."

He smiled. "Ah. A shame. Well, perhaps I will find more reasons to visit Whistle Creek now that you are here." With a jaunty motion, he placed his hat back on his balding head and left.

As soon as the door closed, Blanche said, "You stay away from him, Mary. He's bad news."

But Mary didn't need to be told that. She'd once known a man who'd had the same soulless eyes as this Halligan. In fact, she'd killed him.

The memory of that horrible morning in Winston Kenrick's office washed over her unexpectedly. Her knees felt like rubber. Her throat seemed to close, cutting off her air.

Since her flight from New York, Mary had been mostly successful in distancing herself from the terrible deed itself. She had closed her mind to those dreadful images, mentally acknowledging that she had committed a crime without letting herself remember the particulars. But today she couldn't seem to stop the memories. She seemed to feel Kenrick's hands on her skin. Her heart raced now as it had then. She could smell both his lust and her own fear. She could hear the awful sound of metal meeting flesh and bone, the thump of a body striking the floor.

May God forgive me. I've killed a man. May God forgive me.

"Sheriff, Mary has discovered some serious discrepancies in my records that can only mean one thing. Lloyd has been stealing money in my absence."

It was Blanche's voice that drew Mary back from the edge of despair. In that instant, she remem bered her son. Keary depended upon her. He needed her. She had to be strong. She could not let herself be buried under guilt, no matter what gruesome thing she had done. All her life, she would be forced to live with her sin, but for Keary, she must rise above it. He was all that mattered. Nothing else.

Mary glanced toward the sheriff and was relieved to see he wasn't watching her. If he had been, she was sure he would have guessed the truth about her, for she knew her guilt had been written on her face only a moment before.

Carson frowned at Blanche. "That's a mighty serious charge." His gaze shifted to Mary. "Are you certain?"

Mary wished she'd never told Blanche what she'd discovered. She never should have drawn the sheriff's attention to herself like this. She never should have gotten involved.

She looked at Blanche and knew immediately that she couldn't have done anything differently. This woman had saved Mary and Keary back in New York City. Blanche had voluntarily placed herself in danger for a complete stranger. Mary owed her too much to not help her now.

"Aye." Mary nodded as she met the sheriff's gaze again. "I am that."

"How much has he taken?"

Blanche answered him. "At least four thousand dollars."

Carson whistled softly. "Four thousand? In six months?" He raised one eyebrow. "That would've put anyone else clean out of business."

"I'm not anyone else."

"No, Miss Blanche, you're sure not."

Mary had heard this sort of talk between them before, and it confused her. She wasn't sure if they disliked each other or not.

Blanche placed her ledger on Carson's desk. "Here is the proof, Sheriff. I have no intention of leaving this here, so I suggest you study it now. Then I want Lloyd arrested."

Carson looked at Mary again, his blue eyes serious and searching. "Care to show me what you found?" He motioned for her to come around to his side of the desk.

Mary saw no way to avoid doing as he requested, although the last thing she wanted was to stand close to

68

Carson Barclay. He made her too nervous. He represented the law, and Mary was a lawbreaker, a murderess.

She drew a deep breath and stiffened her spine with determination, then moved to stand beside him.

"Show me," he said, his voice low but commanding.

Her throat went dry. She swallowed, trying not to move away from him as all her instincts commanded her to do. Instead, she flipped through several pages to the first suspicious entry. "'Tis here I found the first error."

"Could it be just an error, Mrs. Malone?" he asked. "Could Lloyd have only made a mistake?"

She pointed to a column of numbers. "I'm thinking not."

He turned his head. She did the same. Their gazes collided. Her breath caught in her chest, and for a moment, she forgot why she was here or that she should be wary of him because he was the sheriff. For a moment, she was aware of him in a very feminine, much more personal way.

"Could you have made a mistake, Mrs. Malone?" he asked, his voice even softer than before, almost gentle.

She wanted to feel insulted by the question, but indignation wouldn't surface. She should have at least remained afraid and wary, especially with him standing so close. Especially with him staring at her with those blue eyes of his. "If you're asking if I know what it is I'm doing, then I'll be telling you I have a fine head for numbers, Sheriff Barclay. 'Tis why Miss Blanche hired me, I'm thinking. But 'twould take no genius to see what was done here." She took a quick breath, then said as forcefully as she could, "If you would be looking at what's before you, you'd be seeing it for yourself."

She thought she would wilt with relief when he

69

finally turned his gaze from her to the book on his desk. And now that his attention had turned where it should, she was free to put some distance between them. She moved around the desk to stand beside Blanche.

It was a long while before the sheriff straightened, a frown creasing his forehead. "I see Mrs. Malone's point. This wasn't a simple mistake."

"So you'll arrest him?" Blanche asked.

"Yeah, I'll head over there right now."

"Good." The woman retrieved the ledger from the desk. "Sheriff, I trusted Lloyd. We go back a long way." Her voice broke. She paused and swallowed hard. When she continued, her voice had deepened. "I've paid him handsomely over the years. I never thought he would do something like this to me."

"The quest for money can make people do strange things, Miss Blanche." His gaze darted to Mary and lingered briefly, then returned to Blanche. "It's one of the things that keeps both you and me in business."

He didn't wait for a reply. He rounded his desk and strode across the office where he grabbed his hat off the peg on the wall. Then he opened the door and left without a backward glance.

Mary suspected his cryptic last words had been as much for her as for Blanche. She just wasn't sure what he'd meant by them. Did he suspect her of wrongdoing? Did he even now know who she was and what she had done back in New York City? Would she soon find herself in one of those jail cells?

"Well, come along, Mary. This unpleasant task is done."

Wordlessly, relieved and yet not relieved, Mary nodded, then followed Blanche out of the sheriff's office.

Late that night, with an angry Lloyd Perkins cooling his heels in a cell downstairs, Carson turned out the lamp and lay down on his bed. He didn't close his eyes right off. He'd always needed a few minutes to get accustomed to the dark. He'd learned the trick as a young boy. Once he felt comfortable with his surroundings, the sense of suffocating would diminish, the walls wouldn't seem to be closing in on him. Then and only then would he be ready to sleep.

But maybe his dread of tight places wasn't what was keeping him awake tonight. Maybe it was Mary Malone.

It wasn't just her sensual beauty or his physical reaction to it. He'd known beautiful women before. He'd known desire before. This was different.

No, it had more to do with the way she looked at him, an underlying sense of fear that seemed to emanate from her. He wanted to know why she was afraid. He wanted to know why she'd come to Whistle Creek, why she'd chosen to live with her son in that saloon. This wasn't a woman who sold her body for money. Not for any reason. This was a woman who chose to go to church on Sunday, even when others shunned her. This was a woman who loved her child.

He closed his eyes now and remembered the sweetness of her lilac cologne. The fragrance had lingered in his nostrils long after he'd stepped away from her this afternoon, long after he'd brought his prisoner back to jail. In fact, it seemed to be lingering still. He also remembered the tiny fishhook curls that bordered her nape, the enticing curve of her neck, the way she held herself erect and proud, the lyrical sound of her voice, the soft pink color of her mouth.

He'd never had a woman take control of his thoughts before. Not like this. He wasn't sure what to do about it.

He wasn't sure he *wanted* to do anything about it.

He wished David Hailey were still alive. His old mentor would have understood, would have known what Carson should do. Sheriff Hailey had been the wisest, kindest, most honorable man it had ever been Carson's good fortune to know. David had also loved and adored his wife, Claudia; he would never have been unfaithful to her, would never have done anything to hurt her. Carson had always thought love like that was a rarity. Perhaps it was because he'd seen too many husbands visiting the rooms above Aldora's dance hall when he was a boy. He'd always known love and marriage weren't in his future.

He opened his eyes and stared at the ceiling. The imprudent direction of his thoughts was getting absurd. He hardly knew the widow Malone. He didn't care if she was the most beautiful woman to ever waltz into Whistle Creek. He wasn't crazy enough to think his attraction to her would ever amount to more than physical desire.

For a moment, Carson was sorry she was only the bookkeeper at the Painted Lady. If she was otherwise employed there, he'd be able to pay for a private visit to her room and he could get her out of his system, once and for all.

But since that wasn't an option, he guessed he'd just have to lie here and stare at the ceiling instead.

Seven

MARY AND KEARY HAD EATEN BREAKFAST ALONE every morning since arriving in Whistle Creek. Therefore, Mary was surprised when she entered the kitchen the morning after Lloyd's arrest to find John seated at the table, sipping a cup of Greta's strong coffee.

"Good morning to you, Mr. Tyrell," Mary greeted him as she settled Keary into the high chair Blanche had purchased at the mercantile.

"Morning."

She looked at him, noting the changes a few days of sobriety had wrought. Although she hadn't seen John at his worst, she knew there was a clarity in his eyes that hadn't been there before. He carried himself with more confidence, and he wasn't so quick to turn the scarred side of his face away when he was speaking to someone. Mary thought Edith had contributed much to the transformation in this young man.

"And how is it you're finding yourself this fine day?"

He ignored her question and asked one of his own. "Is it true Lloyd was stealing from Miss Blanche?"

"Aye, 'tis true." Mary walked over to the stove to pour herself a cup of coffee, then checked the pot of oatmeal that Greta had kept warming there.

"Who'd've believed it?" John shook his head. "I always thought the two of them were sort of . . . Well, you know. Together."

Mary glanced over her shoulder, her eyebrows arched. "Miss Blanche and Mr. Perkins?" It would never have occurred to her.

"Yeah. I heard they came here together. Hasn't ever been another bartender at the Painted Lady. Folks just assumed . . ." He let the sentence trail into silence.

Mary stirred the hot cereal. She wondered how much anyone ever really knew about someone else. Everyone seemed to have secrets of their own. Folks seemed always to be guessing and supposing, one about another.

73

Of course, there were those rare few who could see through a facade to the truth beneath.

Those like Carson Barclay, for instance.

Her pulse jumped. What a terrible thing that would be, if he were to guess the secrets she carried in her soul.

She turned abruptly. "Mr. Tyrell, I'm understanding you used to work out at the mine. Out at the Lucky Lady."

"Yeah," he said, unconsciously scratching his disfigured cheek.

"I'm looking for someone who might work there. Or maybe once did. How would I go about learning if he's there? I know only that he was mining in Idaho. I wouldn't be knowing where for certain. And 'tis long ago since I heard from him. He may have moved on to another place."

"Lots of men work in the Lucky Lady. Lots more have over the years." His brows drew together in contemplation. "I guess the best way'd be for you to go out there and talk to the manager. Fella by the name of Jeff Christy."

She repeated the name softly to herself, then asked, "And how would I be finding the mine and Mr. Christy's office?"

"Easy. The road north of here only goes to the mine. You can't get lost. But you shouldn't go alone, Mrs. Malone."

"Would you go with me?"

John shook his head. "Sorry. Can't."

She realized belatedly that she shouldn't have asked such a thing. It would no doubt be a place of bad memories for him. "'Tis all right, Mr. Tyrell. I understand altogether."

He opened his mouth to say something but was

interrupted by the appearance of Edith in the kitchen doorway. Her blue eyes looked sleepy, her golden hair disheveled. As soon as John saw her, his face turned red. Edith, on the other hand, smiled prettily.

"Johnny, I didn't know I'd find you here."

"Miss Edith," he mumbled, his gaze falling to his coffee mug.

Mary returned her attention to her son's breakfast, feeling suddenly old and jaded. Once she'd believed in love and hope and the future. Once she'd been able to smile like Edith when she thought about a certain young man. But the innocent girl she'd been was gone forever.

Carson patted Cinnabar's side while looking over Abe Stover's shoulder. "What d'ya think, Abe?"

The blacksmith gently lowered the horse's leg and straightened. "I'd say he'd better rest it for a few days. Maybe a week. Swelling's bad, but nothing's broken. I'll treat it with liniment."

Carson nodded in agreement.

"When you takin' Perkins over to Wallace?"

"In the morning."

Abe rubbed the stubble on his jaw. "Sure never thought I'd see Lloyd Perkins in this sort of trouble. Hell, I've known him as long as I've lived here." He shook his head. "Stealing from Miss Blanche. Who'd've thunk it?"

Carson didn't bother to comment. He'd been keeping the law for too many years to be surprised by what people would do.

"Hello? Is anyone here?"

Carson didn't have to look over the top rail of the stall to know the distinctive voice belonged to Mary

75

Malone. It was a voice he'd begun to hear in his sleep.

"Right here," Abe called as he opened the gate and stepped out.

"Good day to you, sir. I'd be asking about the use of one of your fine horses and a buggy to go with it."

Carson looked through the rails and watched as Mary approached Abe. She was wearing a gown of indigo satin, and her midnight hair seemed to shimmer with the same shiny blue tones, looking like satin itself. He wondered what it would feel like to comb his fingers through that lush mane of curls, to see it spill across a pillow, to . . .

"You came to the right place, Mrs. Malone. I've got all kinds of rigs for rent. Reasonable rates, too."

"I'm sorry, but I wouldn't be knowing your name, sir," Mary said. "Have we met?"

"No, ma'am, but I seen you at church on Sunday." He held out a blackened hand. "I'm Abe Stover."

Carson noticed that Mary didn't hesitate to shake Abe's hand, even though it was sure to soil her pale gray glove.

"'Tis an honor to meet you, Mr. Stover." Her gaze drifted around the barn's interior. "I would need the buggy for several hours this afternoon. Miss Loraine said you are to put the charges on her bill."

Abe grinned. "Always glad to help out Miss Blanche. I can have the rig hitched up and ready for you any time you say."

"I'll be needing it in an hour."

"It'll be ready for you, Mrs. Malone."

Mary smiled, and the expression seemed to light up the livery stable. "Thank you, sir. I'll be seeing you then." She turned and walked out, a spring in her step.

It wasn't until she'd disappeared around the corner of

the open doorway that Carson stepped out of the stall.

"Well, if she isn't the prettiest piece of calico I ever laid eyes on." Abe turned toward Carson. "I don't know where she's going, but she sure do look happy about it, don't she?"

"Yeah," he murmured, even as he wondered why Mary Malone would want to rent a buggy for an afternoon. Not that it should matter to him. The roads were open, and it wasn't all that many miles to Wallace to the east or Osburn to the west.

Before he realized he was doing it, he followed after her. It wasn't difficult to catch up, each of his long strides equaling three of her smaller ones.

"Mrs. Malone," he said when he was nearly close enough to touch her shoulder.

She gasped as she whirled about. Her right hand fluttered to her chest. Her eyes were wide. "Faith, but must you be sneaking up on a person? You scared me half to death."

"I'm sorry." There it was. Her lilac cologne. It floated around him and made him lose his train of thought.

"Was there something you'd be wanting from me, Sheriff?"

He gave his head a quick shake. "Yes . . . No . . . I'm not sure."

His reply made her laugh—surprising them both, he suspected. For just that moment, she looked happy and at ease and very, very lovely.

"I was in the livery," Carson continued. "I heard you renting a buggy from Mr. Stover, and I was wondering where you were going."

All signs of her laughter vanished. "Would there be some reason I'd not be free to go wherever I wished?"

Mary reminded him of a yearling filly he'd seen one

time, cornered by a couple of men in a pasture. When the young horse had seen there was no other avenue of escape, she'd simply turned and charged through the barbed wire. He didn't want the same to happen here.

Carson raised his hand, palm toward her. "No. Of course not. I just . . ." He cleared his throat and tried again. "I just thought you might need some directions or something."

"I'm thinking I can find me own way to the mine."

"The mine?" he asked sharply.

She took a small step backward. "Aye."

"You're not planning to go out there alone, are you?"

Mary's demeanor changed right before his eyes. Her chin lifted defiantly. Her shoulders were drawn back like a soldier at attention. "Am I not now? And why would that be, I'm asking? You've only just said I was free to come and go as I please."

"Women," he muttered.

"Aye, a woman I am." She leaned forward, eyes sparking. "And one that will not be pushed about by the likes o' you, Sheriff Barclay."

Carson leaned forward, too, bringing his face mere inches from hers. "I'm not trying to push you around, Mrs. Malone, but if you go out there by yourself and get into some sort of trouble, it's me who'll have to take care of things afterward."

"And just what sort of trouble do you think I'd be getting meself into?"

He cursed beneath his breath, then half shouted at her, "You're a beautiful woman, Mrs. Malone. That mine employs hundreds of men, and some of them have no more morals than a rutting bull elk. Just what sort of trouble do *you* think you'd be getting yourself into?"

Thick silence fell around them. Carson was aware of

78

the rapid rise and fall of Mary's chest. He watched the play of emotions cross her face as she considered his words, saw the widening of her eyes as she realized what he was saying.

"Oh," she whispered.

"Darn right, oh."

Mary glanced over her shoulder toward the saloon. "Maybe there's someone who can go with me," she said, more to herself than to him.

"*I'll* go with you."

"You?" Her gaze swung back to meet his, suspicion in her wide brown eyes.

"Yeah, I've got some business out there myself." He wanted to ask her why she was going to the Lucky Lady, but he thought better of it. It wasn't any of his concern, just as she wasn't any of his concern.

Even though he'd been acting like she was.

He touched his hat brim. "I'll meet you at the livery in an hour." Then he turned and strode away.

Mary knew she should have found someone else to accompany her to the Lucky Lady Mine. Anyone would have been better than Carson Barclay.

He was the law. He would arrest her, should her crime ever be found out. He would have to. He could be the very person who delivered her to the gallows, who would take her son and place him in an orphanage to be raised by strangers, strangers who would never love Keary as she did.

But it wasn't only fear of Carson's legal office that caused her distress as the rented buggy moved along the road toward the mine. It was also her growing awareness of Carson as a man. It was the way he caused her heart to quicken when he glanced at her. It was the

79

tumble of emotions she felt when she looked at his hands, the leather reins looped through his fingers. Just sitting beside him left her feeling breathless and with a terrible ache for his touch.

Saints preserve her! The last thing she needed was to find herself caring for Carson Barclay. She'd made one grievous mistake in her life when it came to trusting a man with her heart. And although that mistake had given her Keary—and she'd not change having her son for anything—she was determined never to make such a mistake again.

"'Tis grand country, this," she said, hoping to turn her thoughts in another direction.

"That's what I've always thought." He paused, then said, "The mountains are all part of the Bitterroot Range. This road follows Whistle Creek there"—he pointed to the ribbon of crystal clear water—"from above the mine all the way down to the river just south of town." He lifted his arm toward a place across the creek and midway up the mountainside. "That's the rail spur up there. Both it and this road only go as far as the Lucky Lady Mine. After that, there are trails fit for pack mules and not much else, but plenty of miners still trek into those backwoods, looking for their own fortunes instead of working for men like Halligan."

"And do they find it? Their fortunes, I'm meaning."

"Not often."

Mary felt his gaze turn toward her, and instinctively, she knew what he wanted to ask her: Why was she going to the mine? Who was she going to see?

Hoping to delay, if not completely avoid, the question, she quickly asked, "How did you come to be sheriff of Whistle Creek?"

"I sort of fell into the job." There was a note of

amusement in his reply.

Curious now, she turned to look at him and was grateful to find him watching the road again. "What would you be meaning by that?"

"I worked cattle on a spread over in Montana for several years, but the owner was pretty near wiped out during the big winter of ninety-two. He couldn't afford to keep on all the cowboys he had working for him. I was one of 'em he had to let go. I'd met a fella who'd been over in Oregon, doing some logging, and he'd liked the work. I thought maybe I'd give it a try."

Carson removed his hat and wiped his brow with his shirt sleeve. He glanced up at the glaring sun, riding high above the canyon walls. Then he set his hat back over his hair and continued his story.

"I was cutting through the mountains south of Whistle Creek when a rattler spooked my horse. Cinnabar was still young and pretty green back then. He took off running like the devil himself had ahold of his tail. Next thing I knew the trail gave way and sent us both crashing to the bottom of a ravine. Broke my leg in two places, and my horse was mighty beat up, too. Even if I could've managed to get back on him, he couldn't've carried me far. Luckily, a couple of miners happened upon me the next day. They brought me into Whistle Creek."

"And your horse?"

He grinned as he looked at her. "Cinnabar's just fine, and thanks for asking."

It was difficult to break eye contact with him. There was something mesmerizing about the blue of his eyes, something all too endearing about his lopsided grin.

She moistened her dry lips with the tip of her tongue, then said, "Go on with your story, Sheriff."

He didn't immediately obey her request. He simply continued to watch her and smile. It was most disconcerting.

"Please, Sheriff Barclay, continue."

Carson shrugged. "Not much more to tell. While I was laid up, waiting for my leg to heal, they learned I'd been a deputy sheriff down in Silver City for four years. The folks here wanted their own sheriff, and somehow I found myself elected. I didn't mean to stay on long, but I discovered I liked it here. I liked the country and I liked the people. And I took to sheriff's work better than I ever did cowboyin'. So as long as the townsfolk want me, I guess I'll stay." He nodded, as if to emphasize his words. "Now it's your turn. Tell me something more about yourself, Mary Malone."

She turned away from him, pretending to study the scenery. "Nothing I could tell would be so interesting."

Sure and that was a lie. He'd likely be most interested if she was to tell him about Winston Kenrick.

"I'd like to hear it anyway." He said the words in a low voice that seemed to vibrate straight into her heart. When she remained silent, he suggested, "Tell me about Ireland. I've never been farther east than the Dakotas."

Mary thought on it a moment, then decided the land of her birth was a safe enough subject. And it would be a far sight safer than listening to the deep timbre of Carson's voice and feeling its affects upon her.

"Do you have family still in Ireland?" he persisted.

"No." She envisioned her parents, Fagan and Maeve Malone, and felt the stinging heartache that always came with missing them. "Me da was a tenant farmer, working the land of the English gentry. 'Twas a hard life, don't ya know, but 'twas not all bad. Me da was a big ox of a man with a laugh that could rattle the rafters.

He and me brother Padriac both played the fiddle, and the rest of us would sing and dance when we had a mind to."

She smiled to herself, remembering the lot of them in front of one of the thatched roof huts they'd lived in over the years, dancing and acting the fools, as if they were as rich and grand as the landlord himself. Sure but those had been bonny times.

"I was the youngest of ten, but there was only six of us who grew to adulthood and me the only girl." She looked at Carson. "Do ya have any brothers or sisters yourself?"

"No." He frowned. "I grew up alone."

"Then 'tis sorry I am for you altogether."

"You said there was no one left in Ireland. What happened to your family?"

"Me ma died when I was fourteen." Poor Maeve Malone, made old before her time by poverty and hardship and heartache. "Da passed on after me twentieth birthday, just." Wonderful, laughing Fagan Malone, his fiddle silenced forever. "I was already in service to the Whartons by then. Ever since I was fifteen, to be sure. After Da died, me brothers went their own ways. Most went to England to find work. Padriac married a Scottish lass and moved to the Lowlands." *And Quaid came to America, but I'll not be telling you that, Sheriff Barclay.* "None o' me brothers was good at corresponding, and I don't know for positive sure where any of them are except Padriac. 'Twould be a miracle if I was to see any of the others again this side of heaven." But a miracle was exactly what she was expecting, although she wasn't telling the sheriff that either.

When she fell silent, Carson seemed content to leave

it that way. He didn't ask any more questions. Mary was relieved, for talking about her family had stirred up too many painful memories.

The Irish had a word for the act of leaving Ireland. It was *deoraí*, which meant exile, not emigration. And Mary understood the word at this moment as she never had before. She could almost smell the sweet green of the Irish hills, could almost feel the crisp sea breeze upon her cheeks. The home of her birth, the land where she'd lived for twenty-four years before fate had taken her away, first to England and then to America.

"I'm sorry, Mary," Carson said. "I didn't mean to make you sad."

She blinked away the tears that had blinded her. "'Tis nothing but a speck o' dust in me eye."

He was silent for another long spell, then broke it by saying, "The mine's just around the next bend."

She was altogether glad of that, for hearing him call her Mary in such a gentle voice had wrought new havoc in her already confused heart. To continue sitting so close beside him without a few minutes to compose herself would have been unbearable.

Eight

THE DRIVE BACK TO WHISTLE CREEK TWO HOURS later took place in complete silence, both parties lost in thoughts of their own.

Mary had learned nothing from the mine manager. Jeff Christy had been friendly enough, but he hadn't been willing to open the mine records to her. He'd promised only that he would look into the matter, see if he could locate her brother's name among the hundreds of others.

Of course, she hadn't called Quaid her brother when talking to Mr. Christy. She'd said Quaid was her brother-in-law, the brother of her deceased husband. What was one more lie among many? she'd reasoned to herself.

Carson hadn't fared any better. While Mary was inside the office, conducting whatever business she had there, Carson had made small talk with some of the workers who were employed aboveground. If there were plans afoot to riot or blow anything up, no one had let it slip to him. Not that he was surprised. The miners might like him. They might trust him. But they also knew he was the law, and if they were up to mischief, they were smart enough to be cautious around him.

Shadows fell across the road in front of them as they came down out of the mountains. The heat of the day was already beginning to lose its grip on the valley below.

When the town came into view, Carson realized his stomach had been growling for the past two miles. Impetuously, he asked, "Would you care to have supper with me at the café, Mrs. Malone?"

For one brief instant, he thought she might agree. Then she shook her head. "I'm thinking I should be getting back to Keary. 'Tis"—she blushed—"'tis past time for him to be having his own supper."

Carson remembered his brief glimpse of Mary nursing her son, and he wished he could see it again. It was a peculiar wish, he thought, but it was a strong one. Why the lingering image of mother and child made him feel warm and content, he didn't know. Wasn't sure he wanted to know.

He turned off the mine road, crossed the bridge over

Whistle Creek, and took the north road into town. He stopped the buggy at the corner of River and Main, then helped Mary to the ground.

"I'll be thanking you for taking me up to the mine, Sheriff."

"No trouble, Mrs. Malone. I was glad to do it."

"Good day to you, then."

He pinched the brim of his Stetson. "Evening, ma'am."

He watched as she hurried across the street and down the sidewalk toward the rear entrance of the Painted Lady. Then he hopped into the buggy and slapped the reins. He didn't have to turn the horse onto Main Street. The animal knew the way to the stables from here.

Carson was just entering the barn when a gunshot broke the peacefulness of early evening. It was followed by a woman's scream. He was out of the buggy and running before the sound faded away.

He found several of Blanche's saloon girls huddled together outside the front door of the saloon.

"What happened?" he demanded as he approached them.

Ruby, a woman with bright red hair to match her name, turned toward him. "It's Lloyd. He's threatening to kill Miss Blanche."

"Lloyd? How'd he get out of jail?" The question was rhetorical. Carson didn't expect or need an answer right now.

He inched along the sidewalk toward the swinging doors of the saloon. Cautiously, he glanced inside, just in time to see Lloyd fire off another round, followed by another scream.

Cold fury swept over Carson as he took in the scene.

Blanche Loraine was huddled behind the bar with two more of her girls, and midway up the stairs was young Edith, holding a squirming Keary Malone in her arms. Lloyd had safely positioned himself out of view of the doorway. Carson wouldn't be able to get a clear shot at him without exposing himself first.

"You there, Barclay?" Lloyd shouted, his voice slightly slurred.

He'd been drinking. That made him prone to mistakes. It would slow his reflexes. It also made him more unpredictable, more dangerous.

"I'm here, Lloyd. Why don't you put that gun down so we can get back to the jail and have our supper? Zeb always rustles us up some good grub."

"I'm not goin' back." He shot some of the bottles just behind Blanche, and glass and liquor splattered everywhere.

A movement at the top of the stairs caught Carson's eye. Mary was standing there, her eyes wide with terror, her hand over her mouth.

Damn!

Lloyd saw her, too. "Get down here, Miz Malone."

"Go back, Mary!" Carson commanded.

Lloyd fired another shot, this one hitting the wall just above Edith's head. Keary started to wail.

"I said, come 'ere!" Lloyd shouted.

Mary hurried down the stairs, quickly stepping in front of Edith and Keary, shielding her son with her own body.

"All the way down, Miz Malone. After all, this is your fault, ain't it? You're the one who told Blanche I was stealin' from her. Ain't that right?"

Blast! Carson couldn't just stand there and watch Mary descend the stairs. There was no telling what

87

Lloyd was going to do next. But if Carson went barging through these doors, Lloyd could fire several times before the sheriff would have a clear shot. Lloyd could kill both Mary and her son, maybe others, too, before Carson could stop him.

Just then, Abe arrived beside him, shotgun in hand. "What can I do?" the blacksmith whispered.

Carson glanced down the sidewalk to the northwest corner of the saloon. The Painted Lady had several windows on the street side ground floor, all of them made from stained glass. It let in light, yet hid the internal goings-on from passersby.

"Stay here," he answered Abe. "When I get inside, you come in. Ready to shoot if you have to."

"How will I know you're inside?"

"You'll know," Carson replied, then he ran in a crouched position toward the far end of the saloon.

"Hush now, Keary me boy," Mary whispered over her shoulder. "'Tis all right we are."

The sheriff is outside. He will help us.

Lloyd fired his gun again, this time toward the ceiling. "I said for you t' get down here, Miz Malone. I mean *now!*"

Mary wasn't sure her legs would carry her safely down the steps. "Mr. Perkins, sir, will you be letting me send the boy upstairs with Edith. He's just a wee babe and can do you no harm."

He replied by firing another shot, this one striking the wall just over her right shoulder.

"For the love o' Mike!" Mary screeched, fear and anger mingling together now. "Have you no pity? What has Keary ever done to you, I'll be asking?"

Lloyd downed another swig of whiskey, then rose

from his chair, still carefully hidden from the front doorway by a wide pillar. "The next shot goes right through you and into the brat's head if you don't shut up and get down here."

"Lloyd." Blanche stood and moved from behind the bar. "It's me you're mad at. Let the others go. This has gone far enough."

"Maybe I'll kill you now," he said as he turned the muzzle of the gun toward the madam.

Mary held her breath. Even Keary quieted.

Blanche stopped and stared straight into Lloyd's eyes. "Shoot me then," she said in a calm voice, "if that's what you mean to do. Just quit terrorizing everyone else. This is between you and me."

Suddenly, there was a great shattering of glass. Lloyd turned just in time for Carson's first shot to tear through his left arm. Still, Lloyd managed to fire his own gun at the sheriff. Carson dropped, rolled, then was on his feet again, Colt revolver blazing. Another bullet hit the bartender, this one striking his chest dead center. An expression of surprise crossed Lloyd's face and was frozen there as he fell backward, dead before he hit the floor. Blanche let out a choked cry, then rushed toward the fallen man, her hand over her mouth.

Keary started to wail again at the top of his lungs. Mary felt like crying right along with him. Her knees gave way, and she sank onto the step, shaking all over as she took her son from Edith and hugged him to her bosom. She closed her eyes, wanting to shut out the image of the dead man lying on the floor of the saloon. She rocked back and forth, and after a while, Keary's crying quieted to an occasional whimper.

"Are you hurt, Mary?"

She opened her eyes, surprised to find Carson

89

standing in front of them. She wanted to answer him but couldn't seem to form a reply.

"Are you hurt?" he asked again as he leaned forward and placed a gentle hand on her shoulder. "Is Keary okay?"

She shook her head, then nodded. Her vision suddenly blurred.

"Thank God," he said softly. His hand left her shoulder as he straightened and looked behind him. "You don't belong at the Painted Lady."

She swallowed the lump in her throat and blinked away her tears. When she could see clearly, she followed Carson's gaze. Blanche was kneeling beside Lloyd's body and holding his hand as she talked softly.

"I must be going to her," Mary said as she rose.

He placed his hand on her shoulder a second time. "I think she'd rather be alone."

"'Tis true, then? Mr. Perkins and Miss Blanche?"

"Yeah, it's true. Long time ago though." He took a step down, then grimaced and touched his right thigh. When he looked at his hand, it was scarlet with his own blood. He muttered an oath beneath his breath.

Mary's heart jumped at the sight. "Faith and begorra! You're wounded, you are." She looked behind her where Edith had been, but the girl had slipped away unnoticed. Glancing at the gathering of people inside the doorway of the saloon, Mary called out, "Someone send for the doctor. The sheriff is after being shot."

"It's nothing," Carson objected.

"I'll be having none of it. Sit down, Sheriff Barclay, before you fall down." She tugged on his arm. "Do as I'm telling you." When he'd followed her order, she added, "Here. Hold Keary while I tend to you." She shoved her son into Carson's arms, then lifted her skirt and tore off a length of petticoat.

"It's nothing," he repeated as she knelt on the step and tied the white cotton strip around his thigh. "Just a flesh wound."

"You wouldn't be knowing that for certain. Now would you?" She glanced up. Her pulse skipped, this time not from alarm but because of his amused smile. In defense against the emotions racing through her, she huffed, "I'm not seeing anything to smile about, Sheriff Barclay."

"Can't help it, Mrs. Malone. You're mothering me like you do Keary."

She stood, then grabbed her son. "I'm doing no such thing. I'm thinking that wound has made you daft."

He laughed aloud. His skin crinkled near the outer corners of his eyes, blue eyes that sparkled despite the pain he was in.

She loved his laugh. She loved the crinkles near his blue eyes. She loved . . .

Faith and begorra! It was herself who was daft, and there'd be no mistaking it.

She was rescued from her unsettled feelings by the timely arrival of the town's physician. As Dr. Ingall set his black leather bag on the step next to Carson, Mary tried to escape up the stairs.

"Mary Malone," the sheriff called after her.

She stopped but didn't look back. "Aye?"

"I meant what I said. You need to move out of this place. It isn't safe for Keary." He paused. "Or for you either."

Heaven help her. The last thing she needed was Sheriff Barclay caring where she lived or if she was safe.

She continued upward without comment, not trusting her voice nor knowing what she would say if she tried to speak.

Tibble Knox squinted at the notepad in his hand. "Miss Malone was living with a couple by the name of Nolan and Siobhan Dougal. They've got a coldwater apartment on the Lower East Side."

Winston impatiently tapped his fingertips on the glass-covered surface of his desk. His head was pounding, and the stitches were beginning to itch. He wished the investigator would hurry up with his report. So far he hadn't told Winston anything he didn't already know.

"She was living with a Ryan and Cora Maguire when her baby was born. From what I could learn, Ryan was a cousin to Seamus Maguire, Keary Malone's father. Seamus left a widow here in New York as well."

Winston cocked an eyebrow. Interesting but nothing more. "Go on, Mr. Knox."

"Keary Malone was delivered early, and for a time, the midwife didn't think the boy would live."

"Yes, yes, yes. But have you learned anything of value?"

Tibble Knox removed his spectacles and cleaned them with his handkerchief. "Actually, I have." He hooked the wires over his ears again and peered at Winston. "It seems Miss Malone formed a rather close friendship with two other immigrants during the voyage across the Atlantic. She has kept up a rather steady correspondence with them for the past fifteen months."

"Splendid!" Winston straightened in his chair. "She probably went to stay with one of them. Where do we find them?"

The detective shook his head. "Unfortunately, Miss Malone did not leave any of the letters behind, and I have yet to uncover the women's whereabouts."

"Damn it, man! Then what good is the information?"

Tibble Knox rose from his chair, slipping the small notebook into his vest pocket as he did so. "Don't worry yourself, Mr. Kenrick. I *will* locate them. You can be sure of that."

"Let me remind you, Knox. When it's time to confront Miss Malone, I'm going with you to wherever it is she's hiding. Is that understood? I will be the one to speak to her, not you."

"You made that clear at our first meeting. I haven't forgotten."

"Good." Winston reached for a cigar. He used to keep them in the box Mary had stolen, but it wasn't cigars that made the blasted box so important to him. Without that box, his future would be ruined. It was crucial he get it back, and he had to get it back soon. Most importantly, he had to make sure that Irish witch hadn't discovered what was hidden inside.

Louise Schmidt drew herself up to her full, imposing height, her arms crossed over her ample bosom. "I'll remind you that I run a respectable boardinghouse, Sheriff Barclay. And besides, I'm all full up. There's no room here for that woman and her baby."

"But Mrs. Schmidt—"

"You heard me. There's no room available." And with that, she closed the door in Carson's face.

Favoring his right leg—it was only a flesh wound, but it still hurt like the dickens—he stepped off the boardinghouse porch and walked back toward the jail. Evening had fallen over Whistle Creek, and shop windows were dark while residences had come to life with golden lamp light. At the far end of town, music

93

and laughter spilled from the open doors of the Painted Lady Saloon. Except for the window that had been boarded over, no one would think anything unusual had happened there a few hours ago.

Carson stopped in front of his office, his gaze locked on the saloon.

Mary Malone didn't belong there. Keary Malone didn't belong there. They both could have been killed today. But if Mrs. Schmidt wouldn't rent Mary a room, what was she to do? She had a job and was being paid a wage for it. A better-than-average wage, more than likely, since Miss Blanche seemed to like her so much. If Mary was to leave the Painted Lady, what sort of work might she find? Nothing in Whistle Creek, that was for sure. She'd probably have to go clear over to Spokane.

But if she went to Spokane, who would keep an eye on her? Who would protect the widow and her son? Who would she turn to if Keary needed something? At least here, she had a friend in Miss Blanche. No, it was better that Mary Malone stay in Whistle Creek.

Better for whom he didn't allow himself to think about.

And then the idea came to him right out of the blue. His cabin. It was sitting empty. He could let her have use of it for free. It was no more than a quarter of a mile up the draw. It was an easy walk, and if necessary, he could help her get a horse and cart for transportation.

Of course, she would be out there by herself, but there were plenty of widow women who lived on their farms and homesteads all alone. He could show her how to use a rifle, just in case. He was convinced she would be safer out there than she was at the Painted Lady.

And Keary . . . What about the boy? Mary needed

someone to care for her baby while she was at work. Keary shouldn't be staying at the Painted Lady, watched out for by Edith or any of the other *ladies* who worked there.

He remembered the blowzy Miss June back in Idaho City, a woman long past her prime with sagging breasts and heavy makeup that caked in the creases of her face. Miss June had loved to cuddle and fuss over Carson. She'd smelled of sweat and worse, and for a moment, it seemed he could still smell her body odor. He wrinkled his nose in distaste, wondering if he'd ever be rid of that scent in his nostrils.

Miss June had always offered to look after Carson when Aldora wanted her son out from underfoot. But Miss June, as kind as she'd tried to be, had been worse than having no one at all.

No, Keary didn't belong in that saloon, and if Mary Malone didn't have the good sense to get her son out of there, then by damn, Carson would do it for her.

With determined steps—and only a slight limp—Carson set off for the Painted Lady and a meeting with Mary Malone.

Holding a sleeping Keary in her arms, Mary sat in the rocking chair, humming softly. She stared down at her son's face, thinking how sweet he looked, how precious and beautiful. He might have been killed today. When she recalled the terror of those few minutes—minutes that had each seemed an eternity long—she felt a sick twist in her stomach.

"I'm thinking, Lord, that you might have made a wee mistake," she prayed. "Maybe 'tis not here we were meant to be, and I'd not be disappointed if you were to send another miracle our way."

The last words were hardly spoken when a knock sounded at her door.

"'Tis open," she called.

She glanced over her shoulder, expecting to see Edith or Blanche. She definitely wasn't expecting Carson Barclay.

"Good evening, Mrs. Malone," he said as he removed his black hat. "May I come in? I need to talk to you."

She held her son more tightly, feeling a familiar twinge of fear at his words. A *sheriff's* words. "Aye, you may come in, Sheriff Barclay."

Carson stepped into the room but left the door wide open. Then he walked toward her, stopping in front of the rocker so Mary didn't have to crane her neck to look at him.

"How are you?" he asked, his voice low and concerned.

"I'm all right, just." It was an honest reply. But would she be all right after he told her why he'd come to see her?

Carson slid his fingers around the brim of his hat, his expression thoughtful. "Mrs. Malone, you might tell me again that it isn't any of my business. I suppose it isn't. But I don't think you and this baby of yours should be living in this saloon. It isn't safe. It's one thing for you to work in the back office, keeping Miss Blanche's books for her. That's bad enough. But living in this place with Keary . . . Well, it's not the best situation."

Mary stiffened, but tried to swallow the anger that sprang instantly to life. "Would you be saying I'm not a fit mother? Haven't you said as much before?"

"No, that's not it. Maybe once I thought that, but no more, Mrs. Malone. I just want to help if I can. I've got that cabin sitting empty. It would suit the two of you

96

mighty well, I think."

"Your cabin?" She pictured the log house and the pretty meadow filled with wildflowers. Then she remembered her prayer of moments before. *I'd not be disappointed if you were to send another miracle our way.* Had the Almighty answered her prayer so quickly?

"Look," Carson continued, his tone more forceful now, as if arguing to convince her, "I don't know what Miss Blanche is paying you to keep her books. I'm sure it's fair, but it probably isn't enough to rent a house from someone else, even if there was one available. But I won't charge you rent. It would be better for me to have someone out there, looking out for the place, than just have it standing empty. You'd be doing me a favor, actually."

"A house of me own," she whispered. "I scarce can believe it."

"You can believe it."

She shook her head. If she moved into his cabin, she'd be beholden to the sheriff, the very man she needed to stay clear of. This couldn't be the miracle she'd been praying for . . . could it?

"Mrs. Malone, believe me, a saloon is not where Keary should be living. It isn't safe." The expression on his face was one akin to anger, but she suspected it wasn't really because of her. "Please, use my cabin."

He was right, of course. This wasn't the place she should be raising her son. As much as she liked Blanche and Edith and a few of the other women, she knew this wasn't where Keary belonged. He deserved better than this. It seemed her decision was made.

"Sure and I'll be thankful to you altogether, Sheriff Barclay. This is a kind offer you've made, and I'll be accepting it with gratitude." She rose from the chair,

97

then cradled Keary with one arm just long enough to shake Carson's hand.

A tingle raced up her arm the moment their fingers touched. It caused her pulse to jump and her breathing to momentarily cease. She was relieved when he released her hand and stepped back from her.

"I'll ride up there tomorrow morning. Make sure everything's in order." He placed his hat on his head. "Then I'll borrow a wagon from Abe Stover and help you take your things up there in the afternoon."

She thought to say he wouldn't need a wagon to help her move, her belongings being so few, but he left before she could speak.

Sure and she hoped this was the miracle she'd prayed for. If not, it was the devil giving Mary her due for the crime she'd committed.

It was surely one or the other.

Nine

Saturday, 30 July, 1898
Whistle Creek, Idaho

Dear Beth,
It is less than a week since I posted letters to you and to Inga, but it seems longer as so much has happened.
First I would have you know I have begun to search for my brother Quaid. The manager at the Lucky Lady Mine, Mr. Christy by name, has promised he will ask about to see if Quaid ever worked at this mine. If not, I will be finding a way to visit the other mining operations in these

98

mountains and be asking the same questions. I feel it in my heart that I am meant to find my brother, and there will be no changing that belief.

Last week there was a bit of trouble at the saloon. Keary might have been hurt were it not for the sheriff. I knew then and there that this was not the place for my baby to be staying, but I did not know where we would go.

Once again it was the sheriff himself who helped us. He has allowed us use of a small house he owns but has not lived in for some time. It is rustic, but far better than the places where my brothers and I lived in Ireland, to be sure. I have made new curtains for the windows, green to remind me of the land of my birth. There is a shed nearby that houses an artesian well. The water is cold and sweet tasting. The stove is a sad use of iron, but I am thinking I will be able to cook our meals on it without burning down this house made of logs.

Sheriff Barclay has visited us daily since we moved here three days ago. He is always bringing something he thinks we need. I would rather he did not continue to do so for I have no wish to be beholden to him or any other man, but I am not knowing how to tell him to stop. He has a real affection for my son, and Keary has taken to him altogether.

You would be surprised, Beth, were you to see me working with Miss Blanche's books and ledgers. My da always said I had a good head on my shoulders, and I am thinking he was right. Not that I would be bragging and puffing myself up. But it is pleased I am when the work is through at *the end of the day. I like it altogether better than dusting handrails and mopping floors and carrying laundry up and down a back staircase, day in and day out.*

Today I mean to plant some flowers near the house, and then we are going to search for huckleberries, for I am told they are delicious in a pie.

I remain your affectionate friend always,
                    Mary Emeline Malone

With her hair in a braid and wearing her most threadbare dress, Mary knelt in the dirt in front of the cabin and attacked the hard-packed earth with a spade. She'd been told in the mercantile that the growing season was half-gone. But she knew the wildflowers in the meadow would soon be gone, and she was determined to have a garden of flowers to enjoy until the first frosts of winter.

Of course, she might not be in this house come winter. She might find Quaid, and then they would go away from here. Her brother would take her to a place of safety, a place where she didn't have a sheriff lending her a house and watching over her all the time, where she was far away from anyone who might suspect her of committing murder.

Her hand stilled and a shiver raced up her spine. She hated remembering what she'd done. She liked it much better when she could pretend that nothing so horrible had happened to her. But even worse was thinking what would happen if she was ever found out. Keary would grow up in an orphanage. He might grow up mistreated and hungry. She would rather live with the knowledge of her sin weighing on her shoulders than ever have her

100

child suffer as he might if she were arrested and hanged or imprisoned for her crime.

Which brought her thoughts directly back to Sheriff Barclay. How was she to dissuade him from taking on the role of protector? How was she to tell him she didn't need his help—especially when it was so obvious that wasn't true? She'd needed his help several times already. She would never have been able to start a fire in that miserable stove without his careful instructions their first day here. She wouldn't even have this little house to live in without his generosity.

"Sure and I'd like to know what it is I should be doing?" she whispered with a glance heavenward.

But no answer was forthcoming.

Keary's cheerful jabbering caused her to sit back on her heels and glance to her right. Her son was seated a short distance away in the center of a child-sized corral Mary had made from some lengths of lodgepole pine. And with Keary was the mangiest-looking dog she had seen in her life. The large beast was brindled in color, tawny with spots of black and streaks of white, its long hair matted and its tail drooping. It had one blue eye and one black and an open mouth large enough to swallow Keary's hand and arm—which at the moment were painfully close to the dog's sharp fangs.

"Keary!" Mary shouted as she jumped to her feet.

Her son squealed with laughter and pounded the dog on the head with both of his hands.

"Faith and begorra! Keary, stop!"

The dog lay down, pressing its chin onto the ground between its forepaws, and whined.

Mary jumped over the low barricade and whisked her child into the safety of her arms. She was just preparing to race in the opposite direction when she took another quick look at the dog. What had looked so dangerous to her seconds before now looked pitiful. Her breathing slowly returning to normal, she took one step closer to the ugly canine.

"I'll be thinking you're a poor thing, you are. Look at you, will you now." She hunkered down, then tentatively reached out and stroked the dog's head.

It rolled its eyes upward, the better to see her leaning over it, and its tail flopped once in the dirt. Otherwise, it didn't move.

"Aye, 'tis starving you are beneath all that hair or my name isn't Mary Emeline Malone."

"Ba, ba," Keary chanted merrily as he tried to touch the dog again. "Ba, ba, ba, ba."

"Do you think that's the name, Keary lad? Well, tis a bath for Baba before you'll be touching him . . . or her . . . again. But I'm thinking it won't hurt to share a bite to eat first. Would that be to your liking, Baba?"

The dog sat up, then cocked its head to one side, ears flopping forward. Mary couldn't help laughing at the expression on its face. She was quite certain no amount of soap, water, or brushing would improve Baba's looks by much.

"If you'll stay there, I'll be bringing you some food, Baba. If you've a mind to go on, then so be it."

She carried Keary into the house and set him in his high chair. Then she put together a plate of food—chunks of cheese and some scraps of ham and beef—for their guest. When she went outside, she found the dog sitting exactly where she'd left it.

"Come here, Baba, and fill your belly, for you look like you'd be needing it."

The dog immediately obeyed. It seemed she—for Mary could see now that the animal was female—was quick of mind even if she was a sore sight to look upon.

"I'll be putting a kettle on to boil, and when the water is hot, we'll rid you of the dirt and vermin, we will. If you've a mind to stay with us, then you'll not be dragging fleas into me house."

A half hour later, with Keary standing alongside the washtub that Mary had dragged down next to the stream and half filled with cold creek water, warmed slightly by hot water from the kettle, Mary set about scrubbing Baba. She knelt beside the tub, the front of her skirt tucked into her waistband to protect it from the dirt. Baba stood still, head drooping and without complaint, while Mary worked the soap into a lather, then rinsed several times. Keary stood on tiptoes and splashed merrily. When Mary paused to watch her son, Baba decided to shake off the water from her long coat.

"Stop, Baba!" Mary shouted, putting up her hands in defense of the flying beads of water and turning her face away.

In seconds, Mary and Keary were as soaking wet as the dog.

Mary would have laughed, but another beat her to it. The deep male laughter seemed to reverberate in her chest, making her heart leap.

She looked over her shoulder at her not-unexpected visitor. She knew the burbling brook and Keary's splashing had drowned out the sound of Carson's approach, but the reaction of her heart had little to do with her surprise at his sudden appearance.

"Quite a sight," Carson said, a chuckle lingering in his words.

Mary rose quickly and turned toward him. Too late, she remembered her skirt was hiked up, revealing her now-muddied petticoat and too much bare leg. Wet hair straggled around her face and neck. Her bodice clung to her body like a second skin. She was a sight to be sure, just as he'd said, and a poor one at that.

The sheriff, on the other hand, looked altogether too handsome, standing there beside his horse, so tall and lean and whipcord strong, his golden brown hair reflecting the rays of the afternoon sun, his blue eyes twinkling with amusement.

"Will you be laughing at me, then?" she demanded, ready to be insulted, *wanting* to be insulted.

He shook his head. "Now be honest, Mrs. Malone. You've got to admit you couldn't be more wet if you'd all three jumped into the creek." He tried—and failed—to suppress his grin. "Aren't I right?"

Mary glanced at Keary and Baba, then down at herself. And then she laughed, too. "Aye, you are that."

"Where did you get that ugly mutt?" Carson left his horse's reins trailing the ground and walked toward Mary and the washtub.

"I wouldn't be knowing where she came from. Baba just showed up at me door, hungry and dirty."

"Baba?"

She lifted Keary into her arms. "'Twas me boy who named her." She felt her cheeks grow warm. "'Tis only babble, but I'm thinking he knows what it is he's saying."

"Ah." Carson stretched out an arm and ruffled Keary's hair with his hand. "I'm sure he does. You're a smart one, aren't you, Keary?" Then he looked at the dog again. "She probably belonged to some miner. Maybe he died or abandoned her."

"Aye, that's what I'm thinking. She seems gentle enough, though she frightened me at first, big and ugly as she is."

"Come here, girl," Carson said, patting his thigh with his fingers.

Baba didn't budge. Except for one side of her mouth, which twitched as if she was about to snarl.

"'Tis all right." Mary mimicked the sheriff by patting her own thigh. "Come here, Baba."

The dog immediately jumped out of the tub and came to stand in front of Mary. Baba sat and cocked her head to one side, looking up, as if waiting for another command.

"Looks like you've got a protector, Mrs. Malone."

I'm wishing you'd call me Mary again. Her pulse skipped, and she felt short of breath. "Aye, 'twould seem so." *Carson,* her traitorous thoughts finished for her.

"Probably a good thing. I sometimes worry about you being out here alone, even though I know it's better than living over the saloon."

"And quieter altogether."

"Yeah, I imagine it is." The blue of his eyes seemed to darken as he stared at her. After a long moment, he cleared his throat. "Well, why don't I dump that water and carry the tub back to the house for you? It's plenty heavy for someone as tiny as you."

She longed for him to stay. She wished he would go. She wanted him to do everything for her. She wanted nothing from him ever again.

"I'm used to hard work, Sheriff Barclay," she said stiffly, trying to hide her confusion. "I brought that tub out here meself, you know. I'm not so weak I can't take it back the same way."

His smile returned, accompanied by his warm laughter. "Sometimes you're as prickly as a porcupine, Mary Malone. Has anyone ever told you that before? I wasn't criticizing you. I was merely offering to help."

Softly, "Maybe I'm thinking you've already helped enough."

Maybe she was also thinking she liked his help too much. Maybe she was forced to admit she looked forward to his visits too much. Maybe she knew she was not wary enough of this man of the law. Maybe she knew the danger was not in losing her freedom but in losing her heart.

Faith and begorra! It wasn't her heart she'd lost but her blooming mind!

Carson watched as Mary turned away from him and walked swiftly toward the house, her skirts flipping up just enough to reveal her bare feet. He had an almost overwhelming urge to go after her, take her in his arms, and kiss her soundly. The way a woman like Mary should be kissed.

A woman Like Mary . . .

He wasn't sure what he meant by that. He didn't know Mary. Not really. She was just a widow woman who needed a bit of help. That's all she was to him. Nothing more.

He thought of the way she so often faced off with him, head held high, her eyes sparking in defiance, her knuckles resting just above her pleasantly rounded hips. Even when she was afraid, Mary Malone didn't back down. She was full of spit and fire. She was beautiful and smart. She was gentle and loving. She was many things, and most of them were still a mystery to him. A mystery Carson wanted to solve.

He grabbed the washtub and set it up on its side, watching as water spilled out onto the ground and rushed in a dozen rivulets toward the mountain stream.

So the truth was, he admitted silently, that Mary had

become more to him than a widow needing assistance. He just didn't know what that "more" was. Was it merely desire he felt, a physical response to her earthy, sensuous beauty? Or was it something less definable— and more disturbing?

He looked toward the house. Mary and Keary and that mongrel dog had disappeared inside. The door stood open, as did the windows. New green curtains, the color of a Douglas fir, fluttered in the gentle summer breeze. Mary had accomplished much in just three days, turning a bachelor's cabin into a woman's home. Carson had always been proud of the one-room log house. He'd built it with his own hands. It was the first place he'd ever been able to call his own, and he'd liked living here. But it had never felt like it did now. Now it felt like a home.

As Carson picked up the washtub and strode toward the cabin, he wondered about the absent Mr. Malone. Mary never spoke about her deceased husband. He'd never heard her say how long they'd been married. He wondered if she'd loved him. He wondered if she still mourned him. He wondered what had caused her to leave her home in the East and come to Whistle Creek, Idaho, to work at the Painted Lady.

In the open doorway, he paused a moment, letting his eyes readjust to the dim light of the interior. Mary had curtained off the sleeping area of the cabin, and over the top of the blankets and rope strung from wall to wall, he saw her arms rise above her head as she donned a clean gown.

His body immediately reacted to the image that played through his mind. He cleared his throat loudly. "Here's the washtub, Mrs. Malone."

Baba nosed her way through the curtain and growled

107

at him.

Carson decided he wasn't going to like that dog.

"'Tis all right, Baba," Mary said softly.

The sound of her voice flowed over Carson like warm honey, and he knew it would be better if he took his leave before he did something he'd regret later. Heck, he hadn't even mentioned what he'd come here for. He'd forgotten as soon as he'd seen her down by the creek.

"Listen, Mrs. Malone, I've got to be getting back to town. But I came out here to bring you a rifle. I thought you should have one handy, just in case."

The curtain moved aside. "A rifle?"

"Yeah."

"Are you thinking I'll be needing one?"

"Look, I know you'd never intentionally hurt anybody. You even take ugly dogs under your wing. But you need to be able to protect yourself and your boy if you have to." He shrugged. "Like I said before, I wouldn't have brought you out here if I didn't think you'd be better off, but all the same, you should know how to use a rifle."

Her voice had an odd, strained quality as she replied, "I would protect meself and Keary if I had to, Sheriff. Make no mistake of that."

"So do you know how to use a rifle?"

She shook her head.

The urge to hold her and kiss her—and more—shot through him again. He swallowed hard. "Like I said, I've got to get back to town. How about if I leave the rifle with you, and I'll come out tomorrow after church and give you lessons. Would that be okay?" He hoped by tomorrow he'd be able to rein in his raging desires.

"I'm thinking that would be all right."

"Good. I'll get the rifle. It's on my saddle." He headed for his horse.

"Sheriff?"

He turned, saw her standing in the doorway. Her hair had been freed from the braiding, and it spilled over her shoulders like a black waterfall, damp and shiny in the afternoon sunlight. Her dress was a dark lavender calico that emphasized the narrowness of her waist and the womanly rounding of her bosom and hips.

He had a sudden vision of her, naked in the moonlight, imagined how one of her breasts would fill his hand. His body reacted, almost painfully. His mouth and throat went dry.

"Would you be staying for dinner tomorrow?" Her smile was hesitant, unsure. "You'd be welcome for all that you've done for Keary and me."

I'm not sure that's a good idea, Mrs. Malone, he thought, knowing he should refuse the invitation. *I just might become the man you need that rifle for.*

"I'll be frying a chicken," she added.

"Thanks, ma'am. I'd be obliged."

Ten

MARY AWAKENED ON SUNDAY MORNING TO A SKY covered with dark rain clouds and a chilling wind that felt more like November than the last day of July. Staring out the window at the gloomy weather, she suspected her shooting lesson with Sheriff Barclay would be canceled. Which was probably just as well.

"I'll be losing me mind altogether," she whispered as she turned toward the stove and the breakfast she was preparing.

109

I know you'd never intentionally hurt anybody . . .

The sheriff didn't know how wrong he was, and that was just one more reason to discourage him from coming around. She needed to make it clear that she preferred to do for herself, that she didn't want his help or even his friendship.

And what if he was wanting more than friendship?

She felt the flutter in her stomach. Merciful heavens! It would be a dreadful thing were it to happen. Him the law itself and her in hiding from the law. It was one thing to lie to protect her son, but she had no right to involve an honest man like Sheriff Barclay in her deceptions.

Well, then. It was up to her to make sure Carson understood she didn't want him in her life. There were plenty of girls at the Painted Lady who'd be more than happy if he was to call on them. But Mary Emeline Malone didn't feel the same way. Seamus Maguire and Winston Kenrick had taught her all she cared to know about men.

With her thoughts still churning, Mary fed herself and Keary, then got them both dressed and ready for church. She was thankful Blanche had included a warm cloak with a hood among the clothes she'd given her. Mary suspected she would need it to stay dry until they were home again.

When she set off walking toward Whistle Creek, Baba insisted on following at her heels. Mary tried several times to order her to wait at the house, but for the first time since the dog had appeared, Baba refused Mary's commands.

"If 'tis sitting out in the rain you want to be, then you'll be getting your wish," she muttered as she quickened her stride, Baba continuing to follow along.

110

Mary's pulse accelerated as she entered town and walked toward the church. Last week, the members of the congregation hadn't been all that welcoming. Mary had known it was because she was living at the saloon, but it hadn't made their rejection hurt any less. Still, she wouldn't be missing church just because there were those who turned up their noses at her. She had sinned enough in her life without leaving the church altogether.

Mary, girl, there's nothing that can't be forgiven if you'll be but asking.

"Not murder, Ma," she whispered in reply, as if her mother were actually there with her. "Maybe for lying down with Seamus and giving birth to Keary with no husband in sight, but not for murder." She was quite certain the glowering, hellfireand-brimstoneshouting minister back in County Armagh would agree with her.

Mary was one of the first to arrive at the church that morning. After telling Baba to lie down at the side of the building beneath the shelter of the eaves, she went inside and slipped into the back pew, sliding over to the- far corner. She didn't turn her head or watch as others entered the small sanctuary. She'd decided she would mind her own business and let them mind theirs.

But when she heard a sharp gasp and saw the heads craning from those seated at the front of the church, she couldn't help looking to see what the commotion was all about. And there was Blanche Loraine, her brassy orange-red hair piled high on her head in a cluster of curls more suited to a girl than a middle-aged woman. She had forgone the use of face paints, which made her look more sickly than ever.

Blanche smiled faintly when she found Mary. Then she slid into the same pew. "Good morning. I hope you don't mind if I join you."

"Sure and you're welcome, Miss Blanche. But 'tis mighty surprised to see you, I am."

"I'm a bit surprised myself. I saw you coming into town this morning, and all of a sudden, I decided it might do me some good to see the inside of this place at least once before I go."

Mary heard the low murmur of voices. It wasn't hard to catch the words that were meant to be heard. Harlot . . . Scandalous . . . Jezebel . . . Whore . . .

Anger flared in her chest. How dare they judge Blanche Loraine? They didn't know the woman had a good heart, that she had rescued Mary and Keary, strangers to her. They didn't know what she'd been through, what she was going through now. She was dying of a disease of the lung, and she had seen a man she'd once loved-perhaps still lovedshot down in her saloon only a few days before.

"I don't mind, Mary," Blanche whispered.

"But I'm thinking I do."

"There's nothing they can say that isn't true, I reckon."

"Miss Blanche-"

The other woman shook her head slowly as she laid her right hand over Mary's left. "I've never claimed to be a saint. In fact, I've had a right good time being a sinner." She offered a half smile. "But a body gets to thinking and..." She shrugged. "Anyway, I'm here."

Mary nodded, a sudden lump in her throat making it impossible to reply.

"Here. Let me see the boy." Blanche held out her arms for Keary. She made a funny face, then rubbed her nose against the toddler's. "You two still like it out at that place of the sheriff's?"

"Aye. You should come see us. We even have

ourselves a dog now."

"A dog?"

A door behind the pulpit opened at that moment, stopping Mary's reply, and a black-garbed minister stepped through. He was an elderly gentleman, thin and short, with a shock of pure white hair combed back on his head. He wore spectacles on the bridge of a nose that could only be described as hawklike.

"Good morning," he said in a whisper thin voice while his gaze scanned the congregation, pausing briefly on the two women in the rear pew.

Mary wondered if he would ask them to leave.

But before he could open his mouth again, a tall teenage boy burst into the church, stopping in the aisle near Blanche. "There's been a cave-in out at the mine!" he shouted. "There's men trapped below."

In an instant, all the men—including the minister—were running out of the church. They were quickly followed by women and children.

"Come on, Mary. Even I'm tolerated when there's trouble like this. They'll need everyone's help. We'll get back to the saloon and gather up blankets and food and lanterns, then drive out to the mine."

For a moment Mary couldn't move. She thought of Seamus, who'd been killed in a cave-in back in West Virginia. Then she thought of Quaid. What if her brother was working at the Lucky Lady? What if he was trapped in that mine? Maybe Jeff Christy hadn't checked the records to see if her brother was working there. What if . . .

"Come on," Blanche repeated. "Time's a-wasting."

As Mary followed after the other woman, she tried to reason with herself. She'd learned there were many mines in this region known as the Silver Valley. Quaid could be anywhere, in any one of them. He might not even be in Idaho. There was no cause for her to think the worst.

And yet her heart wouldn't stop pounding in dread.

Carson broke into a cold sweat just stepping close to the elevator cage filled with volunteers, their hands grasping picks and shovels. As the hoist engine fired up and the cage began to disappear into the adit, Carson felt the same shortness of breath that he imagined those ten miners trapped below—at the two-thousand-foot level, he'd been told—were feeling. He watched the cable slide through the pulley and silently called himself every name for a coward he could think of.

"We'll get them out," Jeff Christy said, but he sounded cautious rather than confident.

Carson glanced at the mine manager. "Do you know yet what happened?"

Jeff shook his head. "They were driving another horizontal tunnel off of number nineteen. They weren't blasting at the time. The wall just gave way."

"Are you sure any of them survived?"

Again the other man shook his head. "Too much came down. Can't hear a thing. It could take us several days to reach them."

Carson didn't need to be a miner to envision what had happened. He'd spent most of his life in mining towns. Most of his friends and acquaintances had been or were miners. His one brief experience in a mine filled any gaps that their stories left unexplained.

There would have been the sounds of breaking timbers and a grinding rumble. Then there would have been a violent rush of air, followed by an eerie silence. Any survivors—and God willing, there were survivors—

would have been plunged into total and complete darkness, their carbide lamps extinguished.

Carson smelled the smoke from the day's blasting, just as the men below must smell it. It seemed he could also hear the water dripping from the ceiling of the tunnel and trickling out of the walls. The miners' clothes would be uncomfortably damp. The heat would be unbearable. Whatever food they had with them, if uneaten, would quickly spoil in the moist, hot air. And whatever matches and candles they had with them would be gone in a few days.

Then they would be trapped in darkness again, listening to the dripping walls and the beating of their own hearts.

Suddenly, Carson needed air. He quickly strode toward the mine entrance. Once outside, he paused and took several deep breaths. A measure of strength returned to his legs, and his pulse began to slow. He was thankful for the cool, fresh air that brushed his damp, perspiring skin and filled his starved lungs.

It was hard for him, this weakness in his character. He had a healthy respect for fear in its proper place. He'd never gone up against a man with a gun without knowing he could die, but fear in such instances only seemed to sharpen his thinking.

His terror of close, dark places was another matter entirely. It left him feeling helpless. It numbed his mind. It was cowardice, pure and simple, and he hated being a coward.

He removed his hat and wiped his forehead with the sleeve of his shirt. As he placed the Stetson back on his head, he heard someone calling his name. He turned and saw Edith, the young girl from the saloon, hurrying toward him.

"Sheriff Barclay," she said in a breathy voice, "have you seen Johnny?"

"Tyrell? No."

She glanced toward the mine entrance. "He was coming out here this morning. He was gonna talk to a friend of his about something important, he said." Her gaze swung back to meet Carson's. "His friend is one of them trapped below. I just heard. Do you . . . do you think Johnny went down into the mine with him? His friend, I mean. I . . . I can't find him anywhere."

Carson would have had to be blind not to see what Edith was feeling. And in that moment, he also saw that she was more than just one of Miss Blanche's girls. She wasn't just a whore who sold her body to men. She was a young woman with a heart, a girl able to love and care just like any other. The notion surprised him, for he had never thought it possible. Not just about Edith. About any of the women like her. Certainly it hadn't been true of Aldora Barclay.

He put his hand on Edith's shoulder. "I'll ask Jeff if he knows anything about John. But I doubt he'd have gone down into the mine. He's probably up here somewhere. Or maybe he's with the volunteers."

"I hope so," she whispered, furiously blinking her eyes as she fought tears.

Briefly he wondered what it would be like to have someone worried about him the way this girl was worrying about John. And then, for some reason, he thought about Mary Malone with her wild mane of black hair and her flashing dark eyes. What would it be like to have Mary worry about him?

As if summoned by his thoughts, Mary broke free of the crowd of those waiting for word of the miners and hurried toward Carson and Edith.

When she arrived beside them, her gaze met with his only for a moment before she turned her attention to Edith. While balancing Keary on her hip, she put her other arm around the younger woman's shoulders.

"Would you be helping us, Edith? We're putting together food to send down to the volunteers, and Greta is complaining she's only got two hands."

Edith nodded, her lower lip quivering.

Mary glanced at Carson once again. "You'll be looking for John, Sheriff?"

"Yeah, I'll look for him."

"Thank you," she said, then gently guided Edith away.

Carson seemed unable to tear his gaze away from Mary's back. He'd never known anyone like her before, but it was hard to define what made her different.

It occurred to him then that Mary Malone could make a man want marriage and a family. It was a surprising—and unwelcome—revelation.

Other than Claudia Hailey, who had been a surrogate mother to him in the years he'd lived with her and David, Carson had believed himself incapable of loving any woman. He was sure he could never trust a female enough to marry one. Besides, he'd seen how Claudia suffered when her husband was killed by a drunk with a gun. Carson had decided the night David died that lawmen shouldn't have wives, because then they wouldn't leave behind widows.

He gave his head a swift shake. He didn't know what had gotten into him, but this sure as heck wasn't the time to be mulling over his personal philosophies. Not when there could be men dying two thousand feet beneath him.

Rain started to fall in the early afternoon and didn't seem inclined to ever let up. Blanche and Mary handed out many cups of coffee from beneath a canvas shelter held up with poles, ropes, and stakes while Edith watched Keary within the shelter of a tent.

At first the women among those waiting for news— most of them miners' wives—refused to come near Miss Blanche and the others from the Painted Lady. But as time went on, even the most self-righteous among them needed the warmth of a cup of coffee to ward off the chill.

It was odd, the way she was feeling, Blanche thought as she filled another tin cup with the black brew Greta kept boiling over the campfire. There had been other disasters in Whistle Creek through the years, and Blanche had helped then, too. But she had done it with an angry attitude, a sense of flaunting who she was and what she did in the faces of those women who judged her and her kind. Today, there wasn't any anger on her part. She felt only sympathy for them.

Blanche supposed it was because her end was near. It changed a person's perspective, made one look harder at the things that were important and the things that weren't. It also probably had something to do with Lloyd's death. She'd been hurt by his stealing from her, but she hadn't really been surprised. She'd loved him once, more than a woman like her had a right to love. She supposed there was a part of her heart that would always love him. She wished she'd told him so. Maybe then he wouldn't have been killed.

She glanced over to her right and saw Mary speaking softly to a woman who was weeping. "I'm thinking you must be strong," Mary said. "Don't go losing your hope."

Mary had made a difference in the way Blanche looked at things, too. The young woman was a strange combination of fiery temper and gentle spirit, and she was like Blanche in a few ways. She wasn't defeated by the hand life had dealt her. She just took the cards and played them the best way she knew how. Blanche understood that about her. But there were other things she wanted to know.

Why hadn't Keary's father married her? Had the scoundrel deserted her? Or hadn't she loved him? Was he really dead, or was she on the run from him? Was that why she was hiding here in Whistle Creek? And why, if she'd been hurt or betrayed, was she still willing to care for others?

"I'd be most grateful, Miss Loraine, for a cup of your coffee."

She turned her head toward the man who'd spoken, interrupting her musings. And there stood the Reverend Mordecai Ogelsby, whom she'd never spoken to even once in all the years she'd been in Whistle Creek. Not that their paths had crossed. He'd sure never walked into the Painted Lady, and until this morning, she'd never darkened the door of his church.

"It was good to see you at services." He had a thin, parchmentlike voice. "I regret you didn't have the opportunity to hear the sermon I'd prepared. It was one of my better efforts, I believe."

Blanche wondered how he could be heard from the pulpit with such a soft voice, even in a church as small as the one in town.

"It's good of you to do this, Miss Loraine," he continued. "I'm afraid we're in for a long wait."

She shrugged, uncertain what to say to this man of the cloth. A year ago she would probably have said something crass, would surely have tried to embarrass him. She wasn't tempted to do anything of the sort now.

He reached out, touched her shoulder lightly. "If ever you wish to talk to me, about anything, I would consider it a privilege."

Blanche was suddenly overtaken by a fit of coughing. It took several minutes before she could control it and draw a relatively peaceful breath. By that time, Mary had come to stand beside her, watching her with a concerned gaze.

"I'm all right, Mary," Blanche whispered hoarsely once she was able. Then she cleared her throat as she looked at the minister. "Thanks for the offer, Reverend Ogelsby. Maybe I'll take you up on it. There are a few things I wouldn't mind having answers to before it's my turn to go." She suspected he'd already guessed that her turn wasn't far off.

"I look forward to it, Miss Loraine." With that, he walked toward the group that was standing closest to the mine entrance, an assembly made up of the wives and children of those trapped below.

For days, the town of Whistle Creek held its collective breath. Rescuers worked around the clock, digging and chipping away at the rubble of rock and timber.

By the second day, Edith had taken to her bed in a state of mourning. John Tyrell was nowhere to be found, and everyone agreed the only explanation was that he'd been in the mine when the cave-in occurred. Edith was inconsolable, convinced that her Johnny was lost forever.

By the third day, the attitude of those waiting for news changed noticeably toward Mary. While Blanche's presence was never entirely accepted—she had been an outcast for too many years—Mary was another matter. It was the sheriff who'd made the difference. Whenever the opportunity arose, Carson explained the exact nature of Mary's job at the saloon, making it sound more respectable than the townsfolk had imagined. He also made it a point to explain that Mary had lost her husband in a mining accident, thus putting her on more even ground with the other wives.

Of course, Mary didn't know she had the sheriff to thank for the warming attitude toward her. She only knew the women spoke to her more freely and without so much censure in their eyes, and she was grateful for it.

Sheriff Barclay himself rarely spoke to Mary in those long days of waiting, but she was always aware of him. He helped organize the shifts of volunteers. He rounded up more equipment. He consoled the families. Mary could see how much others respected him, how much they listened to him, and for some unexplainable reason, she was warmed by the knowledge.

It was on the fourth day of the agonizing wait that Mary met Fenella Russell. Twelve-year-old Nellie, as the girl was called, was the only child of Dunmore Russell, a Scotsman who had worked at the Lucky Lady for the past seven years. Dunmore was among those trapped by the cave-in. Nellie's mother had died many years before, and so Nellie waited alone for news of her father. Seeing that the child needed something to occupy her time and her mind, Mary asked her to watch after Keary and Baba.

The ploy worked the majority of the time. Baba didn't need watching, of course, but the active toddler kept Nellie constantly on the go, too busy to fret. Mary was glad. She remembered well what it was like to lose her parents. She knew the pain the girl was suffering. She hoped and prayed that Mr. Russell would be spared, just as she hoped and prayed for John Tyrell and all those other men.

The fifth day dawned with the first clear skies they had seen since Saturday. Steam rose up from the rain-dampened earth as warming rays of morning kissed the ground. Perhaps it was only because of the sunshine, but there was an air of anticipation that spread through those camped out near the mine entrance. And at noon, the words they had all been awaiting arrived.

"They've broken through! They've found survivors!"

Mary held Nellie in her arms as the child cried in heartbroken sobs. Mary was crying, too. Only one man had perished in the cave-in, and that man was Dunmore Russell. Nellie was left all alone in the world at the age of twelve.

A short while before, Mary had overheard Reverend Ogelsby say something about an orphanage in a town to the west of Whistle Creek. The very notion caused her heart to break. Nellie in an orphanage? She couldn't wish that on any child. Especially not Nellie, whom she'd already learned to care for.

"Would you like to come home with me, Nellie?" she asked gently as she smoothed the girl's scraggly hair back from her face. "Keary has taken to you, as have I. You'd be welcome altogether. And Baba likes you, too."

Nellie looked up with huge, sad eyes. Her nose was running, and her dirty, freckled cheeks were wet with tears. "Can I really? Can I really come stay with you?"

"Sure and I couldn't be wanting anything more."

The girl pressed her face against Mary's chest again.

122

"Why'd he have to die?"

"I don't know, love. I don't know."

Holding Nellie tightly, Mary looked around her. Women and children were hugging their husbands and fathers, smiling and laughing and rejoicing. The gloomy, fearful atmosphere from the last few days had changed dramatically to one of celebration. Only here, beside Blanche Loraine's tent, was there sorrow.

She saw Carson striding toward them, and her arms tightened even more around Nellie. Before he reached them, she said, "You'll not be taking Nellie to an orphanage, Sheriff Barclay. She'll be coming to live with me and Keary." She lifted her chin stubbornly, daring him to challenge her decision. "'Tis settled, and I'll hear nothing more about it."

His expression didn't reveal what he thought of her announcement. He simply stared at her for a few moments, then asked, "Are you sure this is what you want?"

"Didn't I say so?"

"Nellie?" He touched her shoulder. "Is that what you want, too?"

The girl nodded without looking at him.

"You're sure there's no other family we can contact? No aunts or uncles or grandparents?"

Nellie started to sob again.

Carson's gaze returned to Mary. She saw then that he was saddened, too. That he wished he could stop the child's pain and make it all come out right again. He had a tender heart, this man of the law. It seemed a strange contradiction for one who was so able with a gun.

"I'll help break camp," he told Mary, "and then I'll see you all back to town."

"We'll be getting her things together."

He nodded, then moved off.

"Nellie, would you show me where you live? We'll need to get your clothes."

The girl sniffed as she pulled back from Mary's embrace. "I'll show you."

Blanche volunteered to keep an eye on Keary, who was napping soundly in the carriage. Then Mary and Nellie, with Baba at their heels, set off toward the small shacks that lined the foot of the mountain on the opposite side of the Lucky Lady compound.

The Russell shack, a single room with a potbelly stove, two cots, and an unsteady table with two chairs, was tidy and uncluttered. Mary was quick to discover there was little for Nellie to retrieve. Most items inside the shack belonged to the mining company. There were only a few articles of clothing, the well-worn family Bible, brought to America from Scotland a generation before, and a fading photograph of her mother and father on their wedding day. Nellie was able to carry it all herself.

Mary fought the thickness in her throat and the welling of tears in her eyes. It was like seeing herself again after her ma died. She remembered the mean, dark tenant's but with its thatched roof where Maeve Malone had breathed her last. She could see her own threadbare clothes and dirty bare feet. Mary had been fourteen at the time, tiny and skinny and raggedy. She hadn't been alone in the world like Nellie. She'd had her brothers and her da. But she'd felt alone, all the same.

"I'm thinking you'll like our house," she said, forcing a smile as they left the shack and walked toward the carriage. "Keary and I moved into it a week ago just, and 'tis a fine home for us."

Nellie's only reply was a loud sniff.

"Well, now. I guess you'll be seeing for yourself soon enough." She patted Nellie's shoulder, letting her hand linger in a gesture of comfort.

The road back to Whistle Creek narrowed as it left the Lucky Lady Mine, passing through a canyon with high, rocky walls. Carson drew in on the reins and pulled his horse back behind the Loraine carriage.

John Tyrell sat beside Blanche in the rear seat. He was dirty and hungry, but he was alive. In fact, some of the miners had called him a hero, saying it was his quick thinking that had saved many of them from dying along with Dunmore Russell. When they'd praised John, Carson had seen something new in the younger man's face—hope, pride, a sense of renewed worth—and he believed John was going to be okay from here on out. Those things didn't take away the disfiguring scars from his face or give him back the use of his arm, but they restored something of greater value. Add to that Edith's love . . .

Yes, he reckoned John would be okay from here on out.

Carson's gaze shifted to Mary. She sat in the front seat, driving the horses, Nellie and Keary beside her. She'd worked tirelessly over the past few days. She'd camped out at the mine as if she had a loved one trapped below. She'd been a constant source of comfort to those around her. He knew because he'd found himself observing her whenever possible, taking comfort himself in her presence.

He wondered if Mary had loved her husband with the same sort of passion as Edith apparently loved John. He wondered if Mary had camped out for days by the mine

125

in West Virginia. He wondered if she'd wept inconsolably when she'd learned her husband wouldn't return to her and her child. He wondered if she would ever be willing to love again.

It was a crazy thing to wonder. Especially since it had nothing to do with him.

Nothing to do with him?

Dang right! And he would do well to remember it.

Eleven

WHATEVER WAS I THINKING? MARY WONDERED as she cut the mutton into fairly large pieces.

Why had she invited the sheriff to supper again? The disaster at the mine had saved her from honoring her first invitation, but then she'd issued another. Yesterday, when Carson had brought her a rooster and six laying hens, the request had just slipped out, as natural as you please, and there'd been no way she could take the words back.

There was no mistaking it. She'd gone daft. Completely and utterly daft!

Mary began to peel and slice the potatoes and onions for the Irish stew she was making, her thoughts still churning.

She was becoming much too dependent upon Carson. She was certain she should refuse all the kind things he did for them. First it was the use of this cabin, then it was the stacks of firewood he'd chopped. And in the week since the miners were rescued, he'd done even more. He'd brought supplies from Chuck's Mercantile, saying it was because Mary had taken Nellie in and would need the extra food, then he'd repaired the outhouse and patched a spot in the roof. Next he'd put up a chicken coop, and now he'd supplied the chickens, too. Carson had never said anything untoward to Mary, never indicated he wanted anything—respectable or otherwise—in repayment. He always waved off her thanks, saying he would do this for anybody.

She wasn't convinced that was entirely the truth.

Perhaps Mary didn't listen to her better judgment because it was so obvious Keary was smitten with Carson. Or maybe it was because the man seemed to be just as smitten with the little boy.

Or maybe it was because Mary herself . . .

But she wouldn't even consider *that*!

With the back of her wrist, she swept wisps of hair away from her forehead. Then she put a layer of potatoes in the pot, followed by a sprinkling of parsley and thyme. She covered the potatoes with sliced meat and onions and seasoned it with salt and pepper. Then she repeated each step, topping it all with a layer of potatoes. She poured a measure of water over the meat and vegetables before covering the pot and setting it on the stove to simmer gently.

Faith, but she hoped Carson was fond of Irish stew and potato-apple dumplings.

Baba's barking and Nellie's laughter filtered through Mary's troubled thoughts and drew her toward the open doorway. The August sun glared down on the meadow from a cloudless blue sky. It would be more than an hour before it dipped behind the mountains to the west and gave them respite from the heat of the day. Mary was surprised to find the air was nearly as hot and still outside as it had been inside the cabin. She shaded her eyes with one hand as her gaze sought and found the children.

Nellie sat on the ground, her back leaning against a tree. She held Keary in her arms and pointed at Baba, who was trying to catch a butterfly. In her futile pursuit of the insect, the galloping dog barked and jumped and tumbled, ears flapping like hairy flags in a strong wind. Mary laughed aloud at the sight.

Baba's chase was interrupted by the sound. Looking, Baba saw her mistress and bounded over in her direction. The dog plopped down in front of Mary, tongue hanging out one side of her mouth. Mary would have sworn Baba was grinning.

"Ah, you're a corker, you are," Mary said as she stroked the dog's head. "A real corker."

Baba barked in agreement.

Glancing up again, Mary saw Nellie and Keary walking toward the cabin, Keary's little legs moving just as fast as he could make them go. A feeling of pure, unadulterated joy shot through her.

How had it happened, all of this? She had a home of her own and work she enjoyed because it challenged her mind. She had a healthy son. She had friends in Blanche and Edith and John. She had Nellie, who was both someone she could help and someone who could help her. She had one of the ugliest dogs in the world, who loved them all. She had chickens in the coop and food in the larder. She had lovely clothes, like nothing she'd owned in her entire life. And with every passing day, she believed a little more that she would never be found and tried for the crime she'd committed. She felt a strange peace, a belief that the future would work itself out. She had no right to feel this way, and still she did.

Tomorrow would bring problems, to be sure. Even now Blanche was sick and dying. How would Mary get along without her beloved friend and generous benefactress? What would happen to the Painted Lady when Blanche was no longer alive? Would Mary still be employed?

And yet, even knowing there would be more worries in the days to come, she felt oddly secure. There was a rightness about the here and now, a joy in simply being alive.

How had it happened, that she should know such happiness? It went beyond anything she'd anticipated when she first came to America.

As if in answer to her question—or perhaps, as one more example of the blessings she enjoyed—Carson appeared on his dun gelding, looking dashing in his black Stetson, a white shirt with a string tie around the collar, and black trousers and suit coat. He didn't normally wear such fancy clothes, and so she knew he had dressed up for this supper with her.

Her heart flipflopped, then began to race. He was early. He wasn't supposed to come until six o'clock. Mary wasn't cleaned up. Her hair was a shambles and she probably had flour on her cheeks. Her dress was soiled from her cooking and cleaning. And the stew wouldn't be ready for another two hours.

"Nellie," she said quickly, "be keeping an eye on Keary and welcome the sheriff while I put myself to rights. Tell him I'll be out directly." Then she stepped back and swung the door closed.

Faith and begorra!

She was so nervous she could scarcely make her fingers unbutton her bodice. There was no call for her to be feeling this way, but there it was. She did feel it. All aflutter. Excited and nervous. The way she used to feel when Seamus . . .

Her careening emotions were stopped by the cold

dash of reality. Carson was nothing like Seamus, and she was no longer the foolish girl who had fallen for an Irishman's blarney. Besides, something told her Carson would be far more dangerous to her heart than Seamus had ever been.

She sank onto her bed and closed her eyes as she faced another truth.

She was guilty of a grievous crime, whether the law ever found her or not. Even if she let herself fall in love with Carson, nothing could come of it. The fear of discovery would always stand between them. He was too good. He deserved better than that from her. If Mary were to give her heart again, it would have to be with complete honesty. She could never be honest with Carson.

"Then I shall be making him me friend," she whispered. "'Tis possible between a man and a woman and would be enough." She stood and hastily began to change her clothes. "'Tis friends we shall be, then."

By the time she was dressed and her hair once again pinned in place, Mary had convinced herself there was nothing to worry about. She was convinced she felt nothing more for Carson than friendship and appreciation for all he'd done to help her. She was convinced of it right up until the moment she opened her cabin door and saw him holding her giggling son high above his head.

Then her heart called her the liar that she was.

From the comer of his eye, Carson saw the door open. He lowered Keary, holding the toddler against his chest, and turned toward the house.

He'd thought Mary beautiful the first time he'd seen her. He thought her even more so today. She was wearing a blue gown the color of camas flowers, a gown that accented all her lovely curves. Her cheeks were flushed a becoming pink. She had captured her long, thick hair in a bun, but wisps curled at her nape and near her temples. She looked deceptively fragile.

"Sure and you're too early for supper, Sheriff Barclay," she said.

"I know. I thought I might chop some more wood for you."

Her gaze slipped down and up the length of him. "In your fine clothes, will you now? I'm thinking not. 'Tis too much you've done for us already. How will I ever be repaying you?"

He thought to tell her she could give him a kiss. He'd been thinking about that a lot lately—how she would taste, how her lips would feel against his. And maybe he would have asked for that kiss if Keary hadn't suddenly squawked a demand to be put down.

Just as well, Carson thought as he lowered the boy to the ground.

Keary hurried toward Baba. When he reached the dog, he buried his face in the canine's coarse coat and hugged her around the neck, then took off in a jerky run, giggling as Baba followed.

"That's the ugliest dam dog I've ever seen," Carson said with a shake of his head. Then his gaze returned to Mary.

"'Tis the truth." Her smile was repeated in her eyes. "But we none of us have much to say about that. We are born to look the way we'll look."

He couldn't stop himself from saying, "And you, Mrs. Malone, were born to look particularly beautiful."

She blushed and glanced away, turning her eyes toward her son. "'Tis kind of you to say so, Sheriff."

"Not kind. Just the truth."

"'Tis the dress Miss Blanche gave to me." She ran the palms of her hands over the skirt, and he saw they were trembling.

Was it possible she felt the same nervous excitement when they were together as he did?

He removed his Stetson, then took a step toward her. "It isn't the dress, though it's pretty enough. It's you, ma'am. Just you."

Her gaze swung back to him. "I'm thinking 'twould be better if you weren't saying such things."

He reckoned she was right. It would be better. But the cold hard fact was, he *wanted* to say them. He *needed* to say them. He was feeling things he'd never felt before, things he'd never expected to feel, and he wanted to explore them. Would he change his mind about lawmen marrying? He didn't know. Did he believe he could fall in love with Mary? He didn't know that either. But he wanted to find out. For the first time in his life, he wanted to see where an attraction for a woman would take him—besides into her bed. It went without saying that he wanted her that way already.

Take it slow, Barclay. She's looking mighty skittish.

He turned away, saying, "I'm gonna put my horse in the corral."

And then, he finished silently, *I'm going to chop that firewood. 'Cause if I don't keep busy, I'll probably say—or do—something I shouldn't.*

The Kenrick mansion on Madison Avenue, built twenty years before and paid for out of the vast fortunes of Pendergast Industries, was a model of good taste. The grand dining room was no exception. Hundreds of electric lights glowed brightly from crystal chandeliers.

Gilded mirrors lined two walls. A third wall was solid glass, looking out onto a private garden of sculptured hedges and colorful flowers.

That evening, as Portia Pendergast Kenrick looked down the long table set with fine china and beautiful silver, her thirty guests seated in a carefully selected order along both sides, she thought how very content she had been in this house. She and Winston owned other residences, of course, but it was this house she had always preferred. Invitations to Portia Kenrick's supper parties were eagerly sought after. It was a well-known fact in New York society that one wasn't anyone unless one had been a guest in the Kenricks' Madison Avenue home.

At the far end of the table sat Portia's husband. Even without her glasses, which vanity precluded her from wearing when entertaining, she could see that Winston was flirting with the women on either side of him. In fact, if Portia wasn't mistaken—and she wasn't—she believed the woman on his right, Amelia Pedersen, was his most current lover. She wondered if Mr. Pedersen had also guessed of the clandestine visits these two had participated in.

But it wasn't Winston's latest sexual conquest that caused Portia's brow to furrow in thought. It had more to do with her husband's ever-increasing obsession with finding Mary Malone and the silver cigar box the foolish girl had taken. Winston's behavior in the past few weeks was quite out of character. It was far more than mere anger that Mary had struck him— undoubtedly well deserved, if Portia knew her husband, and she did. No, there was an underlying sense of panic in his actions, in his words. And that was very unlike Winston.

Now, why would he be afraid? What would give him cause to want to find that silly cigar box so desperately? Oh, it was valuable, but only relatively so. It could be replaced with a quick order to the silversmith, and Winston knew it. The excuse of sentimentality that he continued to use didn't ring true. So why?

There was much more to this matter than Winston wanted Portia to know. Which, of course, was precisely why Portia was so determined to discover the truth.

It was also why she was paying Tibble Knox—paying quite handsomely, she might add—to report to her before he reported anything to her husband. Tomorrow the gnomelike detective would tell Winston that he had located Mrs. Inga Bridger in Uppsala, Iowa, and it was Mrs. Bridger who might hold the key to finding Mary. Portia knew Winston would insist on accompanying Mr. Knox to Uppsala to meet with Mrs. Bridger. What he didn't know was that Portia was going to insist on going with them as well. She could already imagine what his reaction would be.

She smiled at her guests as she motioned for the serving to begin. Then her gaze returned to the far end of the table and to her husband.

Yes, she could just imagine what Winston's reaction would be.

Her smile broadened as she engaged in a bit of conversation with the gentleman on her left.

Shadows were growing long in the protected valley as Mary and the others sat down to supper. Carson had carried the table and chairs out of the cabin and set them beneath the spreading branches of an ancient Rocky Mountain maple, and it was there they dined on the thick and creamy stew, brown soda bread, and the old-country pudding, made with a potato paste filled with apples, cloves and sugar, and topped with butter.

Baba positioned herself between Nellie and Keary, having quickly learned that this was the place where she would benefit the most. Keary always threw food on the floor when he was no longer hungry, and Nellie just couldn't resist slipping a bite to the dog every now and then.

Mary turned a tolerantly blind eye on the shenanigans. The Whartons, the Wellingtons, and the Kenricks would never have allowed pets in their fancy dining rooms. But Mary didn't care. Come to think of it, none of her former employers would have allowed *children* in their fancy dining rooms.

What mattered to her were the smiles on Keary's and Nellie's faces. Especially Nellie's. The girl was always willing to help, and she adored Keary, had become almost a second mother to him. But she was often teary-eyed, and sometimes she had nightmares. Today was the first day since she'd come to stay with Mary that Nellie had truly smiled and enjoyed herself, earlier when Baba had been chasing the butterfly and now as they sat around the table.

"How come you're not a miner?" Nellie asked Carson all of a sudden.

He leaned toward the girl and, in a stage whisper, said, "Because I'm scared to death of the mines." Then he smiled, the look assuring them all that he was teasing. As he straightened, he asked, "Would you like to hear how they found the silver in these parts?"

Nellie nodded.

"Seems old Noah Kellogg and a few friends of his were prospecting up in this district when Kellogg's jackass wandered away. So Kellogg and the others went off after it. They found all sorts of traces of that jackass, wads of its hair where it had scraped up against timber and such, so it wasn't hard to follow. Tracks plain as day. Well, when they finally caught up with it, there it was, standing on the side of a hill, staring off across the canyon, its eyes fixed on something and its ears set forward. When those men got over to that jackass, it didn't run off again. Just kept staring across the canyon at what turned out to be an ore chute that was reflecting the sun's rays like a mirror. The sheer glitter had that pack animal mesmerized, so they say. Made Kellogg a mighty rich man." He grinned at Mary. "I keep setting that horse of mine loose in the hills, but he never has found me a vein of galena. Guess I'll just have to keep sheriffin' for a living."

Mesmerized. That was a good word to describe the way Mary felt beneath the blue of his gaze. Mesmerized. Scarcely able to breathe.

"Is that story true," Nellie asked, "or are you just spinning yarn?"

Carson glanced lack at the girl. He drew an X over his chest. "Cross my heart." Then he winked at her and said, "'Course, even plumbers and house-wives know full well that silver and lead lose their brightness when exposed to the air. Just turns a drab gray like most of the other rock around here. So I expect most of the tale is pure moonshine. But it does make for good storytelling."

Nellie scowled. "If I told a whopper like that, my father would've tanned my hide for lying." Her eyes immediately welled with tears. She hopped up from her chair and raced off, disappearing around the side of the house.

Carson started to rise. "What did I say? I—"

"No," Mary said quickly. "Stay here. She's just needing some time to herself. Let her be."

He looked at her. "But what did I—"

"'Twas nothing you did or said, Sheriff. 'Tis only when she remembers her da. Then the crying comes on her. I'm thinking it will pass soon enough. Time'll do what words cannot." She stood up even as he sat down. "You just be staying there while I pour the coffee."

"If you're sure." He sounded unconvinced.

"Aye, I am that." She offered a gentle smile. "I'll be but a moment." She turned and walked toward the house.

The rooftop of the cabin was splashed in gold as the last rays of sunshine reached into the valley. In a moment, evening would arrive. Dusk was mere minutes away. It would soon be time for Carson to leave, to ride back to town before darkness fell. Mary knew she should hurry and send him on his way. But she was reluctant to have him go. She'd enjoyed this meal more than she wanted to admit.

Perhaps because, in admitting so, she would realize exactly what it was she could never have.

Twelve

CARSON DREAMED OF MARY IN A BLUE GOWN, HER wild mass of hair falling free. She was running through a meadow of wildflowers, and her laughter drifted back to him on a breeze. He ran after her, stretching out his arm to touch her. But try as he might, he couldn't catch her. He ran and ran and ran, but she was always out of reach.

Always just out of reach.

Hot coffee splashed over the rim of the cup and onto Carson's left hand, scalding him.

"Damn!"

The tin cup clattered to the floor, splattering coffee in a wide swath. Quickly, Carson returned the pot to the stove. He shook his hand, as if trying to throw off the pain. Then he grabbed a towel and mopped up the mess he'd made, muttering all the while.

It was that blasted dream. He just couldn't get it out of his head. He couldn't think straight, couldn't even pour himself a cup of coffee because of it. Even now, if he closed his eyes, he would see her, running through that flowering meadow, looking beautiful and wild and free.

Maybe his dream was trying to tell him something. That he was supposed to catch her? That he would never catch her?

He muttered another oath, angered by his persistent thoughts. After all, he wasn't the sort to put stock in the meaning of dreams. That was for Indian shaman and old European gypsies. Not for a practical man like him.

Before he'd left the cabin last night, he'd invited Mary and the children to have supper with him in town this evening. He couldn't cook, but Zeb Brewer over at the Whistler Café could. He was aware that taking Mary out to supper would cause plenty of talk, if there wasn't plenty of it already. In all the years he'd been sheriff of Whistle Creek, Carson had never paid court to a lady. He'd never been interested before now.

That was no surprise, of course. There weren't many single females in these parts. At least not the kind one didn't pay money to spend time with. Still, having supper with Mary and her little brood would be grist for the gossip mill.

Suddenly it occurred to him that he didn't care what the gossips said.

He sat back on his heels, his hands braced against his thighs, while he mulled over this unexpected discovery.

It was true. He really didn't care what folks said or thought. He wanted to be with Mary Malone. The more often, the better. He wanted to know everything about her, what caused her to laugh, what caused her to cry. He wanted to run his fingers through her thick cascade of ebony hair and he wanted to kiss the fullness of her innocently seductive mouth. He wanted to listen to her sweet Irish brogue and breathe in the soft scent of lilacs that always lingered near her. He wanted to see the twinkle in her wide brown eyes when she looked after Keary.

Oh, the little Irish colleen had gotten under his skin something fierce. He didn't know if what he felt was love, but it had to be something darn close to it.

He shook his head slowly. There was no denying it any longer. Carson was thinking along the lines of matrimony.

Marriage. Carson Barclay was actually thinking about marriage. A home, family, roots, obligations. He waited to feel a sudden chill, a return to old truths about the untrustworthiness of most women, old beliefs about lawmen never marrying. They didn't come.

Instead, he felt a lightness of heart such as he'd never felt before. Smiling, he stood, tossed the towel into a box near the stove, then grabbed his hat and left the office. He even found himself whistling softly as he strode along the sidewalk toward the café. He hoped Zeb would be amenable to cooking up something special tonight.

A woman ought to have a special supper on the night she received a proposal of marriage.

Mary hurried along the trail toward home. She was feeling somewhat anxious. For the first time, she'd left Keary behind that morning while she'd gone into work at the saloon. She knew Nellie was a responsible sort. She'd observed how well the girl took care of Keary. Still, Mary had found the hours agonizingly long and would be glad to get home and see for herself that both children were all right.

Then, of course, there was the added anxiety about tonight. It seemed she was doomed to ignore common sense. Otherwise, why would she have accepted Carson's invitation to take supper with him in town? Why would she be anxious about what dress to wear and how to fix her hair and whether or not Keary would be on his best behavior?

"Mrs. Malone!" an unfamiliar male voice hailed from behind her. "Wait!"

She stopped and turned. She recognized the mine owner as he rode toward her.

"Good day, Mrs. Malone." Bryan Halligan grinned as he drew near.

"Good day to you, Mr. Halligan," she answered, hoping her intuitive dislike for the man didn't show in her tone of voice.

"I'm honored that you remember me, ma'am." His grin broadened. "And I'm glad I caught you before you made it all the way home. I just missed finding you over at the Painted Lady."

His words caused her to tense. "You were looking for me, sir?"

"I was, indeed." He dismounted, then faced her again.

"I've been up at the Lucky Lady Mine, overseeing the investigation into that unfortunate collapse of the tunnel"—his gaze flicked over her appraisingly—"and I found myself hungry for some delightful female companionship. I was hoping you might consent to have supper with me."

As was true the first time she'd met this man, Mary found herself reminded of Winston Kenrick, and a chill shivered up her spine. Instinctively, she took a step backward. "I cannot, Mr. Halligan, but 'twas nice of you to ask."

One corner of his mouth twitched before Halligan said, "Please reconsider, my dear Mrs. Malone."

There was something menacing in his eyes, a look that once again reminded Mary of her former employer.

"Sure and 'tis not possible, sir." She wanted to light out for home, but she hated the idea of him following her there. She hated the idea of him even knowing where she lived—which he apparently already did.

"I won't be in Whistle Creek long. My work at the mine is nearly finished."

"Then I hope you'll be having a safe journey back to Spokane." She started to turn away.

He laid his hand on her arm, not grasping, yet somehow holding her there. "Mrs. Malone, it would be a mistake to make an enemy of me." He spoke softly, but it didn't disguise the threat in his words. "Now, agree to have supper with me. You'll be glad you did."

Her temper flared hot. "I'll have you taking your bloody hand off o' me." She tried to jerk away from him.

"Just who do you think you are?" His grip tightened.

"I'm thinking I'm Mary Emeline Malone," she answered through gritted teeth. And then she kicked him in the shin just as hard as she could.

Halligan yelped in surprise. He released his hold on her arm and stumbled back a step.

Mary's instincts shouted at her to run, but she stubbornly held her ground. She was tired of running scared.

"I'll not be bullied by the likes o' you, Mr. Halligan. You're not me master. I'm a free woman, I am, and I'll not be having supper with you tonight or any other night. Will you be understanding that plain enough now?"

Halligan's eyes narrowed. "You'll be sorry you did that."

She gave her head a tiny toss in reply, a show of bravado she wasn't feeling on the inside. "I'm thinking you're wrong."

For a breathless moment, he continued to scowl at her. Then, abruptly, he turned, remounted his horse, and rode away.

The fury drained out of Mary in an instant, leaving her shaken and weak in the knees. *Control your temper, Mary girl*, her da had always told her, but she'd never learned to follow his advice. If she had, she wouldn't be living in Idaho, hiding from the law.

Carson stepped into the darkened church. "Christy?" he called softly. "You in here?"

A shadow toward the front of the building moved. A moment later, it became the clear shape of a man walking toward him.

"What's this all about?" Carson asked once he could see the mine manager clearly. "Why'd you send a note for me to meet with you here? You could've come to my office." He continued to speak just above a whisper, he

142

supposed because this meeting place seemed to demand it.

"Halligan is somewhere in town," Jeff Christy answered, "and I didn't want him to see us talking."

"Why not?"

Jeff jerked his head toward the nearest pew, and the two of them sat down.

"What's up?" Carson prodded when the other man still didn't answer his previous questions.

"Sheriff, I think Halligan's going to blame that collapse in tunnel nineteen on the miners. The ones who have vocally supported the union in the past. He's going to make it look like the cave-in was intentional rather than an accident, like those men were trying to cause trouble."

"Why?"

Jeff raked the fingers of both hands through his hair while he stared down at the floor. "He wants to force the miners to go out on strike."

"Strike? But why—"

"So he can bring in scab labor for a pittance of what he pays these men. You know how cheap new immigrants will work. Especially the ones who don't speak English. That, in turn, will drive down wages."

"Is Halligan *crazy*? Doesn't he remember what happened in this district six years ago?"

Jeff nodded slowly. "He thinks they'll give in, accept the lower wages he wants to pay before the strike stretches out too long or real rioting begins. And if it does, he's confident the governor will step in like he did before. In the meantime, he can get rid of those union organizers."

Carson muttered a few choice words about Bryan Halligan and his ancestors.

"Look, Sheriff, I don't have any proof of any of this. It's just a gut feeling." He paused, then added, "But if I'm right, this whole town could explode."

"I know."

"I've got a lot of friends working out at the mine. I don't want to see any of them hurt, maybe killed. Losing Dunmore was bad enough."

Carson frowned thoughtfully. "You don't think Halligan was behind the cave-in, do you, Christy?"

There was a pregnant pause before the manager answered, "There's no evidence that says he was. It still looks to me like an accident."

"Hmm."

Jeff Christy rose from the pew. "Listen, I've got to be getting back to the Lucky Lady. Do what you can, Sheriff."

"Yeah," he answered, but he hadn't a clue what that would be.

He waited while the other man slipped out the back door of the church, forcing himself to sit still until enough time had passed for Jeff to be long gone from town. In the meantime, he searched his mind for a solution to the problem.

Carson didn't like Bryan Halligan. Never had. He was the sort of man who cared little for human life—except for his own, of course. And he made no bones about thinking all underground workers made too much money at three dollars a day, especially since anything they made cut into his own personal profits.

But would Halligan really try to *cause* a strike?

Last time there was trouble in the Coeur d'Alene district, the strikebreakers had come under attack. One man had been killed and many more injured in an explosion caused by an ore car filled with a hundred

144

pounds of dynamite. Part of a stamp mill had been demolished. The governor had called up six companies of the National Guard, and President Harrison had sent twenty companies of United States infantry. Six hundred miners and their supporters had been imprisoned for several weeks without trial or hearing.

It was hard for Carson to believe anyone would want to intentionally cause something like that again. But if anyone would, Halligan was the man.

Carson left the church, still mulling over the situation. Out of habit, he followed his circuitous route around town, taking Church Street to the depot, then heading east along Lucky Street toward River Street and the rear entrance of the Painted Lady.

He supposed it wouldn't hurt to stop in at the saloon. It was possible he might overhear something that could be of use to him. If Jeff suspected Halligan of trying to place the blame of the cave-in on the miners, he supposed others might be thinking the same thing.

He came to an abrupt stop when he saw Halligan himself riding out of the draw that led to Carson's cabin—the cabin where Mary and the children were now staying. Reflexively, his fingers tapped against the gun strapped to his thigh.

What reason, except to see Mary, would have taken Halligan up that trail? he wondered.

The answer was, none.

He started walking again, quickening his pace so he would arrive at River Street about the same time Halligan rode over the bridge crossing the Coeur d'Alene.

"Hello, Halligan," he said, making sure his voice didn't reveal the distrust he was feeling.

"Sheriff."

"I heard you'd been out at the mine."

"Yes." Halligan reined in.

"Have you discovered what caused it? The accident, I mean." He'd chosen his words purposefully, and now he waited to see what the mine owner's reaction would be.

Halligan shook his head. His expression remained neutral. "Nothing yet."

"Too bad."

"Don't worry. We'll find the cause."

Carson was getting nowhere fast. He decided to change course. "I see you were up to my old place. I didn't know you and Mrs. Malone were friends." He couldn't keep the edge out of his voice, no matter how hard he tried.

"I wouldn't say friends exactly." Halligan leaned down and rubbed his shin with his fingertips before dismounting. When he faced the sheriff again, he said, "I hope you're keeping your eyes and ears open for troublemakers. Like I told you before, I'm sure something is afoot with the miners. I think that cave-in is just the beginning." He started walking toward the center of town, leading his horse behind him.

Carson didn't fall into step beside Halligan as was surely expected. He simply stood and watched the other man walk down River Street, then turn west on Main, disappearing behind the barbershop and bathhouse.

Jeff was right. Carson had no doubts left. Halligan meant to put the blame on the miners. He meant to *cause* trouble at the Lucky Lady and in Whistle Creek, not avoid it.

But what had Halligan wanted with Mary? he wondered as his gaze turned up the draw. For some reason that question concerned him even more than the possibility of riots and strikes.

It shouldn't have, but it did.

So for the second time in as many days, Carson headed up the draw several hours before he was expected.

"Oh, you poor thing," Mary whispered when she saw the gelding. She completely forgot the reprimand she'd been forming in her head, about Nellie and Keary wandering so far from the cabin.

"I told you," Nellie said. "How long you think he's been there?"

"Sure and I wouldn't be knowing."

The swaybacked pinto stood with his left foreleg lifted off the ground, the knee swollen more than twice its normal size. The knotted end of a frayed rope was snagged in a fallen tree, keeping him from lifting his head above knee level. His black and white coat was crisscrossed with tiny cuts and scratches, probably from the branches and thick underbrush of the mountain trails that had brought him to this place, but it looked to Mary as if a whip had caused the welts on his rump.

"Poor laddie," she crooned as she took a step toward him, half expecting him to try to bolt.

But when she looked into the horse's eyes, she knew that was a needless worry. This animal hadn't the strength to run. Mary wasn't sure he would survive another hour.

"Well, boyo, 'tis a fine mess you've got yourself into altogether. Let's be seeing if we can get you free." She circled behind him, then leaned down and freed the snared lead rope.

The horse nickered softly. It sounded a bit like gratitude.

"How're we gonna get him home?" Nellie inquired.

Mary could only shake her head. She knew little about horses. She was able to drive a buggy but had never felt a great deal of confidence when holding the reins. Her da had been too poor to own much in the way of livestock. A few chickens and a goat for milking. Certainly never a horse.

Cautiously, she touched the swollen knee. The horse gave a sort of grunt but didn't strike out at her. She decided to probe a little more, and when she was finished, she was fairly convinced that nothing was broken.

"'Tis a bad sprain, I'm thinking," she told Nellie as she straightened. "If we go slow down the trail, we could get him back to the house and see that he's fed and watered. Will you be leading the way with Keary?"

"Sure."

"Well, then." Mary took hold of the lead rope as she stepped out in front of the animal. Then she stared him straight in the eyes. "'Tis some walking you'll have to do, if you've a mind to go home with us."

As if he understood, the horse gingerly set the hoof of his injured leg on the ground and limped forward.

Nellie grinned. "Look at him, Keary! He's coming home with us."

Keary squealed merrily.

They followed a well-worn deer track down the mountain. It was narrow and slippery with tiny rocks and shale. The going was slow. Mary's skirt got snagged once, suffering a small tear before she had it freed, but other than that, they all managed to reach the meadow without mishap.

"Sure and we're here," Mary said as she patted the horse's neck.

The sound of thundering hooves alerted her to the

presence of another. She turned just in time to see Carson slide his steed to an abrupt halt.

"Where have you been?" he demanded as he vaulted to the ground. His gaze swept from her to Nellie and Keary, then back again.

Mary was too surprised by his sudden appearance to be insulted by his demanding tone of voice. "Nellie found this poor horse up on the mountain."

"And you went up there without the rifle I gave you?" he half shouted.

"The rifle?"

"What if there'd been a cougar or a bear? You shouldn't be traipsing around in the forest without protection."

Her anger came as swift as ever. "I'll be going where I like, when I like, and 'tis not you who'll be telling me otherwise, Sheriff Barclay."

He stepped forward, towering over her, his blue eyes glowering as he stared down. His hands gripped her shoulders, firm but not painfully so. "Don't you know how worried I was when I couldn't find you?"

"Sure and you've no cause to worry about me." She tried to jerk away.

His fingers tightened. The kiss came as suddenly as her anger, but was more unexpected. It was over just as quickly.

She should slap him, she thought as he backed away. She should tell him he'd had no right to do that. She should tell him she wanted nothing to do with him. Not now. Not ever.

But her treasonous body wouldn't listen to the wise counsel of her mind. Not while her lips tingled from the pressure of his. Not while she could feel the rapid beating of her heart. Not while the heat of wanting was coiling in her loins.

"I'm sorry," he said—but he didn't sound so. He still sounded angry. "I shouldn't have yelled at you. But when I didn't find you here . . ." His words trailed into silence.

This could not happen, this attraction that crackled between them. She could not allow it to happen. It was dangerous for her, and it was unfair to him. She needed to stop it now, before it was too late. Before he learned the truth about her. Before she told him any more lies.

Send him away, Mary, her conscience demanded.

But she couldn't. Not yet.

Because her heart was demanding that she let him stay.

Carson wanted nothing so much as to pull Mary back into his embrace and kiss her again. Slowly this time. As brief as it had been, that first kiss had shaken him to the bottom of his soul. Now he wanted to savor the taste of her soft lips against his. He wanted to test the emotional upheaval in his heart and see if it was real.

"Sure and you must not do that again," Mary said softly, confusion in her wide, brown eyes.

"I didn't mean—"

Nellie's giggle interrupted him.

Mary blushed. "I'm thinking it would be better if we didn't go to supper with you, Sheriff Barclay." She stepped around him, still leading that limping rack of bones she called a horse.

"Mary, wait." He touched her shoulder, then pulled back his hand. "I'll say it again. I'm sorry. I just lost my head. I was afraid something had happened to you and the children."

She glanced at him.

"Please, have supper with me."

Nellie chimed in, "Please, Mary"

Carson offered an apologetic grin. "I promise to be on my best behavior."

Mary shook her head slowly. Then she looked at Nellie. "Take Keary back to the house."

"But—" the girl began to object.

"Now, Nellie." Her tone brooked no argument.

"Oh, all right. But I don't see why."

Mary waited until Nellie had obeyed before she turned and met Carson's gaze again. "'Twould be a mistake for you to think there is more than friendship between us, Sheriff Barclay."

He would have been disappointed, except he could see that she was wrestling with her own feelings. He was certain she felt something more than friendship for him, even if it was only a kindled desire. He wasn't giving up yet.

"Mary—"

"No." She raised her hand to stop his words. "'Tis on me own I wish to be. Just me and me son."

"And Nellie and Baba and now this miserable pinto." He smiled again, appealing to her sense of humor. "After all these other strays, outcasts, and orphans, won't you take pity on me, too?"

"You're no outcast," she argued, "and you're too old to be an orphan."

His smile vanished. "But I am alone, Mary."

She caught her breath.

He couldn't help it. He reached out and drew her to him, holding her body close against his. "Don't you know there is something special between us?" he asked, his voice low and husky. "I've never felt anything like this. Have you?"

151

"No," she whispered, shaking her head, her gaze never leaving his. "No."

"It *is* more than friendship." He brushed his lips against her cheek. "Admit it. It is more."

She closed her eyes, and he felt a quiver run through her. "'Twould be a terrible mistake to admit such a thing."

"Why?" He kissed her forehead.

"I cannot say."

"Why?" he repeated.

Her reply was so soft, he could scarcely hear her. "Do not ask me, Carson."

Perhaps it was because she'd used his Christian name. Perhaps it was the catch in her voice. Or perhaps it was the note of quiet desperation he'd heard therein. Whatever the reason, Carson understood he had pressed her too far.

"All right, Mary, I won't ask." He rested his cheek against the top of her head. "But it doesn't change what I feel, and it won't change what I want. Remember that, will you?"

"Aye, I'll remember."

Thirteen

Monday, 15 August, 1898
Whistle Creek, Idaho

Dear Inga,
It was good to receive your most recent letter and to learn your wonderful news. I know how much you have hoped and prayed for a baby of your own, and God has heard your prayers.

152

Today I am driving over to a neighboring town and the mine there where I will inquire about Quaid. It is becoming more imperative that I find my brother, for I am unsure how long I will be able to remain in Whistle Creek. I am thinking it is not good for us to stay much longer. The sheriff's interest in me is one I cannot return.

When I was little, my da was forced from job to job, and he took his family with him. I do not know how many places we lived through the years, but there were many. I used to wish for one home where I could live forever, like the titled families who owned the lands he worked. And to be honest altogether, I would love to stay in this little cottage in the mountains. It is perfect—or as near to perfect as I have ever known.

But to stay would be unfair to the kindest man it has been my good fortune to meet. Aye, it is true. Carson Barclay is a wonder of a man, handsome and tall, strong and kind and honest. The sheriff is a man of integrity, he is. I am believing he means to propose marriage, but I cannot accept. I cannot tell you why anymore than I can tell him why. So I know it would be better if I should take myself from this place and soon.

My Keary turned a year old last week. He no longer walks with unsure steps. He runs instead. And he jabbers constantly, though he makes no sense as yet. He is such a handsome lad, and he holds my heart in his wee hands. There is not anything I would not do to protect him and keep him from harm. Now that you will soon have a child of your own, I know you must be understanding how I feel.

153

I must close this letter and be about my day's work. I pray that all goes well with you throughout your confinement. Do write again soon, and give my love to your parents and sisters.

With affection always,
Mary Emeline Malone

A seemingly endless fit of coughing left Blanche wilted and longing for the simple luxury of one deep breath of air. Why was it, she wondered as she leaned against the pillows at her back, her eyes closed, that folks seldom knew what really mattered until it was too late?

"Should I send someone for the doctor, Miss Blanche?"

She opened her eyes. "No, Martin," she answered hoarsely. "We haven't finished our business."

The lawyer shook his head, but he didn't argue with her. Instead, he flipped over another page of the thick document, then handed it to her. "There is the new paragraph regarding the Painted Lady Saloon. You already know how I feel about this change you've made."

"Yes, I know." She frowned as she carefully read everything through. It wasn't that she didn't trust Martin Burke. She did. But Blanche had learned long ago that it was she and she alone who had to take responsibility for her business and her own well-being. Sometimes the learning had come hard, but she *had* learned.

Martin leaned forward. "At least allow me to find out a little more about Mrs. Malone. I could send out a few inquiries. You say you met her in New York. Why not—"

"No!" She gave the man a cross look, then resumed reading.

The lawyer bounced his heels off the floor while restlessly tapping his fingertips against his knees. Blanche had to concentrate hard to ignore the irritating movements, but finally she was convinced everything was exactly as she wanted it.

"Give me a pen, Martin and bring in the witnesses. I'm ready to sign it."

"I still think you're making a mistake, Miss Blanche. This place could bring you a small fortune if you were to sell—"

"Martin."

He sighed, defeated. "All right. I'll do as you ask."

"Thank you." She smiled wearily. The business of dying, she was finding out, wasn't any less complicated than the business of living.

A short while later, with her revised will signed and duly witnessed, Blanche bid her lawyer a good afternoon and watched as he took his leave. Then Greta brought her a fresh pot of tea.

"Tea," Blanche muttered as the cook poured the fragrant brew into a cup. "Who'd've thought I'd ever take up drinking tea instead of brandy?"

Greta clucked her tongue.

Blanche turned her gaze out the window toward the thickly treed mountains beyond. Her eyes filled with tears, much to her irritation. It seemed she was becoming a sentimental fool in her last days.

"No place else like here," Greta said.

Blanche didn't try to respond. There was nothing to say. After all, she agreed. There wasn't any place else like her glorious Silver Valley. This was home. She was going to miss it for all eternity.

In silent understanding, Greta patted Blanche's shoulder before quietly departing.

Alone again, Blanche tossed off the light coverings on her bed and sat up, then lowered her feet to the floor. With great effort, she stood and made her way across the bedroom to the window. Each breath came with difficulty, and she concentrated hard not to give in to another coughing spell.

At the window, she leaned her forehead against the glass and stared out at the sunny afternoon. Below her lay the town of Whistle Creek. The dusty streets were quiet, usual for a Monday afternoon. She wondered how many of her neighbors had heard that the infamous madam was dying.

And dying soon, she thought as she listened to her own belabored breathing. *Very soon.*

She sighed and closed her eyes. She supposed it was time for that little chat with the good Reverend Mordecai Ogelsby.

Carson tugged on his hat brim, the better to shade his eyes. The air was still and hot and the sky blindingly clear, but a sixth sense told him they were ripe for a thunderstorm come evening. Not a welcome possibility with things as dry as they'd been. It only took one lightning strike to start a raging forest fire.

And they had trouble enough without adding Mother Nature into the mix, he thought with a frown.

"Halligan's gonna do it, ain't he?" John asked. "He's gonna pin the blame on me."

The two men were riding west toward Osburn. Carson had heard a rumor that Halligan had a man bringing in cheap labor for the Lucky Lady, just in case there was a strike. He wanted to see for himself if it was true.

Just in case.

"Yeah," he answered John, "I think that's what he's planning to do."

The younger man shook his head. "You know it ain't true, Sheriff Barclay. I didn't go into the mine to cause trouble, and I'm sure a heck of a lot smarter than to blow up a tunnel with me in it. What happened to me"—he pointed at his scarred cheek—"was an accident. But if I was settin' something on purpose, I'd know exactly what I was doin' and I wouldn't get caught neither."

Carson believed him. But it didn't matter what Carson believed. Besides, Halligan wasn't after the truth. By picking John Tyrell to take the fall, Halligan had chosen well. Accuse the hero of the cave-in of wrongdoing, and he would have the trouble he was after.

"We've got to make the men see reason, John. If they'll hold onto their tempers—"

"Sheriff, it ain't just me. If Halligan fires those other men, the ones tryin' to organize the union, all hell's gonna break loose."

Frustration made Carson grind his teeth. There should be something he could do, but he felt helpless to stop what was coming. When trouble flared, Halligan was going to demand protection, and it would be Carson's job to provide it. The National Guard would probably come in. Scab labor would work the mine. Good men would be out of work. Families would be thrown out of their homes, and innocent people could get hurt if violence became part of the package. In the end, the miners who kept their jobs would go back to work for a reduced wage, and Halligan would take his and his partners' increased profits back to Spokane to enjoy.

The two men rode on in silence for the better part of half an hour. The whole time, Carson searched his mind for a solution, for some way to stop the trouble before it began. But every idea that came to him was quickly discarded. It seemed to him that Halligan held all the cards.

They were almost to Osburn before John spoke again. "I asked Edith to marry me."

"What?" Carson reined in abruptly.

John grinned. "You heard right. My brother's givin' me a small section of land to build a house on. Miss Blanche says I can keep on at the saloon, and if I get tired of that, Wade says I can work the farm with him."

"You sure you're not rushing into things, John? You're just beginning to get your feet under you."

"You mean I haven't been sober all that long, and you're wondering if I'm gonna stay that way."

Carson shrugged.

"Or maybe you're wondering if Edith's gonna want to be a farmer's wife."

"Would she?"

John took quick offense at the comment, and his voice revealed it. "She hasn't always kept company in a saloon. Edith grew up on a farm over in Montana. She knows what the life is like. And she knows she loves me, too."

"Look, I didn't mean—"

John waved his hand, dismissing whatever Carson had been about to say. "No, it's okay. I shouldn't've got mad so fast. Edith ain't no innocent girl. That's true enough. But she's got her a good heart, and she loves me just like I am. I reckon that's all I need to know."

"Then I'm glad for you, John. I mean it. I'm happy for you both."

The younger man grinned. "Thanks. Now how about you?"

"Me?" Carson clucked to his horse and moved out.

John quickly caught up. "You think everybody in town hasn't noticed you've got eyes for Miz Malone? When're you gonna ask her to marry you?"

He shot the fellow a look that clearly said, *Lay off.* He hadn't talked to Mary since the night he'd kissed her. She'd been avoiding him and doing a dang good job of it.

But he'd sworn to himself that he would be patient. Holding her in his arms as he had that night, feeling her heartbeat next to his, he'd known he would have to move slowly if he was to win her. He'd sensed then that she was more fragile and jittery than he'd thought her at first. So if it was time and space she needed, he was determined to give it to her.

He just hadn't known it would be this blasted hard.

It was nearly six o'clock by the time the rented horse and buggy carried Mary along the road back toward Whistle Creek. Much later than she'd intended to return from Wallace. But she was too excited to care.

Today she had found a man who once worked with Quaid. True, it had been two years ago, but the man had known her brother. He was pretty sure Quaid was still in Idaho. He'd even promised to ask around for her, see if anyone knew of Quaid's current whereabouts.

Sure and it would be perfect altogether if she were to find Quaid now. She would leave Whistle Creek. She would go to live with her brother. She would be safe from the law.

And Carson Barclay would be safe from her.

Her heart skittered, and her emotions plummeted, her joy and excitement immediately forgotten.

It was a terrible thing, the way she had lost her heart to the sheriff, and there was no denying it, not even to herself. It was bad enough that she had weakened in her resolve never to play the fool for a man again. It was worse that it had happened with this particular man. "

Carson was going to ask her to marry him. She sensed it. He'd made it clear in a dozen different ways. But no matter how much she cared for him—or precisely *because* of how much she cared for him—she would have to refuse. She couldn't marry the sheriff. Even if the truth about New York and Winston Kenrick never came out, she couldn't live that particular lie. As Carson's wife, always fearing the day of discovery would be a hundred times worse than anything she lived now.

She closed her eyes, giving the horse his head, and remembered the way Carson had kissed her. The brief touch of his lips upon hers shouldn't have affected her so greatly. It had been over in an instant.

No, it hadn't been over in an instant.

It still wasn't over.

She drew in a shaky breath, trying to ignore the tingling in her body as she recalled the way Carson had held her close against him, the brush of his lips against her cheek and forehead, the gentleness in his voice.

"You thought Seamus a good man," she scolded herself. "You thought you loved him, too."

But her argument didn't work. She knew Carson was different. She knew he was exactly the sort of man she had dreamed of when she was a young girl in service. Seamus had lied to get her into his bed. Carson would never do such a thing.

Mary opened her eyes and stared up at the darkening sky. "Why now?" she demanded. "Why did I find him after it was too late?"

As if in reply, the wind rose, drowning out the clipclop of the horse's hooves and the music of the river.

You could tell him what you've done.

Before the thought had scarcely registered, Mary rejected it. She couldn't tell him. Carson would be honor bound to turn her over to the authorities back east, and then what would happen to Keary? It was the same fear, the same question, the same quandary, she'd always had. Nothing had changed. There were good people in Whistle Creek who might take him in and raise him, but no one could love her son the way she did. No, she could never tell the truth. She would have to live with her crime until her dying day.

And that would mean living without Carson.

"I'll be finding Quaid," she whispered to herself. "'Tis why fate sent me to Idaho. I'll be finding me brother and we'll all be going away from here, and I'll forget Sheriff Barclay altogether."

She was silent for a long time before adding, "And 'tis a fine liar you've become, Mary Emeline Malone, if you'd be believing that 'tis true. A fine liar."

The storm swept up the valley with a sudden vengeance that surprised even the old-timers. There was little warning. First there were a few clouds on the western horizon, and then came the battering wind, with gusts strong enough to knock a man right off his horse.

Carson listened to the walls of his office creak and moan and was thankful he and John had made it back from Osburn before the storm hit. He hoped Mary and the kids were okay.

He rose from the chair behind his desk and walked to the window, gazing out at a huge cloud of dust rolling down Main Street like a giant tumbleweed, driven by the furious wind. The sky had grown as black as midnight in a matter of moments, and the clouds looked ready to drop a deluge of rain on the small town. But at least there hadn't been any lightning thus far.

Maybe this storm would cool things off around here. And he didn't mean just the weather.

He turned away from the window, his thoughts straying to what he'd learned in Osburn. Halligan had gathered himself quite the little workforce over there. Right now they were just standing around in the saloon, swilling beer and whiskey. But eventually . . .

Beside him, the door flew open, crashing back against the wall. A strong gust of wind sent the papers on his desk flying like a dervish.

"Sorry!" John shouted as he grabbed the door and pushed it closed again.

Carson raised an eyebrow, then strode across his office to retrieve the strewn papers.

"I thought you ought to know. Miz Malone ain't back yet, and Edith's getting worried."

Carson stopped abruptly, then turned toward John. "What did you say? Back from where?"

"From Wallace."

"What was she doing over there?"

John shook his head. "Edith didn't say. I just know Mary left Keary and Nellie with Edith and rented Stover's buggy. She told Edith she'd be back before dark."

Carson muttered an oath beneath his breath. Dang fool woman. What business did she have over in Wallace? Especially on a day like this. He could've told her it was going to storm. Besides, he'd warned her these mountains were full of disreputable men, and she shouldn't be traipsing around by herself. Why hadn't she listened to him?

"I'll go find her," he grumbled, jamming his hat on his head.

"I'm comin', too."

Carson nodded, then pulled on his slicker, although he doubted it would help much, from the look of the storm clouds. He figured they'd all be half-drowned before they got back to town.

Blinded by swirling dust, pebbles, and dried pine needles, Mary drew back on the reins, stopping the buggy in the middle of the narrow road. She couldn't expect the horse to continue on in this. They had to find shelter of some sort. At the very least, she needed to turn the animal's back to the wind until the worst was over.

She climbed down from her seat and felt her way forward, holding onto the harness as she went. Just as she reached the horse's head, a blast of wind knocked Mary a step backward. Her skirt flew up, slapping and snapping like a flag. Above the noise of the storm, she heard the horse whinny in alarm. It reared, striking out with its hooves. Mary took another quick step back—

And felt the earth give way beneath her feet.

Carson's heart nearly stopped when he saw the Stover rig come flying along the road without a driver. He didn't try to stop the runaway horse. He figured the horse would make it back to Whistle Creek on its own.

"Come on!" he shouted at John, then dug his heels into Cinnabar's ribs and set off at a gallop. It didn't take

163

him long to realize he would miss any sign of Mary if he didn't slow down, even though taking his time was the last thing he wanted to do.

As he reined in, he glanced over his shoulder at John. The younger man simply nodded in understanding. Then John guided his horse over to the mountain side of the road, his gaze sweeping the underbrush amidst the trees. Carson turned his mount toward the side of the road that overlooked the turbulent white water below.

The wind at his back continued to stir up whirlwinds of dirt, making it difficult to see clearly. He almost wished it would go ahead and rain. Maybe then . . .

He stopped abruptly. A sixth sense told him something was not as it should be. It took him a few moments to realize ground at the edge of the road had fallen away, crumbling down the steep slope to the river.

"Mary!" he shouted, his hands cupped near his mouth. "Mary, can you hear me?"

The wind grabbed his words and carried them off before even he could hear them.

He dismounted and carefully approached the edge. "Mary?"

He tried telling himself there was no reason to believe she had fallen here. She could be anywhere. She might be perfectly all right, standing under a tree farther up the road. The horse might even have run away from Wallace. Mary could be stranded but safe.

And then he saw her, clinging precariously to a jagged outcropping of rocks, her legs and skirt immersed in the churning, foaming river.

"John, she's here!" Carson cried as he grabbed his lariat from his saddle.

Quickly, he made a loop and dropped it over the

saddle horn. He cinched the other end around his waist. By the time he was ready to start his descent, John was there, too. The younger man took Cinnabar by the reins.

"Pull us up when I give the signal," Carson shouted over the wind.

John nodded that he understood.

The moment Carson stepped over the edge, more earth came loose. Pebbles and dirt showered Mary below. Carson swore beneath his breath but kept going.

"Hang on, Mary," he called to her, hoping she could hear him.

She didn't move.

Several anxious moments passed before Carson reached Mary's side. Her bonnet, if she'd worn one, was missing. Her head was turned toward him, her right cheek pressed against a cold, damp rock. Her hair, wet from the constant spray off the river, was plastered against her left cheek. Her eyes were closed. The knuckles of her right hand were white from her tight grip on the stones, but her left arm and hand were limp at her side. She was shivering uncontrollably.

"Mary, I'm here."

Just as the words came out of his mouth, jagged lightning brightened the stormy sky, followed by a loud crash of thunder.

Carson saw Mary's whole body tense, but she still didn't open her eyes. He looked upward; he could barely see John. Then he glanced at the lariat tied around his waist. He sure hoped the knot would hold, because he was going to have to let go.

He took a quick gulp of air, then released the rope and reached for Mary, gripping her firmly by the upper arms. Only then did she open her eyes. They were glazed with fear and pain.

"I've got you, Mary," he said loudly. "Let go of the rock. Take hold of me."

She didn't budge.

"You can trust me, Mary. Let go."

Another flash of lightning.

Another boom of thunder.

Mary loosened her death grip on the rocks, and he pulled her into his embrace. She wrapped her right arm around his neck and held on tightly.

"Are you hurt?" he demanded, but he knew the answer already.

She nodded mutely.

His right arm tightened around her as he gripped the rope with his left hand. "Pull us up, John," he shouted. Then to Mary he said, "Don't worry. I'll get you home all right."

She laid her head against his shoulder and closed her eyes again.

If it had been up to Carson, he would have kept her there the rest of their lives.

Fourteen

"SURE AND THERE'S NOTHING MUCH WRONG WITH me, Dr. Ingall," Mary said as the physician gently manipulated her right knee. She tried and failed to hide the flinch of pain.

"Hmm," was his reply.

"I cannot be lying in bed when there's so much work to be done," she persisted. "I've been down too long already. Miss Blanche will be needing me to look after her ledgers, and Edith is planning her wedding and—"

"Mrs. Malone, if you put weight on that leg before it's ready, you could do permanent injury to the knee." He pointed to her left arm. "And I don't want to see your arm out of that sling for another week."

Mary let out a deep sigh.

With a shake of his head, Jakob Ingall straightened. "Sheriff Barclay warned me you would be a stubborn patient."

"He did, did he? And I'd like to know what he—"

The doctor chuckled as he touched her shoulder. "Don't go having a conniption. He only said it out of concern for you, Mrs. Malone."

She sighed again, her burst of temper gone. She knew Carson cared. He cared too much.

And so did she.

Dr. Ingall closed his black leather bag. "Nellie Russell seems to be thriving here. It's a kind thing you've done, giving her a home with you."

"She's a sweet girl altogether. I'd not want her anywhere else."

The doctor headed toward the cabin door.

"Dr. Ingall?"

He stopped and looked back at her.

"How is Miss Blanche? Edith will only say I'm not to worry meself."

For a moment she thought the man would shield her from the truth. But finally he said, "I don't believe she has much longer, Mrs. Malone. Perhaps a few weeks. Perhaps less."

"She's been very kind to me," Mary whispered, her throat tight.

Jakob Ingall nodded again, then exited through the open cabin door. It wasn't long after he left before Nellie and Keary appeared in the same doorway.

"How are ya, Mary?" the girl asked.

"Well enough and tired of all the fussing."

"Sheriff Barclay said he's bringing us supper from town. Can we eat outside again?"

Mary's heart did its familiar little flutter in response to Carson's name. "Aye," she answered softly. "We can eat outside again."

Keary pulled free from Nellie's hold on his hand and ran across the room to climb onto the bed with his mother. Mary smiled as she helped him up and snuggled him in the crook of her right arm. He jabbered something nonsensical.

"The sheriff said I could try riding Cloud pretty soon," Nellie commented, referring to the horse they'd found the previous week. "He says I'm light enough, I can't do Cloud no harm. I think his leg's doing better than yours."

Mary raised an eyebrow.

The girl laughed. "Well, it's true."

"Is it now?"

"Can I leave Keary here while I go brush Cloud? I'd like him to look good when the sheriff comes."

"Aye."

"Thanks, Mary." She vanished in a heartbeat.

Mary stared at the empty doorway. She was gladdened by Nellie's high spirits, but she knew the mood could shift suddenly, as it often did, leaving the child in tears. Carson did much to help, she admitted reluctantly. He never failed to say something to Nellie that made her smile or laugh. He had an uncanny understanding of children.

"Why does he have to be so perfect altogether?" she asked her son softly. "And why is it I have to . . ." She hesitated, knowing everything would be changed once she confessed her feelings, even only to herself. But there was no denying the truth any longer. "Why is it I have to love him when there's no hope for the two of us?"

Keary shook his head, as if he'd understood.

Mary smiled, but there was no happiness in it. Loving Carson Barclay would only bring her more heartache. How had she let it happen? How had she let him become such an important part of her life?

She remembered the moment he'd rescued her from the edge of the river. *You can trust me, Mary*, he'd said to her.

Could she? Could she trust him? She wanted to. With everything within her, she wanted to trust him. But how could she? Or rather, how could she allow *him* to trust *her*, after all she'd done? He was a good and honest man. And she? She was an unmarried mother with a past full of mistakes. He represented the long arm of the law. She was in hiding from the law. What possible future could they have?

She heard Nellie shout a greeting, and Mary knew the man of her thoughts had arrived. Her pulse quickened as she sat up straighter. Keary wiggled, trying to get down, having heard Carson's reply to Nellie. In a flash, he slipped from her one-handed grip and off the bed and rushed toward the door.

Just as Keary reached it, Carson stepped into view. He scooped the toddler up, tossing him high and catching him, eliciting a squeal of joy from the boy.

"Where are you off to, Keary Malone?" Carson's gaze met with Mary's, and she momentarily lost the ability to breathe. "And how are you, Mary?"

"I'm fine altogether," she answered, the words barely audible. She took a quick breath, then said, "The doctor was just here."

"I know. I ran into him on the trail. He says you're *not* fine altogether, and you're to stay off of that leg. And that's just what you're going to do."

"Well, if you know so much, Carson Barclay," she snapped, "why would you be bothering to ask me?"

"Have I made you mad at me again, Mary?" he asked with a teasing grin.

She started to nod, then shook her head. She didn't know what she felt at the moment. Everything within her was at odds.

Carson's grin widened. "I'll be right back." Then he disappeared from view, Keary still in his arms.

Mary let her head fall against the pillows behind her. She recalled the terror she'd felt when she'd been clinging to those jagged rocks, trying not to be swept away in the river. She was a poor swimmer. She would have drowned if she'd lost her hold and gone into the water. And that was precisely how she felt now. Like she was drowning. Like she was helpless against the swift current that was carrying her away.

Carson returned, pausing a second time in the doorway. This time, instead of holding her son, his hands held a large bouquet of purple, yellow, and white wildflowers. "I thought these might brighten the place a bit."

"Aye," she whispered, "they will that."

He stepped toward her. "Mary . . ."

"There'd be a jar in the cupboard. You should be putting them in water."

He arrived at her bedside and went down on one knee. He placed the flowers on the floor near his boot, then removed his hat and set it next to the flowers. "Mary, I have something I want to say. I've been wanting to say it for quite a while now." He took hold of her right hand as he spoke.

As she looked into the blue of his eyes, Mary felt that drowning sensation again. She had a nearly irresistible urge to touch the tiny scar in his left eyebrow, to run her fingers through his golden brown hair, to feel the afternoon shadow of his beard on his jaw.

"I've never done anything like this before," he said as his fingers tightened around hers. "I never wanted to."

"Carson, don't."

He ignored her protest. "I don't know any fancy words, so I'll just come right out and say it. You know I love you, Mary Malone. Last week, when I realized I could have lost you, I knew I couldn't wait any longer. I want to marry you. Say yes, Mary. Say you'll marry me."

"Oh, Carson," she sighed.

There were no words to describe what she felt, hearing his simple declaration of love. It was like the heavens opened up and poured joy directly into her heart. Only the joy was brief, for he offered her something she could never accept.

"I think you love me, too, Mary."

She shook her head. "I can't."

He smiled, and his eyes teased her. "Yes, you can. I'm not entirely unlovable, am I?"

"Oh, Carson," she repeated. Then to herself, *I didn't mean I couldn't love you.*

"Marry me." He drew closer. "Marry me soon."

He kissed her then. His mouth was tender upon hers, gently plying the flesh of her lips. Then it deepened, became more forceful, more demanding. Became more. Became all.

Her heart skipped, stumbled, raced. It seemed that she had been resisting this moment and longing for this

171

moment from the first time she'd laid eyes on him. The first and last kiss he'd bestowed upon her had been nothing like this. It had merely promised it.

A surge of wanting rushed through her. Not just a physical wanting but a desire for all the things she knew a woman would have with a man like Carson. Peace and contentment. Safety and comfort.

Things she didn't deserve.

She pulled her right hand free from his, then placed it on his chest and pushed him away. She stared into his watchful eyes, saw the love, knew he could see hers, too.

"I can't marry you," she said hoarsely.

"Why not?"

Mary closed her eyes. Another sigh escaped her lips. "There are things you don't know about me. If you did, you would not be saying you love me."

"Try me." He captured her hand again.

She shook her head.

His grip tightened. "Look at me, Mary" His voice was soft but firm.

She thought if she ignored him, he would eventually give up. He didn't. The seconds flowed into minutes, and he didn't move, didn't release her hand. He just waited. Finally, she had to look at him as he'd demanded.

"You do not know who I really am," she told him. "I am not good like you."

"Is that what this is about?" He kissed her again, this time with tenderness. Then he stood and walked over to the doorway where he stared outside at the golden afternoon. "I guess you don't know much about me either."

I'd be knowing I love you, Carson. I love you and I shouldn't.

Carson had never liked remembering the past, let alone talking about it. As he stared outside, memories flitted through his head, things he'd rather leave forgotten. But if it meant persuading Mary to be his wife, he'd recall every sordid detail of his life and recount them for her. Now that he'd discovered love, he wasn't about to let it slip away from him. He wasn't going to let *her* slip away.

"There wasn't much good about my childhood," he said honestly. "I grew up in a place a lot like the Painted Lady. My . . . mother"—he couldn't keep the bitter edge from that word—"owned it. That's why I hated having you and Keary at the saloon. Because I know what it's like for a boy to grow up in a place like that, living around women like . . . my mother."

He didn't tell her he'd once thought she might be like Aldora or how mistaken he'd been. Never had he known two women more dissimilar than Aldora and Mary.

"I took off on my own when I was thirteen. I had a real chip on my shoulder, too. By the time I was fifteen, I could play poker with the best of them, including dealing from the bottom of the deck. I could handle a gun as good as any man, and I wasn't afraid to aim and fire, even if it meant killing somebody. I wandered from one small mining town to another, hating them all but not knowing anything else. When I could find work, I worked. When I couldn't, I stole. Usually I stole."

He glanced over his shoulder. Mary was watching him, listening.

"I wound up in Silver City when I was sixteen. It's about three, four hundred miles south of here. It was winter, and I was cold, hungry, and without money. So I decided to take a few things from the general store."

He remembered that large hand slapping down on his

173

shoulder as he'd shoved a pair of gloves into the waistband of his trousers.

"I was caught stealing by Sheriff Hailey." He smiled to himself, recalling David's grim expression. "He could have just thrown me in jail and let me serve my time, but for some reason, he took a liking to me. I'll never know why. I had a foul mouth. I was dirty and scruffy. And I had an attitude that said to hell with everyone. But for whatever reason, he decided I was worth saving."

He took a step toward the bed and Mary.

"My point is, I'd probably be either dead or sitting in prison somewhere if it weren't for the Haileys. They took me in, David and Claudia. Let me live with them. Became my family. They turned my life around. I did plenty of bad things when I was a kid that I can't ever change. That's something I just have to live with. But that's not who I am now."

He wondered if she understood what he was telling her, then figured she didn't. He raked the fingers of one hand through his hair, frustrated by his seeming inability to express himself better.

"Mary, it doesn't matter to me who you were or what you did before you came here. It just matters to me who you are now. And that's who I'm in love with."

Silence followed. Carson waited and watched. He saw the different emotions flitting across Mary's face—fear, hope, frustration, longing, despair.

Despair most of all.

"'Tis no use, Carson. It wouldn't be right. 'Tis not the same what you did and . . . and what I did."

He took another step toward her. "Try me."

Another lengthy silence filled the room.

"Mary, nothing you could ever tell me would make

174

me stop loving you. Nothing."

"Not even if you were to know Keary's da's name was Maguire, not Malone?"

For a moment he didn't understand what she was saying. And then he did.

"Aye, 'tis true. We were never married, Seamus Maguire and me. 'Twas Miss Blanche who called me Mrs. Malone, but in truth, 'tis unmarried I am and unmarried I have always been."

Carson could see Mary steeling herself for his judgment and condemnation. And a few short weeks ago, he probably *would* have judged and condemned her. But not now. Not when he loved her like he did. Loving her had changed him.

"It doesn't matter," he said, hoping she could hear the earnestness in his voice. "I'll raise Keary as my own. I'll love him as my own. I'll be his dad."

She turned her face toward the wall. A sigh escaped her. "I'm thinking you should go, Carson."

"You're a stubborn woman, Mary Malone."

"Aye, that I am."

He sat on the edge of the bed, took her hand once more, forced her to look at him again. "I can be just as stubborn as you. I'm not going to give up. I'm not going to stop loving you. I'll just wear you down until you don't have a choice except to say yes. You'll see."

Winston drained the brandy snifter, then set it beside his dinner plate. It had been a disappointing day. They had returned from Uppsala to Des Moines after nightfall with nothing to show for their troubles. He was now intent on drowning his aggravation in alcohol.

He glared across the table at his wife, who was having an intense but muted discussion with Tibble Knox.

175

Winston couldn't hear what they were saying, but he didn't care.

He glared at Portia, despising the sight of her. It didn't matter how elegantly she dressed, his wife would never be anything but the plain, plump daughter of an uneducated buffoon who'd gotten lucky and made a fortune. Winston had been shackled to her for twenty-four years. Far too long, in his estimation. He wanted out. He was desperate for a way out. But he couldn't go without money and plenty of it.

"What now, Knox?" he suddenly demanded, causing not only Portia and the detective to look his way but people at the surrounding tables in the hotel dining room as well.

"We could wait and return to the Bridger farm next week," Tibble answered him. "It's possible Mrs. Bridget might be able to tell us something her little sister couldn't. But I suspect it would be a waste of time. I don't think Miss Malone is in Iowa now nor that she came here after leaving New York."

"What makes you so sure?"

"Let's call it a hunch."

Winston grunted. "Like the one that brought us here?" he asked sarcastically.

"Hardly." The little man patted the corner of his mouth with a linen napkin. "I was able to gain some helpful information from Mrs. Bridger's sister." He grinned. "Including the whereabouts of Elizabeth Steele, Miss Malone's other shipboard friend. Mrs. Steele is living in Montana. I recommend that we go there next."

"It could be another wild-goose chase," Winston muttered.

The detective appeared unruffled. "It could be. Might

176

I suggest you and Mrs. Kenrick return to New York City while I do my job? Then you wouldn't be wasting your time if it turns out there is nothing to be learned from Mrs. Steele. I will gladly send you daily telegrams, if that's what you want."

"No, Mr. Knox," Portia said before Winston could speak. "I believe we shall continue on with you. I have never been out West. I should like to see it, regardless whether or not we find Mary."

Winston filled his snifter with more brandy and took another deep swallow. In his heart he cursed women. All women. Especially two—Portia Pendergast Kenrick and Mary Malone. Damn them both!

His plan had been working so well. Right up until that ill-fated moment in his study. He'd been so close to escaping the clutches of his wife. He'd been so close to secreting away a fortune for himself. But without those papers hidden in the secret compartment of the silver box, he was doomed. He'd be tied to Portia until the day he died.

What if Mary doesn't even have it anymore?

As always, the thought made him shudder. It was possible Mary had sold the valuable box for cash to pay for her flight from New York. It was possible she had dropped it in a ditch somewhere, not wanting to keep the weapon she'd used against her employer.

But Mary was his only hope of recovering it, and so he was determined to find her. No matter what it took, he was going to find Mary Malone, and when he did, he was going to make her pay for all the trouble she'd caused him.

Fifteen

CARSON WAS AS GOOD AS HIS WORD. HE DIDN'T give up. He kept on asking Mary to be his wife. Every time he saw her, he proposed again. And she was sorely tempted to accept. After all, she loved him, and he loved her. Why shouldn't she take hold of the happiness he offered?

Lying on her bed, waiting for her leg to heal, gave her a great deal of time to think about marrying him. She discovered countless reasons to agree, and she found just as many reasons to refuse. But it always came down to Winston Kenrick and that day in his study. She knew she could never marry Carson because of that one crucial moment in her past.

She tried telling herself that if the authorities hadn't found her after more than a month they weren't ever going to find her. She tried telling herself that the law didn't even suspect her, that they were looking for someone else entirely. She tried telling herself that if she didn't get caught it made it all right.

But it didn't.

Again, she considered telling Carson the whole truth. She wanted to believe he would understand, as he'd promised.

But would he?

It was a hot August Sunday afternoon. Carson came out to the cabin after church, once again bringing a bouquet of flowers. The first thing he did upon arrival was tell Mary he loved her. Then he gave her a kiss that left her breathless and gave Nellie the giggles.

"It's too hot to be stuck in here," he announced

suddenly. He scooped Mary into his arms and headed outside, calling behind him, "Nellie, bring Keary. We're going into town."

He carried Mary to the buggy he'd driven out. Then he stood waiting for Nellie and Keary to catch up rather than setting Mary on the seat immediately.

"You can put me down," she told him, hoping he wouldn't. She loved the feel of his arms around her.

"Not yet." He gazed into her eyes. "Are you ready to change your mind, Mary Malone? Are you ready to marry me?"

"Sure and I've told you I can't."

"Sure and you have told me that," he said with a grin, mimicking her accent. "But 'tis unwilling I am to believe you, me darlin' girl."

"You'll be making fun of me now."

His smile faded. His voice softened. "Ah, Mary. Don't you know I'd never make fun of you? I love you too much."

Why not give your consent, Mary? a small voice whispered in her ear. *'Tis happy you'd be with him. 'Tis happy Keary would be, too.*

She closed her eyes as she laid her head against his shoulder. She knew the answer to her own question. She couldn't tell him the truth, and she couldn't marry him with such a lie—even a lie by silence—between them.

"What is it we'll be doing in town?"

"I thought you might like to see Miss Blanche. John says she's been asking for you."

Mary felt a catch in her heart. She was afraid she knew what that meant. Blanche must not have much longer to live. "Have you seen her?"

"Not recently," he answered.

"I'm wondering why it has to be this way," she whispered, more to herself than to Carson.

He didn't answer.

She lifted her head from his shoulder and met his gaze. "She has a good heart, no matter what else you might say about her."

"She brought you here." He brushed his lips across her forehead. "How can I have anything against her now?" His words were true. Mary had changed the way he felt about Blanche. Mary had changed the way he felt about lots of things.

Nellie and Keary arrived at the buggy just then. Reluctantly, he set Mary on the buggy seat. Then he lifted Keary and placed him in his mother's arms while Nellie scrambled up onto the rear seat.

As Carson stepped into the buggy and settled beside Mary, he considered the picture they made. They must look like a family.

His family.

And by darn, he wasn't going to let Mary Malone or her son or young Nellie get away from him. Carson was laying claim to his family. Whatever impediments kept Mary from agreeing to be his bride were going to be torn down. He didn't know how, but he did know it would happen. He was going to *make* it happen.

He slapped the reins against the horse's backside, and they set off toward Whistle Creek. The journey was made in silence, each of them lost in their own thoughts.

When the buggy pulled up at the rear entrance of the Painted Lady, Carson glanced over his shoulder and said to Nellie, "Why don't you take Keary over to Chuck's Mercantile while Mary and I go see Miss Blanche?" He reached into his pocket and pulled out a

180

couple of coins. "Here. You can buy some peppermint sticks or some licorice or whatever you like."

"Thanks, Sheriff Barclay!" the girl exclaimed.

"But you have to keep a close eye on Keary." Carson cautioned.

"I know. I always do. I'll make him hold my hand the whole time."

Carson hopped to the ground, then handed Keary to Nellie. He watched for a moment as the two of them started down the boardwalk, Keary's short legs churning to keep up with Nellie. When he glanced toward Mary, he found her watching the children, too, her expression pensive.

"A penny for your thoughts," he said.

Her gaze shifted to meet his. "I'm thinking 'tis blessed I am altogether, and I'd be greedy to be wanting more."

He decided against arguing with her, even though he understood what she was saying to him. "Come on. Let's get you inside." He lifted her once again into his arms, cradling her against his chest, and carried her toward the back entrance of the saloon.

Blanche heard the door open, heard the footsteps drawing close to her bed, wondered who had entered her bedroom this time.

"Miss Blanche? 'Tis Mary. I've come to see you."

She opened her eyes with effort. Everything was an effort for her now. But she smiled when she saw Mary in Carson's arms. "Hello, Mary," she whispered, her voice raspy. "How are you?"

"I'm fine altogether." Mary looked at Carson. "Set me down now."

He lowered her to the chair beside the bed. Then he

181

glanced at Blanche. "I'll just step out into the hall. Leave the two of you alone for a while."

Thanks, Blanche mouthed.

Carson nodded.

When he was gone, Blanche reached for Mary's hand. "I don't have much time."

The younger woman shook her head. "Don't be saying that. 'Tis not true."

"Let me say my piece while I've got the breath to do so." She concentrated on not coughing. "The truth is the truth."

Tears glimmered in Mary's eyes. It surprised Blanche how it made her feel, seeing Mary cry for her. Blanche had never expected anyone to sorrow at her passing. She'd never expected anyone to miss her or care when she was gone. She'd lived a hard life. She'd sinned in countless ways. She'd mocked society and its rules. She'd never cared what others thought of her. Or, at least, she'd believed she didn't care. Until now.

"Mary, you've become my dearest friend."

"And you mine." Mary's fingers tightened around Blanche's hand.

"I know there is something troubling you, something you fear that drove you away from New York."

Mary visibly paled.

"It doesn't matter to me one whit what it is that caused you to run. I've done it all myself anyway. But I want you to be safe and happy when I'm gone. You and your boy."

"I'm thinking we'll be fine, Miss Blanche."

"I think you will, too." She tried to smile even as she fought for more air in her lungs. "Especially knowing that the sheriff has taken such a shine to you."

The tears returned to Mary's eyes.

"It might help if you were to talk about it," Blanche suggested. "It might free you from it."

Mary shook her head. "I can't."

"I'll take it to my grave, whatever it is."

The words only served to upset Mary more. Her tears fell, leaving damp tracks down her cheeks.

"Tell me, my dear girl."

"I . . . I killed a man."

Blanche nearly responded with a denial. It was too outrageous to believe. Mary? Gentle Mary?

"'Twas an accident. I wasn't meaning to kill him, but no one would be believing that."

Blanche waited patiently, certain Mary would continue now that she'd begun. She wasn't disappointed. Like a dam bursting, the words spilled out of Mary. She told Blanche about Seamus Maguire's betrayal. She told her about the hardship of her pregnancy, alone in New York City with only the kindness of strangers to help her through. She told Blanche about the hope that had come when she was employed by the wealthy Kenricks and the way Winston Kenrick had stalked her and the day he'd tried to force himself upon her. Mary told her about the moment she realized her employer was dead and her flight into hiding. And she told Blanche of her hope of finding her brother Quaid, who had once lived in Idaho.

The confession exhausted Mary. When she was finished, she laid her forehead on the bed at Blanche's side. Her shoulders shook as she wept, but she made no sound.

Blanche stroked Mary's head with her free hand, wordlessly offering what comfort she could. She knew from experience that it wasn't words she needed so much as quiet acceptance

In truth, Blanche wasn't shocked by Mary's story. She had heard too many with a similar theme. The details were different, each story carrying its own tragedy, but the result was the same. A woman's life destroyed. A heart losing its ability to trust and to love. Children abandoned.

"Mary?"

The younger woman lifted her face toward Blanche.

"Promise me you'll stay here in Whistle Creek. Don't run away again. Stay here. The sheriff won't let anything happen to you."

"If he was knowing the truth about me—"

"Carson won't let anything happen to you, Mary. I know it." She felt herself growing weaker and resented it. There was still so much to be said. She lifted her hand and touched Mary's cheek with her fingertips. "Don't shut up your heart. You'll only regret it when you're old and dying."

Blanche released a sigh as her hand dropped to the bed. She closed her eyes and listened to her own agonized breathing. Death had spread its shadow over her, but strangely, she wasn't afraid. Not after her talk with Reverend Ogelsby. She knew a peace in dying that she'd never known in living.

But there was still something she wanted to accomplish, and so she kept dragging air into her failing lungs, praying that her opportunity would come.

Carson wasn't sure why he returned to the Painted Lady after taking Mary and the children back to the cabin. It wasn't like he and Blanche had ever been friends. Still, he couldn't shake the feeling that he needed to talk to her one last time.

He arrived at the saloon during the quiet time of early

evening, when the sun hovers in the western sky and the air is still and mild. Because it was Sunday, the streets were empty, most folks in their homes.

It was a teary-eyed Edith who led Carson into the madam's bedroom.

When Blanche saw him, she whispered, "You came back . . . I was hoping . . . you would."

Carson nodded, not sure what to say, not sure why he was there.

Blanche glanced at Edith, who understood and withdrew, closing the door behind her.

"Come." Blanche patted the bed at her side. "Sit down, Sheriff. . . . There isn't . . . much time."

The sound of her belabored breathing caused his own lungs to ache.

"Do you . . . love her?" Blanche asked without preamble.

"Yes."

"Look after . . . her."

"I will."

She closed her eyes, and for a moment, he wondered if she was gone.

Then she spoke again. "There is much . . . I'm not at liberty . . . to tell you . . . But this much . . . I can . . . Mary has . . . a brother."

"She has several brothers. She told me about them."

Blanche looked at him. "No, she has a . . . brother . . . in Idaho . . . in the mines . . . She came here . . . to find him . . . Help her . . . find him." She coughed faintly.

Carson could see she was fighting hard to say what she wanted to say.

"His name . . . is Quaid . . . Quaid Malone . . . Don't . . . let her know . . . that I told you."

He nodded to indicate he'd heard.

185

Weakly, she lifted her hand and placed it on his arm. "Give her time . . . She is . . . afraid."

"I know, but not why."

"I can't . . . tell you more." Breath rattled in her throat and lungs. "She must . . . tell you herself."

"But—"

Clawlike, her fingers tightened on his arm, and she raised her head. "Mary always . . . treated me . . . like a friend." Then she fell back against the pillows.

Carson heard a whisper of air escape her lips, but there was no corresponding drawing in. Blanche Loraine was gone.

He hadn't expected to feel a lump in his throat. But then he would never have guessed the madam's last words would show concern for another instead of for herself. He hadn't known this woman. Not really. He'd simply judged her—like everyone else in Whistle Creek—and his judgment had been harsh.

Maybe if someone had offered Blanche a hand in friendship years ago, her last years might have been different. That someone could have been him, he realized with a twinge of regret.

Maybe Mary was right not to tell him her secrets. Maybe he wasn't as fair and forgiving as he liked to think he was.

Carefully, he straightened the sheet over Blanche, then placed her hands, one on top of the other, on her abdomen. Finally he rose from his chair and walked to the door. When he opened it, he found Edith in the hallway. John was with her, his arm around her shoulders. She took one look at Carson's face and began to weep in earnest.

"I'll let Doc Ingall know," Carson told John.

His feet felt heavy as he descended the stairs and

went out the back door. He paused on the boardwalk and drew in a deep breath, thankful that he could do so. Then he headed toward the doctor's home.

He wondered suddenly if Aldora was still alive. It had been twenty-one years since Carson had taken off from the Golden Eagle Dance Hall with his few belongings wrapped in a bedroll. He'd never looked back, never returned to Idaho City. Not even once. He wondered what Aldora would think of the man he'd become. Would she be proud of him? It was a strange thing to wonder, and one that made him uncomfortable. It was easier not to remember his mother at all.

With a singleness of purpose, he turned his thoughts in another direction. Back to Mary Malone.

Blanche had asked him to take care of Mary. That's what he intended to do. But how was he to do it if she refused to marry him?

The answer was simple. She had a brother in America. In Idaho, if Blanche was to be believed. Now Mary's visits to the Lucky Lady and to Wallace made sense. She'd been searching for Quaid, a miner by trade. And that was how Carson would begin to help her. He would locate her brother for her.

But there was more to be done than find Quaid Malone. Blanche had said so, and he knew it was true. Carson needed to discover what it was that Mary feared so much. It was more than just folks finding out she was an unmarried mother. That might have brought her censure, but by itself, it wasn't enough to quell Mary. She was more courageous than that. She'd proved it in countless ways since her arrival in Whistle Creek.

So what was it that at times caused the look of a hunted animal to come into her eyes? What was she so afraid of?

187

Carson knew he would have to find answers to those questions before he would ever convince Mary to become Mrs. Barclay.

Sixteen

AT THE FUNERAL, CARSON STOOD WITH MARY AND the children, offering support by his presence. The pastor, who had returned to Whistle Creek especially for this purpose, prayed for Blanche Loraine's immortal soul and spoke words of comfort for those who mourned her passing. There were not many. Edith, John, Mac, and a few others who had worked for Blanche at the Painted Lady. Some of the miners. A smattering of townsfolk. Not many to show for the years she had lived in Whistle Creek.

There should have been more, Mary thought as she watched the casket being lowered into the ground.

She missed Blanche even more than she'd expected she would. Her heart ached with it. She had lost a friend, the person who, like the Good Samaritan of old, had reached out to a stranger and helped in a time of need. Now Mary was alone once again.

As if he'd understood what she was thinking, Carson's hand tightened on her elbow. She glanced up and found him observing her in that piercing manner of his.

You aren't alone, his eyes told her. *I'll take care of you and the children. Marry me.*

Aye, she could do that. It would be so easy. She loved him with her whole heart. Without a shred of doubt, she knew it would be a pleasure to live with him, to lie with him as his wife, to give birth to his babies and watch them grow. He would protect and cherish her. She had been on her own for many years. It would be heavenly to rest in his arms, to be taken care of by Carson.

But just as always, the wisp of hope was shattered by the image of Winston Kenrick, lying on the floor of his study, a crimson stain spreading across the carpet.

It would be better if she left Whistle Creek. Better for the sheriff whose wife, when he took one, needed to be above reproach. And better for Mary, too, because as it was, she was tortured by what she wanted and couldn't have.

When the brief service was over, Martin Burke approached Mary and Carson. "I'll be reading Miss Loraine's last will and testament tomorrow afternoon in my office," the attorney said. "She requested that you both be present. Shall we say two o'clock?"

Mary nodded.

"We'll be there," Carson replied.

We'll be there. He made it sound so simple. We. Carson and Mary. A couple. A family. Yes, it was indeed a cruel twist of fate, finding what she wanted and knowing she could never have it. If Carson were anything other than a lawman . . .

But he wasn't, she told herself with resignation, so there was no point dwelling on it. It would be much better if she ended any association between them, once and for all.

Carson's fingers tightened on her arm again. "I'll see you and the children home."

"No." She withdrew from his grasp. "I'm thinking 'twould be better if we went on our own."

"Mary—"

"Don't you be arguing with me, Sheriff Barclay. 'Tis

189

how I'm wanting it."

He frowned. "You're a stubborn woman, Mary Malone."

"Aye." She lifted her son into her arms. "So you've told me before. More than once."

He stopped her with a gentle touch on her shoulder. "There's no need to—"

"I'll be leaving Whistle Creek soon," she interrupted as she looked into his eyes and felt her heart breaking. "I'm thinking 'twill be better that way altogether. I'll be thanking you for your kindness and the use of your house and all you've done for me and me children here."

She glanced down at his fingers, still resting on her shoulder. After a long moment, his hand dropped away.

"Where will you go?"

"I wouldn't be knowing just yet."

"Why are you running away?" He paused a moment, then added, "From me."

She shook her head.

"Running never solved anything, Mary. I know from experience."

She believed him, but she also believed staying would be worse.

"Come, Nellie," she said to the girl. "'Tis time we went home." *Before I start to cry.*

Carson watched the three of them go, Nellie carrying Keary, and he felt a wave of frustration wash over him. Why wouldn't she see reason? Darn stubborn female! Things had been a whole heck of a lot simpler when he'd wanted nothing to do with women or marriage. He should have stuck to that way of thinking.

He spun on his heel and strode toward town. He walked with a purposeful stride and an air that said, *Don't talk to me.* Nobody did.

Didn't he have enough troubles right now? There were the scab workers Halligan had hired, loitering over in Osburn. There were the whispers of accusations against John and the other miners who'd been trapped in the tunnel. That was enough trouble for any sheriff without adding a woman to the mix. Whistle Creek and the Lucky Lady Mine were like tinderboxes, just waiting for something to ignite them so they could burst into flames. If not for Mary, Carson would have been concentrating on keeping the peace, making sure nobody struck that particular match. But because of her, he'd been picking wildflowers instead of doing his job.

He should have had more sense than to go soft for a woman. He'd seen few enough men made better by infatuation with a female. What man could ever figure what a woman was thinking, let alone what fool thing she might do? You couldn't trust them. They weren't logical. They didn't think and reason like men.

So let her go, he told himself. Who needed her? He hadn't been looking for love before she came here, and he would get along just fine without it once she was gone. She could go find her brother without his help. He didn't owe Mary Emeline Malone a dang thing. Not one single dang thing!

By the time he stormed into his office and slammed the door behind him, Carson was in a fine fury. For a short while longer, he continued to silently rail against women in general and Mary in particular, and he almost believed the words he mentally spouted.

Almost.

Finally, he sank onto his chair, braced his elbows on the desk and lowered his forehead onto the heels of his hands. How had she done this to him? he wondered. How had that tiny slip of a woman created so much confusion in his mind in so short a period of time?

He leaned back in his chair and stared up at the ceiling. Up until the last month or so, he'd never been given to introspection, but now he saw with sudden clarity a few truths about himself. David Hailey had rescued him from a life of crime and set him on a better path, but Mary had awakened his heart. Claudia Hailey had removed much of the bitterness he'd harbored, but Mary had taught him to truly care about others.

He thought about John. Carson had helped the troubled young man, but it had been to keep peace and order in Whistle Creek, in Carson's town, not because he'd really known John, not because he'd truly been concerned about him. At most, he'd been following David's example. But his reasons had changed after Mary arrived from New York City. Carson had learned to care. Not just about keeping peace and order and not just about John. He'd begun to care about all the people of this town in a new and different way.

Mary was the reason for the change.

The office door opened, and Mac MacDonald, the card dealer at the Painted Lady, stepped inside. Carson was relieved to have a diversion from his prevailing thoughts.

Usually a smiling, devil-may-care sort of fellow, Mac wore a somber expression at the moment. "You got a minute, Sheriff?" he asked as he removed his hat.

"Sure. What do you need, Mac?"

"Well, I'm leaving Whistle Creek later today."

"Sorry to hear that," he responded—and discovered he meant it.

Mac shook his head, then shrugged. "It was time to move on. I never stayed so long in one place in my life as I have here. Only stayed because of Miss Blanche.

Anyway, 'fore I go, I thought you should know something. I heard Halligan's gonna be back in town in a day or two. I don't know what he's plannin', but I don't expect it'll be anything good."

Carson nodded. This wasn't news to him.

"There's a chance he might bring the federal marshal in with him. That's the rumor."

Carson raised an eyebrow. "For what reason?"

"Tyrell. He seems to have it in for the boy."

Again Carson nodded.

"It's easy enough to see why. The miners are calling Tyrell a hero. They blame the cave-in on unsafe conditions, and that's Halligan's fault. Tyrell's got the power right now to rally the miners behind the union supporters if he wants to. Halligan can't afford for that to happen."

"No," Carson agreed thoughtfully, "he can't."

"Well, that's all I come to say." Mac put on his hat. "Good luck, Sheriff."

"Thanks, Mac. I imagine I'll need it."

Actually Carson suspected the whole town was going to need it before this was over.

Portia was delighted with Bozeman, Montana. It was like stepping into a dime novel. The majority of men on the streets wore boots, wide brimmed felt hats, and gun holsters strapped to their thighs. For the most part, the women were dressed simply in calico and bonnets, but then there were the more brazen of the saloon girls, out walking in plain daylight, their faces painted, clad in bright silks and satins and wearing ostrich feathers in their hair.

Yes, the Wild West was everything Portia had hoped it would be and more. She imagined the ladies and gentlemen who attended her glittering soirees and supper parties would be scandalized to know just how much she was enjoying herself. Certainly her husband was not of the same mind. Winston was positively taciturn, if not downright morose.

It had taken some doing, but Portia had finally persuaded Winston to remain in Bozeman with her while Tibble Knox journeyed north to New Prospects. "If Miss Malone is there," she had told her husband the previous day, "Mr. Knox will return for us before confronting her. If she is not there, we will have saved ourselves the discomfort of a stagecoach ride."

And in the meantime, Portia was able to entertain herself with a variety of pastimes, not the least of which was tonight's bawdy performance by a traveling theatrical troupe. Oh, yes. Her society friends would be scandalized, indeed.

Portia cast a sideways glance toward Winston. He was slumped in his box seat, his forehead creased in thought. She was certain he hadn't seen a minute of the uproarious comedy. Poor dear man. Whatever was the matter with him seemed to be growing worse by the day. The tension in him was palpable.

For an instant, she felt sorry for him. Her husband had hungered after many things in his life, things that had remained just beyond his grasp. His problem, of course, was that he thought the world and all that was in it was his due, simply because he was born a Kenrick. It had never occurred to him that he should have to work for the things he wanted or the things he already had.

And when he looked at his wife, Portia knew, he saw someone of less value than he simply because she came from the working class. Her father hadn't inherited his money as a gentleman should but had earned it by the sweat of his brow. Winston had married Portia for her inheritance, had lived off of her wealth, but he had resented her because of it.

She turned her attention back on the stage, but her thoughts soon wandered.

Portia had always considered herself a pragmatist. She had long ago accepted that she and her husband would never share love. She had put up with his affairs and dalliances, looking the other way rather than upsetting the applecart—as her grandmother would have said—with accusations and recriminations. Didn't it follow then that she was as much at fault for the state of her marriage as Winston?

The question left a bad taste in her mouth. The answer was no more comforting when it came to her.

Portia had settled for the type of marriage they shared because she'd thought Winston was right. She'd thought he was better than she, just because he was a Kenrick. She'd thought the glittering life of proper society he'd offered was worth sacrificing herself to obtain.

She glanced at him again and knew a sudden sadness. What might her life have been like if she hadn't sold herself so cheaply?

"I need a favor, John."

"You know I'll do whatever I can for you, Sheriff."

Carson looked around the deserted saloon. The Painted Lady had been closed for several days, out of respect for Blanche Loraine. Still, he lowered his voice, just in case someone was on the staircase or on the other side of the door. "Mary has a brother, and there's a good chance he's working in one of the mines in the panhandle."

"A brother?" The eyebrow on the unscarred side of John's face lifted. "Why hasn't she said something before now?"

"She still hasn't said anything. She doesn't know that I know."

John made no comment, but curiosity flickered in his eyes.

"Mary's been looking for him. That's why she went up to the Lucky Lady a while back, and that's why she was over in Wallace the day she got hurt. She's been trying to locate her brother. Anyway, for whatever reason, she hasn't wanted to ask anybody's help. But I don't want her getting hurt again. I was hoping you might look for him."

"Why me?"

One thing Carson had learned about John Tyrell in recent weeks was that he was nobody's fool. Now that he'd stopped drowning himself in self-pity and booze, John had also proven he had a fair amount of pride in doing for himself. He wouldn't take it kindly were he to guess he was being sent out of town for his own protection. So Carson needed to choose his words carefully; he had to be convincing.

He glanced toward the doorway, then returned his gaze to John. "You were right about my feelings for Mary," he confessed. "She means a lot to me, and I don't want to lose her. But she's determined to leave Whistle Creek now that Miss Blanche is dead. I think it's got something to do with her brother, but I won't know what until I can find him and talk to him myself. Only I can't leave town right now." He leaned forward. "I need somebody I can trust, John. I also need somebody that other miners will be willing to talk to. If

I go asking questions, they'll be suspicious 'cause I'm the law. But not you. They'll talk to you 'cause you're one of them."

John nodded thoughtfully.

"His name's Quaid Malone."

"Malone?" There was no judgment in the younger man's voice, just a request for clarification.

Carson nodded. "Malone."

"What else do you know about him? How long's he been workin' the Idaho mines? What's he look like? Anything like that."

"I don't know much," Carson admitted. "I think he probably came to America back in about . . ." His voice trailed into silence as he tried to remember what little Mary had revealed about her family. Her brothers had gone their own way after their father died, she'd said. "Must be back about ninety or ninety-one," he finally concluded, "although I don't know that for a fact."

John leaned back in his chair. "How soon do you want me to go?"

"Today be too soon? I'll supply the horse and the money you'll need. If it takes you longer to find him and you run out of funds, I can always have it wired to you wherever you are."

John responded with a grin. "You do have it bad for her, don't you, Sheriff?"

"Yeah," he answered, a reluctant smile curving the corners of his mouth.

Why kid himself? He wanted to help and protect John, but this search for Quaid Malone was all about Mary. If she left Whistle Creek, Carson would be a lost man. He wanted her in his life. He wanted her in his home and in his bed. He wanted to raise Keary as his own son. He wanted them to have more children, a

197

house full of them. *Two* houses full of them, if that's what Mary wanted.

"Yeah, I've got it bad for her," he said, his voice lowered to a near whisper.

John's chair slid back from the poker table, and he rose to his feet. "Well then, I guess I'd best go tell Edith I'll be gone for a while. I won't tell her why, just that I've got a job to do for you."

Carson stood, too, and offered his left hand. "Thanks, John. I appreciate this more than I can say."

"I'm glad to do it." John shook the proffered hand, no hint of a smile remaining on his face, his voice serious. "It's little enough I can do after what you did for me."

Carson wished he'd be able to convince Mary to stay as easily as he'd been able to convince John to go, but he figured the chances of that were about as good as Cinnabar's leading him to silver like Kellogg's jackass was supposed to have done.

Not very doggone likely.

Seventeen

Wednesday, 24 August, 1898
Whistle Creek, Idaho

My dear Beth,

My heart is filled with sadness as I write this letter. Dawn is just lightening the sky. The children still sleep innocently in their beds. Oh, how I wish I could sleep as they do, but it is not to be.

Yesterday, we buried my special friend, Miss Blanche Loraine. She departed this world on Sunday last, taken by the consumption that had

198

eaten at her lungs for so long. It is only for myself that I mourn. To wish her back would be cruel, for I know at last she is no longer in pain. Her suffering was great in her final days.

The time has come for me to leave Whistle Creek. My work at the Painted Lady is done. The records are all in order, and while others here hope to continue working for the new owner, whoever that may be, I have no wish to do so. I am thinking it was Miss Blanche who made the work so enjoyable to me and not the work itself.

So now I must be asking a favor of you, dearest Beth. I have only just discovered how near Whistle Creek is to New Prospects. If we would not be a burden to you and Mr. Steele, I would be asking if Keary, Nellie, and I might be staying for a week or two on your ranch, just until I can decide where I should go and what I should do.

It is a lot to ask, I know, but I do not know where else to turn. I do not seem to be any closer to finding Quaid's whereabouts, so I cannot depend upon family for assistance. And I cannot stay here. To do so would be a grave mistake.

I must confess to a wee bit of selfishness as well. I am eager to hold your babe in my arms and see for myself if she looks like your husband as you have claimed in your letters. Already your Regan is three months old, and if I do not come soon, she will be walking like Keary before I see her. I know you must find that hard to believe, but it is true. She will be running with Janie before you turn around.

But as much as I long to come, dearest Beth, you must be honest with me. If our coming will prove a *hardship to you in any way, you must tell me so. Talk with your husband, and then send me word by telegraph. I will await your answer for the next two weeks. I do not feel I can wait any longer than that before I must go.*

Your affectionate friend,
Mary Emeline Malone

The morning air was crisp. The smell of approaching autumn drifted on a breeze that whispered through the meadow grass and caused the branches of the pines and aspens on the hillside to wave gently. Puffs of clouds, pure white and dazzling, floated against an azure canopy. A bald eagle, his wings spread wide, rose elegantly, lifted by an unseen hand, soaring above the mountaintops. In the corral, Cloud snorted, then bobbed his big black and white head and pawed at the dirt with one hoof. Down near the creek, Baba chased a squirrel along the bank, barking noisily in her hopeless pursuit.

Mary stood in the open doorway of the cabin and stared at the familiar scene. There was a terrible homesickness welling up inside of her, and she hadn't even left yet. Instinctively she knew it would be much worse than when she'd departed Ireland. She also knew the reason it would be worse.

This time, she would be leaving Carson.

She closed her eyes and remembered the last time he'd kissed her. Even now, she could imagine his lips upon hers. She could still feel the tingling sensation that coursed through her body in response to him. How wonderful it would be to give herself completely to him. Not just physically, although she longed for that, too. No, she wanted to give him her most secret thoughts, to reveal her true self to him as she had to no other.

She imagined him speaking, heard his voice as clearly as if he were actually with her. *It doesn't matter to me who you were or what you did before you came here, Mary. It just matters to me who you are now. And that's who I'm in love with.*

She sighed as she opened her eyes, then turned and closed the door.

It *would* matter to him if he knew what she'd done. It would *have* to matter to him because he represented the law of this land. And so Mary had no choice but to leave. She was never to know what it would be like to be his completely. That was her punishment for killing a man—to be denied the love and happiness Carson offered her.

Mary gave her head a tiny shake. There was no point in feeling sorry for herself. It wouldn't change anything. It wouldn't change anything at all.

"Nellie, we must be getting ourselves ready. We're going to town."

The girl looked up from the book she was reading to Keary. "Will we see the sheriff? Keary and I've made somethin' for him. It's just some pine cones and such nailed to a piece of wood, but I think he's gonna like it."

Mary felt the tightness in her heart. "Aye, we'll be seeing Sheriff Barclay at Mr. Burke's office later today, and I'm sure he'll like whatever you made. But first I must post a letter and then see to some final details at the saloon."

"Can I ride Cloud into town?"

Another image flashed in Mary's mind, this one of Carson leading the pinto while Nellie sat on the horse's bony back. Both Carson and Nellie had grinned broadly, as if they'd achieved something of enormous proportions. The memory was from only a few days before, but so much had happened since then, it seemed much longer.

Mary could hear the strain in her voice as she asked Nellie, "Did Sheriff Barclay say it would be all right to ride Cloud so far?"

"He didn't say I couldn't."

Mary raised an eyebrow.

The child lowered her eyes, and her shoulders sagged. "Well, I suppose he didn't say it'd be all right."

All this over leaving the horse behind for a few hours. What was going to happen when Mary told Nellie they were moving and couldn't take Cloud with them? And who would want the pitiful, swaybacked animal? What if he were to be mistreated again? What if . . .

But she couldn't think about that. It wasn't to be helped.

Mary's head started to ache, a persistent pressure near her temples. She pressed her fingertips against her forehead and closed her eyes for a moment. When she opened them, Nellie was watching her with a confused expression.

She forced a smile. "Well, I'm thinking we'd best be hurrying. There is much to do."

Carson stood on the sidewalk outside the mercantile, his shoulder braced against the building as he listened to the idle conversations of Dooby Jones, Chuck Adams, and Abe Stover. Abe's wolfhound lay sleeping beneath the bench upon which his master and Dooby sat. Occasionally the dog whimpered and his legs twitched, but he never opened his eyes. As they talked, Chuck washed the mercantile window, a useless war against dust and grime but one his wife insisted upon.

"Shore am glad t' see the weather coolin' off," Dooby said. "Been a hot summer."

"Yup," Abe agreed with a quick glance at the sky.

"We could use some more rain, too. Forest seems mighty dry. Sure would hate to see any fires startin' up. I'm guessin' the first snows are still several weeks away."

Chuck dropped his soapy rag into the bucket, then placed his fingertips against the small of his back and arched backward. When he straightened, he said, "Abe, you'll be complaining that the snow came too soon once it starts. You always do."

"I ain't never complained about snow."

Dooby and Carson both laughed.

Chuck snorted. "You must think I'm the forgetful sort. There you sit, over at the Painted Lady, sipping your beer and wishin' summer'd come."

Dooby glanced at Carson. "Say, Sheriff. You heard what's gonna happen to the saloon now that Miss Blanche is gone?"

"Haven't heard."

"I reckon Burke knows," Abe interjected. "He's been her lawyer ever since he come to Whistle Creek."

"She have any family?" Chuck asked as he resumed his scrubbing duties.

Carson shook his head. "Not that I heard of."

"Wonder why she and Perkins never married?" Dooby didn't really mean it as a question, nor did the others attempt to answer it as such.

"Well, all I can say is, we'll be in a heck of a mess if the Painted Lady closes down," Chuck continued. "That saloon brings more miners to town than anything else, and when they come for a drink, they pretty near always spend some of their money elsewhere, too. I'd have to shut down this store and move without a saloon in

203

town."

Abe and Dooby murmured their agreement.

Privately, Carson thought they had worse things to worry about than the Painted Lady shutting its doors. Like miners going on strike. Or worse, rioting. Now that's what made his blood run cold.

And speaking of blood running cold, he thought when he recognized Bryan Halligan riding in their direction.

Halligan drew his sleek black gelding to a halt in front of the mercantile. Touching the brim of his hat, he said, "Morning, gentlemen. Nice day, isn't it?"

"What brings you to Whistle Creek again so soon?" Carson asked, striving to keep his voice neutral.

"Mine business," was the man's noninformative reply. He glanced away, looking toward the saloon. A smile curved the corners of his mouth. "And maybe something personal."

Carson followed the direction of Halligan's gaze just in time to see Mary and the children crossing Main Street. He wondered what had brought her to town so early. They weren't due at the lawyer's for several more hours.

He continued to watch as the threesome moved along the boardwalk to Whistle Creek's post office, then disappeared inside. When he turned, he saw that Halligan's gaze had followed them, too. He bristled, wanting nothing more than to inform Halligan that Mary was his.

Only she wasn't his. She'd made that clear enough.

His eyes narrowed. Maybe something personal, Halligan had said. Well, he'd be hanged before he'd let Halligan anywhere near Mary. Something personal, his aunt Gertrude!

And Mary *was* going to be his. He wasn't going to let

her leave Whistle Creek. He didn't care if he had to hogtie her and lock her in his jail until she agreed to marry him. She loved him, and he wasn't going to lose her. Not to her own fears and sure as heck not to another man.

Carson pushed off from the wall of the mercantile. "If you fellas will excuse me, I've got things to see to myself." He stepped off the sidewalk and headed across the street, ostensibly toward his office. His real destination was the post office.

"Sheriff," Halligan called after him, "could you wait a minute?"

Carson stopped and turned. Halligan nudged his gelding forward, and Carson waited in silence for the man to speak again.

"I was wondering if you could help me. I'm looking for John Tyrell."

Carson remembered what MacDonald had told him. He cast a furtive glance up the street, wondering if the marshal was in town. Was that why Halligan was on horseback? He usually took the train from Spokane. Maybe he'd ridden in with the marshal.

"Haven't seen him today," he answered as he looked at Halligan once more. "What do you need him for? Maybe I can help."

"I just have a few more questions for him. About that *accident*"—skepticism dripped from the word—"at the mine last month."

"I'm surprised you haven't wrapped up your investigation yet, Halligan."

The mine owner's mouth flattened, and a tic appeared at the corner of his right eye. After a moment's pause, he said, "The miners haven't been cooperative, but I will have the answers I want soon, Sheriff. I

205

promise you."

The air was heavy with their mutual animosity.

Carson forced himself to relax. "You know, Halligan, now that I think on it, seems to me I heard John was called out of town on some sort of business. Don't know where he went or when he'll be back, though."

Halligan cursed. "You sure he's coming back? You sure he's not on the run?"

"I'm sure." Carson grinned. "He's getting married in a few weeks."

"Married?" Halligan's tone implied, *Who'd have the cripple?*

"Yeah, married." He was itching to take a swing at Bryan Halligan. Just one good punch would improve Carson's mood immensely. "Got himself a real sweet girl, too. He'll be back. You can bet on it. But by then we ought to know who is *really* behind the trouble at the Lucky Lady. Shouldn't we." He tugged on his hat brim, pulling it lower on his forehead. "See you around, Halligan." He walked away before the other man could reply.

Simmering anger and a load of frustration made Carson's stride long and quick. For a lawman who preferred his town and his life to be peaceful, quiet, and orderly, he wasn't having much success at keeping things that way lately.

Mary smiled at the postmistress. "Thank you, Mrs. Finley. I am hoping you'll feel yourself again soon." She glanced over her shoulder at Nellie, who was attempting to keep Keary out of mischief.

"You're lucky to have that girl's help," Susan Finley commented. "I'm wore out just watching that boy of yours. My girls are near grown, and I've forgotten what

206

it's like to have small ones under foot."

"Nellie's been a real blessing, to be sure. 'Tis sorry I am she lost her kin, but I'll never be sorry she's come to live with us. I love her like me own."

"You know, Mrs. Malone, the ladies of our church circle would be right pleased if you'd join us some time."

Mary turned toward the postmistress again.

She must have looked surprised, because Mrs. Finley quickly added, "We'd all like to get to know you better. You were such a godsend when the accident happened out at the mine. We all heard about it in town. And then you took that little girl in. Such a Christian thing to do."

Mary knew it was by way of an apology, and she was touched by it. Only it had come too late. Here she was, fixing to leave Whistle Creek just as others were starting to accept her into their midst.

For just a moment, she entertained the fantasy. Mary Barclay, wife of the sheriff, pillar of the community. She envisioned herself in a gracious home, surrounded by well-behaved, well-dressed children, all them with their father's golden brown hair and stunning blue eyes.

"Keary!" Nellie cried, shattering the daydream. "Come back here!"

Mary whirled around just in time to see Keary dart out the door. "Keary!" She hurried after him, knowing how quickly he could move. If he should run into the street when a horse or wagon was coming—

She stopped on the sidewalk, arrested by the sight before her.

It wasn't the first time she'd found her son in Carson's arms. In that moment, it seemed as if Keary was always running toward trouble, and the sheriff always managed to be there to stop him.

"What's the matter with you?" Carson snapped at her. "Why weren't you watching him closer? What if he'd run out in front of a wagon or something?"

Mary drew back, surprised by the anger in his voice. "He slipped away from Nellie, and I—"

"That girl's not his mother. You are. I may not always be around to rescue him when you're not paying attention."

Her own temper flared hot. "And are you thinking I don't know that altogether?" She stepped forward and held out her arms. "I'll be thanking you to give me boy to me now. Sure and I wouldn't be troubling you any further."

He ignored her outstretched arms, looking behind her. "Nellie, come here."

The girl hurried forward as commanded, her face pale and her eyes wide.

"Carson Barclay," Mary warned, "don't you dare frighten her."

He still paid her no attention. "Here," he said to Nellie. "Take Keary over to the Painted Lady. Shut yourselves in Miss Blanche's office and don't you move until Mary or I come for you. You hear?"

Nellie nodded.

Carson set Keary on his feet and passed his hand into Nellie's.

Before Mary could react or try to stop what he'd put in motion, Carson grabbed her hand, spun on his heel, and pulled her along with him as he headed for the sheriff's office. She was breathing hard by the time they reached their destination.

Carson opened the door, then put her in front of him and gave her a gentle push inside. Once he was inside, too, he closed the door firmly behind him.

Mary turned, sputtering like a wet hen. "Now see here—"

She was in his arms before she knew what was happening. His lips captured hers, ending her objections. Her anger melted beneath the onslaught to her senses. This was a different type of kiss from those they had shared before. There was no tender persuasion here. This was fierce, hot, demanding. This kiss left no room for thinking. It filled her, overwhelmed her, possessed her.

His tongue teased her lips until they parted. A strange feeling curled in her stomach. Heat spread through her veins. She heard a soft mewling sound, then realized the whimper had come from her own throat.

With a fluid motion, Carson turned, taking her with him, then pressed her back against the door. He began to rain kisses over her cheeks, her ears, her throat, then he returned to drink of her mouth again.

Mary had no sense of time or space. She didn't know if it was minutes or hours before he ceased his wondrous assault. When he withdrew slightly, she knew she would have fallen were it not for the door at her back and the arms that held her still.

"I'm sorry I yelled at you," he said, his voice low, husky, enticing. "I didn't mean to take out my frustration on you or Nellie. You know I wouldn't hurt any of you for anything. Don't you?"

She nodded, mesmerized by the intense look in his eyes of blue.

"Now, let's get something else straight between us, Mary Emeline Malone. I've always hated disorder in my town. I've worked hard to keep things nice and peaceful ever since I was elected sheriff. I'm trying dang hard to

209

keep it that way right now, but there's unrest brewing out there. Plenty of it. I can feel it, and I can smell it. I'd like to be able to count on just one thing."

Despite herself, she whispered, "And what would that be, I'd be asking?"

"You." His lips brushed over hers as he spoke, as faint as the touch of butterfly wings.

She closed her eyes. "Me?" she said on a sigh.

"Yes, you." He kissed her again, slow and deep. When he was through, he asked, "Now, are we finished arguing about this? Are you going to agree to marry me or am I going to have to do some more convincing?"

"Carson, you wouldn't be understanding. I can't. You don't know—"

"Hmm." He cut her off with kisses. He raised his hands to cradle her face, spread his fingers through her hair, dislodged her bonnet.

I'll be leaving Whistle Creek, Carson Barclay. I cannot marry you. It would be wrong for me to do so, and if you knew the truth, you'd think it wrong, too. So I'll be going away from here and from you. It'll be better altogether. You'll see.

"Marry me, Mary Malone," he whispered near her right ear.

"I cannot."

"Marry me," he whispered again, this time near her left ear.

"Oh, Carson, you—"

His tongue sparred with hers. Longing filled her, burned in the secret most place of her.

"Marry me. I need you, Mary. I need to love you. I need you to love me."

There was a reason she had to refuse him. What was it?

"I've been patient. I've tried to give you plenty of time." He pressed his mouth against the pulse point of her throat. "I don't want to wait any longer."

She knew there was a reason she must refuse him.

"I've been a loner all my life, Mary. I don't want to be alone any more."

Sure and I don't want to be alone meself.

"Marry me."

She sighed, feeling herself relenting. She hadn't the strength to resist him. It was useless to try, loving him as she did.

"Marry me."

A heartbeat more of hesitation, and then, "Aye."

He drew back mere inches, stared down at her. "What? What did you say?"

Her heart quickened as she met his gaze, her capitulation complete. "I said, aye. I'll marry you." She swallowed hard, then added, "And I'm hoping you'll never regret it, Carson Barclay."

He let out a whoop of joy, then effortlessly lifted her and whirled her around the room. When he set her feet on the floor, he kissed her again.

"I love you, Mary," he whispered when their lips parted at last, "and I'll never regret it. Never."

"She's in a town called Whistle Creek," the detective reported. "It's across the border in Idaho. Maybe three hundred, maybe three hundred and fifty miles from here. The railroad's got a regular run up there, although it's not the most direct route. Still, it would be faster than hiring a rig and going over the mountains."

Winston was on his feet, pacing, his heart pumping. "At last," he muttered.

"When can we leave, Mr. Knox?" Portia asked in her

usual calm and cool manner.

"We'll take the next train to Pendleton, Oregon, spend a night there, and then head north. We'll be in Whistle Creek by Friday afternoon."

Winston stared out the window of their hotel room. By Friday afternoon, he thought. By Friday they would find her. He clenched his hands at his side. He was going to make that Irish witch pay for the trouble she'd caused him.

"What is Mary doing there?" his wife inquired of Tibble Knox.

Winston glanced over his shoulder.

The detective consulted his notepad, then answered Portia, "It seems she is working at a saloon."

"The little slut," Winston said, remembering the way Mary had fought him in his study. And now it seemed she was selling herself to other men.

Portia sent him a censuring glance. "Vulgarity is unnecessary, dearest."

He swallowed his angry retort. As soon as he got those papers he'd hidden away, he would be free of Portia. He wouldn't have to listen to his wife or look at her a moment longer. All he needed were those papers, and then he would be free.

And heaven help Mary Malone if he didn't find them.

Eighteen

MARY STARED AT MARTIN BURKE, UNABLE TO speak.

"Well," the attorney said as he closed the file, "except for a generous bequest to the orphanage in Wallace and another to the Whistle Creek Community Church, that is everything." He removed his spectacles and pinched the bridge of his nose between thumb and index finger, muttering, "Though what I ever did to make her leave that spoiled dog to me . . ." He let the words trail off as he glanced toward Nugget, asleep in his soft bed in the corner of the office.

Carson cleared his throat. "Why would she do this, Martin? Why did she single us out?"

"Because she liked both of you," Martin answered, all business again. "A great deal, obviously."

"But to leave me the Painted Lady. . ." Mary shook her head. "I was here such a short time."

The attorney frowned. "I'll be honest with you, Mrs. Malone. I tried to talk Miss Blanche out of that particular addition to her will, but she was determined. She told me she trusted you to do what was best for all concerned."

"But what if I don't stay in Whistle Creek?"

"It is yours to do with as you please," he answered. "And, as I said, she trusted you to do what is right."

It was too much to comprehend. The direction of Mary's life had changed in a matter of hours. First she had agreed to marry Carson, a man she loved with her entire heart and soul. Now she found herself the owner of the Painted Lady Saloon and a wealthy woman in the bargain.

She could see that Carson was just as overwhelmed by what Blanche Loraine had left him a large section of land, complete with a lake, plus a healthy number of shares in the Lucky Lady Mine. Even Mary, who had kept Blanche's books, hadn't known the complete extent of the woman's holdings.

Carson rose from his chair and offered his hand to

213

the lawyer. "Well, we thank you, Martin. I guess it'll take a while for it to sink in." The two men shook hands, then Carson turned toward Mary. "I think we should talk about this." He helped her rise with a gentle hold on her arm.

After a soft farewell to Martin Burke, Mary allowed Carson to steer her out of the office. Neither of them said a word as they crossed Main Street, then followed the sidewalk through the center of town.

It just didn't seem possible, any of it. Less than two months ago, Mary had been working as a maid, making barely enough to support herself and her son. She'd been alone and friendless in an uncaring city. And now . . .

She remembered the day that had sent her fleeing from New York. She remembered that moment on the train when she'd met Blanche. She remembered the way she'd felt when Blanche mentioned Idaho as her destination. She'd thought it a miracle. She'd thought she would find Quaid here. Only it wasn't her brother she'd been meant to find. The miracle had been finding Carson. The miracle had been making friends like Blanche and Edith and John and bringing Nellie to live with her.

"I'm thinking I won't ever believe it," she said as they entered the sheriff's office. She turned toward Carson. "Sure and I still can't think why she would leave the Painted Lady to me."

He shook his head. "I'm pretty surprised myself." He removed his Stetson, then raked his fingers through his hair. "I always wanted to find a way to shut that place down. I never figured it would happen this way."

She stared at him, confused.

When he saw the look on her face, he stared back at

214

her. "You do understand that you'll need to close it down, don't you?"

"And why would I be doing that?"

"You know why."

Oh, her temper was a cursed thing. She only barely held it in check now. "No, I wouldn't be knowing why. Explain it to me, if you'd be so kind."

"It was one thing for you to keep the books for Miss Blanche," he answered as he stepped closer to her. "It would be something else again for you to own and run the business. Especially now that we're to be married."

"And if that's what I choose to do?"

"Be reasonable. You know—"

"In me own country, there's no shame in owning a pub."

Carson shook his head. "It isn't the liquor. It's the women."

He was right, of course, and Mary did understand what he was saying. She knew what Blanche's girls did in those upstairs rooms, and what they did had made Blanche a rich woman. And now because of it, Mary was a rich woman. But she couldn't just close the doors of the Painted Lady and turn everyone out into the street. There were many things to be considered before she made any decisions.

She turned away from Carson and walked to the window. She looked out at the street, noticing for the first time that there was a larger number of miners in town than was usual for a week day. Which meant a lot of business for the girls at the Painted Lady. Which reminded her of what they were discussing.

She turned around. "I don't fancy you thinking you can tell me what I must do, Carson," she said stiffly. "I'll be no mealymouthed wife you can order about as you

215

please, and you'd best be knowing it now, before it's too late."

He stared at her for a moment, then surprised her by laughing aloud. When he was able, he said, "If that was the sort of wife I wanted, I'd never have fallen in love with you, Mary." His eyes twinkled with amusement. "You're the most stubborn, hard-headed woman I've ever met." The way he said them, the words sounded strangely like a compliment.

Despite herself, she smiled back at him.

"Let me try again." He stepped toward her, took hold of her upper arms and drew her close. Looking down into her eyes, he said, "Mary dearest, I think you should close the Painted Lady. But the business belongs to you, and you'll have to do whatever you think is best."

"You'll be making fun of me now."

All traces of his smile vanished. "No, Mary, I'm not. I mean it. Miss Blanche trusted you. So do I."

Mary leaned her cheek against Carson's chest, suddenly as serious as he. *And may you never be regretting it, love. May you never regret it.*

It was late by the time Mary got both the children to sleep. She knew she should crawl into bed herself, but she was too keyed up. So much had happened that day. She still couldn't take it all in.

She grabbed a shawl and threw it over her shoulders, then stepped outside into the blanket of night, closing the door behind her. She was quickly enveloped by silence. Though the air was cool, there was no wind tonight. Stars twinkled gaily in the heavens. There was no moon to dull their brightness, and they reminded her of jewels spread across a black cloth.

Mary took a deep breath, letting the night air fill her

lungs. After releasing it, she walked toward the corral. Baba joined her, following at her heels. Cloud lifted his head and snorted, then crossed to where she stood.

"'Tis married I'm to be," she told the horse as she stroked his muzzle. "Would ya fancy that."

Cloud's ears flicked forward.

"And the Painted Lady is mine," she added. "But what am I to be doing with it?"

She hadn't needed Carson to tell her that owning a bawdy house was quite different from running a pub. The citizens of Whistle Creek had slowly come to accept Mary, but what would happen when the word got out about the Painted Lady? It certainly wouldn't be good for the sheriff's wife to operate such an establishment. Nor did she want to, if truth be told.

But what about the women who lived and worked there? What would happen to them if she suddenly closed the Painted Lady? She didn't approve of how they made their living, but she understood how many of them had come to be there. They were women who'd been pushed to the edge, surviving the only way they thought they could. It might have happened to her, if circumstances had been different. What would she have been willing to do in order to protect Keary?

"I have done much worse," she whispered as a shiver raced through her.

She shook her head, driving off the unpleasant image. She wouldn't entertain thoughts of the past tonight of all nights. She had too much to be happy about. She wasn't going to let her past spoil her joy.

She set her thoughts on Carson. She remembered the first time she had seen him, the day she'd stepped off the train. Oh, how he'd frightened her, the tall handsome man with a badge and a gun. Now he was to be her husband.

She placed her forearms on the top rail of the corral, then rested her chin on her right wrist and closed her eyes.

Her husband. Carson Barclay, her husband.

She envisioned the two of them, lying together in bed. She pictured him touching her, caressing her, loving her. She was no innocent virgin. She knew what happened between a man and a woman. But she suspected she had yet to discover all there was to know about the act of loving. She suspected there were pleasures still to be experienced, pleasures she couldn't even imagine now.

But soon . . . soon she would know them.

A deep sigh escaped her.

"Lovely," a male voice said out of the darkness.

Baba growled as Mary whirled around, a gasp of surprise on her lips.

"What do you want?" she asked breathlessly as her gaze found the man on horseback, his silhouette a shade darker than the night around him.

"I came to see you, Mrs. Malone."

She recognized his voice then. Bryan Halligan. She glanced toward the house, wondering how quickly she could run to it.

Halligan dismounted.

Baba growled, more menacing this time.

"Call off your dog," he said. "I'm here to talk."

"At this hour?"

He chuckled. It was an unpleasant sound. "I admit it is a bit late. But I only just heard the news about Blanche Loraine's will, and I wanted to discuss it with you."

"And what business would that be of yours, Mr. Halligan?" She moved away from the corral, taking a

218

couple of steps toward the house, then stopped, hoping he wouldn't notice.

He noticed. He moved in the same direction. "I'd like to make you an offer for the Painted Lady."

"An offer?" It wasn't what she'd expected him to say.

"I'd like to buy it from you. I'm willing to pay a good price, and you'd be free to do what you want. Besides, you don't know anything about running a saloon in a mining town. Keeping the accounts for Miss Blanche was one thing. Keeping those whores . . ." He had the audacity to laugh softly. "Pardon me. Managing those *soiled doves* is another matter."

Mind your tongue, Mary, she seemed to hear her da caution as her temper sparked, but as usual, she didn't heed the voice from her past. "There's nothing that I'd be selling to the likes o' you," she snapped, her contempt obvious, "and now I'd have you leave me place."

"But you haven't heard my offer."

"Sure and I have no intention of listening to anything you have to say, Mr. Halligan. I'm thinking you're a hateful man, with no good intent for anyone but yourself. I'll thank you to be going now."

He chuckled again. "All right. If you don't want to talk business, maybe we should consider something more pleasurable to us both."

His comment deserved no answer. She marched toward the house, her head held high in a show of disdain.

Suddenly, Halligan had her by the shoulders and spun her around. When Baba moved in with an ominous growl, Halligan served the dog a vicious kick in the ribs, sending her flying into the darkness.

"Baba!" Mary cried.

"I'm losing my sense of humor," Halligan snapped as he gave Mary's shoulder a hard shake.

Before she could respond, before her temper cooled and fear could replace it, she felt something rush past her. Then Halligan grunted and fell backward to the ground.

"You leave Mary be!"

For a moment, Mary didn't believe what she'd heard. "Nellie?"

Nellie's and Halligan's shadows rolled away from her. "Nellie!"

By the time Mary moved forward, Halligan had already gained the upper hand. He dragged Nellie up by her hair. Profanity issued from him in a scalding stream of words, barely heard above Nellie's shrieks. Even in the darkness, Mary could see him give another violent yank on her hair.

"Stop! You're hurting her," Mary screamed.

"I'll do more than hurt her."

Nellie tried to kick him.

He slapped her with his free hand.

Just as Nellie had done moments before, Mary threw herself at him. And just as Nellie had done, she caught him unaware and knocked him off his feet. With a thud, they hit the ground. Mary was prepared for a struggle, but there was none. Halligan stopped fighting. Apparently, he'd had enough.

She jumped to her feet and reached for Nellie. "Are you hurt?" she asked, cradling the girl's head between her hand and leaning low.

"No," Nellie whimpered. "I'm okay."

Mary glanced over her shoulder. Halligan still hadn't moved. She felt a tiny shiver of alarm. "Go in the house, Nellie."

"Not without you."

"You'll be doing as I say."

"No! I'm stayin' with you. You might need me."

Mary thought to argue, then decided against it. It might be better not to be alone. "Then stand over by the house." She gave Nellie a little push to send her on her way.

Taking a deep breath, she turned again. She saw Baba, obviously not seriously harmed by the kick, standing over Halligan, sniffing at the man's still body. Unnaturally still, it seemed to Mary.

Could it have happened again? Just as she'd dared to hope for happiness, could it have happened again?

She stepped toward Halligan, her thoughts swirling. She seemed to be in two places at once—in a book-lined study in New York City and in an open meadow in the mountains of Idaho. She could see two men, both of them lying deathly still because of something she'd done. Because of her temper. She'd escaped her guilt the first time. But now. . .

Halligan moaned.

Baba growled.

Mary gasped, surprised, then thankful, and then angry all over again.

She whirled about and raced into the cabin, where she grabbed the rifle Carson had provided. She was breathing hard by the time she returned to stand in the light spilling through the doorway.

"I'm thinking you should leave now, Mr. Halligan," she called to him as he staggered to his feet. "And I'll thank you never to return."

He cursed. "You'll regret this."

Sure and I already regret it.

She couldn't marry Carson without telling him the

221

truth. This incident tonight had reminded her that the past would come back to haunt her if she didn't. She would find no peace, no real happiness, not as long as she let the lie remain. No, she either had to refuse to marry Carson or she had to tell him the truth.

She lifted the rifle to her shoulder and aimed it at Halligan. "Leave," she ordered in a voice devoid of emotion. "Just leave."

She didn't lower the rifle until he'd mounted his horse and ridden away. Even then she stood staring out into the night. Her heart ached. She felt lost and confused.

Finally, she forced herself to draw a steady breath. "Come, Baba," she called to the still-wary dog. Then she placed a hand on Nellie's shoulder and guided the girl inside.

Bright and early the next morning, Carson rode out to the property Blanche had left to him. As he sat astride Cinnabar, staring down at the crystal-clear lake, morning sunlight glittering over the surface of the water, he felt an astounding sense of gratitude.

He couldn't imagine what he'd done to deserve such perfect happiness. Mary would soon be his wife. He would have a son in Keary and a daughter in Nellie, and hopefully, there would be more children in his future. He had good friends he could trust. He had the newly inherited interest in the Lucky Lady that made him a man of some means. And now he owned this beautiful section of land, where he would build Mary the finest house she could ever wish for.

No, he'd never done anything to deserve all this. But miraculously, it was his, and he was thankful for it.

It was too late in the year to start building the house,

222

of course. The first snowfall was probably no more than a month away. Winters came early in these parts and lasted long, but those winter months would give him plenty of time to design exactly what he wanted Mary to have.

It would be two stories with an attic and a porch that wrapped around two sides of the house. He would paint it white with green shutters at the windows. The front would face the lake and the sunrise. Mary could sit on the porch in the morning and see the golden light flickering on the water, just as he was doing now.

He grinned at the image in his head. He'd never been much for daydreaming, but he'd discovered there was pleasure to be found in it.

He straightened in the saddle and turned his dun gelding toward the road. He wanted to see Mary. He wanted to hold her in his arms and kiss her like he had yesterday. They hadn't set a wedding date yet. Today he was going to convince her it should be soon. Real soon. Maybe next week.

He nudged Cinnabar into a lope, eager to see his bride-to-be. It seemed in that moment that nothing could go wrong ever again. His life was perfect and seemed destined to stay so.

Fifteen minutes later, just as the east end of Whistle Creek came into sight, he found out how wrong he was.

Nineteen

THE MINERS POURED INTO WHISTLE CREEK, THEIR voices raised in anger. Dozens of them. Well over a hundred, it looked like. Some carried guns or rifles. Others toted tools of their trade. A few of them rode

223

horses or mules. Most were on foot. There were even a few wives and children in their midst.

"Where's Halligan?" someone shouted. Others picked up the cry. "Where's Halligan? We want Halligan."

A knot formed in Carson's belly as he approached the front wave of the mob. He drew Cinnabar to a halt, bumped his hat brim with his knuckle, tipping it back on his head, then leaned his forearm on the saddle horn in a deceptively relaxed pose. His eyes focused on Pete Edwards, the apparent leader of the group.

The surge of miners slowly came to a stop. Silence spread from the front of the mob to the back. All eyes were fastened on the sheriff.

"What's going on, Edwards?" Carson asked the leader, keeping his voice neutral.

"Halligan's fired Grigg and the others that were trapped with Russell and Tyrell."

The announcement didn't come as a surprise. Carson had been expecting it for some time now.

"And he's cut our wages, too," someone else interjected.

Carson felt the knot in his gut twist. "That's rough, fellas," he said evenly, keeping his gaze on Edwards, "but that's no reason to come swarming into Whistle Creek, making it unsafe for folks to walk down the street."

"We come to find Halligan. We want to talk to him."

Carson shook his head, then shrugged. "Why didn't you talk to him at the mine?"

Edwards spit into the dust, then replied, "Because the coward had Christy do his dirty work for him. That's why."

Well, Carson thought, at least they weren't blaming Jeff Christy for the bad news. And nobody had mentioned the scabs waiting over in Osburn. Maybe they didn't know about them yet.

"We heard Halligan's in the saloon."

Carson straightened in the saddle and once more swept the mob with his gaze. "I'm not having any trouble here," he told the men, raising his voice so he could be heard at the back of the crowd. "Go on back to your homes. If you want a meeting with Halligan, send a representative or two. There's no need for all of you to be here." His gaze swung back to Pete Edwards. "And there's no call for guns, either."

"You sidin' with Halligan, Sheriff?" Edwards demanded.

A murmur of discontent rose and fell.

Carson's eyes narrowed. "I'm siding with the law," he answered without hesitation. "And those who break it will have to answer to me. That goes for Halligan and it goes for all of you. Is that clear?"

There was more grumbling, but Carson saw men beginning to turn and walk away. He waited, unmoving. He saw the angry glances that were exchanged amongst those closest to him, and he knew he'd won only a momentary victory. One thing he'd learned over the years: Trouble rode a fast horse. It would be back, and he would have to face it down again.

When the last of the mob began to drift away in small clusters, Carson turned Cinnabar toward the Painted Lady. He found Bryan Halligan sitting at Mac MacDonald's old table, nursing a whiskey. He was alone.

Carson pulled out a chair opposite the mine owner, turned the chair around, then straddled the seat. "You surprised me, Halligan. I expected you to cut wages *after* you had to call in the National Guard."

Halligan scowled at him as he rubbed the back of his head, wincing as if something hurt.

"And when are you bringing in the scab labor? They must be costing you a pretty penny to keep over in Osburn."

"Shut up, Barclay." Halligan took another gulp of liquor.

"I don't see what you have to gain from all this."

"And I don't see that it's any of your business."

Carson leaned forward, pressing his chest against the back of the chair. "It becomes my business when it causes trouble in Whistle Creek."

Halligan was silent for a moment, then said with a smirk, "Maybe all you care about is the value of those shares you inherited from Miss Blanche."

Carson didn't figure the comment was worth a reply.

"What did you do to earn them, Barclay? Cut Miss Blanche a deal? Maybe the good folks of Whistle Creek should know you've been on the take."

Carson hoped his eyes didn't reveal his inner fury. He didn't want Halligan to know what he was thinking or feeling. He'd learned long ago that a cooler head always prevailed in situations like this.

Halligan sloshed more whiskey into his empty glass and abruptly changed the subject. "I want you to arrest John Tyrell."

"On what charges?"

"Destruction of property, to start with."

Carson didn't have to ask what Halligan meant. He had a good idea where this was going. But he asked anyway. "What property is that?"

"You know damn well what property." Halligan drained half his glass of its amber contents. "Mine property. He was the cause of that cave-in at the Lucky

226

Lady. That bastard took dynamite down into the tunnel and tried to blow up the entire section. Only he got trapped by accident. Him and the others."

"What reason would he have to try to blow up the mine?"

"Because he's a bitter drunk. Because he's a damn cripple and he blames the mining company for it. Because he's a fool." Halligan's voice rose a notch in volume with every sentence. "How the hell should I know what's going on in his head? Now are you going to do your job or do I have to call in the federal marshal to do it for you?"

There was more behind Halligan's words and actions than simply trying to reduce wages and make a larger profit for himself and the other owners. But for the life of him, Carson couldn't figure out what it was. It didn't make sense. What Halligan was doing would cost the owners far more in the long run than what they would save in reduced wages.

"Well?" Halligan demanded. "What are you going to do?"

Carson rose to his feet. "You bring me some proof of your suspicions, and I'll arrest him. But not until then."

Halligan hopped up, knocking his chair over backward in his haste. "The word of Bryan Halligan is all the proof you need," he shouted.

Tension knotted the muscles in Carson's neck. "Maybe in Spokane that's how it works, but not here. I don't arrest somebody without just cause. In Whistle Creek, a man is still innocent until proven guilty."

"You won't arrest him because he's your friend," Halligan accused.

"You're right. John Tyrell is my friend. But I'll arrest him if there's reason to. I've arrested him before. You

227

bring me evidence of his involvement, and I'll put him in jail until a trial can be arranged." He rested his knuckles on the table top. "In the meantime, you watch what you do and what you say. *I'm* the law in Whistle Creek, and don't you forget it. You hear me, Halligan?"

The other man's face turned bright red.

Carson paused a heartbeat, then spun about and left.

Mary had wrestled with her decision throughout the previous night, sleeping little. She'd silently debated with herself all morning as well. She knew she had only two choices: Tell Carson about Winston Kenrick or refuse to marry him and leave town as she'd originally planned. One or the other.

But which was she to choose? Which would be the better thing to do? For Carson, for the children, for herself.

She loved Carson. She longed to spend the rest of her life with him. Keary loved him, too, and she knew Carson would make a grand father for her son.

But what would he do if she told him about her reason for fleeing from New York City? She'd realized, sometime during her many hours of contemplation, that it wasn't jail she feared most. It was causing Carson to go against his ideals, to compromise his own integrity. She feared that much more than a prison cell.

And if she left suddenly, disappeared into the western wilderness, what would that do to him? Would he search for her? Would he learn to hate her?

And, as always, there were the children to consider. Who would care for them? Would they forget her if she was taken away? Worse, would they learn to despise her?

Mary had a hundred questions and no answers. She'd

228

found no way to predict the future. She knew she would have to make her choice, and soon. She just didn't know how she would make it.

In the midst of her confusion, she cursed Bryan Halligan. Not for his assault last night but for forcing her into this untenable position. For making her face what she'd managed to avoid since accepting Carson's proposal of marriage.

It was now after lunch, and Mary felt no closer to a decision than she'd been last night. Keary was down for his nap and Nellie was quietly working on some embroidery, something Edith had taught her how to do.

"Sure and I think I'll be taking a walk," Mary told the girl, trying her best to sound casual. "Will you keep an eye on Keary while I'm gone?"

"'Course," Nellie answered without looking up from her sewing.

Mary felt a welling up of anxiety, a fear of what the future might bring. "You're a good lass, Fenella Russell," she said huskily, her voice filled with emotion. "I don't know what I'd ever do without you. I'm glad altogether that you've come to live with us. You're like me very own daughter, and that's the truth of it."

The sudden outburst caused Nellie to glance up, her eyes wide with surprise.

"I . . . I just thought you should know the way of it." Mary forced a smile, then hurried outside.

But her escape into the mountains in search of answers was thwarted. As she stepped into the summer sunlight, she saw Carson, riding up to the house. What was she to say to him? she wondered. Was now the time?

But then she noticed his strained expression, and she forgot her own dilemma. "Carson? What's wrong?"

229

He didn't answer her. He simply dismounted, then took her in his arms and held her close.

She could feel the steady beat of his heart. His breath was warm on her scalp as he pressed his cheek against her hair. His strong hands spread wide across her back.

"Carson?" she whispered after a lengthy silence. She drew back but didn't leave the circle of his arms as she looked up at him. "Tell me what's troubling you."

He shook his head slowly, his gaze locked with hers. "Halligan."

Her heart jumped. Did Carson know what had happened here last night?

He kissed her forehead, then whispered, "All hell's about to break loose." He kissed the tip of her nose. "I just needed to hold you, to feel something good before it does." He kissed her on the lips. "I love you, Mary."

She couldn't leave him. She knew in that moment that leaving was not an option. She would have to tell him the truth. Maybe he wouldn't want her any longer. But whatever happened, it would be up to him, for Mary could never walk away of her own volition.

The words she had never allowed herself to speak aloud slipped quietly into the open. "And 'tis you I love, Carson."

He stilled, staring down at her once more, his gaze searching, hungry. "Say it again," he gently demanded.

"I love you." Oddly enough, instead of feeling more vulnerable because of her admission, she was strengthened by it. Her fears about the future seemed to retreat.

Carson's voice was husky as he drew her close again. "You'll never know how I've longed to hear you say that."

"There's more I need to be telling you, Carson. Much

230

more."

He didn't seem to hear her. "Will you marry me next week when Reverend Ogelsby is back in town?" He kissed her again, long and deep, a kiss that left them both in want of oxygen.

When their mouths parted, Mary put her hands against his chest and gently pushed herself away from him. "'Tis talking we must be doing first, Carson Barclay. There's something important I must tell you."

He grinned and the tension left his face for the first time since he'd arrived. "I don't feel like talking, Mary. I feel like kissing some more."

"Faith and begorra," she muttered but was unable to keep from returning his smile. Would one more day matter so much? she wondered as she surrendered to the pleasure of his mouth on hers. Tomorrow would be soon enough to tell him what had to be told.

The moment of peace was shattered by a distant boom that caused the air around them to vibrate. In unison, they broke apart and turned their eyes toward Whistle Creek. A few heartbeats later, an enormous black cloud rose above the hilltops.

"It's started," Carson said as he spun toward his horse. He swung into the saddle, then looked back at Mary. "Whatever happens, you and the children stay here. Understood? Don't leave the cabin. I promise I'll come back as soon as I can. Just stay here until I do."

The black smoke from the burning storage shed—a cavernous building belonging to the Lucky Lady Mine—could be seen for miles. It rose swiftly, a belching dark cloud staining the clear blue of the sky. Ash and embers drifted down on the town. Men and women rushed to dampen rooftops in the hopes of

231

preventing a spread of the fire.

Carson joined the townsfolk in their battle against the raging blaze. Everyone was aware of the danger. Many a city and town had been destroyed by fire. The people who made their homes here, who had their businesses here, stood to lose everything they'd worked so hard to build unless they could contain the flames.

Luckily, the storage shed was located near the railroad tracks. There were no other buildings nearby, and the river formed a natural barrier between the fire and the parched summer forest. Chances were good they could stop it from spreading.

As Carson flung buckets full of water on the fire, he swore to himself that he'd find out who had caused the explosion that started the blaze. All indications would point to the miners, especially after this morning's angry demonstration, but a sixth sense told him that was too obvious. He suspected this was just another part of Halligan's plan. But a plan for what? What did he stand to gain from destroying his own property?

"Look out!" someone shouted, jerking Carson back to the present.

He jumped aside just in time to avoid being struck by a falling timber. Drawing a steadying breath, he decided he'd better concentrate on the fire first and solving the matter of who started it later.

Evening had settled over the mountain meadow like a soft gray blanket. The children were already fast asleep in their bed, but Mary remained at the window, watching. Carson had promised to return, and so she waited.

The moment she spied him, riding toward the cabin, she raced outside. There was nothing shy or reticent

232

about the way she approached him this time. She had been worried sick, and she needed to reassure herself that he was all right.

As soon as she reached him, she laid a hand on his thigh. Even in the twilight, she could see the smudges of soot on his face, the weary sag of his shoulders. "Is the news so terrible altogether?" she asked, not really wanting an answer.

"Could've been worse." He dismounted, then turned toward her. "The only thing lost was the mining company's storage building down by the tracks. It burned to the ground, but we managed to keep the fire from spreading."

"I'm glad you came back. I've been worrying for the sight of you."

"I should be investigating what started the fire." He reached out, tucked a loose strand of her hair behind her ear. "But I wanted to see you."

He sounded more than tired. He sounded defeated, and that was unlike the Carson Barclay she knew. Mary stepped up close, wrapping her arms around his chest.

"I smell smoky," he objected. But even as he spoke, he hugged her to him. Tight, with a grip that said he didn't want to ever let go. After a long silence, he spoke again, "I saw what happened up in this country the last time the miners went on strike. There were riots. People died. Others were arrested. Buildings were blown up. I don't want to see that happen in Whistle Creek. I just don't know how to stop it. I should be able to stop it, but I can't figure out how."

"You're too tired to think straight," she replied as she eased back and looked up to meet his gaze. "Come and sit down. There's a pitcher of lemonade in the springhouse. I'll get some for you."

233

He nodded, and she took his hand and led him to the bench just outside the front door of the cabin. With a wave of her hand, she commanded him to sit. Once he'd done so, she hurried inside for a glass. A quick glance reassured her that the children hadn't stirred.

After going to the springhouse for the lemonade, she returned to where she'd left Carson. She found him leaning against the cabin wall, his head back, his eyes closed. She paused, uncertain if she should disturb him or let him rest.

"I'm not asleep," he said softly, without opening his eyes.

"'Tis sleeping you should be, I'm thinking."

He patted the bench. "Come sit beside me, Mary."

She did so.

He put his right arm around her shoulders, then pulled her close to his side. "I wonder if it wouldn't be better for you and the children to leave Whistle Creek for a while."

"Are you expecting it to be as bad as all that, then?"

Instead of answering, he leaned his cheek against the top of her head, and his grip on her upper right arm tightened.

It was strange, she thought. Not so very long ago, she'd been wanting to leave Whistle Creek. She'd been wanting to take herself and the children away from here. She'd been willing to go into hiding. She'd even thought it would be best for Carson if she were to do so.

But now it was the last thing on earth she wanted to do. Leaving him would be the same as ripping out her heart. She couldn't go away from this place, away from him. She wanted to remain here, in his arms, forever.

"I'm thinking we'll stay," she said at last, "if 'tis all the same to you. I'd not be drawing a peaceful breath were I to put any distance between us, Carson." Her throat was thick with emotion, and she felt the sting of tears behind her eyes.

Carson straightened, took the glass of lemonade from her hand and set it on the ground. Then he gently pulled her across his lap. The embrace seemed natural, comfortable, as if they'd been doing it for years. She looked up into his eyes, and even though she couldn't see him well in the gloaming, her heart quickened.

"I never expected to find you, Mary."

She swallowed the lump in her throat.

"I wish this wasn't happening now. Halligan and the miners, I mean. I want to be thinking of you. Just you."

"Aye," she whispered, wishing the same.

"I don't know a lot of flowery words. The kind a man ought to sweet-talk his lady with. Poetry and such. I wish I did. You deserve them, Mary. I never knew anyone who deserved them more than you do."

Slowly, he lowered his head toward hers until their lips met. The kiss was tender, slow, sweeter than any words could have been. It made Mary's head spin, her heart to flutter.

Carson drew her closer as the kiss deepened. She heard him groan, a sound that rumbled up from his chest, then became a part of her. She felt the hot flare of desire deep in her loins. It overtook her unexpectedly, a terrible yet wonderful wanting to be joined with this man, to be a part of him. It was a feeling unlike anything she had known in the past.

Again Carson groaned, and she knew he was feeling the same desire, the same wanting, as she. He ended the kiss, but his lips continued to hover just above hers. His breath was warm upon her face, feeling even warmer in comparison to the cool night air. With his free hand, he

235

pulled the pins from her hair and let it fall loose over his arm. Then he ran his fingers through the thick cascading tresses, stroking, caressing. Mary hadn't known such a simple act could be an intimate one as well—or so provocative at the same time.

"I wish Reverend Ogelsby was going to be here tomorrow," he said, his voice a husky whisper.

She swallowed, unable to speak, wishing the same.

"I think I'd better go."

She wanted him to stay. She wanted to spend the night in his arms. She wanted to lie naked beside him, to feel the warmth of his body, to . . .

"I'd best go now," he half groaned, half growled.

She couldn't stop herself from whispering, "Stay with me."

He silenced her with another kiss, a brief, quick, frustrated kiss that spoke volumes.

What if she was never to know his loving? What if, when she made her confession to him, when he knew the whole truth, he didn't want her anymore?

"Stay with me," she said again.

More than seeing his gaze, she could feel it. "Don't tempt me, Mary."

"But—"

"Shh." He brushed his lips over hers. "You deserve better. You deserve everything wonderful and perfect."

She felt a warmth in her heart. He didn't need flowery words or poetry to tell her she was cherished, to tell her that he valued her. The knowledge made her feel both glorious and unworthy. No matter what tomorrow might bring, she would remember this moment forever.

Twenty

SWEAT TRICKLED DOWN CARSON'S BACK AS HE rode toward Whistle Creek beneath the hot afternoon sun. He'd spent hours up at the Lucky Lady, ever since early that morning, talking to the striking miners, hoping he could get some answers before it was too late—if it wasn't too late already. Once again, he'd come away empty-handed.

"What would you have done, David?" he muttered aloud.

A better job of things, he answered himself.

David Hailey would have found answers by this time. Carson was sure of it. Of course, it might have been easier if he could control the direction of his thoughts. All too often, when he should have been concentrating on the miners, he'd found himself thinking about Mary.

Stay with me.

Heaven help him! There was nothing he would have liked more than to have stayed with her. Nothing he'd ever done had been more difficult than riding away from the cabin last night without claiming Mary for his own, without seeking solace in the warmth of her body. He'd wanted nothing more than to let his passion have free rein to discover the pleasures he knew awaited him.

But another man had done just that and left Mary with a child. He didn't know the whole story—and he realized now it was a sign of cowardice on his part that he'd never asked her to tell him more about Keary's father. But whatever had happened between her and the man she'd called Maguire, Carson wasn't about to do the same thing to her. When he took Mary for his own, it would be as her husband, all right and proper.

237

Pressing his mouth into a thin line, he shook off her image. Now wasn't the time to let his thoughts stray off course again. He had only to remember this morning's confrontation to know that.

"You'd better find out who started that fire," Halligan had shouted as he'd stood before Carson's desk. "You make some arrests. You do your job. Or, so help me, I'll do it for you. I know you're turning a blind eye to what's going on. I know you favor the miners."

Carson was glad he hadn't made any accusations of his own. He still thought Halligan might have set the fire, but he didn't want the man to know of his suspicions. Not until he had some proof.

Only he wasn't sure he would have the time he needed to get his proof. The mood out at the Lucky Lady was ugly. If the miners weren't behind the fire yesterday, they'd probably be behind the next incident. And he knew there *would* be another incident, just as surely as the sun would rise again tomorrow morning. It was only a matter of time.

He felt the blistering sun beating down on his back and cursed the lingering heat wave. Tempers were shorter in weather like this. Including his.

As the train whistle sounded its mournful cry, Portia stared out the window, watching the passing countryside. She found the scenery breathtaking. The mountains rose like pyramids, covered in green blankets of pine and fir. The sky overhead was a blinding blue. The river ran clear and smooth at times; at others, the rapids made it froth like the mouth of a mad dog. Towns were few and far between, and all of those were small, made up of a saloon or two, a dry goods store or a mercantile, a smithy and, if the town was fortunate,

238

perhaps a doctor's office. There was seldom much else, other than a few homes.

What would it be like to live in such a place? Portia had found herself wondering with each stop. She'd looked at the men and women getting off the train in these "jerkwater towns"—as Winston called them—and she'd wished she could go with them. She knew their lives must be hard. She could see that by their faces. To live in country like this, to fight the elements day in and day out, couldn't be easy. But she wished to experience it for herself.

It came as an enormous surprise to discover she didn't want to go back to New York City once they found Mary. She didn't want to return to her beautiful home on Madison Avenue. From the time she was a little girl, Portia had been given everything her heart desired by the father who had doted on her. Merlin Pendergast had done his best to lay the world at Portia's feet, including finding her the sort of husband who could give her what he couldn't—the right name. Marrying Winston had introduced her to the society she'd thought she craved. But money and position hadn't given her real happiness. Certainly her marriage hadn't given her any. She'd thought the price was worth it. She'd been mistaken.

"Whistle Creek, next stop," the conductor called, interrupting her musings.

"About time," Winston grumbled.

Portia turned her eyes toward her husband. Briefly, their gazes met. His was full of anger and bitterness, and so much more. Loathing, perhaps. For her. She wondered what he saw in her eyes.

She wasn't going back to New York with him, she knew in that instant. It wasn't too late to try to find a shred of the happiness she'd missed. She couldn't change the past, but she could change her future. It was time she became responsible for her own happiness. She intended to start taking that responsibility now.

"Mr. Kenrick . . ." Tibble Knox began. Winston and Portia glanced in his direction. "I suggest you and your wife check into the hotel while I try to find Miss Malone's whereabouts."

"I'm going with you," Winston shot back quickly.

"But—"

"I'm going with you," he insisted.

Portia looked out the window once again, thinking, *Mary came out here, all alone and penniless. If she could do it, so can I.*

When the knock sounded on Blanche's office door, Mary closed the ledger and called, "Enter."

"You wanted to see me?" Edith asked as she stepped through the doorway, a smile brightening her pretty face.

"Aye, that I did. Will you be closing the door behind you, please?"

Edith's smile vanished. "You sound serious."

"'Tis a matter of importance I wish to be discussing with you."

"Is it Johnny?" the girl asked, a note of panic in her voice. "Has something happened to him?"

Mary shook her head. "No, 'tis not your Johnny. 'Tis yourself this concerns."

"Me?" Edith sat down in the chair opposite the desk. "Have I done something wrong?"

Mary laughed softly. "I'm thinking I've alarmed you needlessly. I'm sorry for that altogether. 'Tis your help I want. Nothing more." She held up her hand, stopping the girl from speaking. "Hear me out."

Edith nodded.

"When I came to Whistle Creek, it was because Miss Blanche offered help to a stranger. I had nowhere to go, and I had little enough money to see me through. I wouldn't be knowing why she helped me. I'm thinking she didn't know either. It just happened."

"She helped me, too."

"Aye, I remember you telling me how it was." Mary rose from her chair and went to the window. "Most of the women who work here have similar stories to ours. No money and nowhere to go. 'Tis what's made them desperate enough to live like this. 'Tis what could happen to any woman." She paused, her thoughts wandering for a moment, reliving snippets from her past. Finally, she turned to look at Edith again. "I wouldn't be knowing for certain why Miss Blanche left the Painted Lady to me, but she must have known I wouldn't leave it as it is."

"What do you mean, Mary?"

"The pub can stay. I've no quarrel with serving ale to thirsty men. But I'll not keep women for them to use."

"But—"

"Hear me out," she repeated quickly, then returned to her chair and sat down. She placed her forearms on the desk and leaned forward. "'Tis a safe haven I want to provide, Edith. A place for a woman to go when she's got nothing else. And her children, too, if she's got any."

"I reckon that's right nice of you, Mary, but—"

Again she interrupted Edith. "And I want you to run the place."

"*Me?*"

"Aye. Because you understand what it's like." She

241

lowered her voice. "And so do I. I was never married to Keary's da. I was thinking we were to be married when I joined him in America, but he married someone else before I came here. I don't believe he ever meant to marry me. He died without knowing he'd sired a son and left him without a name."

"Oh, Mary," Edith whispered. "I'm right sorry."

Mary realized there were tears in her eyes. She impatiently flicked them away. "'Tis not Seamus Maguire I cry for. 'Tis knowing what happens to many girls who make the same foolish mistakes as I did. No one cares that there was a man involved, too. He is not blamed. 'Tis only the girl. And then there are other men who think to take advantage of her again just because she's made a mistake in her past."

Edith nodded.

"Miss Blanche made me wealthy by leaving this saloon to me, but I've no need of the income now that I'm to be married meself. I was thinking of selling it. Then last night the answer came to me altogether. We'll make the upstairs a home for women in need. A safe haven, like I said."

There was a spark of interest in Edith's eyes, but she kept it out of her voice as she said, "I'd have to talk to Johnny."

"I was thinking he could manage the saloon, if he'd be of a mind to. I'd make him me partner."

"A partner?"

"Aye, the both of you."

It was Edith's turn to rise, Edith's turn to walk to the window and stare outside. Softly, she said, "I never expected nothing like this to happen. Finding Johnny, that was enough for me. More than I deserved." Her voice fell so low, Mary had to strain to hear. "Johnny doesn't seem to mind. What I've been, I mean. He says it don't matter. That I'm special. He says I ain't gettin' no bargain in him. But I sure wish I could go to him, all clean like instead of like I am. If there'd been some other way for me . . ." Her voice drifted into silence.

"So you'll do it? You'll help me?"

Edith turned. She stared at Mary for a long time before nodding. "Yeah, I reckon I will. And I know Johnny'll want to. You see if he don't." She crossed back to her chair. "What about the girls who're workin' here now? What are you gonna do about them?"

"They'll be offered a place to stay as long as they want it. But they won't be allowed to entertain men here. If that's what they want to keep doing, they'll have to move on. For those willing to learn, we can teach skills so that they can get jobs. Real jobs. Like teaching or dressmaking. Or they could learn to be cooks. Greta could help us with that."

Edith laughed aloud. "Greta? Not willingly, I wager."

"Aye, she will. You'll see."

For the next hour, the two young women enthusiastically discussed all the possibilities and made a host of plans for changes to the property. Mary wanted to close off the entrance connecting the saloon to the rest of the building. She wanted to fence in the property at the back and make a play area for children. Edith suggested enlarging the kitchen and dining areas. She also thought they should turn a large room on the main floor—once used for private high-stakes gambling parties—into a sewing room because of the daylight that came in through the westside windows.

They were still bubbling over with ideas when Shirley, one of the Painted Lady "girls," opened the office door. "There's a couple of men out front asking for you, Miz Malone," she said, then winked at Edith, as if sharing a good joke. "And I wouldn't mind spending a bit o' time with the taller one. Handsome fella if ever I seen one, even if he isn't so young anymore."

"What do they want?" Mary asked, hating to be disturbed while the ideas were still flowing.

"Don't know. Just wanted to talk to the owner. In private, they said."

Mary supposed she shouldn't be surprised. Word that she had inherited the Painted Lady would have carried quickly through Whistle Creek and on to neighboring towns. These men were probably whiskey salesmen or some such, hoping to get the saloon's business. It was a reminder that there were other things she must do. While Blanche had left her plenty of money, it would be costly to run the charitable establishment she had envisioned. She would need the saloon to turn a profit, even if a modest one, if the home was to be of lasting duration.

"I suppose I must be seeing them." She glanced at Edith. "We'll talk more later."

Shirley asked, "You want I should send 'em back?"

"Aye. And thank you, Shirley."

"No trouble, Miz Malone."

Edith rose from her chair and started to follow after Shirley.

"Edith," Mary said, stopping her departure. "When I'm finished with these salesmen, I'm thinking I should have a talk with everyone who works at the Painted Lady. They should be told what I'm planning. They must all be wondering what I'm going to do."

Edith nodded. "I'll see to it, Mary." She smiled. "And don't you worry none either. It's all gonna work out just fine. It's a real good thing you're doing. A real good thing."

Carson slammed the cell door closed. "Cool off, Edwards," he told the older man, "and then we'll talk." He glanced toward Thomas Crane, who was now sitting on a cot in the cell opposite Pete Edwards. Thomas was gently touching his split lower lip, then glancing at the blood on his fingertips. "I'm going to want to talk to you, too, Crane."

The two men had been brawling in the middle of Church Street, just as the three-fifteen was letting off passengers. Rather than having those newly arrived in Whistle Creek thinking there was no law and order in this town, Carson had hauled both men off to jail, not even asking who or what had caused the fight between the two miners.

As he walked into his office, Carson used his foot to shut the door that separated the office from the jail cells. He raked the fingers of both hands through his hair and muttered a few strong oaths beneath his breath. It was time he admitted to himself that he needed help. He couldn't handle this situation alone.

He stepped outside and stood on the sidewalk, glancing up and down Main Street. The afternoon sun continued to bake the town, blistering the paint on storefront signs. Horses stood at hitching rails, their heads hung low, their tails switching slowly. Abe Stover's dog had crawled beneath the raised boardwalk in front of the mercantile, seeking shade.

All was peaceful.

Before he sent a wire to Boise, Carson decided quickly, he'd call in a favor from Sheriff Parks down in Latah County. Maybe with a few deputies and a bit of luck, he could hold trouble at bay awhile longer. Maybe even long enough to get the answers he needed.

He looked toward the Painted Lady and wondered if it was full of miners. Friends of Edwards and Crane. If so, it probably wouldn't matter if he had fifty deputies to help him.

All was peaceful—but only temporarily. It could burst apart at the seams at any time.

His pride was causing him to use poor judgment, he thought grimly. He should have sent for help long before now. He didn't have time to waste, looking for clues all by himself. If the anticipated trouble erupted, Mary and the children—his family—could get hurt. He wasn't about to risk that.

He turned, reached through the doorway to grab his hat off the peg, then headed toward the telegraph office, his decision made.

When she heard the footsteps in the hallway, Mary rose from her chair and stood behind her desk, trying to look sure of herself, trying to look like the owner of the Painted Lady Saloon. But when the taller of the two men stepped into her office, she lost the ability to breathe, to think, let alone to pretend a confidence she didn't feel.

"Hello, Mary" Winston said, a cruel smile curving his mouth. "I guess you didn't expect to see me."

She grabbed for the desk, hoping to keep herself from falling. It couldn't be him. She'd killed him. He was dead. Faith and begorra! Was this his ghost, come to haunt her?

He turned to the man behind him. "Wait for me out in the hall, Knox. I want to talk to Miss Malone in private." When the door was firmly closed, he looked at

Mary once again. "I asked to see the owner. I didn't expect to find you here."

"I . . . I'm the owner," she answered without thinking—and immediately wished she hadn't.

"Indeed?" He smiled again. "Then you have done quite well for yourself in a short time." His gaze moved slowly over her. "Running a bordello seems to agree with you, Mary"

She ignored the obvious meaning in his words. "I was thinking you were—"She stopped abruptly, not wanting to say the word aloud.

"Dead," he finished for her. "No doubt, you wished it so." He touched the back of his head, as if to remind her what she'd done.

"No." She sat down, her legs no longer able to support her. "I was only wanting you to stop."

His smile turned menacing. "Too good for me but not for this?" He waved his hand, then took two steps toward her. "I should—" He swallowed his angry words, but his hard gaze never left her.

She watched him control his rage, saw the cool, aristocratic mask slip into place. She wondered what he intended to do with her now. Many times she had imagined the authorities finding her, taking her back to New York to stand trial for murder. But never in her wildest dreams had she thought she would be facing Winston Kenrick himself.

For just a moment, she felt relief. All these weeks, she'd thought she was guilty of murder. But she wasn't. He was alive. She hadn't killed him. She wouldn't have to confess to Carson that she was a murderer. She could go to him with a clean conscience. She could marry Carson without guilt.

"You did *try* to kill me, Mary," Winston said, as if

247

reading her thoughts. "You could hang for that alone."

A chill gripped her heart. "'Twas only because you were forcing yourself on me against me will."

"And who would believe that?"

"But 'tis true."

He chuckled softly as he settled into the chair opposite her. "Are you naive enough to believe the truth matters? What matters is who I am and who you are. And that is all that matters. Fair or not, that's the way it is in this world, my dear girl."

Carson . . . Keary . . . Nellie . . . She felt her heart breaking as their names whispered in her head. *Carson . . . Keary . . . Nellie . . .*

Winston cleared his throat. "I would be willing to forget what happened if you just return what you stole from me."

It took a moment for his words to seep through her grief. When they did, she was confused. "What I stole?"

"The silver cigar box," he snapped, anger once again in his voice. "The one you struck me with. You took it when you ran, and I want it back."

She shook her head, not because she was denying she'd taken the box but because she was trying to remember what she'd done with it.

Misunderstanding her gesture, Winston leaped to his feet and leaned across the desk, grabbing her chin with one hand and squeezing tight. His face was mottled with fury. "What did you do with the box, Mary? Tell me." He squeezed harder. "Return it to me or, so help me God, you'll regret it."

"I don't know where it is!" she cried out, fearing he would break her jaw in his iron grasp.

"What did you do with it?" There was murder in his eyes. "Did you sell it? Did you throw it away?

248

You fool!"

"No," she answered quickly. "I had it when we got here. I . . . I put it out of sight so I wouldn't be remembering . . . so I wouldn't be thinking on what happened that day. I . . . I just wouldn't be knowing where I put it."

Winston released his grip and straightened. His cool facade slid back into place, and he was once again the calm, controlled gentleman. "I suggest you find it, Mary, and quickly. We have taken rooms at the boardinghouse, since there is no hotel in this miserable town. You bring me that box by tomorrow morning, or I'll have you arrested for attempted murder." With those words, he turned and walked out of her office.

Mary stared at the closed door, her heart hammering, her mind racing.

Where had she put the box?

Her future depended upon finding it.

Twenty-one

BY SATURDAY AFTERNOON, THE WHISTLE CREEK jail cells were bursting at the seams, filled with grumbling, angry miners. Carson no sooner slammed the door behind his latest prisoner than someone would send for him with news of another altercation. Matters had worsened after the arrival of scab labor on Friday's train. Most of those men were holding court in the Painted Lady, waiting for their orders from Halligan.

In anticipation of even more trouble, Carson deputized Wade Tyrell, Abe Stover, and Dooby Jones—and then he prayed that the help he'd sent for would arrive soon.

Carson had just sunk down onto his chair behind his desk and closed his eyes, in hopes of finding a moment of peace, when he heard footsteps running along the boardwalk. He groaned softly, knowing his respite was already over.

"Sheriff Barclay!"

He was on his feet in a flash. "Nellie?"

"Sheriff Barclay, you'd better come quick. It's Mary."

Long strides carried him across his office. "What happened? Is she hurt?"

"No, but she's acting real queer-like. She was up all night, searching through her trunk and the cupboards and Keary's toys. Opening things again and again. She brought us into town before the sun was hardly up, and now she's doing the same over at the saloon. She's got me scared. And Edith, too."

Nellie had to run to keep up with Carson as he hurried toward the Painted Lady.

He didn't know what to make of what the girl had told him. It didn't sound like Mary. Maybe Nellie was reading more into whatever she was doing. Tensions were high. Even a child was sure to feel it.

Once inside the saloon, he paused, unsure where to find her. He looked behind him at Nellie. "Where is she?"

"Upstairs," she answered, jumping in front of him to lead the way.

Before they reached the bedroom, Carson could hear furniture being moved across the floor. Then he heard Mary's voice, soft and mumbling, the words indistinguishable.

He paused in the doorway and looked in. Mary was jerking open the drawers of a bureau, her hands searching the empty cavity she found within. There was a wild, desperate look about her. Even at her most skittish, he'd never seen her like this.

His gaze flicked toward a corner of the room where Edith stood, holding Keary in her arms. She met his gaze and gave her head a tiny shake, the gesture stating her helplessness.

He looked back toward Mary, then said her name softly.

She gasped and jumped away from the doorway, staring at him with frantic eyes.

"Mary, what's wrong?

She shook her head. Then her gaze began to rove around the room, as if she'd forgotten he was there. "I can't find it. 'Tis gone. I can't find it."

"Can't find what?"

"'Twas here. Edith thought it a jewelry box." She turned her back toward him. "Sure and I put it away so I wouldn't be seeing it, and now 'tis gone."

Carson was growing alarmed. All this over a jewelry box? He looked at Edith again, and again she shook her head.

Mary spun around. Tears filled her beautiful brown eyes. "Don't you see, Carson? I've lost it. I've looked everywhere. 'Tis gone, and now—" She choked on a sob.

In three quick strides, Carson was in the bedroom and gathering her into his embrace. "Whatever it is, we'll replace it, Mary. I promise." He kissed the top of her head. "I promise."

"You wouldn't be understanding," she replied as she pressed her face against his chest. "'Tis too late."

No, he didn't understand, but all he wanted at the moment was to stop her tears, to have her know he would do anything for her. "Shh." He stroked her back. "Shh. It'll be okay. I'll buy you a new jewelry box. An

251

even prettier one. Shh. It'll be okay. I promise."

She drew in a ragged breath, then let it out as she whispered, "No."

He heard Edith moving across the room, heard her softly say, "Come along, Nellie. We'll leave the two of 'em be." Then the door closed.

Carson and Mary stood in the center of a room in shambles. He kept her in his tight embrace, his cheek pressed against the top of her head. Neither of them spoke or made a sound, but Carson knew she was crying from the way her body occasionally shuddered.

His heart ached for her, and he wished he could do something to make her feel better, to stop her tears, to take away the desperation. He was a man of action, had always been a man of action. He hated this sense of helplessness. He wanted to fix whatever was wrong. But how could he fix it if he didn't know what it was?

He didn't look up when he heard the door open, assuming Edith had returned for some reason.

"My, my," a man said. "What have we here?"

Mary stiffened in his arms.

"Sheriff Barclay, I presume."

Carson glanced toward the stranger. From his silk top hat to his single-breasted gray walking suit to the shine on his leather-soled shoes, the fellow's attire proclaimed he was a man of means. So did his demeanor.

"You *are* Sheriff Barclay, are you not?" he continued when Carson didn't speak.

"I am." His arms tightened on Mary when she started to pull away. "And who are you?"

The man smiled, but there was nothing friendly about it. "My name is Winston Kenrick." His gaze shifted from Carson to Mary. "And I am here to demand the arrest of Mary Malone."

For a moment, Carson was silent. He suspected this man was the source of all Mary's fears; he just didn't know why. Finally, he asked, "On what charge?"

"Attempted murder and theft."

It took the last remnants of Mary's strength to pull free of Carson's embrace, to raise her head and look into his eyes. She saw the surprise and the questions in their blue depths.

"Well?" Winston continued.

"What proof do you have?" Carson asked, his gaze still locked with Mary's. "When and where was this supposed to have happened?"

"I have all the proof you'll need over at the boardinghouse. There are statements from my physician and from several of my house servants. Mary fled New York because she tried to kill me. She was a maid in my house. She attacked me in my own study. Ask her to deny it."

"Mary?" Carson queried softly.

"I wasn't trying to kill him," she whispered, barely able to speak.

"There!" Winston crowed. "That's all the proof you need to lock her up. She's as good as admitted it. Now ask her what she did with my property."

Carson shot the other man an angry glance, then looked at Mary again. "Tell me what happened."

"Just because the two of you are engaged doesn't mean you can ignore—"

"Shut up, Mr. Kenrick," Carson growled.

Mary knew what her former employer would do. If Carson didn't arrest her, Winston Kenrick would destroy him. He had the money. He had the influence with powerful people. She knew he wouldn't hesitate to use everything at his disposal against Carson.

"Sure and I'm thinking you should take me to jail," she said, blinking to clear her eyes of unwelcome tears.

"Mary—"

"I'll be asking Edith to see after the children. I'd be obliged if you'd look in on them now and again."

Carson grasped her by the upper arms and drew her toward him. His voice was low and stern when he spoke. "This isn't over. Martin Burke will represent you. We'll clear this matter up. You'll be all right."

She could only nod, even though in her heart, she believed he was wrong. She was guilty enough. And even if the law didn't hang her, she would never be able to marry Carson. Not after everyone heard what she'd done—and she knew they would hear. There was no keeping her sins secret now.

Carson had understood Kenrick's not-so-veiled threats, but he hadn't arrested Mary because of them. He'd taken her into custody because he knew it was the only way he could get to the bottom of things.

Since the jail cells were full, Carson took her to his room above the sheriff's office. There wasn't much to it—a narrow cot where he slept, the small stove where he occasionally cooked something to eat, the table with one chair scooted beneath it, the pegs in the wall that held his clothes and his spare Stetson, the two curtainless windows, one looking out on Main Street, the other facing River Street. Still, he thought it was better than a room made with steel bars, so he was thankful he hadn't had to put her in one of the cells.

"Sit down," he gently commanded as he closed the door behind them. When she didn't move, he stepped past her and pulled out the chair from the table. "Sit down, Mary. Please."

She did so without meeting his gaze. She sat stiffly, her back ramrod-straight, her gaze fastened on the closed door.

Carson hunkered down beside her and placed a hand on her thigh. "Mary, look at me."

It took a few moments, but eventually she did as he'd asked.

"Now," he continued, soft and gentle, "tell me what happened with Kenrick. Tell me everything, Mary, so I can help you."

She gave him a sad smile. "I'm thinking you can't help me. 'Tis the truth Master Kenrick told you. I hit him and left him for dead. I was not trying to kill him, mind you, but that's what I thought I'd done all the same."

Carson took hold of her right hand. It was cold as ice. "Start at the beginning, Mary."

She ducked her head. "Then I'd have to go all the way back to Ireland."

He nodded, hoping to encourage her.

Tears welled in her eyes. "I've not been altogether honest with you, Carson," she whispered, and he could hear the pain in her confession. "I've wanted to be, but . . ." She let her words drift into silence.

"I love you. Nothing you say is going to change that."

He could tell she was struggling to believe him, wanting to but afraid to.

After a long while, she began to speak in a soft voice. "The Malones were poor, me da a tenant farmer like I told you before. But me ma was determined to raise us to be clean and upright. We were in church every Sunday. Ma wanted to make sure we wouldn't be tempted into sin." A sad smile flickered at the corners of her mouth. "'Twas difficult for her, her children being as they were. Headstrong and stubborn, the whole lot of us. Always at odds with the world and with each other. Worry made her old before her time. When she passed on, the light went out o' me da's heart. He wasn't ever the same again."

Carson wished he could take her into his arms and comfort her, but he knew he had to wait until her story was told.

"I went into service for the Whartons at their estate near Belfast when I was fifteen. 'Twas the first time I saw for meself how different from the Malones the rich lived. I had me own room on the third floor. 'Twas no bigger than one o' your cells below us, but I had it all to meself and I thought it was heaven on earth. I'm thinking it was then I started to want more than I should." She paused, then whispered, "Rising above me station in life, as me ma would've said."

Carson brushed a loose strand of her hair back from her face, looping it behind her ear. She didn't seem to notice the gesture.

"After me da died, Padriac married a girl from Scotland and moved to the Lowlands. Three of me brothers went to England to work in the coal mines. Me brother Quaid came to America." She glanced up, then dropped her gaze quickly.

"I know about Quaid," he said. "I know you've been searching for him ever since you came to Whistle Creek."

Again she looked at him. "'Tis sorry I am I never told you meself."

He shook his head slowly, telling her with his eyes that it didn't matter.

After a lengthy silence, she continued her tale. "I was all alone in the world after that. Even when I'd been

256

away in service, I'd always known me da and brothers were in our village. Now they were all gone, and I was lonely without them. 'Twas the next year I met Seamus Maguire." She drew a deep breath, then let it out. "Ah, he was a handsome bloke, he was. His hair was auburn, and he had a smile that bewitched the girls from Donegal to Cork. I was no different from the others. For two years, I hoped he would notice me, but 'twas Brenna, the downstairs maid, he took a fancy to. It wasn't until the Whartons went back to England and took both of us, Seamus and me, with them that he gave me a turn."

Mary rose abruptly from the chair and walked to the window. Carson stood but didn't follow her. He could tell it was difficult for her, talking about Maguire, and despite knowing she loved him now, Carson felt the thin blade of jealousy slice through his heart.

"Seamus didn't stay in service to the Whartons once we were in England. He was off to make his fortune, he told me. I thought that was the last I'd ever be seeing of Seamus Maguire, and it would've been better altogether if it had been. 'Twas more than a year later, after I'd left the Whartons and taken a position with the Wellingtons, that he returned to Buckinghamshire. He came to work as a groomsman for the earl, but he was already planning on leaving for America, just as soon as he'd set aside the cost of his passage from his wages."

Mary turned around. He saw her stiffen her spine, recognized the proud lift of her chin.

"Sure and I'll never understand how it was I let him take me to his bed without me being his wife. He had a glib tongue and a magic smile, he did. I believed with all me heart that he loved me and would marry me, just as he'd promised. Only he said we couldn't until I joined him in America. He made it sound like it was best to wait for marriage but not for bedding, and I was fool enough to believe him."

Carson remembered holding her in his arms just two nights before, remembered the temptation to make love to her without waiting on formality. His love for Mary went beyond what a legal piece of paper had to say. It wasn't hard to understand what had happened to her. "It's not unforgivable, what you did, Mary. You were in love." His last words pricked his heart, but he'd had to say them.

It was as if she hadn't heard. "When I realized he'd left me with a wee one in me belly, I came to join him as quick as I could. 'Twas full of hope and dreams I was when the ship landed here. I had no way of knowing Seamus was dead." She took a ragged breath. "Or that he'd married someone else not more than a month after he'd left me behind."

If Seamus Maguire hadn't already been dead, Carson would have hunted him down and paid him back for the hurt he'd caused Mary. First Maguire had misused her, then Kenrick had attempted to do the same. Carson knew, without hearing the rest of her story, that Mary had faced everything with characteristic courage and determination. She might have made mistakes, but he knew she wasn't guilty of any crimes worth imprisonment. It was men like Maguire and Kenrick who deserved that.

Carson strode across the room, took Mary by the hand, and led her back to the chair. With a gentle pressure on her shoulders, he forced her to sit down once again.

"You don't have to tell me any more," he said softly as he hunkered down beside her, covering her folded hands with one of his. "It doesn't matter."

"No," she answered, her voice stronger. "'Tis time you know. 'Tis what sent me here." She met his gaze through a glitter of tears.

After an extended silence, she continued to tell him what had caused her to run from New York City.

The sheriff took Mary to jail?" Portia asked as she watched her husband pace the width of their rented room.

"Yes, and by damn, that's where she'll stay." His face was red with fury. "She refuses to give me the box. I told her I'd forget what happened if she just returned the box."

"Perhaps Mary doesn't have it," she suggested.

He whirled toward her. "Oh, she has it, all right. She has it."

If Portia had ever doubted there was more to Winston's obsession about that box than met the eye, it would have been dispelled by his current behavior. He looked ready to kill.

"I don't trust that sheriff," he continued, renewing his pacing. "Did I tell you he's engaged to Mary? The little Irish witch has cast a spell over him. For all I know, he'll turn her loose in the middle of the night. He might help her escape."

Portia feigned disinterest. "I'm sure that won't happen, dear. Mr. Knox will keep an eye on things." She rose from her chair. "Well, I suppose we shall be stuck here until Mary's trial. I believe I shall have a look at the shops and discover what I might do to occupy my time until it is over." She walked to the bureau. Gazing into the mirror, she settled her hat over her hair and secured it with two hat pins. When she was finished, she turned toward Winston. "Would you care to join me?"

"No," he snapped irritably.

She'd known he wouldn't. She hadn't wanted him to. "Do try not to work yourself into too much of a lather, Winston. I'm sure this will all be over in short order and we can return to New York." She smiled sweetly. "I'll buy you a new box to replace the lost one."

Of course, Winston would never suspect she had no intention of returning to New York with him, let alone buying him anything, but now was not the time to tell him so. She would wait until this matter of Mary was settled. She wanted to know why Winston had been so determined to find the woman. Her instincts told her it was important for her to know, that it would somehow affect her as much as Mary.

Carrying her parasol to shade her from the harsh sun, Portia strolled along the sidewalk. She pretended to be oblivious to the tension all around her, but she wasn't. She took note of the small gatherings of men, grumbling angry-faced men who were everywhere she looked—outside the café and the mercantile, in the shade at the side of the livery stables, and more noticeably, inside the Painted Lady. It seemed apparent that Mary's sheriff had more than enough trouble on his plate without Winston's adding to it.

Pausing on the boardwalk, she peeked inside the saloon. There were paintings of half-dressed women on the walls, and there were real-life half-dressed women standing and sitting throughout the room. An enormous mirror backed the bar. The air was smoky, and voices were loud.

The Painted Lady. What an appropriate name for such a place. And it was Mary's.

Portia smiled to herself as she considered what it would be like to be in Mary's shoes. Now wouldn't that be a lark? Portia Pendergast Kenrick, the owner of a saloon and dance hall. She could just imagine the expressions of her society friends back East if Portia were to become a saloon keeper. They would be aghast at the very idea.

Then again, perhaps they wouldn't be. Most had always thought her beneath them, the upstart daughter of a working class businessman. They weren't really her friends. They were people who wanted to be seen with Portia because of her money and because she was Winston's wife, not because they truly liked her. She had always known that.

Suddenly, she laughed aloud. The sense of freedom she felt was utterly amazing. She didn't need those men and women. She could do as she pleased. There were so many possibilities available to her. She only had to decide what she wanted to do, and she could do it.

Several people inside the saloon glanced up at the sound of her laughter. Portia waved at them, still chuckling, then turned and walked across the street. It was time, she decided, to meet Sheriff Barclay. Perhaps between them, they might find the answers they needed to set both Mary and Portia free.

Mary's throat ached by the time she ended her story. "And I wouldn't be knowing what happened with it after that," she said in a hoarse whisper, referring to the silver box.

It took more courage than she had left to look at him. So she continued to stare at her clenched hands and his hand lying on top of them. She had told him everything. She'd held nothing back, even though her heart was breaking from the telling. He would know now, as did she, that their union was forever doomed. There would be no wedding. She would never bear his name or his children.

After some time, Carson said, "It was self-defense, Mary. You were only trying to protect yourself. Once we show that, you'll be free."

She blinked away tears. "Are you telling me you're believing that?" She smiled, loving him even more because he was trying so hard to reassure her. Now, at last, she met his gaze. "Me, an Irish immigrant, and himself, a man whose supper guests include every judge and magistrate in New York City, I'll wager. They would not be believing the likes o' me, Sheriff Barclay, and well you know it."

He cocked his head to one side. "So are you just going to give up? Are you going to let him take you away from Keary and Nellie?" He paused, then added, "And me?"

A spark of anger made her sit up straighter. "And what is it you'd have me do, I'd be asking? I'm guilty as sin of hitting him, no matter what the reason. And I *did* take the bloody box, may it ever be cursed."

"Yes." His expression turned thoughtful as he rose and began to pace. "Have you stopped to wonder why Kenrick would follow you all the way across the country just to get it back? I haven't seen it, but it can't be worth that much to a man of his means. He's probably spent far more than its value in his search to find you." He rubbed his chin. "Is he the sort of man who would do it just for revenge?"

Mary frowned. She hadn't even considered the why of it. "Aye, he might," she answered at long last.

Carson stopped pacing and turned toward her. "I'm

not going to lock that door, Mary. I'm going to trust you to stay put. I'll tell Edith she can bring the children to see you whenever you want." He stepped toward her. "Stay angry, darling. Keep fighting. I'm not going to let Kenrick or anyone else take you away from me."

He'd never called her darling before, and she found it much to her liking. For just that moment, she forgot she was his prisoner. She forgot that her former employer was determined to see her hang. She forgot that the life she wanted had slipped out of her reach the moment Winston Kenrick had arrived in Whistle Creek.

Unable to stop herself, Mary stood and moved into Carson's arms. He drew her to him, close enough that she could feel his heart beating. She let her head drop back and their lips met in a long, bittersweet kiss.

Aye, she would stay angry, if it was what he wanted. There would be time enough for sorrow after she was forced to tell Carson good-bye forever.

A few minutes later, Carson forced himself to leave Mary in his one-room apartment. He couldn't help her if he stayed there and did nothing.

As he descended the narrow stairway, he said a quick prayer for her safety. Nothing in this world mattered as much to him as Mary, and he knew it would take a miracle for him to be able to protect her. She was right about the likelihood of a judge or jury believing her, the Irish housemaid, over a man like Winston Kenrick. It would take more than her word to free her.

He stopped suddenly, just inside his office. A woman was waiting in a chair near his desk. She looked up when she heard his footsteps. Her gaze was forthright and unwavering. Although not what one would call a handsome woman, she had a pleasantly shaped mouth and intelligent eyes.

After a moment of frank appraisal on both their parts, she said, "Sheriff Barclay?"

"Yes, ma'am. What can I do for you?"

"I'm Portia Kenrick."

His mouth pressed into a thin line, and he knew his gaze had hardened.

She inclined her head to one side, as if acknowledging his feelings. "I am not the enemy, Mr. Barclay. In fact, I hope to be a friend."

"A friend?" He stepped over to his desk but didn't sit down. "And why is that?"

Her voice was determined, almost grim. "Because I am convinced Mary Malone is guilty of nothing except trying to escape my husband's unwelcome advances. And because I believe that box he is so determined to retrieve will give us the answers we both want."

Her words perfectly echoed Carson's own beliefs, but he was still wary. He wasn't about to trust this woman too soon, despite his gut feeling that told him he could.

"Sheriff, I could see that you have some trouble on your hands in this town and probably have little time to search for something as insignificant as a silver cigar box. I would like to offer the services of the private detective I hired, the man who brought us here. Mr. Knox is over at the boardinghouse now. I will pay all of his expenses, but he will be instructed to do whatever you tell him."

"Why?" he asked again. "Why are you doing this?"

"Although not a fashionable thing to do, I made it a point to know all my servants." Portia stood. "I liked Mary, Sheriff Barclay. I would not have Winston ruin her chance for happiness." Her eyes narrowed slightly.

"My husband and I have been married many years. I know him well. There is a reason for what he is doing that goes beyond wanting revenge. I suspect that I need the answer as much as you and Mary do." She held out a gloved hand.

Carson stared at the proffered hand for a few moments, then took hold of it. "I could use your detective's help, Mrs. Kenrick. I'm not going to let Mary be taken away from here."

"No," she said with a wry smile, "I don't think you will, Sheriff Barclay."

Twenty-two

Monday, 29 August, 1898
Whistle Creek, Idaho

My dear Inga,
Much has been happening since my last letter. The secret I have kept from you and Mary and everyone I know has come to light, and I find myself in trouble with the law. My reason for leaving New York City so suddenly was because I struck my employer and had thought him dead. It is with relief that I have lately learned the man lives, but now he has had me arrested for attempted murder.

The matter is made more awful altogether because I recently accepted a proposal of marriage from Sheriff Barclay. Now this same man has been forced to imprison me, and we will never be able to marry because of what I've done. I mourn what will never be. The joy of being Carson's wife is lost to me forever.

I cannot say that my imprisonment has been a terrible hardship, because Carson has placed me in his room above the jail cells, them being full of miners for there is trouble at the Lucky Lady Mine. The room is sparsely furnished, but it has windows and plenty of sunshine and fresh air.

The children are staying with my friend, Edith, and have been to see me twice each day. Keary is too young to know there is anything wrong, but Nellie understands and is frightened. I know Carson has done his best to reassure her, as he does with me. Neither of us are fooled.

I am finding that inactivity is the worst part of my captivity. I wish I could make quilts like you or do embroidery work as Edith does, if only to keep my hands busy. I have tried keeping a journal, but there is nothing to write about except the past, and I would rather not think of it now. Baba, our dog, has come to stay with me, and she is some comfort. I find myself talking to her. If I was to be heard, folks might think me daft, and it is enough trouble I am in without that.

Would you be knowing the worst of it all? My own guilt. Not for the crime, though I am guilty there, too. No, I feel guilt because my thoughts turn to Carson again and again. I am consumed by them altogether. When I think of what the future may hold, it is Carson that I think on most. It is knowing I'll never be with him that causes me pain.

I am ashamed because it is not Keary who troubles my thoughts day and night. I tell myself it is because I now know there are people who will love and care for him if the day comes I am taken

266

from him forever. And since I came into some good fortune because of Miss Loraine's kindness, Keary and Nellie will want for nothing because of lack of money. Still, it is the children who should concern me most, and yet, when I lie here on this cot at night, it is Carson I am longing for.

Sure and I must be awful altogether for having such thoughts at a time like this. Do you think me terrible, Inga?

Your friend,
Mary

Bryan Halligan had heard about Mary Malone's arrest two days before, and the news made him smile. As far as he was concerned, she was getting exactly what she deserved. She'd spurned his offer to buy the Painted Lady, just as she'd spurned his amorous advances. He didn't take kindly to either rejection. He wasn't used to losing, not in business and certainly not when it came to his sexual prowess.

But his satisfaction over Mary's circumstances didn't last long. He forgot her completely when he received a telegram from his business partners. Michael King and Stephen Smothers were coming to Whistle Creek at the end of the week. They wanted to see for themselves what had caused the loss of revenue from the Lucky Lady Mine.

A fine sweat broke out on Halligan's forehead as he reread the telegram. He wasn't ready for this. Things weren't going as smoothly as he'd planned. That blasted sheriff kept getting in his way. No matter how angry the miners, most of them listened to Carson Barclay. Sure, the sheriff had arrested some of the most disruptive men, but real rioting had been averted.

Halligan lifted his gaze from the missive in his hand to look at the two burly men—his bodyguards—seated at the next table. The Whistler Cafe was quiet at this midmorning hour on a Monday, but Halligan was still glad these men were nearby. No one would bother him with them around.

At the same time, his bodyguards made it difficult to go about his necessary business. He couldn't risk their finding out what he'd been doing. If they were to inform Michael or Stephen . . .

Halligan shuddered at the mere thought of it. His business associates would show no mercy if they knew the truth. But, by heaven, he was determined to get them to sell out to him. He *would* be the sole owner of that mine, and one day, he would be the wealthiest man in Spokane. He didn't care what he had to do to make it happen.

He glanced at the telegram again. Perhaps another "accident" at the mine was in order. Nothing that would seriously damage silver production, of course; he had no wish to buy a worthless mine. But if another explosion and cave-in, for instance, were to happen when his partners were in Whistle Creek, they could see for themselves what he had been up against. They would finally support the cut in wages he'd insisted upon. They might even agree with his decision to hire scab labor, something they'd opposed in the past. They would certainly concur with the firing of all union supporters.

But mostly, they might decide that the gain from the mine wasn't worth the trouble that came with it. They might finally agree to sell him their share of the business.

Yes, it was time for another accident at the Lucky Lady.

The second-story room was hot, the air oppressive despite the open windows. Mary lay on the cot, her eyes closed, her thoughts drifting in a state of half sleep.

She imagined Carson, sitting in the shade of a tall tree near his cabin. The creek gurgled and splashed nearby. Carson leaned his back against the trunk of the tree. His long legs were bent, and he rested his wrists on his knees. He was twisting a long piece of grass between his fingers, but he was looking at Mary. His blue eyes were warm with desire.

Her body tightened in response. How she wished she could give herself to him, right then and there. To lie with him in the grass, their naked bodies shaded by the leafy green limbs of the tree. To make love with him to the melody of the bubbling brook. To drink in his kisses. To become a part of him, to be absorbed into him.

Mary moaned softly, then opened her eyes, wishing she could have remained in that dreamy state forever. The dream was so much better than reality.

With a sigh, she sat up, then went to splash tepid water from the washbowl onto her face. It wasn't very refreshing, as warm as it was, but it did help a little. After drying her face with a towel, she glanced in the small, cracked mirror that hung on the wall. The reflection wasn't encouraging. Her cheeks were flushed with heat, her hair resembled a bird's nest, and there were dark circles beneath her eyes.

And this after only two days of captivity. She might go mad before this was over.

Carson had brought her some food at noon and had told her the circuit judge would be in Whistle Creek in early September. Perhaps as early as the ninth, he'd said. But that was almost two weeks away. It seemed a very long time to one who was no longer free to come and go as she pleased.

She heard the creak of boards on the stairs and turned toward the door in expectation. She thought she might welcome a visit from Winston Kenrick himself, just to break the monotony of her confinement.

But it wasn't her nemesis. It was someone much more welcome but much more unexpected.

"Quaid?" she whispered in disbelief. It had been seven years since she'd seen her brother, and time had made a man of the youth she'd remembered. "Is it really you?"

"Aye, Mary, 'tis meself." He grinned. "And happy I am t' see you altogether, Mary girl. Happy I am."

A moment later, they were hugging and laughing. The years melted away in an instant, and it seemed they'd never been apart. For a short while, Mary forgot her worries. She was reunited with her beloved brother, and that was all she wanted to think about.

"How did you find me?" she asked him at last.

"I didn't find you, lass," he answered. "'Twas me that was found." He jerked his head toward the open door. "'Twas your friend who brought me here."

Mary hadn't noticed John Tyrell standing there until Quaid caused her to look. She knew immediately that Carson had sent John looking for her brother. With all the other troubles in the town and at the mine, he'd done this for her.

"Thank you," she whispered. John just smiled in reply.

"Now, Mary girl," Quaid said, drawing her gaze back to him, "I'm thinkin' it's time you were tellin' me why you're kept a prisoner in this room."

"'Tis a long story."

"And I've got nothing but time, me girl."

Mary heard the door close and knew John had left brother and sister alone.

And so she told Quaid all that had happened, sparing no detail, just as she had told Carson two days before.

There was something about the way Portia watched him lately that nearly drove Winston insane. If he didn't know better, he'd think she suspected him of embezzling from her. But she couldn't know. Portia couldn't possibly have guessed what he'd done. His wife wasn't a stupid woman by any means, but she had no grasp for the financial intricacies of the Pendergast empire, as much as she liked to think she did. Besides, he'd been careful not to leave any clues of his larceny, and he'd taken his time. Years and years of time.

Of course, all those years of working and waiting would be lost without the documents contained in the missing box. Those papers gave him access to all that money. They gave him a new identity. They were his future. He had to get them back.

And Mary Malone was keeping them from him.

"Winston dear," Portia said, interrupting his dark thoughts, her voice grating on his nerves, "you seem restless. Why don't we hire a buggy from the livery and take a drive, see some of the countryside?"

"In this heat?" he shot back, irritated by the very suggestion.

Her smile was tolerant. "Perhaps it wouldn't be so hot once we were in the forest. I understand there is a small lake not far from—"

With the sound of splintering wood, the door to their room flew open, crashing into the wall. Portia gasped. Winston spun around in alarm.

The man who stood in the doorway—his feet planted

271

apart, his arms hanging at his sides with his hands curled into fists—was short but built like an oak tree, his chest, arms and thighs heavily muscled. He had black hair and even blacker eyes, eyes that smoldered with barely controlled rage.

"Would you be Winston Kenrick?" the stranger asked, his accent marking him as an Irishman.

"See here," Winston sputtered, finding his voice at last. "What is the meaning of—"

"Answer me. Would you be Winston Kenrick?"

"Yes, but—"

With surprising speed, the fellow was across the room and had hold of Winston by the shirt. Their faces mere inches apart, the stranger said in a low voice, "Me name is Quaid Malone . . . I'm Mary's brother."

Fear burned Winston's throat like bile.

"If you were t' hurt her, I'd have t' kill you. D'ya understand me, man?"

Winston swallowed hard, then managed to say, "You have no right to threaten me." Sweat trickled down the sides of his face. Moisture beaded his upper lip.

"I've got the right of any man whose sister's had unwanted hands laid on her."

From the doorway came another much more welcome voice. "Release him, Malone," the sheriff said with authority.

Quaid Malone didn't obey at once. He continued to stare hard into Winston's eyes, his gaze still threatening even though his voice had been stilled.

"Sheriff Barclay . . ." Winston pleaded, the two words more of a whimper than a name.

"*Now*, Malone," Carson ordered, louder this time.

Quaid let go of Winston's shirt and, with a little shove, took one step backward. "You remember what I said, Kenrick. Hurt Mary and you'll have me to answer to." He turned toward the doorway. "So you'd be Barclay himself. 'Tis you I'd be talkin' to next, then."

"I reckon that's a good idea."

Quaid Malone strode from the room, Carson stepping back to let him pass. Then the sheriff glanced from Winston to Portia and back again before saying, "Mrs. Schmidt will see that someone repairs this door." He bent the brim of his black Stetson toward Portia before walking away.

Winston's muscles seemed to turn to water the moment the sheriff disappeared from view. His legs gave out and it was merely good fortune the bed was directly behind him. He sank onto it, shaking all over. His innards were in knots, and his lungs seemed to have been crushed beneath some great weight.

Through a buzzing in his ears, he heard Portia say, "Should I send for the doctor, dear? You don't look well."

"Shut up, Portia," he whispered before he could think better of it. "Just shut up."

Carson liked Quaid Malone right off. His quick approval of the Irishman might have had something to do with the similarities between brother and sister. There was the same accent and the matching ink black hair. There were also certain words they both used and the unique way they phrased their speech. They shared many of the same mannerisms, too, like the way they sometimes talked with their hands, punctuating their sentences with a gesture in the air.

Carson quickly learned that for a brother who had been absent and out of touch for seven years, Quaid was enormously protective of his little sister and dead set on making sure no one hurt her. He supposed that was the real reason he liked Quaid Malone so much. Both men wanted the same thing—Mary's safety and happiness.

His approval obviously meant nothing to Quaid. It took a bit of fast talking on Carson's part before Mary's brother was willing to believe him. Telling Quaid that he loved Mary, no matter what she'd done, seemed to be what threw the scales in his favor.

Half an hour after Carson had taken Quaid from the Kenricks' boardinghouse room, the two men stood in the shade of a large elm that grew near the northwest corner of the church. Carson stared at the running waters of Whistle Creek as he finished telling Quaid what he knew. "Mary's sure she had that box when she got to Idaho. She says she put it in one of the drawers over at the saloon. That's the last she remembers seeing it." He glanced toward Quaid. "I think someone must've stolen it. Probably somebody who works there. We need to find it. Mrs. Kenrick is certain it will prove Mary's innocence."

Quaid's black eyebrows lifted. "Mrs. Kenrick?"

Carson nodded.

"And why would she be tryin' to help Mary?"

"Because she's nobody's fool."

"I'd not be trustin' her," Quaid muttered.

"I've got a gut feeling we'd better trust her." He looked down the street toward the sheriff's office, his gaze fastening on the window of his small apartment over the jail. "Mary's freedom could depend on it."

They were both silent for several moments, their thoughts unknown to the other. After a spell, Quaid said, "What would ya have me be doin', Sheriff?"

Carson turned his attention back to the Irishman. "First, I'd have you call me Carson. After all, we're going to be brothers." His smile was fleeting. "Then I think I'd like you to join John and Edith in combing the saloon from top to bottom for that blasted box. Other than Mac MacDonald, nobody who was working there when Mary arrived in Whistle Creek has left."

"And if 'twas this MacDonald who took it?"

Carson pondered the question a moment before answering. "I don't think it was Mac. I think it's still there. We just have to find it."

"You could be riskin' Mary's life on a hunch." Quaid's voice was solemn. "What is it you'll be doin' if we don't find the bloody thing?"

Carson had spent most of the last decade trying to serve justice. He'd modeled himself as much as possible after David Hailey, trying to live up to his mentor's standards of honesty and integrity. He'd followed the laws of the land to the best of his ability and had never knowingly defied them. But it was Mary's life Quaid was asking about. This was the woman Carson loved as he'd never thought possible. Would he let a man like Kenrick take her from him?

When hell froze over.

"I won't let them take her," he answered in a low voice, his gaze hard and unflinching. "No matter what."

Quaid held out his hand. "We won't let them take her."

The pledge was made, and the two men shook on it.

Darkness blanketed Whistle Creek, and with the night had come a blessed cooling breeze. Mary lay on her cot, praying for sleep, but her thoughts were running wild as usual.

She was worried about Quaid. After she'd told him what had transpired in New York, he had stormed out of this second-story room in a splendid Malone fury. He hadn't returned. She hoped he hadn't gotten himself into trouble.

Edith had brought both food and the children around six o'clock. They'd eaten together, the four of them, and Mary had held and nuzzled her son, playing with him as if she hadn't a care in the world. It was a fine act she'd put on, but Nellie hadn't been fooled by it. The girl had seemed on the verge of tears the entire time. Before the three visitors left, Mary had pulled Nellie into her arms and promised her that all would go well, that Nellie would always be loved and cared for.

She'd spent the rest of the long evening alone, often standing by the window, looking for a glimpse of Carson as he sought to keep order in the town.

Now, as she stared through the darkness at the ceiling, she imagined Carson joining her here, in his room, on his bed. The images were far too real.

She groaned and pulled the pillow over her face, pressing down until she could scarcely breathe. She didn't want to think about Carson. She didn't want to miss him or need him. She didn't want to love him. It hurt too much. Too much altogether.

That loose board on the stairs alerted her to someone's coming. She held her breath in anticipation, knowing she shouldn't want it to be Carson and yet wanting it all the same.

He rapped softly, then opened the door. "Mary?"

Ah, she loved Carson's voice. Her name never sounded the same as when he said it.

"Are you awake?"

"Aye." She sat up. "Is something wrong?"

"No, I just wanted to check on you." He closed the door behind him, then came toward her.

There was no moonlight for her to see him by, and yet it seemed she could see him clearly. Perhaps it was knowing him with her heart that made the difference.

Carson stopped beside the cot. "I've just left your brother."

"Sure and he isn't in any trouble, is he? You've not had to arrest him?"

"No." Carson chuckled softly. "But he's got a temper a lot like yours, so I suppose it might still happen."

She couldn't help smiling.

Unexpectedly, his hands closed over her shoulders, and he drew her up from the bed and into his embrace. The thin fabric of her cotton nightgown seemed nonexistent as he crushed her close to him. She came willingly, feeling the hardness of his chest against her breasts, running her hands over the muscular plane of his back. She could hear the rapid beat of his heart as he dropped kisses onto the top of her head.

After a while, he gently tipped her head back with his index finger and claimed her mouth with his own. She surrendered to the heavenly moment, wanting to take with her whatever scraps of happiness she could, hoping to gather as many memories as possible.

At long last, Carson broke the kiss. "I love you, Mary," he said huskily. "I wish I knew how to tell you how much."

She almost sobbed, the words both a balm and a torture.

"Reverend Ogelsby got into town today. I went over to talk with him." Once again he kissed her, long and deep. Then, with his lips brushing hers as he spoke, he said, "I've asked him to perform the wedding tomorrow. He agreed to do it. Right here in this room."

She gasped in surprise. "What?"

"Remember last week? I asked you to marry me when Reverend Ogelsby returned to Whistle Creek. Well, he's back and it's time."

"Sure and I never gave you me answer."

She couldn't see his grin, but she knew he was smiling all the same. "How can you refuse me, Mary? You're my prisoner."

Mary didn't find his words or the subject amusing. "Are you completely daft, Carson Barclay? I can't be marrying you. Not now. Not ever." She pulled out of his arms and moved away from him.

"What do you mean, can't marry me now or ever?"

"Just what I'm saying. I can't marry you."

"Why not?" He stepped toward her, reached for her, took hold of her arm.

She shook him off. "You must be knowing why. I'm guilty of what Master Kenrick says. I'll be judged so and sent away. I could hang. What sort of thing would that be, a sheriff whose wife was hanged? 'Tis bad enough they'll all be knowing me boy's got no father to call his own. No, 'twould ruin you, having me for a wife. I'll have no part in it. 'Tis harm enough I've done as it is."

His voice was louder, harsher, when he spoke. "Do you hear what you're saying, Mary? What does one thing have to do with the other? Besides, you're not going to be taken from here and you're sure as heck not going to hang for anything."

"Are you still fooling yourself altogether, then?" she whispered sadly.

"Damn it all!"

She jumped back in surprise.

"You might be the ruination of me, Mary," he continued to shout, his anger clear, "but it won't be because you took something from Winston Kenrick or

278

because you hit him over the head like he deserved. It'll be because you drove me insane!"

She couldn't form a retort.

Carson swore again, then spun away and marched to the door. "Make up your mind to one thing, Mary Malone. You *are* going to be my wife, and nothing's going to keep it from happening. Not even your stubborn, idiotic pride."

A moment later, the door slammed closed behind him.

Twenty-three

THE REVEREND OGELSBY CAME TO SEE MARY THE next day, offering gentle words of advice and comfort, but she made it clear to him that under no circumstances was she going to marry Sheriff Barclay. After that, whenever Carson stopped in to check on her, both of them acted tense and wary, and their frustration showed. By the time he left her alone—always with the same promise that they *would* be married, despite her stubborn refusals—Mary felt drained and exhausted.

But even those painful encounters were better than the monotony that shaped the hours of her captivity. It grew less bearable with each passing day, every one of them seeming a hundred hours long. The sleepless nights were little better. Quaid and Edith and the children came to see her often, their visits carefully interspersed throughout the day, but they didn't come often enough to ease the tedium that stretched in between.

Alone again in her upper-room prison following her afternoon visit with the children, Mary stood at the

279

window, thankful that the heat of late August had vanished with the coming of September. Thin clouds drifted across the sky, swept along by a cool, brisk breeze. Small eddies of dirt whirled down the center of the street. Women fought to keep their skirts down and their bonnets on. Horses lifted their heads, pranced and snorted, made nervous by the changing weather. Even Abe Stover's lazy hound had crawled out from beneath the boardwalk; now the dog was lying in the sun near the corner of the livery stable.

Mary didn't turn when she heard the door open behind her. She knew her newly arrived visitor must be Quaid. It was his turn.

She was mistaken.

"Mary."

With a gasp, she spun around, her gaze clashing with Winston Kenrick's. "What is it you're doing here?" she demanded in a voice made hoarse by surprise.

His face looked somewhat gaunt, his eyes somewhat glazed, and Mary suspected the strain of the past five days had been harder on him than on her.

"I'm here to give you one last chance," he said. "I'm not going to ask again, Mary. After the judge comes next week, it will be out of my hands. Just tell me where you've hidden what is mine and I'll have the sheriff release you."

Reflexively, she stiffened her back and held her head high. She refused to let him see how much she dreaded the day the judge would arrive, certain as she was that she would be found guilty. She refused to give Kenrick an ounce of satisfaction by cowering before him. Silence was her only reply.

He surged forward, crossing the room quickly. She backed away but couldn't escape him. In a voice hardly human, he growled obscenities at her. When she still didn't speak, he slapped her with the back of his hand. The force of his attack knocked her head against the wall behind her. She covered her cheek with her fingers, felt her skin grow hot where he'd struck her. Unwelcome tears—from both anger and pain—blinded her, and they only served to increase her fury.

"I want that box, Mary," Winston ground out through clenched teeth. "Give it to me so we can be done with this."

"*I . . . don't . . . have it.*" She emphasized each word, obviously frustrated, but her voice didn't rise above normal.

He didn't enjoy the same control. Almost shouting, he shot back, "Liar!"

Suddenly, she'd had enough. With a quickness he wasn't expecting, she shoved him away from her. "I'll not be listening to your threats. You'd better be leaving me alone or you'll be the next one the sheriff arrests." She pointed an accusing finger toward him. "'Twas *your* fault I hit you that day. 'Twas *you* who tried to force yourself upon me. You with your money and your fancy house and your fancy clothes. You're thinking you can take what's not yours. You're thinking you're better than the likes o' me. 'Tis a fine name, Kenrick, you're thinking, and you puff up your bloody chest like some peacock. 'Tis a fool you are, and a fool you'll always be. The Malones might be poor but they're a finer family than yours, and proud I am altogether to be one of them. Sure and you wouldn't measure up to the worst in the lot. Me son is already worth more than you'll ever be."

Winston's face turned bright red. For a moment, she thought he might strike her again. But he didn't.

281

Instead, he turned and walked to the door. Once there, he paused, his hand on the doorknob.

"You're not going to ruin me, Mary Malone," he said, his voice low and threatening. He glanced over his shoulder. "Hanging would be too good for you." Then he yanked open the door and left.

Word on the street was that the other two mine owners—who had never before, in anyone's memory, visited the Lucky Lady—would arrive in Whistle Creek the next day. It was anticipated that they would approve Halligan's plan to send scab labor into the mine. In midafternoon, striking miners swarmed into town to search out those who'd been hired to take their jobs. Tempers were high, and there were more than a few men carrying weapons, a sure recipe for disaster.

Carson and his small band of deputies were hard-pressed to keep order. Since the jail cells were already full, the livery had to be commandeered for the new prisoners. With hands bound behind their backs, they were locked up in stalls to await the same judge as Mary.

Carson kept praying help would arrive on Friday's train. If it didn't . . . Well, if it didn't, God help Whistle Creek, because he was pretty sure he couldn't.

It was 4:00 A.M. when Carson finally fell, exhausted, onto the bed he'd made for himself behind his desk in the office. He didn't bother to undress. He settled for removing his hat and boots.

As soon as his eyes closed, he thought of Mary. He hadn't seen her since he'd taken her lunch the previous day. He missed her, but he wasn't about to awaken her at this hour just to say good night. Although maybe if he surprised her out of a sound sleep, he'd be able to talk some sense into her before she realized what he was doing.

Dang woman! He loved her more than his own life. Why was she being so stubborn? Where'd she get this fool notion that she had to save him from himself?

"Ah, Mary" he said with a sigh. "Don't make this so hard on us."

Maybe tomorrow he'd be able to make her see reason. Maybe he'd visit her first thing in the morning, and she'd decide not to torture them both any longer.

Maybe in the morning . . .

Before the thought was finished, he was asleep.

But Carson didn't get to see Mary in the morning. He was awakened after only two hours of sleep to the sounds of gunfire. Instinct brought him out of bed and had him reaching for the gun belt that lay beside his pillow. Assured that the jail itself wasn't under attack, he yanked on his boots, slapped his hat over his head, and was out the door in a matter of seconds.

Near the rear of the Painted Lady, he found John Tyrell leaning over a bleeding man, one of Halligan's scabs. "What happened?" he demanded as he approached.

"Clyde Pugh shot him. When they saw me comin', him and Aldo Hirsch took off up the canyon there toward your old place." John motioned toward the injured man. "Looks like he was unarmed."

"Get the doctor for him. I'll head after Pugh and Hirsch."

"Do want me to come along?"

Carson shook his head. "No, the more deputies we've got in town the better. I can handle these two by myself."

"Right."

Ten minutes later—in the pewter light before dawn, when the whole world is painted in shades of silver and gray—Carson galloped out of Whistle Creek astride Cinnabar, unaware that the greatest danger lay behind him.

Your son will die like his father before him unless you turn over what is mine.

Winston Kenrick

Mary stared at the note, her mind screaming denials, her blood running cold through her veins, her hands shaking. Winston Kenrick had Keary. He was threatening to kill her son.

Edith whispered, "I don't know why I didn't wake, why I didn't hear him. How could he come right into my room and take Keary like that?"

Mary glanced up. Edith's face was colorless and tears traced her cheeks. She was wringing a handkerchief between her hands. Nellie stood behind her, looking just as lost and frightened.

"Carson? Does he know?" Mary asked.

Edith shook her head. "Somebody got shot this morning outside the saloon. The sheriff's up in the mountains, looking for the men that did it. Johnny said he'd go after him. Oh, Mary, this is all my fault!"

"No," she replied hoarsely. "No, 'tis not your fault. 'Tis Master Kenrick's fault, the devil take him."

Your son will die like his father before him unless you turn over what is mine.

As the words ran through her mind, Mary felt as if she should understand something. A clue of some sort. It was there, yet she couldn't quite grasp hold of it.

Your son will die like his father before him unless you turn over what is mine.

Winston Kenrick hated her. Beyond all reason, he hated her. She had seen it in his eyes, heard it in his voice. She had recognized desperation yesterday. But what—

. . . will die like his father . . .

"God have mercy," she whispered as the note fell to the floor.

"Mary?"

Wide-eyed, she stared at Edith. "The mine. He's taken Keary out to the mine. That's how Seamus died. In the mine."

"You can't know that for sure."

"Where else would he be hiding him? Keary'll be crying. He'll be wanting me. Oh, God, protect me boy!" Before the prayer was scarcely out of her mouth, Mary was across the room and racing down the stairs.

"Wait!" Edith cried from behind her.

But Mary paid no heed. She had to find Keary. She had to be there when he needed her.

She grabbed the reins of the first saddle horse she came to out on the street. It was sheer panic that got her up and onto the saddle without breaking her neck, and good luck over any riding skill on her part that the horse didn't throw her off before they were out of town.

Perhaps the animal sensed a mother's terror. Or perhaps it was just ready to gallop after being tied to a hitching post for too long. Whatever the reason, once it was on the road to the Lucky Lady Mine, the horse stretched into an all-out run, ears flat against its head, hooves pounding a relentless beat against the road. Mary gripped the saddle horn and clung to it for all she was worth. Her only thought was to reach Keary before it was too late.

Please, God, don't let me be too late.

The site of the Lucky Lady Mine was drastically different from the last time Mary had been there. Deserted by the striking miners, the place was silent. Eerily so. The only sign of life was a horse and buggy, standing unattended near the mine entrance.

Somehow, Mary stopped her mount, then half slipped, half fell from her precarious perch. Her knees buckled and she pitched forward into the dust and rocks.

"Keary," she whispered as she scrambled to her feet. Then she shouted it. "Keary!"

She ran toward the entrance. She stopped when she saw Winston Kenrick, standing alone in the elevator cage. There was no sign of Keary. Another man stood near the controls of the hoist. Steam hissed from somewhere within the complex machinery, a fitting sound for this nightmarish moment.

"Good morning, Miss Malone," Winston said in that smooth, cultured voice of his, drawing her gaze back to him. He no longer sounded desperate or panicked. He was in control again. "I wondered how long it would take you to figure out where we would be."

"Where's Keary?"

"Where's my property?"

God, help me! she prayed silently. *I don't know what to do or say on me own.*

Winston raised an eyebrow. "Don't tell me you came without it." He clucked his tongue. "Now that was a very foolish thing to do. You know what it means to me."

"I'll not be giving it to you until I have me son." She was surprised by how calm she sounded when all she wanted to do was shriek and scream.

286

"I don't trust you, Miss Malone."

She moved forward, hoping and praying her legs wouldn't give out on her as they had when she'd dismounted. "Sure and I don't see what choice you'd be having, Master Kenrick. If anything was to happen to Keary, I'd not ever tell you where I hid that bloody box o' yours, and well you'd be knowing it."

"Aha!" He grinned. "Then you *do* have it!"

"Aye," she lied. "And I'll be givin' it to you just as soon as I've got me son back. You've me word on it."

"Your . . . word . . ." he echoed softly, drawing the words out. "Hmm."

Mary glanced toward the man at the controls, then back at her tormentor.

As if she'd asked a question, Winston said, "I paid Armstrong there a handsome price to run this cage for us." He grinned.

Mary thought the look an evil one.

"He'll have to run it again if you're going to get your son."

Sick horror twisted her stomach. "You've left him below? By himself?" she whispered, even though she'd known that's what he'd meant to do from his note. Still, she had hoped . . .

Winston motioned her forward. "I'll take you to him, Miss Malone, but understand this." His smile vanished. "If you betray me, you won't get another chance. I'll see that you hang. You know I have the power to do it. And you'll die knowing I'll do even worse to your boy. He'll suffer, and you won't be there to save him. Do you understand me?"

She nodded.

"Very well." He reached for two lanterns on the floor near the cage. He took one in each hand, then offered one to her. "You'll need this. It's dark where we're going."

Keary, me darlin', don't be afraid. Your ma's coming. Don't be afraid.

"Go ahead, Armstrong. Lower us to the same level as before."

Exhaustion pulled at Carson like lead weights. His eyelids were heavy from lack of sleep, and weariness caused the muscles in his neck and shoulders to ache.

He followed his two prisoners along the narrow forest track. They were on foot, their horses having bolted during a brief gun battle with Carson. The slow pace they'd set as they walked toward town was almost enough to lull Carson to sleep.

"Sheriff Barclay!"

The distant shout instantly revived him. He didn't know what had brought John looking for him, but whatever it was, it couldn't be good.

"Here, John!" he yelled in return. Then he glared at his prisoners who had stopped in front of him. "Get moving and be quick about it."

John found the three of them a few minutes later. "It's Keary" he said without preamble as he brought his horse to a stop a few yards up the trail. "Kenrick's taken him. Edith sent me—"

Carson didn't listen to more nor did he say a word. He spurred Cinnabar, and the trusted animal shot forward instantly. Pebbles and dirt flew up behind his pounding hooves. Carson leaned forward, wanting his steed to go even faster, demanding it from him.

Hate roared to life in his belly. If he had to, he'd remove the badge on his chest. He'd remove it just before he killed Kenrick with his bare hands. And if

288

he'd harmed one hair on that boy's head . . .

Edith and Nellie were waiting for him at the bridge over the Coeur d'Alene. The moment she saw him, Edith began frantically waving her arms over her head.

Carson reined in as he drew near.

Edith's eyes were wide with fear. "She's gone after him."

He didn't need to ask whom she meant. He knew. "Where?"

"She thinks he's taken Keary up to the Lucky Lady. The note said Keary was going to die like his father if Mary didn't give him what was his."

Like a sledgehammer, dread hit Carson square in the chest, knocking the air from his lungs. The mine. Kenrick had taken the woman and boy Carson loved into that mine.

Before he could recover his voice, he heard a deep rumbling noise. He would have sworn the ground shook beneath his horse's hooves. His gaze shot north ....

Toward the Lucky Lady.

Don't let it be what I think it is, he thought as he spurred Cinnabar into a gallop once again.

It happened in one horrifying instant.

Mary knelt in the mine shaft, holding Keary tightly in her arms, pressing her face against the downy hair on his head, weeping tears of relief. A frightened Keary, who had been tied with a rope around his waist to a large timber, sobbed and hiccuped. Winston stood no more than five feet away, saying something about going back to the cage.

Suddenly, an enormous roar blasted through the tunnel, deafening Mary. She was knocked onto her side as the earth bucked and rolled. A violent rush of air blew out the lanterns, plunging them into complete and utter darkness.

It lasted an eternity. It was over in the blink of an eye. The silence, when it came, was more deafening than the explosion had been.

Mary righted herself, clutching Keary ever tighter. "Master Kenrick?" she whispered, her throat choked with thick dust and the smell of water-soaked timbers.

There was no reply.

For a moment, Mary was frozen by her own terror.

Had she come all this way—across an ocean, across a continent—only to perish in a mine? Would she die in this horrible blackness, she and her son, too?

She felt a scream rising up from inside, the sort of scream that would never stop once it began. It was Keary, straining against her, that pulled her back to her senses.

"You're right, Keary me boy. I'm thinking we should be getting ourselves out o' here."

She was thankful now for the rope that was still tied around her son's waist. The thought of losing him in this blackness had the power to paralyze her again. She quickly shook off the feeling. She tied the opposite end of the rope around her own waist, then rose to her feet, bringing Keary with her, holding him on her left hip.

As she reached out with an arm, feeling for the wall of the tunnel, she cleared her throat. "Master Kenrick?" she said again, but there was still no answer.

It took her a few moments of groping in the dark, but she did find him, nearly stumbling over his prone body. Kneeling again, she touched his face and hair. She felt the warm, damp blood near the crown of his head. Then she felt for a pulse. There was none.

"May God have mercy on your miserable soul," she

whispered. As she stood, she added, "And may he forgive me, for I cannot be sorry you're dead."

Twenty-four

MARY MOVED AWAY FROM WINSTON'S BODY AND felt her way toward the wall again. Once there, she took a moment to steady herself and get her bearings, forcing herself to think clearly. Both her life and that of her son could depend upon it.

The cage had been lowered deep into the mine shaft—or so it had seemed to Mary. Once the cage had stopped, Kenrick had led her along a dark passage until it branched. Perhaps three hundred yards or so. He'd taken the right fork. They hadn't walked very far from that point before Mary had heard Keary's cries. She'd hurried ahead of Winston then, filled with joy and relief to have found her son. Winston had still been behind her when the explosion took place.

Therefore, she reasoned, keeping in mind where she'd been and where his body was now, she was certain she knew in which direction she would find the elevator shaft. She had only to make her way back along this tunnel, take a left at the fork, and find her way to the main shaft. Then she and Keary could be rescued.

"Carson will come for us, Keary." Saying Carson's name aloud made tears well up in her eyes, even while giving her some comfort. She blinked them away. "We'll be out of here in no time at all. And won't that be grand altogether?"

She drew a deep breath, then began her slow walk in what she hoped was the right direction, feeling her way as she went. The walls were damp, and every so often, drops of water would strike her on the head as they fell from the ceiling. She thought once that she heard the scurry of tiny feet.

An image of rats, surrounding her and Keary in this dark mine tunnel, flashed in her mind. She could almost feel their teeth biting into the flesh of her legs. Her stomach turned over, and she tasted bile on her tongue.

She hated the large rodents. Rats lived in the poor villages of Ireland. They traveled across the ocean in steerage with immigrants. And they dwelled in the tenement houses of New York City. Mary detested the sight of them. In this total darkness, she feared them.

To calm herself as well as her son, she began humming softly. The melody was from a lullaby her mother had sung to her when she was little, the same one Mary had sung to Keary from the day he was born. Strangely enough, she couldn't remember the words now, no matter how hard she sought them. Only the melody came to her.

She pressed on, still humming, reassuring herself that it wouldn't be long before they reached the main tunnel. It only seemed to take forever because of the darkness, because of the strange smells of the mine, because of the horror of what had happened.

Keary seemed to grow heavier with each step she took, but she wasn't about to set him down, not even for a moment, not even with the safety rope around his chubby waist. She shifted him to her other hip and continued walking.

Pebbles crunched beneath her feet. Then she found herself stumbling over progressively larger rocks. At first she was merely surprised by them, knowing she hadn't had to step over any rocks that size on the way in. She supposed the lantern could have made the difference, but . . .

And then, just a second before her hand touched the solid rubble, she understood what had happened. Her way of escape was blocked. The mouth of the tunnel had collapsed.

Mary and Keary were trapped in tunnel number fourteen of the Lucky Lady Mine.

Waiting for a rescue party of experienced miners to be organized was the hardest thing Carson had done in his entire life. If he could have operated the elevator controls and gone down in the cage at the same time, he would have done so.

Horrible scenarios played in his mind as he waited. He imagined Mary and Keary buried beneath rubble. He imagined them falling down a bottomless shaft. He imagined them alone and frightened, and he knew he would go into hell itself to find them.

There was no one to tell him exactly where to find Mary, which only made matters harder for him. Whoever had operated the steam-driven hoist had disappeared before Carson arrived. He was certain it hadn't been Kenrick running the elevator, for it took a skilled operator to run the machinery, enough skill that hoistmen earned a dollar more a day than their colleagues who worked below ground. Besides, Kenrick's horse and buggy—rented from the livery— were still outside, along with the horse Mary had ridden from Whistle Creek.

Kenrick must still be in the mine with Mary and Keary. Carson didn't know whether that possibility made him feel better or worse.

After what seemed a lifetime, he stepped into the elevator cage with Quaid Malone, John Tyrell, and a dozen other men, everyone wearing hats with carbide lamps on top of them, everyone carrying shovels and picks. Expressions were grim and determined. For now, the strike—and all the anger that had gone with it—was forgotten. These miners were joined by a common cause, and they wouldn't rest until they'd found those who were trapped below.

As the men closed in around him, Carson thought his heart might stop. Then his pulse began to race, causing a buzzing sound in his ears. He felt the oxygen being sucked right out of his lungs. His hands were perspiring, making the handles of his tools slippery. The cage started its descent with a jerk amidst the hiss of steam and a rattle and clang as gears and pulleys turned.

I would go into hell itself, Carson remembered thinking only minutes before, and now it seemed to be coming true. He gripped the side of the cage, a familiar icy terror sweeping through him.

Hell itself.

Like the serpent whispering lies in the garden of Eden, a voice of doom warned him, *You're going to die below. You'll never see daylight again.*

In the past, Carson had always given into that inner voice. This time he couldn't give into it. This time he was going after his future. Without Mary and Keary, he would have nothing left that mattered. He wouldn't go back without them. He would rather die in this dark, dank hole in the ground than return to the surface alone.

"You okay?" John asked in a low voice.

Carson swallowed and nodded.

"You don't have to do this," the younger man continued. "There are plenty of others who're willing."

Carson met John's gaze. "I *do* have to do this. It's

Mary and Keary down there."

John nodded in understanding.

"Here!" someone shouted. "This is the level."

The cage jolted to a stop, and the miners spilled out.

"How do they know we should be on this level?" Carson demanded of John as they moved forward. He looked toward Quaid on his other side. "What if they're wrong?"

It was Mary's brother who answered his question. "They brought the cage up from this level. 'Tis here we have to suppose they'd be. Your Mr. Christy showed me the map of the mine. This tunnel drifts to the left, then breaks into three stopes. We'll be dividin' up there and followin' the tunnels 'til we find Mary and Keary"

Up ahead, someone shouted, "We've found someone!"

Carson shot forward, pushing his way through the miners who had come to a halt in front of him. Hope. Fear. Despair. He felt them all before he broke through the crowd and saw one of the search crew bending over a man on the floor of the tunnel.

A man. Not Mary.

"Who is it?" he demanded.

"Bart Gibson." The crew member lowered his voice. "He's lost a lot of blood. Hurt bad. He won't make it."

Carson knelt beside Gibson.

But before Carson could say anything, the fallen man grabbed hold of him by his shirt sleeve. "I didn't know anybody'd be down here. Halligan swore the mine would be deserted today. Nobody was supposed t' be in here when I set the dynamite."

Carson's gut tightened. Halligan. Halligan had hired someone to blow up a section of his own mine. And now it was Mary and Keary, innocent victims, who could be paying the price of his treachery.

Gibson's eyes reflected the glow of Carson's carbide lamp as he pulled Carson's face closer to his own. "I don't hear so good after all the years of blastin'. I thought I was imaginin' things when I heard a youngster's cry." He grimaced, then shuddered. "But when I saw the cage'd been lowered, I knew it was real. I tried to get back in time to stop the blast, but it was too late. I heard me a woman's voice in the tunnel. Then it blew."

Carson caught a glimpse of the extent of the other man's pain, but he felt little sympathy. It was more habit than concern that caused him to say, "Hang on, Gibson. We'll get you out of here."

"Never mind . . . me. I'm dyin'. . . anyways." It took a lot of effort, but Gibson managed to roll his shoulders off the ground and point. "That's the way. The stope ain't . . . deep yet. If they're alive . . . there won't be . . . much air for 'em. She'll be . . . sealed up tight. Get 'em . . . outta there . . . quick." He dropped back onto the hard rock ground and closed his eyes.

Carson glanced up. "He's dead."

The rescue party surged forward and around Bart Gibson. There was nothing anyone could do for him now. The moment they reached the wall of rubble and debris, they set to work with shovels and picks.

Someone shouted, "Miz Malone, can you hear us?"

But the only sounds were those made by the rescuers as they hacked away at the sealed tunnel.

Working beside the other men, Carson sent out a silent cry of his own. *If you can't hear them, Mary, then hear me. Hold on. I'm here. I'm coming. I love you, Mary, and not even this hellhole will keep me from you.*

The air was thin, dank, and hot.

In the complete blackness that surrounded her, Mary had difficulty knowing for sure when she was awake and when she was dreaming. Her thoughts sometimes meandered, sometimes raced. Some made sense. Some were a mystery.

She saw Fagan Malone standing before her, smiling sadly, heard him say, *Ah, Mary, me girl. Would ya never be larnin' t' keep that temper o' yours? Always fightin' with your brothers. Will ya be provin' all by yourself the sayin' that an Irishman is never at peace except when he's fightin'? Sure and 'twill be the death o' you. Mind me words now. 'Twill be the death o' you, Mary girl.*

Her da was right. It *was* her temper that had led her into disaster time and again.

"I'm sorry, Da," she whispered. "I'm sorry I wasn't listening to you."

Fagan shook his head, then with a twinkle in his eye, said, *'Tis a fine lad you're holdin' in your arms, Mary, me girl. You tell him his grandda said so when he's old enough t' hear it. A fine lad altogether.*

She felt the sting of tears in her throat. "Aye, I'll tell him, Da."

Maeve Malone came to stand beside her husband.

'Tis your heart I worry about, me darlin' daughter. You've a stubborn pride, that you have. Don't be breaking a shin on a stool that's not in your way, Mary Emeline.

She thought she felt her mother's fingertips stroke her cheek. "Ma . . ." She reached out to take Maeve Malone's hand, but all she grasped was air.

Her brothers appeared next. They talked amongst themselves, laughing and poking and punching and shoving as boys were prone to do. They called to her in teasing voices. Ah, how they loved to prod their little sister into a fight. But they loved her fiercely, of that she was certain, and so she didn't mind it much. She wanted to join them now but couldn't make herself rise. She felt altogether too tired. Too bloody tired.

Mary.

She gasped. Her heart quickened.

Carson was there, watching her with those brilliant blue eyes of his. She saw the tiny scar that split his left eyebrow, saw the golden highlights in his thick brown hair, saw the slightly crooked curve of his smile.

"Me ma was right," she said to him. "Ah, me darlin', I wish I could be telling you how much I love you. I should have done it long ago. You've held me heart in your hands almost from the first. Forgive me stubborn pride."

I'm not letting you go, Mary. His smile broadened. *I'm not ever letting you go. Just hold on tight. Trust me.*

"I trust you, Carson."

Hold on. I'm here. I'm coming. I love you, Mary, and not even this hellhole will keep me from you.

A weak smile played across her mouth, then she slipped into a well of nothingness.

"We're through!" someone shouted.

But Carson had already tossed aside his pick and was digging at the small hole with his bare hands, working to make it larger. Large enough for a man to crawl through. He pushed and scratched at the rock and rubble. He didn't even stop to yell her name. He had to get to her. He felt it in his heart. He had to get to her now.

Quaid joined him. "Mary!" he called through the opening. "Are ya there, lass?" After a moment, he laid a hand on Carson's shoulder. "Listen!"

Carson stopped his frantic digging. Everyone in the tunnel stilled, waiting breathlessly. And then they heard it. The soft whimper of a child.

"Keary!" Carson, with Quaid's help, lit into the wall of dirt, rock, and shattered timbers with double the effort. "Mary, I'm coming!"

Within a few minutes more, he and Quaid had widened the hole to almost shoulder width. Carson didn't stop to ask if it was safe. He didn't ask if more of the tunnel might come crashing down at any second. He wasn't even thinking of the dangers he'd always known lurked in the mines. Mary and Keary were inside. That was all he knew. That was all he cared about. He had to get to them.

Sweating profusely in the intense heat, his hands torn and bleeding, he squeezed through the tight opening. Jagged pieces of rock snagged his shirt and scratched his skin. He didn't notice. On the other side, with nothing to grasp onto, he fell headfirst toward the ground, breaking his fall with his outstretched arms. His miner's hat fell off and rolled a few feet away, but the lamp stayed lit.

And there, in the light of that blessed carbide lamp, was Mary, curled up in the corner against the rubble, Keary held tightly in her arms. Nothing had ever looked so good to Carson in his life as the sight of mother and child.

"Mary?" he called softly as he crawled toward her.

Her eyes were closed. She looked ghostly pale, but he could see the gentle rise and fall of her chest. At least he knew she was alive.

Keary began to cry, drawing Carson's attention to him.

"It's okay, little fella. It's okay. Your dad's here now."

He untied the rope around the toddler's waist, then rose and carried him to the opening.

"Quaid," he called, "take Keary. Get him up to the doctor." He passed the child through to his uncle's waiting arms.

"How's Mary?" Quaid asked.

"She'll be okay," he replied, not allowing himself to consider any other possibility. Then he hurried back to her, kneeling down and taking hold of one of her hands. "Mary? It's me. Carson."

Her eyelids fluttered, then opened. For a moment, she seemed disoriented. Finally, her eyes focused on Carson's face, and a gentle smile played on her lips.

"Ah, 'tis you, me love," she whispered. "I knew you'd come back."

"I've come to take you home, darling." He kissed her, needing to feel her breath on his skin, needing to reassure his heart that she was really okay as he'd told her brother.

"Aye, take me home, Carson."

He drew her into his embrace.

"'Tis finished I am, breaking me shin against a stool that's not in me way."

Carson smiled, not knowing what she meant but not caring. He was holding her once again in his arms. That was all that mattered for now.

Twenty-five

BRYAN HALLIGAN WAS APPREHENDED IN SPOKANE a few days after the explosion in tunnel number fourteen and was destined to spend many years in prison. His former business partners, Michael King and Stephen

Smothers, brought an end to the strike, promising not only fair wages but better working conditions for the miners.

Accompanied by Tibble Knox, Winston Kenrick's body left Whistle Creek, shipped in a pine casket to New York City where he would be interred beside other members of his family. In the casket with him was the silver filigreed box he had sought so desperately in the final weeks of his life. It had been found in Lloyd Perkins's old room, apparently stolen while Mary still lived above the saloon.

Portia Kenrick did not go with her husband's remains. The evidence of Winston's betrayal, discovered in a cleverly disguised secret compartment of that silver box, had dispelled any remnants of responsibility she might have felt toward her husband of twenty-four years. Now, she decided, it was time to live for herself, and that was precisely what she intended to do, immediately following the anticipated nuptials of Whistle Creek's sheriff and the owner of the newly established Blanche Loraine Refuge for Women and Children.

There were so many people who came to see the wedding on that Saturday in late September that they couldn't all squeeze into the Whistle Creek Community Church. So they gathered—men and women who had been bitter enemies a few weeks before—beneath the open windows on the sides of the building and listened from the narthex at the rear of the church.

Around and behind the bride and groom stood those dearest to them. Quaid was there, of course, beaming at his little sister with pride. Edith Tyrell, a recent bride herself, watched it all with a bloom of happiness on her cheeks. Claudia Hailey, Carson's foster mother, had traveled up from San Francisco to be there for the occasion; Carson had been surprised and pleased beyond words to see her again, though he'd tried to hide just how much it meant to him.

John Tyrell served as Carson's best man, and he held himself with pride, no longer ashamed of the scars on his face or his useless arm. Beth Steele had come with her family from Montana to serve as Mary's matron of honor. The reunion of the two young women who'd come all the way from England together, their futures unknown, had been a joyous one.

But as the wedding ceremony began, Mary was only vaguely aware of the presence of others. She had eyes for Carson alone. He stood beside her as the parson read from the prayer book, looking tall and rugged and incredibly handsome. He held a smiling Keary in his arms while Nellie stood beside him.

Her heart welled over with joy and love at the sight of the three of them. Never in her wildest dreams had she imagined she would find so much happiness in the wilderness of Idaho. She thought of the many small steps that had steered her course in this direction and knew it was a miracle, indeed, that had brought her to this place, to this man, to this moment. Things that she had thought were disasters and insurmountable mistakes had all been used by a loving and divine hand to send her toward her destiny. She could look back at everything now and see the path so clearly.

Fighting's not the only place an Irishman finds peace, Da, she thought, staring into beautiful eyes of blue. *Sometimes we find it in love. And I'm thinking I'll be proving that with Carson.* She smiled as she added, *Though I suppose we'll do our share of fighting, too.*

Reverend Ogelsby's thin voice continued to lead them in their vows.

I'm thinking you'd be fond of me Carson, Ma. Sure and I know you would. I'll not be breaking me shin again, I'll promise you that.

"And so, by the power vested in me . . ."

As the parson proclaimed them man and wife, Carson handed Keary to Quaid, then placed the fingers of his right hand beneath Mary's chin and tipped her head slightly backward. With infinite tenderness, he kissed her for all to see.

For a moment, there was only silence and the rapid beating of Mary's heart in response to Carson's kiss. Then the church erupted in shouts as miners and townsfolk, family and friends, began to cheer the bride and groom. Men tossed hats high into the air and whooped and hollered like drunken cowpokes. Mary found herself separated from Carson, passed from one person to another, hugged and kissed on the cheek and wished well by those she knew and those she didn't.

It seemed far too long before she returned to Carson's side. When she did, he put an arm around her waist and held her close, and she knew he'd been feeling the same. She knew he wasn't going to allow her to be swept away a second time. The realization made her pulse jump in anticipation for the night yet to come.

It was dusk by the time Carson carried his bride across the threshold of his cabin. He stopped in surprise at what awaited them. Ferns and pine branches and late summer flowers filled the room, changing the interior from a rustic cabin to a sweet smelling bower. His old bed had been removed, replaced by a new wider one with a thick, soft mattress covered in smooth sheets. A lamp burned low on a stand beside the bed.

Carson's mouth went dry, and his body turned hot with desire. Tonight he would lie with Mary. Tonight he would make love to her as he'd longed to make love to her almost from the first day she'd stepped off that train. Soon he would see her glorious body without any covering. Soon he would caress her breasts and feel the silky smoothness of her skin. He wanted to carry her straight to the bed and make love to her this instant. It seemed he had waited so long.

"Someone's been mighty busy planning for this night," he said as his gaze turned to Mary.

Her cheeks were flushed, and he realized with more than a little surprise that she was nervous. In a flash of insight, he knew she had never been loved the way a woman should be loved. In many ways, she was still a virginal bride. She deserved to be wooed and won by her groom.

He checked his raging passion. This was not a night to be rushed. This was Mary he held in his arms. This was a woman to be treasured, to be savored. This was the woman he loved. He would not miss one precious moment because of his own haste.

Carefully, he lowered her feet to the floor, then drew her into his arms. "Are you hungry?" he asked softly. "Do you want me to rustle up something to eat?"

She shook her head, her gaze never leaving his.

"Would you like me to leave you alone for a while?"

Again she shook her head. There was a light in her brown eyes, a light that revealed the hidden corners of her heart. With her gaze, she told him she loved him, she trusted him, she would be forever a part of him. Her eyes told him that together they would face whatever life brought their way, that they would be one, from now until the end of time.

When she looked at him like that, it made it hard to remember he meant to go slowly. Passion smoldered within him, a passion much stronger than mere lust. This was more, so very much more, than just a physical need that could be sated by the joining of two bodies.

He searched his mind for the right words, regretting that he wasn't an educated man, a man who could quote sonnets and poetry. Mary deserved those things.

Her smile blossomed, warmed. "You're everything I'll ever be needing or wanting, me darlin'. Just as you are."

And because he hadn't the right words, he claimed her mouth with his instead.

The kiss was long, slow, sweet, and Mary became lost in it. The scent of pine swirled in her head as tiny glorious shudders raced through her veins. She drew closer to Carson, holding on, her legs suddenly unsteady beneath her, the white heat of desire curling inside her, waiting for her husband's touch. She moaned softly, although it didn't sound like herself in her own ears.

His fingers began to free the tiny buttons down the back of her wedding gown. Inch by inch, the fabric parted. The cool evening air swept in through the still open doorway and touched her heated flesh. She shivered, but not from the cold.

When his hands reached her waistband, he gently broke the string of kisses and turned her away from him. Slowly, ever so slowly, he slid the bodice from her shoulders and down her arms until it fell away. Then, with the same tender care, he plucked the pins from her hair.

The sensations resulting from his fingers brushing against her scalp were all out of proportion to the significance of the action. In some rational corner of her mind, she knew that was true. But this was not supposed to be a rational moment. This was a moment to be savored, to be experienced, to be treasured, not to be thought through. She hadn't known this before. She hadn't known being with a man—even before the physical intimacies of lovemaking—could be filled with such all-encompassing joy.

She laughed softly at the wonder of it. She let her head fall slightly back, then moved it from side to side, causing her hair to sway against her back.

"What's so funny?" Carson asked, his lips near her ear.

Gooseflesh rose all along her arm even as her skirt followed the bodice into a puddle around her feet.

He switched to her other ear. "Are you laughing at me, Mrs. Barclay?" Deftly, he removed her corset.

"No," she answered, suddenly breathless.

He turned her toward him again. His blue eyes promised her the world. She was ready to accept it from him.

The ribbons holding up her petticoats came loose with a quick tug, and suddenly she was standing before him in only her chemise and drawers. He lowered his mouth to her collarbone and trailed soft kisses along the edging of her chemise, just above the swell of her breasts. Her laughter faded, becoming only a memory.

When he straightened, the two of them stared at each other for a long time without moving, simply gazing at the other with love and longing, their quickened breathing the only sounds in the small mountain cabin.

Mary felt a sudden need to feel the warmth of Carson's skin against hers. It was a need that couldn't be denied. Hesitantly at first—for this was untried territory, to be the aggressor—she pushed his suit coat from his shoulders before loosening his collar and tossing it aside. Then, with fumbling fingers, she tugged the hem of his shirt from the waistband of his trousers and raised the shirt over his head.

She paused, then reached forward with both hands and laid her palms against his muscular chest. She sucked in a tiny breath when she first touched him, let it out when she felt the beat of his heart beneath her fingertips.

"Mrs. Barclay, beware," he warned in a hoarse voice. His eyes blazed with an inner fire. "I am only a man, and I love you too much."

It was not a warning she would heed, nor did he truly want her to, and she understood that. Besides, how could she stop when he called her by her new name, when in doing so he laid claim to her, body and soul?

All remnants of shyness vanished, along with any lingering doubts that he might find her wanting because she didn't come to him pure and untouched. With a new clarity, she understood that his love was complete and unconditional. When he'd told her he didn't care about her past, he'd meant it. When he'd told her he would be Keary's father, he hadn't meant stepfather. He'd meant just what he'd said. She'd accepted these truths in her head long before her wedding, but in this one moment, they became crystal-clear in her heart as well.

Mary rose on tiptoe, offering Carson her lips. They drank each other in, like those wishing to get drunk with wine. And when they had sated their thirst, they parted briefly and removed the remainder of their clothing.

"You're more beautiful than I imagined," Carson told her in a reverent voice. His fingertips, still rough from the day he'd dug through a mountain to save her, brushed over her collarbone.

She grabbed hold of his hands, kissed those lifesaving fingertips, then guided them to her breasts and held them there. "Feel me heartbeat, Carson?" she asked.

He nodded.

"'Tis beating for you."

In a swift but gentle motion, he swept her legs off the floor and carried her to the bed with its soft sheets and the golden lamplight.

Time passed in a haze. Whether long or short, Mary didn't know. She only knew the touch of Carson's hands as they explored, caressed, teased, tutored. He created a spark that glowed warm within her, then fed that spark until it became a roaring wildfire only he could quench.

And when neither of them could bear to remain two any longer, Carson rose above her, entered her, and they became one in the flesh. They moved together in an ancient dance and yet one that was peculiarly theirs alone. Their skin glowed damp in the lamplight. Their breathing kept pace, so in unison that it sounded as if they breathed for each other. A thousand lights exploded behind her eyelids. Her muscles tautened as they strove toward the pinnacle she hadn't known existed.

In one breathless, shattering moment, Mary cried out, and before the sound had faded from the room, Carson did the same. A short while later, they lay motionless, their bodies still joined, Carson bracing himself above her with his forearms. They stared into each other's eyes, waiting for their breathing to return to normal, caught in the wonder of the moment. Their lovemaking had been beyond what either of them had expected. Beyond what any mortal might hope for.

And in the silence of their honeymoon bower, they

each became aware of a very simple truth. It was the mingling of their hearts that had brought great beauty to the physical act.

Carson rolled onto his side, taking Mary with him. She lay with her head on his shoulder, running her fingertips over the planes and valleys of his chest and abdomen. She thought she might like to remain like this forever. She'd never felt so safe and secure as she did now.

She smiled as she softly asked, "Would you be knowing I was afraid of you when first we came here, Keary and me?"

"Yeah, I knew. But not why."

"'Twas because I thought I was running from the law." She rose up on her elbow, looked down into the face of the man she loved beyond measure.

He understood and smiled in return. "And you ran straight into the arms of the sheriff of Whistle Creek."

"'Tis a good thing," she said with a sigh, then nestled back into his embrace. "For 'tis here I always want to stay"

Epilogue

Whistle Creek, Idaho
April 1907

IT WAS LATE AFTERNOON ON ONE OF THOSE spring days that made a person want to dance and sing for joy just for being alive. The sun was a golden orb in a cloudless heaven. A warm breeze carried the kiss of summer yet to come. The pines seemed greener, the earth more umber, the sky a crisper shade of blue.

Mary laid her pen next to the two completed letters and felt another wave of contentment wash over her.

Ten years. It had been ten years since she, Beth Wellington, and Inga Linberg had arrived in America. She closed her eyes and envisioned those three young women who had rushed to the railing of the RMS *Teutonic* for their first glimpse of the Statue of Liberty and New York Harbor.

There was Beth. Lady Elizabeth, as Mary had called her then. So beautiful and fragile in appearance. So recognizable as a member of the English aristocracy.

There was Inga, tall and willowy, with hair as pale as prairie wheat. Inga, the minister's daughter, who had always thought of others before herself and who had told stories in her splendid quilts.

And there was Mary, headstrong, stubborn, and fiery-tempered, always breaking her shin against a stool that wasn't in her way.

Would any of them have guessed where they would be on this day, a decade into the future? No, she answered herself with a smile. Those three immigrant girls could never have imagined what lay ahead.

These days, Beth Steele helped her husband run a thriving cattle ranch in Montana. From her letters, it was clear there was little, if anything, left of the English noblewoman who'd arrived ten years before. Beth rode, roped, and branded right alongside Garret, a true woman of the American West.

Quiet, submissive Inga Bridget had become famous because of her quilts. Requests and orders poured in from around the country, far more than she could fill. Dirk Bridger had also made a name for himself and had great hopes for one of his fine thoroughbreds in this year's Kentucky Derby.

And as for Mary herself . . .

"Penny for your thoughts," Carson said softly, his breath whispering against her neck.

A delicious shiver shot up her spine as she twisted on her chair. "I didn't hear you come in."

"I know. Where were you?" With possessive but gentle hands, he drew her up from her chair.

"Sure and I was thinking of Beth and Inga. 'Twas ten years ago today that we arrived in America."

He kissed the tip of her nose. "I wish I'd been there. In New York, I mean. I wish I'd seen you when you first walked off the boat. We'd have had ten years together instead of only eight and a half."

"Oh, that would've been perfect altogether, me belly big and round with Keary." She laughed. "You'd have loved me for sure then."

His smile faded, replaced by the intense, loving look she cherished so. "Yes, I would have loved you for sure then, Mary Emeline Barclay. I couldn't have helped myself."

There was no point arguing with him. Carson had forgotten long ago what he'd thought of her when she'd arrived in Whistle Creek. And she was willing to let him forget if it made him happy.

Her husband glanced toward the hallway. "The house is quiet. Where are the children?"

"They've gone to stay the night with the Tyrells."

"All of them?" Carson raised an eyebrow in surprise. "Even David?"

He was referring to their two-year-old son, the youngest of the Barclay children. It caused Mary to do a quick count of all her blessings. Nellie was a woman grown; she had married the previous summer and was now expecting her first child. Keary Barclay was almost

311

ten and growing more like the man who had adopted and raised him with every passing day. The twins, Fagan and Maeve, were nearly seven, and if ever there were children filled with blarney, it was those two. Claudia, at five, was as sweet and loving as her namesake. And David, as was true of any child his age, kept his mother running from dawn to dusk.

And there was Carson, her greatest blessing, the man who held her heart.

"And just what will we do with all this peace and quiet, Mrs. Barclay?" he asked with a twinkle in his eyes.

She smiled, her joy uncontainable. "Whatever it is, Mr. Barclay, I'm thinking it will be perfect altogether." She stepped closer into the circle of his arms. "Aye, perfect altogether."

Dear Reader:

I hope you enjoyed reading this Large Print book. If you are interested in reading other Beeler Large Print titles, ask your librarian or write to me at

Thomas T. Beeler, *Publisher*
Post Office Box 659
Hampton Falls, New Hampshire 03844

You can also call me at 1-800-251-8726 and I will send you my latest catalogue.

Audrey Lesko and I choose the titles I publish in Large Print. Our aim is to provide good books by outstanding authors—books we both enjoyed reading and liked well enough to want to share. We warmly welcome any suggestions for new titles and authors.

Sincerely,